# Where Nightmares Ride

## R A Baxter

*Appropriate for Teens, Intriguing to Adults*

Immortal Works LLC
1505 Glenrose Drive
Salt Lake City, Utah 84104
Tel: (385) 202-0116

**Cover Art by Warren Design**

**ISBN 978-1-7339085-7-3 (Paperback)**

**ASIN B07YBNZN1Q (Kindle Edition)**

*For James Wymore, for inspiring a concept
so rich in potential.
R.A.B.*

# PART 1

# THE SECRETS WE DREAM

Dark forms materialized, silhouetted against a backdrop of billowing yellow-gray smoke.

"Not again!" Jack Park spun around and searched for his tormentors. He found the shadowy figures, swathed in bright colored silk robes, standing in a wide ring around him. His instincts warning him to run, he charged their linked arms, but all the force he could muster couldn't break through their combined strength. They caught him and flung him like a ragdoll back into the center of the circle.

Jack landed, sprawled at the feet of a squinty-eyed hag. She wore a brilliant magenta dress and carried only a mulberry hand fan adorned with the image of a bird among white flowers. Yet her presence radiated an inexplicable power that compelled him to cower before her. He held back tears. What would she subject him to this time? A pack of wolves? An ogre? A gang of street thugs? He pulled himself up on his feet and glared at her, sweat dripping from his blond-tipped, spiky black hair.

The old woman smiled.

*How dare she smile!* "What's it going to take?" Jack tightened his fists. "You know this is pointless! I can't do what you want! You're wasting your time." He laughed in despair. This woman had no concept of reason.

"Pak Jaegi ya!" she said in a high-pitched voice. "Bring peace to an old woman's mind. Tell me you have obeyed. Tell me you've been honing your skills in your waking hours."

Jack clenched his teeth and fought the urge to clock the old crone. "How many times do I have to tell you? I'll never fight anything for you, especially not some imaginary 'Dark Mind' you keep rambling about."

"What I want is irrelevant, young one. The Dark Mind is coming. Your destiny will find you whether you prepare for it or not."

Jack had heard all this before. "The only future I want is one far away from you."

The woman frowned. "Your defiance is regrettable. You've learned nothing of honor or duty."

Tears filled Jack's eyes. "Why can't you just leave me alone? You don't know anything about me."

"You have forgotten who you are. You must defeat your fear. Were your fate unknown to me, I'd gladly leave you to waste your life—but I know your destiny. I tried to defeat the Dark Mind myself and failed. Zaqar spoke not of me. He spoke of you. It's you who will defeat the Dark Mind."

"I won't do anything for you!"

"Enough!" The woman stepped aside, revealing the towering form of an immense winged lion, a manticore. The huge yellow eyes of its human-like head glared into Jack's trembling face. Its snake-like tail writhed in the air and the animal roared, revealing three rows of shark-like teeth.

It rose into the air and soared in a ring around the boy, its hungry gaze fixed on Jack.

"You people are crazy!" Jack took a defensive Taekwondo stance, fully aware of his limited skills. He feigned an attack, then turned and made another dash toward the human fence, attempting to hurtle over their arms. They merely backed up and caught him, then swung him back into the fight. He saw no hope of escaping, and even less of defeating this monster. His only task was to determine the least painful way to die. He closed his eyes and stretched out his arms, thinking it best to end this charade quickly. He awaited his demise.

His captors, however, wouldn't even tolerate self-sacrifice as a means of escape. The screaming of a woman compelled him to open his eyes. A half dozen robed men dragged a brown-haired girl into the circle and forced her back against a massive stone slab. The girl, clothed in a light blue dress, squirmed and kicked at the men but couldn't stop them from clamping shackles to her arms and legs and chaining her to the rock.

The manticore descended and hovered before the offering, its heavy wings raising clouds of dust. Its face stretched into a savage, toothy grin. The girl screamed and yanked at her restraints. She turned toward Jack, her teary brown eyes pleading for help.

Fury carved the lines of Jack's face. The devils were using this innocent girl again to force him to stay and fight. Either he battled the manticore, or this innocent young woman would die. Jack glared at the old lady. "Leave her alone!"

"Katie's fate is in your hands now." She handed Jack a long, curved scimitar. "Defeat your fear and save her!"

Jack wanted to strike the woman down, but her inexplicable power stayed his hand. Terrified, he couldn't move, let alone attack the monster. Then the girl's gaze met Jack's eyes and fortified his resolve. He turned and faced the beast, aiming his sword between its eyes.

The old hag nodded to the creature, and it turned toward Jack and roared, its glare burning with hatred and rage.

Jack dropped his sword and it clanked against the rocky soil, then he stumbled backward into a multitude of hands. He scrambled to retrieve his scimitar, but now it magically transformed in his hand into a flaming firebrand.

"What's going on?"

The manticore landed in front of him and raised its furry head. Jack swung his firebrand back and forth at the snarling beast and it stepped back, then solidified into stone, its joints crunching and scraping. It lumbered toward him, shaking the earth with each step.

"Fight it!" The old woman's eyes went wild with anticipation. "Defeat it!"

"I can't kill a block of stone!" He charged the creature, seeing no other options, and ducked below each strike of its claws, his firebrand falling meaninglessly across its stone chest. The body of the stone beast transformed again, stubby horns and bat-like ears emerging from its skull. Its grin stretched wide and it glared at Jack with the deep-set eyes of a grotesque gargoyle.

Jack couldn't explain the intense terror that now overcame him. He recognized this beast. The thought had hardly entered his mind before the gargoyle pounced and Jack screamed, raising his hands to protect his face. His world exploded in a flash of bright red-orange flame.

×

KATIE'S WRISTS THROBBED, raw and aching from pulling against the thick black chains binding her to the cold granite slab. She'd avoided death by the manticore before it transformed into stone and shrunk into the form of a flaming gargoyle. She turned away and shut her eyes, unable to bear the terror in the Asian boy's face.

Even closed eyelids couldn't dim the light from the flames or block the sudden blast of hot air. The warmth decreased fast, and she peeked through squinting eyes to find both the boy and the monster had vanished, along with many of the people who'd been tormenting him. The old lady shook her head. Her remaining followers gathered around her.

Katie didn't waste a second. "Let me go! You got what you wanted! Unchain me!"

The old woman stared at her, then approached her at a slow pace, her cohorts assembling behind her. "You've nothing more to fear from us, Miss Frost. It's regrettable that we had to treat you so cruelly, but it couldn't be avoided. We thank you for your sacrifice."

"Sacrifice? You kidnapped me! You killed that boy! You're monsters!"

"I don't expect you to understand, young one. Trust me, there was no other way."

Katie's face contorted with rage and she yanked at her shackles. "Let me go!"

The woman nodded to a green-robed man next to her and he slid a key out of his robe, then proceeded to free Katie's ankles.

"We sought no pleasure in your suffering," the old woman said. "Find contentment that your fear brought about much good."

"Contentment?" Katie yanked her left hand away from the green-robed man the second he unlocked the shackle.

"Before we remove the last restraint, I wish for you to understand something. You're here because you're a woman of special abilities. Your presence lent great power to Pak Jaegi. We, however, aren't the only ones benefitting from your ignorance regarding your power. For your own safety, I beg you to speak to your father and ask him to enlighten you."

"So, you care about my safety now? Keeping a lion-faced monster away from me didn't cross your mind?"

"You were in no danger, young one. The boy simply needed to believe you were."

"You talk about him as if we didn't just watch him die!"

The old woman smiled. "Remember what I said, speak to your father." She nodded to the green-robed man and he unshackled Katie's other arm.

Katie rolled off the stone and stood up. She stared fire at the old woman.

A brown-robed man standing nearby unsheathed a gleaming scimitar and handed it to the old woman, who then bowed to Katie before twisting sideways and raising the blade high above her right shoulder. Katie stepped back, her eyes wide, but could do nothing to block the blade swinging toward her neck.

⚔

KATIE PRIED her eyes open and found herself lying beside her four-poster bed, her cheek pressed against a cold hardwood floor. She gained consciousness and discovered her nightgown wadded up and twisted around her chest, mingling with a chaotic mass of linens and pillows.

"It happened again." She wondered why she never remembered previous nightmares during the current ones.

Sunlight glowed through her window blinds, making her squint. She tilted her head to shield her eyes and spied a pair of glossy black Mary Janes, white knee-highs, and white lace bordering a pastel green dress. Looking up, she met the smiling round face of a complete stranger. The girl's shoulder-length, blonde pigtails bobbed when she giggled. She looked like a child, although clearly a teenager.

"Why are you in my room?" Katie wrestled with her bedclothes and stood up with no small difficulty. "Who on earth are you?"

Jack Park yelled and writhed to the left and right, blinded by the light of an expanding ball of fire. He tried to free himself from an unseen force preventing him from backing away from the inferno, but the anticipated bath of searing pain never came. He peered through raised fingers and watched the flames soften to the marbled gray glow of an overcast sky, viewed through the water-spotted windshield of a silver Ford Fiesta.

Cold moisture flowed down his left leg, melted ice cubes freeing themselves from a toppled paper cup trapped below his left arm. Jack turned to the tall, lanky young man driving the car and awaited the inevitable sarcasm. His friend, however, merely gave him a concerned stare, shifting his attention between Jack and the road.

"Sorry I dozed off, Taylor. Want me to take another turn at the wheel?" Jack shoved the ice aside, then dabbed his leg with a paper napkin he found on the console.

"No, we can switch after lunch. You alright, dude? You had that nightmare again, didn't you? Let me guess: A beautiful girl was going to die if you didn't obey an old hag and fight off some horrible monster?"

Jack nodded and turned to stare out the window. Red, flat-topped mesas formed the backdrop of a wide field of pink soil, sprinkled with pale green sagebrush and scattered bursts of scrub oak. "How long was I asleep?"

"About an hour. I can't believe we left Los Angeles six hours ago and it's not even noon yet."

"Where are we?"

"Utah. You just missed Saint George."

Jack nodded. He spotted a glossy red brochure on the center console and grabbed it and shook off a few stray ice chunks. The cover page displayed an image of young campers smiling over roasted marshmallows next to a large green banner that read, *Camp Farley.*

Jack thumbed through the brochure, looking at the words rather than reading them, then felt the press of Taylor's hand against his shoulder.

"Snap out of it, bro. Now's not the time to give up. We're heading to the one place that can fix your nightmare problem. Unless that brochure is bogus, they've got the world's top experts on dream tech. You may have just dreamt your last chance to kiss that brunette girl."

Jack forced a smile. He usually appreciated Taylor's attempts to lighten the mood, but these repetitive nightmares had taken their toll. "She's the only thing I'd miss if these nightmares went away. I'm sure everyone at school thinks I've cracked. Maybe I have." He pressed his hands over his face.

"No one thinks that, bro. Okay, there was that time you woke up screaming in the middle of chemistry class, but no one cares. Everyone sleeps in that class."

Jack pulled a lighter out of his denim pocket and flicked the flint, then stared at the flame. He wasn't a smoker. He wasn't even a pyro, although Taylor often accused him of being one. He really had no reason for carrying around a lighter. Truth is, he couldn't explain his infatuation with fire. He just loved staring at flames. It brought peace to his mind and calmed his nerves.

"I'm sorry," Taylor said. "I know I'm not much help. Honestly, I never knew anyone could have nightmare problems like yours."

Jack let the flame flicker out, then shoved the lighter back into his pocket. "Dude, you help me more than you'll ever know. No one else would put up with me ranting about my mental problems every day. You totally surprised me this morning when you said you were coming with me. It almost didn't work, though. When you asked me to stop by at four in the morning just to tell you goodbye, I almost didn't do it. I was sure you couldn't wake up that early."

"I don't blame you. Until this morning, I thought sunrises were a myth. I'm glad you came by."

"So am I. Actually, I'm shocked they even let you register at the last minute."

"Someone must have cancelled, and I didn't do it just for you. I'm looking forward to this. According to their website, half of the cabins are for girls. I know the food will be good. They've got canoes and an archery range. This'll be fun."

"I just hope their dream tech works."

"It'll work," Taylor said. "Just getting away for a few days will help. Think about it, a whole week in the woods without your parents stressing you out. That's probably all you need."

"You might be right. It would've been a lot easier if my parents weren't arguably insane. When I told them about my nightmares, you would've thought I'd told them I had the Ebola virus. I've never seen my mom flip out like that, screaming in Korean, throwing food, charging up and down the stairs."

"It was awkward."

"Then my father tried to tell me my nightmare had upset my mom because it reminded her of some experience she'd had when she was little. He's never lied to me like that before."

"Frankly, I think your parents are the ones with the mental disorder."

Jack grinned and nodded. "I'm sure it runs in the family. Whatever's the case, I couldn't tell them about the dream tech at this camp."

"So, what did you tell them? Didn't they read your invitation?"

"I tore off the page that mentioned the dream tech."

"Good thinking. It's cool that the camp specially invited you. You're way smart. Your dad must've been proud they chose you."

"He was more excited than I was. The people at Camp Farley knew exactly what to say to win him over." Jack turned to the brochure. "Advanced training in computer modeling. Credits toward college. All-in-one seven-day summer camp. My dad doesn't even know I'll be getting five thousand dollars for participating in their dream research."

"Man, I wish they'd invited me. I'll have to talk them into letting me do the research with you. On the other hand, I hope we don't have to do work the whole time."

"I doubt we will. They have three instructional sessions every day, but most of the time it's just boating and crafts and hikes and stuff. It doesn't sound like work."

"I wonder how the camp pays for it," Taylor said. "It's got to cost a ton of moolah providing free week-long camps for people all summer long. And that's in addition to what they're paying everyone in the two research cabins."

"They're loaded, believe me. The camp's run by Montathena Research. They're the ones that do research in advanced dream technology."

"What do they sell?"

"Beats me," Jack said. "I couldn't find a single product or service they provide, but they make billions of dollars every year. They could finance a thousand Camp Farleys."

Taylor slowed the car in answer to an approaching line of stopped vehicles. Fifty cars ahead, a middle-aged man stood in a florescent orange vest holding a metal pole with a stop sign on top.

"I hope we won't to have to deal with delays like this the whole way there," Jack said.

✖

THE YOUNG BLONDE girl stared down at Katie, her lip quivering. "I'm sorry if I woke you. Uncle Vance told me to fetch you."

"Look. Maybe you didn't notice, but this happens to be my

bedroom. I'm sorry if I'm not used to people barging in on me this early in the morning."

"But it's one-thirty."

Katie glanced at the curtains, glowing with sunlight. "Whatever." She studied the pouting girl. "Did you say, 'Uncle Vance'? You're not Clara, are you?"

The girl bobbed her head.

"Wow, I haven't seen you in ages. You were a lot smaller back then. I haven't seen you since your dad..." she stopped herself. "It's been what, seven or eight years?"

Clara nodded again, still frowning. "My mommy keeps saying daddy's coming home soon, but it's been so long. I think he's forgotten us."

Katie's jaw dropped. After all these years, Clara still believed her father was alive somewhere. She remembered how Clara's mother had disappeared with her the day before the funeral. Judging from Clara's clothing and childish demeanor, she wondered if she'd even seen the outside world since then.

Happier memories seeped into Katie's mind and she remembered many good times with Clara when they were kids, exploring the neighborhood, pretending they had magic powers, and running around on the Boston docks chasing seagulls.

She grabbed Clara's hands. "I didn't mean to hurt your feelings. You caught me in the middle of the worst nightmare, and I wasn't expecting you. Blame my dad for not telling me you were coming. What did he want, anyway?"

"I think he wants you to give me a tour of your huge house. My mommy and I get to live here with you. I get to sleep in the room right next to yours, but I'll bet we can have sleepovers every night. I'm so excited. This is the best thing that's ever happened to me."

"Live here? You can't have that room. That was Abby's room!"

"That's okay. I'll sleep anywhere you want. I'm sure we'll be best friends again. I've never really had any friends before. Mommy doesn't let me. She likes you, though. She told me so, dozens of times. She forgets a lot of things lately, but you shouldn't worry. She won't be any trouble. I could've taken care of her myself, but Uncle Vance's friends wouldn't let me. He says you get to take care of me."

"What?" Katie stiffened, then grabbed Clara's arm and dragged her into the dark corridor of the Victorian mansion. She led her down two flights of curving wood steps, past century-old paintings, antique rugs, flowered wallpaper, and stained wood cabinetry that heralded the excessive wealth of the old Bostonian estate. She arrived at her father's office on the ground floor and yanked the oiled-bronze door lever before barging inside.

"How dare you!" Katie flung Clara forward like evidence before a judge.

Katie's father, Vance Frost, an overweight man in a black suit, leaned over his wide mahogany desk, his eyebrows raised. Two men sat to either side of him in red, leather-clad chairs. Katie knew Fenton Murdock, a business associate of her father's, sitting to his left. He gave Katie a blank stare and pushed his wire glasses further up the bridge of his nose.

"Not acceptable!" said a sallow-faced, elderly stranger to her father's right. He glared at Katie with contempt and clutched the silver octopus-head handle of his cane; the creature's tentacles seemed to emerge from the man's bony fingers and wrap around the collar of the cane. "Mr. Frost, detain this woman before I'm forced to summon my own security detail!"

K atie riveted her eyes on her father. Vance Frost stood and
faced the man who spoke up, a nervous twitch in his forced
grin. "I apologize, Mr. Lynch. This is my daughter, Katie. I'm afraid
she wasn't aware of this emergency meeting." He turned to her. "We
can discuss whatever's bothering you later, Katie. Get along now. I'm
sure you and Clara have a lot to catch up on."

"I have my own life, Dad. You know how much I hate it when you
try to force me into things. I'm not a child. If you want to invite
people to live with us, that's fine, but you could at least tell me before
you volunteer me to take care of them."

Now that she'd said her piece, she scanned the rest of the room
and noticed Fenton's only son, Damien Murdock, leaning against a
bookcase behind her. He grinned, clearly finding her display thor-
oughly entertaining. Then she saw her reflection in a decorative
mirror behind him and she wanted to evaporate. She'd dashed into
her father's office in her nightgown, with no makeup, and hair like a
rat's nest. It was her anger, however—the raw, ugly rage in her face—
that caused her the most distress. When had she become so cold-
hearted and calloused?

Her father stared at her for a moment before speaking. "Young lady, I'm in the middle of an important meeting. If you have something to say to me, I suggest you first remember who puts the food on the table in this house. I want you to run back upstairs, take a shower, and get dressed. Then come back here when you're ready to speak to me in a tone of voice that will convince me you're a mature human being. If you can do that, I'll be happy to discuss the matter with you privately."

"There's no privacy in this house! Stephanie told me. Your security guards are always watching us. We can't do anything without your board's permission. I never asked for any of this!"

The elderly stranger perked up. "What else did this housekeeper tell you?"

"Excuse me, Mr. Lynch. This will just be a moment." Katie's father rushed to Katie's side and grabbed her arm. "We will discuss this in the hallway."

"I don't care where we discuss it. I'm not the one with all the secrets." Katie strode past Damien, trying not to look at him.

Vance glared daggers at her and closed the door, yet the lines of his forehead told more of worry than anger. "You mustn't talk like that in front of my associates."

"I don't care what they think. I have a right to control my own life!"

"But that's just it, Katie. You don't control it. You sleep in every day past noon. You refuse to finish school. You won't get a job. You've alienated yourself from your friends. Believe me, I know my company makes our lives difficult, but this behavior cannot continue."

"My life is my business."

"What life?" He let the acid of those words sink in. "Perhaps I should've told you your aunt and cousin were coming to live with us. Frankly, I didn't tell you because I'm fed up with arguing with you over every little thing. It seems like that's all you ever want to do anymore. It hurts me to see where your life is heading. It's like you want nothing more from your day than for it to be over with. I know it's been hard for you since your sister died. It's been hard for both of us, and I know you miss your mother."

"I don't miss her."

"Don't say that."

"I hate her, and so should you! She took away everything I care about and left me with a father that doesn't care about anything but his stupid company! Stephanie was more of a mother to me than Mom was!"

"The fact remains that after all these years, we finally located your aunt and Clara. Your aunt's mental health has deteriorated. The state wanted to put Clara into a foster home. We have a nurse for your aunt Virginia, but I can't take care of Clara. I have a business to run. We're the only family she has. We can't just abandon her. She needs your help. I spoke with my associates and they agreed that keeping her here wouldn't interfere with our work as long as I have your help."

"You talked to them, but not me?"

The door swung open. "I've heard enough!" Mr. Lynch's sallow face stretched with indignation. "Montathena Research takes pride in the way we run our business, young lady. I'm appalled at your insubordinate and disrespectful behavior. We have shown leniency to your father, in light of the tragedies you've recently endured, but your attitude has convinced me that the game is up. It's time to start your training."

"Out of the question!" Vance's face showed fear.

"Fenton had Damien trained years ago. You don't see any more attitude from him. Who's to say what your devious little housemaid shared with your daughter?"

Katie's father pointed a pen at Mr. Lynch like a sword. "I said no! I've taken every precaution to protect Katie from this business. She's no threat."

"This isn't only coming from me," Lynch said. "Your brother is on the executive board now. It was his personal request. If you don't want her recruited, take it up with him."

Vance's eyes widened. He looked pale as he led Katie back into the office. She noticed him staring at an old family photograph hanging on the far wall. It was from a Labor Day picnic six years past. Vance was sitting on a blanket with his loving arms wrapped around his smiling wife, Trisha. Abby was glaring comically over her mother's shoulder at a homemade strawberry pie. Trisha was holding baby Marcy, who was half-asleep. Katie was leaning against her mother and laughing. It all seemed like a dream.

"Alright, we'll do what we have to do." Vance lowered his eyes.

Katie scanned every face in the room. "You've got to be kidding me! You people really think I'd work for Montathena Research?" She glared at Mr. Lynch. "I don't even know you. You presume to stand there and tell me what my future has to be?"

"Katie," her father said, "you can't blame Mr. Lynch or Montathena Research for what happened to our family."

"So, what? That means I can't blow my nose without their permission?"

"You don't understand."

"I hate all of you!" She ran out the door and down the hallway, until her strength abandoned her. Her heart wrenching, she dropped at the foot of the wooden stairs. She felt abandoned and alone. Where was the doting father she once knew? Even orphans probably had *someone* to comfort them.

Muffled words crept from her father's office. "You might as well just kill her now," her father said.

"Don't be ridiculous," Lynch said. "They almost always survive assimilation. I'm astounded that a man of your rank and experience would allow his daughter to remain an ignorant sheep. The Intershroud is her best hope of attaining any real power in this world."

"Power! What good is power when you're just a pawn of the Intershroud?"

"Come now, Vance," Mr. Murdock broke in. "I was just as concerned as you are when they made me send Damien to camp but look at him now. His future is set. He'll be running his own research facility soon. It's not as bad as you're making it out to be."

"Don't tell me that! You know what happened to Clara's father, my wife, my daughter, Abby! Don't you ever try to tell me it's not as bad as I think! I know it's useless to fight my brother on this, but I won't force my only remaining daughter to go to that camp!"

"I'll have Damien talk her into it," Fenton Murdock said. "Son, go see what you can do."

Before Damien reached the door, Katie swung it open wide. She stood before them, cheeks wet, eyes reddened and expressionless.

"When can we leave?"

Wisps of smoke played with the crescent moon that hung low over the sharp-tipped logs that formed the twenty-foot-tall palisade around the campground. Unintelligible voices echoed in the cool pine-scented breeze, through staggered pine trees attempting to conceal the fence.

"Slow down, bro," Taylor ran to catch up with Jack, gravel crunching below his feet. "We're three hours late. A few more minutes won't make a difference."

Jack stopped and let his red-and-blue-canvas duffle bag flop onto the rocky ground. "I guess you're right. I was hoping we'd at least catch the end of the opening ceremony, but I hear too many people talking. It must be over. I can't believe there was so much road construction. We should've started the drive last night."

Taylor swung his green backpack over his shoulder and rubbed his arms against the cold. "We'd have been hating it if we did that. We probably took too many rest stops, too, but so what? We enjoyed ourselves. It's not like they're going to send us back home."

"I hope you're right. It's dark though, and we don't even know where we're sleeping."

They started walking again, taking care not to slip on the downsloping gravel path leading to the entrance. A pair of tall wooden gates stood open, sandwiched between two totem poles. A large wooden sign hung above the entrance, bearing the name *Camp Farley* below a giant painted eye rising in place of the sun.

Deep shadows within the trees played with Jack's imagination.

Taylor stopped. "Whoa, what's that?" He pointed at a patch of scrub oak near the gates.

Jack looked. "I don't see anything."

"I thought I saw someone running through those trees. I didn't hear anything, though. My mind must be messing with me."

"We both could use some sleep." Jack peered up at the border fence. "What are we getting into? There's barbed wire up there. Why would they need so much security?

"They're probably just keeping bears out. I'm okay with that."

"With razor wire?"

They passed through the gate, then clomped across a painted wooden bridge which stretched over a burbling stream that ran along a stone-faced wall on the inner side of the fence. Jack's eyes went wide at seeing the eerie darkness of the campground, bathed in the harsh light from two powerful stadium lights at a hillside amphitheater several hundred yards to their right.

A large crowd of campers stood in a clearing ahead of them, their excited eyes entranced by traces of white smoke flowing from the windows and doors of a nearby white clapboard building. The harsh lighting distorted everyone's faces in half silhouettes, giving them an appearance reminiscent of a low-budget horror movie.

"This place is in chaos," Jack said. "I'm totally having second thoughts about this."

The two boys sauntered forward and joined the crowd.

Someone had scrawled *Farley Must Die* in black paint across the front wall of the little structure. Two men carried a desk away from the building and dropped it next to four previously rescued desks, then stepped aside, making room for two women dragging out a wooden table. Other men and women rushed out with boxes and stacks of paper. They were all staff members, judging by their identical tan neckerchiefs, knee-length khaki shorts, and dark-blue polo shirts.

A man with a well-trimmed beard exited the building and set a box of papers on a nearby desk. He climbed on a table and placed a small megaphone to his lips. "We apologize for this interruption to our Opening Ceremony. It appears that someone pulled a prank on our camp's founder. The damage to our main office building isn't as bad as it looks. Right now, I want all staff members with cabin assignments to make sure their assigned campers make it to their cabins. Then return here to help with cleanup. Breakfast starts at seven, so I'd advise you all to get some sleep." The man leapt down from the table and rushed back into the building.

Jack took a moment to survey the campgrounds. He counted ten cabins, each nestled among pine trees, no two of them standing on the same level plane. He figured there were more cabins up a hill to his left, where a portly woman was ushering a group of girls. To his right, the land dropped at a steep slope toward a glassy lake that reflected a mirror image of the distant mountains and the semicircular concrete amphitheater that hugged its east side. A smattering of wood pavilions and fabric canopies surrounded the clearing.

Jack recognized the two-story, cedar-wood lodge from his brochure. Its glass front reflected the stadium lights and rose a story higher than the main offices next to it. He saw a row of two-story cabins across the stream and behind the lodge, likely serving as housing for staff members. Heavily trod paths circled every object, all leading to a clearing where he stood.

"We've got it under control. Get to your cabins," a scrawny staff member urged eight boys down a path toward one of the cabins near the lake.

"Let's find out who's in charge," Taylor said. "I need some sleep."

"There's the guy with the megaphone." Jack pointed to the bearded man now exiting the building with a white box of papers.

A wiry, thin-haired man walked up to him. He'd been standing with his arms crossed and staring at the building, his lip set in a sneer. Pockmarks covered his angular face but couldn't compete with the reddened burn mark that covered the upper left side of his scalp.

"Derek," the sneering man said to the bearded man, "find the security guards that were supposed to be watching the front gates. Send them to the lodge."

"Already done, Mr. Farley. They're waiting for you. I looked around the office. The vandals planned the attack well. They blocked up the fire sprinkler in your office with wads of clay and they knocked the cameras off the walls and disarmed the fire alarm. They pulled all the papers out of your desk. The fire did some damage, but most of the papers survived. Your bug collections were smashed. They must've stolen the clay and paint supplies from the lodge. They painted death threats all over the lobby."

"Threats against me, I assume," Farley's voice was gravelly from too many years of smoking. "Thanks, Derek. I haven't been back to this camp in nearly five years. Someone obviously told them I was coming."

"Told who? Do you know who did this?"

"I know exactly who did it, but someone helped her. Look how dark it is." Farley gazed up at two cracked light fixtures dangling from light poles near the lodge. Jack followed the man's gaze and saw at least four more damaged light fixtures nearby.

"There are a lot of broken lamps," Derek said. "The lights at the lodge are out, too."

"Someone here wanted it dark," Farley said. "Let me know if you hear anything. Get some staff together and move my belongings to the research facility. I'll be safer there. Call headquarters and tell them we need some crews here to repair the office and improve the lighting. By noon tomorrow, I don't want to see any sign of this attack. And let's put stadium lights outside the perimeter. That should keep her away."

"Keep who away?"

"Just do what I ask."

Jack turned to Taylor. "Why would lights keep vandals away?"

"That's what I was wondering," Jack said. "People with the guts to attack during the opening ceremony aren't going to be afraid of lighting."

A hand clamped around the nape of Jack's neck. He winced and turned his head enough to see Taylor's neck in the same predicament. The hands shoved them forward and let them go. Jack massaged his neck, then faced the leer of an elderly man with an unshaven, weatherworn face. He had a small *Camp Counselor* logo on his left pocket and a nametag that read *Avard Slake*.

"What are you two doing, sneaking around in the dark after we told you all to get to yer cabins?" He shoved Jack and Taylor again, forcing them forward until they stumbled next to Mr. Farley.

"Dude, we just barely got here," Taylor said.

"We don't have a cabin yet," Jack said.

Avard squinted and offered a half grin, then pointed at Jack. "You must be the Korean kid we've been waiting for. Pack Jaygee, is it?"

"That's Pak Jaegi." Jack wondered how the man knew the Korean version of his name. "Actually, I prefer 'Jack.' This is my friend, Taylor Bowman."

"Yer friend? That's irregular," Avard said.

"You weren't invited here, were you boy?" Farley sneered at Taylor.

Taylor shook his head and gave an awkward smile.

Jack winced. He should've known Taylor might try something like this. He was always trying to bend the rules to his advantage.

"What?" Farley said. "Did you think you could just show up and we'd all just bend over backward to make room for you?"

"The online registration wasn't working." Taylor produced cash from his pocket. "I'll pay if I have to. I don't even care if I have to sleep on the floor."

"Online registration wasn't working because you weren't qualified! We don't open the gates to every punk with a computer. We investigate people. I invite them personally."

"I'll have someone drive him to Kalispell," Avard said. "He can find his way home from there."

Jack's eyes widened. "It's a thousand-mile drive to L.A.!"

"Maybe he should've thought about that before he tried to invite himself," Avard said.

Taylor turned to Jack and shrugged. "Sorry, dude. It's a summer camp. I was expecting Kumbaya and group hugs."

"Don't be sorry, Taylor. This is strike three. Nothing's worth this." He turned for the gate and Taylor followed him.

Farley rushed to block them. "Wait, wait. Avard doesn't give the orders around here. Someone attacked our Main Office. We're all on edge. I can actually appreciate someone willing to challenge the rules. I'm sure we can work something out. Derek, find a cabin for the boy. Avard, take their car keys and have someone drive his car to the satellite parking area. I'll be in the lodge." Farley walked away.

"What a freak," Taylor said.

Avard presented a hand. "Keys?"

Jack dug his keys out of his pocket and presented them to Avard, then a gut feeling hit him, and he withdrew his hand. "Actually, I'd rather hold on to these if that's okay. Where's the parking area? I can walk back."

"Listen here, pal. We deal with hundreds of kids at this camp. If doing as I say is too much for you, yer free to turn around and hightail it back to yer mommy."

Jack didn't intend to put up with this kind of treatment all week. He leaned into Taylor's ear. "Let's get out of here." He turned around and met Derek's outstretched hands. He brushed them aside and started walking.

"You don't have to convince me," Taylor stepped up next to Jack. "Your nightmare problem can't be worse than dealing with these people."

Jack stopped and stared down at his keys. He turned to Derek and looked him in the eyes. "Your brochure said something about dream technology. Would you be able to help me with my nightmares?"

Derek nodded and smiled. "That's one thing I can promise you."

"Fine." Jack tossed his keys to Derek. "I'll give you people one day to make good on that promise. Otherwise, I'll be wanting those keys back."

"It's a deal." Derek handed the keys to Avard, who then walked away. "Follow me!" He walked to a table and dug through a cardboard box before pulling out two envelopes. "It's good to finally meet you, Jack. Farley assigned me to your cabin. You missed the opening ceremony, but you'll be fine. Everything you need is in this envelope."

He handed one of the envelopes to Jack. "There's a document in there for you to sign, assuming you want to be paid for the dream research. And there's an ID tag you'll need to wear at all times. It lets us know you belong here and it's the electronic access card you'll need to enter the research facility over there." He pointed to a building hidden behind trees up the hill.

"Your cabin's up there too, east of the research facility. Don't wander beyond your cabin, though. The other cabin up there is for the girls on the research team. We're strict about people staying out of other people's cabins. After Farley's opening remarks tomorrow morning, you'll need to go to the research facility with the rest of the boys in your cabin."

"What about me?" Taylor said. "Can I stay with Jack? Like I said, I'll sleep on the floor."

"No," Jack said. "You deserve better. Just go where they tell you for tonight and we'll make better arrangements tomorrow, if we're even staying here after tomorrow."

Derek turned to Taylor and handed him an envelope.

"Is this my lunch money?"

"Very funny. The only cabin with beds available is cabin twelve. It's the farthest one south of the lake. I'll get you an ID tag tomorrow. Now, if it's okay with you, I've got some calls to make. Get to your cabins and read through those info packets. I'll see you in the morning."

"Just one thing," Jack stared at the writing on the office building where three men stood scrubbing at the graffiti. "This vandalism seems too extreme for a prank. Why is someone attacking Farley?"

"You didn't hear it from me," Derek said, "but the guy has no friends. Literally anybody on staff could've been behind this. I don't know how they pulled it off, though. Everyone I know was at the opening ceremony."

"What do they have against him?" Taylor swatted at a mosquito.

"People blame Farley for an explosion that went off at a mine near here the year before the camp opened. A lot of people died. It's a sore point for him, so don't bring it up. I've really got to go now. It was good to meet you. Now, get to your cabins." Derek rushed off toward the lodge.

Taylor joined Jack in the climb up the path toward Jack's cabin. Jack frowned and kicked a rock along the ground.

"You okay, dude? Don't let that Avard dork upset you. I doubt he'll steal your car."

"I know. I just wasn't expecting the first people I met here to be a cranky old geezer and a weird guy who everybody hates."

"I know what you mean. Let's get some sleep. Maybe it'll be better in the morning."

F our rows of semicircular concrete seating lay embedded in the hillside facing a curved, wooden stage in front of Farley Lake. Fire tickled the air in a central pit. Nearly a hundred campers straggled in after breakfast, packing the arena and filling the air with overlapping conversations and laughter.

Jack stood on the top step and watched for Taylor, shading his eyes from the early morning sun.

"There he is," Jack said to the olive-skinned Asian boy standing next to him. Jack waved until Taylor spotted him and waved back.

"How you doing?" A smiling red-haired girl passed in front of Jack on her way down the steps. She joined three other girls, giggling and wrapping their arms around each other's waists.

"I swear, they only invited good-looking people to this camp," the Asian boy said.

Jack scanned the seats. Four boys, a few seats forward, laughed and shared photos on their phones with two girls. Two other boys tossed a blue foam football to each other over the crowd. Everywhere he looked, boys and girls were smiling, laughing, and telling stories. They were all sharply dressed, physically fit, and undeniably attractive.

"You know, Ming, I think you're on to something. Weird thing is, none of us knew each other until last night, yet everyone acts like they've known each other their whole lives. I feel out of place."

Taylor worked around the crowds on the gravel path behind the seating, stopping when he came upon eight boys facing each other in a circle. The boys stood frozen in ninja poses until the burliest young man of the bunch said "Ultimate!" Each boy then struck a new pose. The boy who'd yelled then slapped the wrist of the boy next to him. "You're out," he said.

Taylor eased around the boys and bee-lined for Jack. "They're playing Ultimate Ninja. I played it with the guys in cabin twelve last night."

"You missed breakfast," Jack said.

"I know. Its cruel and unusual punishment to force people to choose between sleep and food. Who's this?"

"This is Ming. His bed's next to mine. I wanted to tell you, we have two leather couches in our cabin. I'd be glad to sleep on one if you want to stay in our cabin."

"Couches?" Taylor looked confused. "My cabin is lame. I'm talking old mattresses on plywood bunk beds along the walls, and that's it. Cold concrete floor. No furniture whatsoever. The door doesn't even latch."

"Wow," Ming said. "Our cabin has a hardwood floor and six beds. We each have our own nightstands and our cabin has a shower."

"Not fair," Taylor said. "I'm there, but I'm taking the couch. I don't want to be a jerk and kick you out of your bed. I like the guys in my cabin, though. Who's in your cabin?"

"That guy's Travis," Jack pointed one row ahead at a muscular blond boy who'd wedged himself between a tall black girl and a petite girl with blue-dyed hair. The black girl stood up and traded places with the heavyset redhead sitting next to her.

"The girl with the blue hair is Marina and the black girl is Barbara," Ming said. "The red-head is Alison. Their cabin is next to ours. They're the only girls on the research team."

Alison turned around. "Actually, two more are coming today. If things don't get better soon, though, I'm out of here. This place has electricity and running water, so why don't they have Wi-Fi or cell service? My mother never would've signed me up for this if she knew we'd have no contact." She turned and continued complaining to Barbara.

Jack turned to three boys sitting on the other side of Ming. "These three share our cabin, but I've only met the guy on the far end. His name's Jorge. He's from Peru. I don't think he speaks English very well."

Jorge looked up and smiled.

"The boy with the book is Tony," Ming pointing to the short boy next to him who didn't take his deep-set eyes off the book he was reading. He had wide shoulders, hardly any neck, and a babyish face.

"I don't know the guy next to him," Ming said.

The tall boy turned and stood up, holding out his hand. His crooked smile revealed gapped teeth on his acne-scarred face. His mop of blond hair made him look top-heavy. His unattractive face seemed out of place at this camp.

"Name's Vandal Hearthstone," he said with a fake English accent. "Nice to meet you."

Tony looked up from his book and sneered, shaking his head. "His name's Carl. His dad works with mine at Baxton Financial."

Carl huffed. "Vandal Hearthstone's my penname, you dweeb. Thanks for ruining it for me." His accent disappeared.

"Pennames are for authors, idiot. Why do you think it has the word 'pen' in it?"

"I am an author. Anyone who writes is an author."

"Well, I don't consider someone an author until they're published. You don't know how to write, let alone get something published. You barely even read."

Derek stepped up on the stage with a folded wooden tray table under his arm and an open laptop in one hand. The boys turned their attention to him. Derek set up the scissor-legged table and set the laptop on it with the screen facing the audience. He turned on the computer and then left the stage.

"That's one of those Nebula 940 gaming laptops," Taylor said, unable to control the excitement in his voice. "They must be starting the computer aided drawing training they talked about on your invitation."

"My invite didn't say anything about that," Ming said. "Mine said we'd be doing animal research. I only signed up because I want to be a veterinarian."

Jack and Taylor looked at each other.

"Mine didn't say anything about animal research," Jack said.

"Attention everyone!" Farley stepped onto the stage, wearing a dark trench coat. His voice blared over a loudspeaker. "Welcome to your first introduction to true self-realization!"

The campers clapped in unison, but Jack ignored them. The campfire mesmerized him. Out of habit, he stroked the smooth steel lighter in his jacket pocket. He heard Farley's words, but understood nothing. The fire called to him. He fought the urge to swim within the flames. He often imagined something living in them, hiding in plain sight. He needed to know what it was.

A hush settled over the audience. Farley waited for complete silence, then spoke. "You're looking at a Nebulas 940 wide-screen gaming laptop. It would go for upwards of thirteen-thousand dollars in today's market."

Taylor's eyes went wide. "I told you there was a heaven." He elbowed Jack in the ribs, shaking his attention away from the campfire.

"This marvel of innovation includes all the latest cutting-edge technology. Everything you could ever dream of is integrated into its design: forty-eight-hour battery life, noiseless cooling system, eighteen-inch swiveling screen, Wi-Fi, internet, 3D movie capabilities, two-way video cam, three brands of gaming capability, voice recognition, motion sensors—you name it. Would anyone like one?"

Everyone's hand shot up.

Farley's expression turned devilish, and he pulled a twenty-pound sledgehammer from under his trench coat.

Ming and Taylor jumped up amid a chorus of gasps and shook their heads.

Farley hefted the sledgehammer over his head and planted it into the laptop. The computer shattered along with the table below it and crashed against the concrete, its parts scattering across the stage. Only shards of broken plastic, crushed metal casings, and splintered wood remained, mingled with power connectors, memory chips, slots, sockets, and fans, shorn from the computer's fractured mainboard.

The campers froze. Silence fell. Even the birds stopped chirping.

Farley savored the stillness.

"Each of you already possess a technological marvel that far surpasses any piece of human ingenuity. It's a technology so great, so powerful, so incomprehensible, that it renders all other technology insignificant." He dropped the sledgehammer, its heavy thud echoing throughout the arena.

"I speak, of course, of your minds. At this camp, you'll learn to see reality in a new light. Montathena Research is committed to helping you rewire your minds to escape the false notions that have plagued your thoughts since the day you were born. We specially selected you because you're the best this world has to offer. You're the successful, the achievers, the winners. Let no one tell you otherwise."

Farley clapped, urging the campers to join him. They did.

Taylor leaned toward Jack. "This is dumb. He's just telling everyone what they want to hear. Never trust someone who flatters you when they don't even know you."

Jack felt a tap on his shoulder. Turning to his left, a boy in a yellow t-shirt smiled at him from across the aisle. "I know we just had breakfast," the boy said, "but would you and your friends like some caramel corn?" He handed Jack a gallon bucket of caramel-coated popcorn and pointed back at another boy sitting five seats away. "Joe's mom made it. Pass it down."

"Thanks." Jack scooped out a small handful and handed the bucket to Taylor. "Take some and pass it down."

"Awesome," Taylor said. He grabbed as much as he could fit in his hand and handed it to Ming.

Jack turned back to the row of boys next to him. They were still clapping, sitting up straight with their heads held high. All five boys were smiling.

"Taylor," Jack said, "have you noticed anything unusual about these people?"

"Like what?

"Everyone here is so, I don't know, so perfect. I feel like such a loser."

"What're you talking about, dude? We're awesome. I agree it looks like they invited every football star and head cheerleader in the country, but what's there not to like about that? So, we get to live in heaven for a week. Let's have fun with it!"

"Yeah, you're probably right."

Jack did a double take when Taylor handed him back an empty bucket a few seconds later. Glancing at the ground, he found popcorn scattered all around their feet. Tony, Carl, and Jorge each held large piles of popcorn against their chests, their hands being too small to hold all that they'd taken. They hadn't passed the bucket on beyond themselves.

"You know, Taylor, I take it back. Farley's right. These people are winners, but I doubt he meant the guys in our cabin. We're the only ones I've heard complaining or being rude or selfish."

"Give it some time," Taylor said. "Once you get to know everyone, you find out they're not all that perfect either."

Jack blushed when he turned and handed the empty bucket back to his neighbor.

"Thanks," the boy said. He glanced at the popcorn on the ground but said nothing about it. "Hope you enjoyed it."

Jack smiled and nodded.

The clapping stopped, and Jack turned to the stage where Farley now stood, frowning and scanning the crowd.

"I tell you," he said, "your minds are a masterpiece. Yet I'd bet my house not one of you kids knows what is really going on in the cruel, merciless world we live in. Your government is hopelessly corrupt. They lie. They cheat. They'll steal your last dime and expect you to thank them for it.

"My goal is to teach you the street smarts you'll need in life. You've probably heard it a million times and never believed it, but it's absolutely true. Nice guys definitely finish last."

"That's not true!" Alison stood up. All eyes turned to her. "Sure, there are corrupt people out there, but you can't make blanket statements like that. There are plenty of good people in the world who aren't 'finishing last.'"

From where he sat behind Alison, Jack could see the fury in Farley's eyes. His expression softened. "Now that's what I like to see. Question everything. You've stumbled upon the first step to survival. You have to awaken your animal instincts. You've been told your conscience is your friend. I, however, implore you to fear anything that has influence over your mind—including your own conscience. Your conscience creates guilt. You must overcome enslavement to guilt. Guilt is just fear, fear of that which is part of your true nature. I'll teach you to rid your minds of this destructive indoctrination. Selflessness, by definition, will never be in your favor.

"Power equals corruption. But we all desire power, don't we? We fight wars to obtain it. We need it! We must, therefore, abolish from our minds this lie that suggests that we can have power and not be corrupt. People grow their businesses out of no other motivation than greed. Politicians are like demons, lusting to control the masses—to mold it to their way of thinking. Make no mistake about this! If you want power, your only option is to embrace that which the powerful have falsely labeled as corruption. How else could they keep you down?

"Reject the deceptive whisperings of your own ignorant conscience. People who foster obedience to their guilt are the lambs upon which the jackals of the world gorge. The cruel man always gains the upper hand. The spoils go to the crafty, the manipulators who care nothing for what others think."

Alison jumped up. "This is outrageous! I'm not going to listen to this crap!" She scooted past other campers. Dozens of other kids followed her lead, each standing and shaking their heads before leaving.

Farley smiled. "You're welcome to leave, but if you think about what I've said, you'll admit I am right."

An approaching helicopter sounded overhead. Farley's face lit up.

"I'll have to let you go early today—free time until lunch. There's boating at the waterfront. The archery is open, and there are crafts and art projects at the pavilions and at the lodge. Those of you on the research teams need to head to the research facility. I'll see you tomorrow." Farley left the stage, walking speedily toward the helicopter landing in the clearing.

"Wow, this place is a dustbowl," Ming said as a dirt storm wafted over the crowd.

Taylor nodded. "Yeah, that's pretty much why I left my A-Star chopper at home. They make such a mess."

K atie found the cabin to be nicer than she'd expected. It included little more than beds and a shower, yet it felt warm and inviting. Soft, brown leather sofas hugged the walls on either side of the doorway. Full-sized beds lay side-by-side on high wooden pedestals, three on each side of the room, with the head of each bed snug against the sidewalls. Pillows and comforters, decorated with images of plants and wildlife, covered each bed. Wooden side-tables with branches for legs stood to the right of each pillow. Rustic wood-paneled walls supported the pinewood beams that held up the slatted board ceiling. Beige curtains bordered the wide, sliding windows.

Katie looked up from the largest of the three pieces of luggage on her bed and watched Clara spinning around and admiring her bright yellow dress. "That dress is too big for you, but it'll have to work. Next, those pigtails need to go. We can't have you running around camp looking like a five-year-old."

"Can we go to the research facility now?"

"We just flew halfway across the country. I need a rest." Katie heaved aside one of her black bags and flopped onto her bed.

Clara dropped onto the bed next to hers and rolled onto her back, a smile ever-present on her face. "This bed is heaven. So's this cabin. I love it here. And best of all, I get to spend a whole week with you without my mommy telling me what to do."

"Mom," Katie said. "I told you, teenagers don't say 'mommy.'"

Clara sat up and nodded her head. "I keep forgetting." She gathered a stash of small rocks off her night table and studied them one at a time. "I collected these on the way to our cabin. Aren't they beautiful?"

Someone rapped on the door. "Hello," chimed a cheerful soprano voice. "May I come in?"

Clara jumped from her bed and ran to door, opening it for a portly woman with auburn hair and a warm, friendly round face.

"You must be Clara," the woman said. "I'm Sherry. I'm in charge of your cabin and just wanted to welcome you to camp. I also head the medical team, if you need anything." She looked over at Katie. "And you must be the famous Katie Frost." Sherry wiped her feet on a black mat next to the door before stepping onto the glossy hardwood floor.

Katie stood up, looking like a model in her draped, mixed-print top, light-blue jeans, and open-toed, leather boots. "I'm about as far it gets from famous. Glad to meet you."

"I don't know about that." Sherry turned to Clara. "Has she told you how they almost named this camp 'Camp Frost'? It's true. Her sister Abigail started it all."

"She did?" Clara's eyes lit up.

"Yep. This place would've been a much better camp if she'd lived. Anyway, the other reason I'm here is to invite y'all to the research facility. You're both part of the research team and our first meeting is about to start. Would y'all mind following me?"

Katie grabbed a water bottle off her nightstand. "What've we got to lose? Come on Clara."

They followed Sherry out the door and down a narrow gravel path. A chorus of songbirds echoed in the shivering aspens. Moments later, they turned down a switchback on the trail and a two-story, stone-clad structure peeked from behind spreads of vines and tall bushes. Its tiny windows made it seem massive, though its green metal roof rose only a few feet higher than the surrounding terrain. Curving river-rock walls sandwiched the steep path to the metal entrance doors.

"That's an odd building for a summer camp," Katie said. "You'd think they built it to withstand a nuclear war."

Sherry nodded. "You'll find this camp is full of surprises."

"Katydid," a male voice called from behind them. Katie turned to see Damien Murdock strutting down the path, his eyes on Katie. He stepped past them, arriving first to the building's front doors, and slid an ID card from the left breast pocket of his black blazer. He passed it in front of the infrared scanner mounted on the wall near the door frame. A slight electromagnetic buzz preceded the sound of large bolts sliding back into the door.

Sherry held the door open while the others entered.

"Wow." Clara's mouth hung open. Sunlight from the clerestory windows reflected off the polished marble floors. Warm cherrywood clad the walls and ceilings of the air-conditioned building, matching the stile and rail-wood doors. Clara darted past the lobby to try out one of the soft brown-leather benches that lined the wide hallway, then she stood up and darted to admire a series of abstract paintings hanging on the walls: large Jackson Pollock canvases, Hans Hoffman studies in fields of green and red paint, and works by Mondrian with their bold primary colors divided into rectangular areas by thin black lines. A life-size bronze statue of Carl Jung posed in the middle of the lobby.

"Only Montathena Research would waste this kind of money on a summer camp." Katie gave a wry smile and shook her head.

"You're in a good mood," Damien slowed down to let Katie and Sherry move on ahead. "I haven't seen you like this in years."

"I feel like a new person. It's been so long since I've been out from under my dad's thumb. I feel like they released me from prison. Montathena has been smothering me ever since my mom left. I can't do anything without them tagging along. I even dream about their operatives watching me. I've started having nightmares the last few months and I'm sure it's because of stress caused by my dad's business."

"Nightmares? Wait, that's the first I've heard about that. Have you told anyone?"

"My dad won't let me enter the research lab in my own basement. Why should I tell him anything? He doesn't care about me."

"Of course he cares. You should've told him. What happens in these nightmares?"

"It always starts with my dad's people guarding me, same as when I'm awake. I try to hide from them out in the gardens, but then some old Asian woman shows up. Next thing I know, I'm in some dark place where the woman's followers are holding me down and encouraging monsters to attack me. At some point, a boy shows up and the old lady orders him to save me. The boy loses the fight every time though, then he disappears in a burst of fire."

"Do you know you're dreaming when it happens?"

"That's what's frustrating. I never remember in the dream that I've had a similar dream before. I don't know what it means."

"You should've said something. We have tech that could've helped you."

"I don't want your technology. For all I know, my dad's experiments are *causing* my nightmares."

"If you hate the technology so much, why did you offer to come here?"

"Why did you? Two years ago, you were threatening to run away from home. You hated your dad's company. Then he sent you to this camp and you returned with a completely different attitude. I never understood it. But my father opened my eyes. He made it sound like I might not survive this camp. But I don't care. Either it'll kill me, or I'll learn to be happy about it like you seem to be. Anything's better than what I've been going through."

With glistening eyes, Katie turned and rushed down the hallway towards a set of blue-carpeted stairs where she'd last seen Clara.

Jack plopped a juicy red grape in his mouth and savored its sweet goodness, waitng for Taylor and Ming to finish filling their plates. The boys from Jack's cabin, and three girls from the cabin next door to theirs, hovered over an assortment of fruit, crackers, and exotic cheeses on a green marble countertop at the back of the circular room. Jack, Taylor, and Ming took their plates of food and melted into the soft chairs at the back of an arrangement of soft leather couches and lounge chairs. Derek stood at the front of the room studying his watch and leaning back against a stone fireplace next to a big-screen TV.

"Finally, a taste of the good life," Taylor shoved a triangular slab of Zamorano in his mouth and rolled his eyes in ecstasy.

Jack savored a slice of Comté cheese, then smiled and nodded. "I don't know what this is, but I like it."

Carl, Tony, and Jorge stacked their plates high before wandering to their seats. Travis, dressed in white slacks and a white sports jacket, held his plate as though it were a glass of wine at a high-end party. He leaned over from behind Jack's chair. "Just so there's no confusion, I have dibs on the Frost chick."

Jack scoffed. "Is that the rich girl that arrived on the helicopter this morning? I'll be surprised if she gives you the time of day."

"That goes for all of us," Ming said.

"Are you kidding?" Travis smirked. "I don't know about you guys, but I intend to leave this camp flying to my new job at Montathena Research, in my own helicopter, enjoying hors d'oeuvres and a foot massage from Katie Frost."

"Getting a head start on the dream tech are we, Travis?" Taylor shook his head. "Where is she, anyway? The sooner this class is over, the sooner we can go shoot some arrows."

Alison turned around. "No doubt Her Majesty deems herself too mighty to join us today. You should've seen all the bags they lugged to our cabin. She's probably never seen dirt before."

Marina bent forward and peered around Barbara. "Come on guys. Give the girl a break. We've hardly had a chance to get to know her."

"Don't defend her," Alison said. "People like her think they can do whatever they want."

A thumping sound echoed on the blue-carpeted stairs. All eyes turned to a bright-eyed blonde girl skipping into the room. She circled the room, taking in every detail, her braids flipping back and forth in time with her steps.

"This place is amazing!" She grinned wide. "Oh, look at that fireplace." She ran to the front of the room and slid her hand slowly across the rocky surface.

Sherry arrived and dropped into a chair near the stairs. "Katie will be here in a minute."

"Great. Let's find a seat, everyone," Derek said.

Barbara raised her hand. "Could I just ask one question before we start?"

Derek nodded. "I don't see why not."

"I just want to know, why did you select us, of all people, for this research team? I've seen some impressive people here, but I don't see what makes us so special. I'm just sayin'."

"That's just it. You're not special in most people's eyes. Montathena Research looks for kids with significant personality flaws, but who also have the type of mental abilities needed to improve themselves. You'll be using dream technology to overcome your character defects."

"Character defects?" Alison's face turned red as her hair. "Who are you people to judge us? This is ridiculous!"

"It isn't personal. Everybody has defects." Derek pointed at Travis. "Some of you are egotistical. Narcissistic." He then pointed at Ming. "Some are self-centered. One of you is afraid of bats." Then he waved a hand toward Jack. "And some are afraid of enclosed spaces and are cowardly, unwilling to fight their own battles. But these are common flaws, nothing we can't handle. We'll either help you overcome these defects or help you learn to accept them. That's what we do here. By the time we're finished with you, you'll be unstoppable."

Every face stared at Derek. Jack felt stunned and turned red with embarrassment. *How could they know about my claustrophobia?* It bothered him that the camp knew enough about his private life to judge him as a coward. They couldn't have found that info on the Internet. Somebody gave it to them. He felt betrayed.

"If everybody is just as defective as we are," Jack said, "how'd you get our names?"

"People recommended each of you to us."

"Seriously? Who recommended me?"

"In your case, Jack, the person asked to remain anonymous. I'm sure, however, Montathena wouldn't have invited you if they thought you wouldn't benefit from it."

Jack became distracted when he caught sight of an attractive girl, who he surmised to be Katie Frost, entering the room from the stairs and stepping softly behind the crowd. The girl blushed when she found Clara piling her plate high with crackers and cheese, and she rushed over to her.

"This is the best stuff I've ever tasted," Clara said. "You've got to try this."

"You're taking way too much," Katie said. "Put some back and come sit down. I told you, you can't act like this." Shaking her head, she waited for Clara to return some of the food before guiding her to a chair.

Clara ate her cheese with such excitement, no one could stop watching her except Jack, whose focused his attention entirely on Katie. Her beauty overcame him, her tanned complexion smooth as silk. Her tawny hair swept her broad shoulders whenever she turned her head and revealed her pearly smile. Her white floral top hugged her well-toned figure and complimented her casual blue jeans and stylish boots.

But it was her face that struck him the most. He knew it—every curve, line, and beauty mark. Time stopped. Then a light flickered on in his head.

*It's her!*

A dream had come to life. Every fiber of his being pulled toward her, but he resisted. Her deep brown eyes held him mesmerized in her lightest glance. His strength abandoned him at the subtlest curl of her full lips.

"That's all of you," Derek said. "Let's get started."

Fearful of making a bad impression, Jack forced his gaze toward Derek, but couldn't resist throwing brief glances at Katie at every opportunity.

"First, I don't want you to think you'll be missing out on activities with the rest of the camp. You'll only spend an hour or so here each morning. Here, we'll show you how to eliminate aspects of your thinking that impede your ability to realize your potential. Thanks in part to dream analysis work by Carl Jung, we now understand how to expose the thought patterns that keep us from performing at our highest level. Sherry, would you hand out the journals?"

He pointed to a stack of lime green notebooks resting on the mantle. Sherry grabbed them and shoved them under her arm.

With Katie facing away from him, Jack chanced a longer stare at the fullness of her silky brown hair. Three times, he brushed aside an object that kept pressing against his left arm.

"This is for you," Sherry said, pushing the book at him one more time, its pebble-surface tickling his fingers. Jack read the words etched in gold lettering: *Personal Dream Journal.*

"Dreams provide a window into our minds," Derek said. "Here's what we want you to do. First, before you bat both eyelids twice in the morning, record your dreams in these journals. Record every minutia of detail. After that, you'll come to the computer lab upstairs and enter the data into the dream assessment program.

"The programs aren't like any you've seen before. Once you input your dream, the program searches for every possible interpretation of it. No single dream provides an accurate analysis of your subconscious. Over time, however, a pattern will develop. That pattern will increase the accuracy of the assessment and enable it to pinpoint the aspects of your subconscious that are holding you back."

Alison rolled her eyes. "You mean to tell me this camp is all about analyzing dreams? I don't believe this."

"It's much more than that. The subconscious exposes the issues that are crippling your conscious mind. Our program uses your dream patterns to simplify what is happening in your mind on a subconscious level, so you can then take steps to correct any problems."

Jack caught fragments of Derek's words, but he had more important concerns. He snuck another glance at Katie, but this time found her glaring back. He turned away at lightning speed, but the disapproval he'd seen on her face wrenched at his heart.

*Crap! Crap! It's over now. She thinks I'm a loser.* He kept his gaze firmly on Derek and hoped she'd assume he had only glanced at her that one time.

"Alright, let's head up to the computer lab now," Derek said. "It's up the stairs and across the hall. You'll find your name on the computer we've assigned to you. Enter your dreams from last night into the program. After that, you're free to join the activities around camp. Just be aware that we won't pay out the five-thousand-dollar check if you fail to do what we've asked."

The campers stood up. Jack stared at the floor, then at Taylor, and then at Ming—any direction sufficed as long as Katie couldn't catch him staring at her. He tapped Taylor on the shoulder and rushed to the stairs, brushing Tony and Carl aside.

Taylor and Ming followed him up the stairs and across the hall.

They walked through the open double doors into the computer room and looked around. Wood-paneled walls matched the hallway. Four large computer screens stood in a row on a wooden table, sandwiched between two identical tables with four screens each. Twelve soft, black-leather office chairs hugged the tables next to each monitor. Masses of wiring ran under the tables on the hardwood strip floor.

"I've never seen computers that size," Ming said. "They're like twice as big as normal. I can't wait to see what they can do."

Taylor marched over to Jack and stopped him before he could sit down. "Okay dude, what's up with you?"

"It's her," Jack said. "That rich girl. She's the one I kept dreaming about!" Jack's spirits fell when Taylor and Ming looked at each other with doubting eyes. "I'm not making this up, guys. I dreamt about her so many times, her face is etched into my brain. I know it's her. I just don't know why."

VIII

Katie leaned back in her chair, watching Clara peck at her keyboard with two fingers. She leaned forward to read over Clara's shoulder. "You can't possibly remember this much about your dreams," Katie said. "You've been typing for hours. They're almost done serving lunch."

"I'm almost through. You have no idea how much happened last night." Clara turned to Katie. "Everyone depends on me in my dream. I can't even find time to journey to the misty castle, I'm so busy. Last night I had to make the pine trolls unblock the silver river so the water faeries and prairie dwarves could get water. A whole fleet of the Needling's ships were grounded when the water dried up. Then the harp trolls started forcing the weaver nymphs to pay a toll on the main road through their territory. Saltasha told me about a rebellion among the brownies…"

"Wait, Clara. What are you talking about? They don't want you to make up a story. Just write down what you dreamed last night."

"That is what I dreamed. There's always tons of things happening in my kingdom."

Katie stared at her and shook her head. "If you're serious, we need to get you to a therapist. You should be dreaming about things that happen in your daily life, not these weird fantasy stories. I'm seriously worried about you."

Clara frowned. "Some of the boys were laughing at me. I thought everybody dreamed this way."

"Don't feel bad. It isn't your fault. Your mother kept you isolated for all those years. You probably created those dreams to make your life tolerable. Let's quit this and get some lunch. When we get home, I'll talk to my dad about getting you some help."

LEAFY VINES TWISTED EVERYWHERE through the wooden trellis that hung over the outdoor eating area sandwiched between the lodge and the camp's main office. A dozen campers remained, finishing off their chicken quesadillas, bread sticks, and chocolate pudding. Jack squeezed his empty plastic plate into a pile of trash that rose above the rim of a metal-strip trash receptacle. Ming and Taylor did the same.

"Self-defense session is next," Jack said. "I'm looking forward to that."

Jack sauntered across the clearing with Ming and Taylor, toward four blue-and-white canopies. They slowed to step around three men raising a light post into a metal sleeve in the ground. A shiny white coat of paint made the main offices look newly built. Jack focused on a group of campers already gathering below the canopies.

"She isn't there, dude," Taylor said. "You're looking for Katie, right?"

Jack reddened and looked away. "She's avoiding me, I'm sure of it. I haven't seen her since the computer lab this morning."

"You're making too much of it, man. Girls like her are used to boys staring at them. I doubt she's given you another thought. She doesn't show up to things because rich people don't like hanging with us common folk. Now Clara, on the other hand, she's worth getting to know. Katie, not so much."

"Don't let some girl ruin your whole experience here," Ming said. "You seemed a lot happier this morning before she came along."

"You're right," Jack said. "I need to get her out of my head. I'll never see her again after this week anyway. I had a good reason to be happy this morning. I didn't have a nightmare last night. I haven't slept that well in months."

"That's great news," Taylor said.

"It might be the dream tech," Ming said. "You guys missed the opening ceremony last night. Derek said we might notice changes to our dreams while we're here. He said that when we on the research team do the sleep lab, our dreams will become even better."

"Sleep lab? Sounds creepy," Taylor said.

"I know," Ming said. "It's some kind of brainwave study that rewires our dream quality."

"No one's hooking anything up to my head," Jack said.

The three boys arrived at the canopies and searched for open spaces on the ground among the forty campers already sitting around a large square section of plywood flooring. Avard sat on a black metal chair, along with six burly, tattooed men and women.

"Looks like we'll be learning self-defense from a biker gang," Taylor said.

Avard stood and stepped forward. He didn't bother to introduce his companions.

"No point waiting any longer," he said. "This session is about defending yerself. If yer expecting the kiddie stuff yer used to seeing in the movies, yer going to be unpleasantly surprised. We're about preparing you for survival. When we're done with you, yer going to be tough, alert, ready for whatever comes at you. Now, who here thinks they know a few things about self-defense?"

Two-thirds of the campers raised their hands, Jack being the only one from his cabin. Avard zeroed in on him.

"My friend, Mister Park, knows a few things, does he? Mind stepping up here to show us a few tricks?"

Jack stood and walked over to Avard, then turned to face the campers. "I can't claim to be an expert. I never made it past the color belt ranks in Taekwondo. But I could show you a few kicks..."

Without warning, Jack found himself lying on the plywood board, confused and unable to breathe, his left side searing with pain.

"You sucker punched him!" Taylor jumped up, but two of Avard's tattooed cohorts grabbed his arms and pinned him against a thick tree trunk.

"There ain't room in this world for the weak," Avard said. He stepped over Jack and kicked him in the ribs. The speechless campers looked on with dropped jaws. Avard snarled at any camper who made eye contact with him.

"You kids have been taught yer whole life to cry to yer mommies every time somebody breathes in yer direction the wrong way. Stub yer pinky toe and you call a lawyer. Gotta sue someone. Well, we don't train babies here. Only the tree that endures the hurricane survives to see the next storm."

Alison stood up, her face red with rage. "You can't go around abusing people! You assaulted that boy! My mother's a lawyer. Your career is over."

The other campers watched her, their eyes wide. Jack couldn't blame them for sitting still and motionless. No one knew what Avard and his crew might do next.

"Look around you, Missy," Avard said. "This camp is surrounded by tall fences and barbed wire. You have no contact with the outside world. No phone service. Why do you think we hid your vehicles away? Wake up! For one week, we own you. We're going to strengthen you whether you want it or not."

"My mother wouldn't have signed me up for this abuse," Alison said.

Avard laughed. "This is exactly what she signed you up fer! Same fer all you pitiful wimps. We told yer parents every aspect of our methods, and they couldn't wait to send you here. No one wants you toughened up more than yer parents do."

"That's a lie!" Alison turned, and bee-lined toward the Main Offices.

A tattooed bald man started after her, but Avard held a hand to his chest and stopped him. "Let her go. She'll just run to Farley where she'll find out he's on our side." He turned to the campers who still sat staring at him. "The sooner you all learn that there's no place to run, the better off you'll be." He grinned and nodded to his friends to let Taylor go.

Taylor yanked his arms free, ran to Jack and pulled him to his feet. Jack held his ribs, his beet-red face wincing with every movement.

"You won't get away with this," Taylor said. He walked Jack away from the canopies.

"I couldn't breathe," Jack said in a raspy voice. "I'm going to kill that jerk."

KATIE SAT ALONE with Clara at the eating area and nibbled on a bread stick. Campers filed out from the canopies of Avard's self-defense session. Katie turned her head when Damien exited the lodge nearby. Spying Katie, he strolled over to her.

Clara stood up. "Can we go to the self-image session? It's in the lodge. Marina said the staff took pictures of everyone yesterday for it."

"Go ahead. I'll catch up in a minute."

Clara darted off, barely avoiding a collision with Damien.

He grabbed an aluminum chair and set it next to Katie, then sat down. "Weren't you supposed to be at self-defense training? Of all the crap they teach here, that's one you could've benefitted from."

"Clara wouldn't go. I think she's scared of Avard. Besides, we both know I'm not here to learn self-defense. I'm here to fall in love with Montathena Research. When does the brainwashing start?"

Before Damien could answer, Sherry emerged from a side door of the lodge with Jack and Taylor at her side. Jack had a bandage wrapped around his chest.

"You're lucky you escaped with just a few bruised ribs," Sherry said to Jack. "Go to your cabin and rest for a while. You have my permission to skip Avard's sessions from now on."

"Thanks, Sherry," Jack said. "If I never see that creep again, it'll be too soon." He and Taylor walked slowly up the hill toward their cabin. Jack glanced at Katie for a second and quickly looked away.

Katie turned to Damien. "Who's that Korean boy? He works for my dad, doesn't he?"

"Jack Park? Not that I know of. I've never seen him before. He lives on the west coast."

"You can stop lying to me, Damien. My dad hired him to spy on me, right? I know that's why my dad sent you here."

"Look, I have no reason to lie to you. I don't know anything about Jack Park, but he seems pretty ignorant to me. And I freely admit that they ordered me to look after you. Your dad all but begged me to keep you from joining his company. But Mr. Lynch ordered me to make sure you joined."

"So, what are you going to do?"

"It isn't up to me. You need to understand; there are some dangerous people at Montathena Research, and Lynch is one of the worst. So is Farley. My dad's scared to death that something could happen to me if I don't do what Lynch wants."

Katie sighed. "If I'd known they were threatening you, I'd have joined without coming here. What do I have to do to keep Lynch off your back?"

"There's a sleep lab he wants you to take. If you do that, he'll be satisfied. You could go home tomorrow."

"Why would that matter? People do those all the time. My dad has sleep apnea."

"It's not a sleep apnea assessment. The lab uses Montathena tech to manipulate your dreams, so you can see with perfect clarity how beneficial their technology is. It's pretty awesome if you ask me."

Katie stood up. "Seems like little to ask to keep Lynch away from you. Sign me up. I'm going to see what this self-improvement session is about."

"I don't see how it could apply to you, but I'll join you if you don't mind."

Katie smiled and they both made their way to the lodge.

R ustic cedar timbers held up the high, wood-slatted ceiling of the lodge's vast lobby. A three-part, bowed window formed the wall facing the center of camp. The other log walls housed cubicles and shelves strewn with scissors, paint, bottles of glue, stacks of leather, and many other craft supplies.

Over fifty campers covered the beige, carpeted floor, facing a large whiteboard. Katie located Clara sitting between Marina and Barbara at the back of the room. Damien blazed a path for himself and Katie until they arrived at an open spot behind Clara. They both stood, leaning against the back wall.

An attractive brown-skinned woman, in a navy-blue, knee-length dress with long, lacey sleeves, swaggered to the front of the room. She moved slowly. Two other staff women passed by her and stood fidgeting, waiting for her to catch up.

"My name is Media," she spoke with unnatural slowness, her accent revealing her Indian heritage. She took her time writing her name on the board. "That's Meh-dee-yah, not Mee-dee-yuh. Ten points from anyone that mispronounces my name. In addition to instructing you on the importance of maintaining a proper image, these women and I will run the competitions and activities here. Any cabin that loses too many points will spend their time cleaning toilets. We'll provide prizes for the cabin that gains the most points at the end of each day."

Katie turned to Damien. "Why does she talk like that? I've never heard anyone talk so slow. It looks like it's torturing her to have to talk so much."

Damien shook his head. "It's sad, really. She was talking as fast as anyone back when I attended the camp. She's real smart, too, has a PhD in Neuroscience."

"So, what happened to her?" Katie waited for an answer, but Damien just stared at the floor. She sensed he was holding something back.

"Something happened to her mind," Damien finally said. "Montathena has its risks. I can tell you more after you join the company."

Katie shook her head.

"This first woman to my right is Jenny," Media said. She pointed at a petite, shapely woman with long black hair, her pink one-piece swimsuit visible under her unbuttoned staff shirt. She smiled and waved.

"You may have already met her. She oversees the waterfront. This other lady is Tamera. She runs our research facility and helps with the science and nature sessions."

A tall woman with perfect posture stepped forward and smiled, then nodded. Katie admired the auburn hair she had tied in a bun. Her blue eyes twinkled behind her large red glasses, and a short red dress peeked through her open lab coat.

Media started to sway back and forth, and her mouth twitched. "In our sessions. In our sessions, we'll focus on beauty and perfection. Looks equal success. And we'll have. We will..." She stared at the crowd for several seconds.

Tamera ran up behind her and grabbed her around the waist, just stopping her from falling over. She lifted Media's arm and placed it around her shoulder, then lowered her into the chair and turned to the campers.

"I suppose I'll be handling things from here," Tamera said, with perfect enunciation. "As my friend was saying, the first impression you make is of extreme importance. It will define who you are in the eyes of every individual you meet. The destructive effect of your imperfections should never be underestimated and should not be tolerated."

Tamera snatched a remote control from a nearby countertop and turned on a white projector hanging from the center of the ceiling. An image of the lodge appeared on the whiteboard.

"As each of you arrived yesterday, we took photos of you for this presentation. Weaker minds often accuse us of being mean and insensitive. My hope, however, is that you all will be mature enough to accept constructive criticism. You will not survive in this world if you cannot accept the truth about yourselves. Those who would spare your feeling merely rob you of the opportunity to empower yourself against their unspoken criticism."

She pressed a button and a highly magnified photo of a wart appeared. Katie looked away. A young black-haired girl gasped and slapped her hand over her cheek. She looked around the room with wide, horrified eyes.

"A seemingly insignificant blemish, like this one, will be the difference between acceptance and rejection in the world you face every day."

The next image exposed dark curves below a girl's brown eyes. "You may think you're getting away with staying up late, but you can't hide the hideousness of baggy eyes from a boy you may have hoped to impress. Unacceptable." A Hispanic girl sat still in the center of the room, her mouth hanging open.

The next image displayed a close-up of the crooked upper teeth of a skinny boy.

"When you go for a job interview, who do you think will get hired? The man with glistening white teeth, or this guy, who looks like he has been chewing on a tire iron?"

Scattered laughter erupted and the boy with the crooked teeth stood up. He clamped his mouth shut and, with glistening eyes, ran out the door. Jenny followed the boy. Tamera gave her an angry glare and wagged her head.

"Like I said, we can pretend we are doing people favors letting them think they're perfect, or we can be honest so they can commence their journey to perfection. That boy may be embarrassed now, but I guarantee you, he will be begging his mother to take him to the dentist next week. Then no one will be quietly disgusted by his face. Now, look at this character."

The next slide displayed the short legs of a stocky blond boy. "Human or chimp? Your call."

Katie felt confused, and a little sick. She'd always believed people needed to be more honest with each other, but now she doubted that philosophy. This woman wasn't just speaking hard truths. She was hurting people. Truth could be a devastating weapon.

"Can we go?" Katie yanked Damien's arm.

"In a minute," he said.

"Why? What are they trying to prove by humiliating people?"

"They know what they're doing. They're creating resilience. You'll see."

"Tell me this doesn't look like a hoard of giant splattered insects," Tamera said. A freckled neckline adorned the projection surface.

"I hate you," a petite freckled girl said, startling Katie. "This camp is like living in Hell!" She stood up crying before stumbling over people in her desperation to exit the building. Four other girls followed her, their faces contorted with rage.

A young blond boy stood with his arms folded. "You have no right to treat people like this! I don't know what you're trying to prove, but I'm not putting up with it." He motioned to four boys next to him and they all stood up and followed him out of the room.

Tamera showed no concern. She even smiled when they left. She continued the session in the same manner: criticizing moles, wide hips, frizzy hair, a chipped tooth. Some of the kids enjoyed it. Carl, Tony, and Travis laughed loudly at Tamera's comments. Carl grinned and made a face when the gap between his upper teeth made the show.

A tall brown-haired girl moaned and dropped her face into her hands when the slideshow exposed a birthmark on her neck.

"Who would ever hire a girl with a dump-truck blotch staring at them? Do you really think you can succeed in life with a stain like this blaring in everyone's face?"

Clara shot to her feet. "I don't care what you," Clara said. "you're just mean and I'm leaving."

Katie had never seen her so serious. She raised an eyebrow at Damien.

He nodded. "Alright. Let's go." He and Katie followed Clara outside.

⚔

JACK AND TAYLOR marched past several cabins on their way toward the amphitheater. They passed two girls sitting on a log and hugging a third girl who was crying and holding her hand over her cheek. A hundred yards later, they moved out of the way of two boys who were shoving at each other.

The larger boy charged at the other and pinned him to the ground. "You mention my teeth again and I'll bite your eyes out," he said.

Farley smiled, watching the fight from a chair in front of the main office.

Jack gave Taylor a confused look. "What is going on? Those are the same guys that shared the popcorn with us this morning."

"Maybe that self-improvement session was no better than Avard's so-called self-defense training. I say we skip Derek's session. Sherry said you could have the rest of the day off."

"I don't care about his session. I just want to ask him some questions."

Many other campers now joined Jack and Taylor, heading to the green canopies on the south side of the lake. Ming and Travis caught up to them, then Alison walked past them.

"Hey," Taylor said to Alison. "I thought you'd be long gone by now."

Alison turned with fury in her eyes. "I just spent an hour in the main offices arguing with that buffoon, Farley. The front gate is bolted. They wouldn't let me use my phone. We're literally prisoners here! When this week is over, you're going to see the lawsuit of the century!"

"Why go to Derek's session then?" Jack swatted a fly from his nose.

"He's my last hope of going home today. At least he seems more rational than Farley."

They arrived at a set of four canopies arranged similarly to Avard's set up. These canopies, however, had blue tarp walls that enclosed six rows of black metal chairs. Derek stood behind an oaken table, in front of a freestanding whiteboard. Pads of lined paper and orange pens lay on each chair. Campers took their seats and Jack settled in one at the front. He noticed Katie enter and take a seat at the back, sandwiched between Damien and Clara.

"Good afternoon," Derek said. "Today, I'll be instructing you on the value of self-marketing. My goal is to show you what it takes to move up the ladder and stay there. Nothing is more important than your reputation. It affects everything you're able to attain in life. It's needed to impress employers or attract friends. Reputation, however, is not about who you are. It's about who other people *think* you are."

"You want us to lie about ourselves?" Barbara laughed at her own comment.

"Truth is irrelevant," Derek said. "Once you've convinced people you're invincible, reality makes no difference. The Egyptians learned that even a young boy could rule the world, if the world believed he was a god. Only you know who you really are. Everyone else sees you the way you make them see you. Whether you choose to admit it or not, we all are liars by nature. Isn't it about time we accepted it and embraced it? It's not a question of whether to lie. It's a question of how to lie."

"This whole camp is a lie," Alison said. "My invite said I'd be given guidance toward a law career. I haven't heard a word about it."

"I've been wondering about that, too," Jack said. "When do we start the 3D computer modeling?"

"Mine said we'd be doing animal research," Ming said.

"Is this some kind of joke?" Travis stood up. "I better be getting assistance in business management. What's the deal?"

"This is bogus!" Alison folded her arms. "This camp is a fraud! You lured us here with lies! You snared us like animals!"

"We can't even call home," Barbara said.

Alison shook with anger. "This isn't legal, and you know it! You may think you have us trapped, but this hoax won't last forever. You might as well start looking for a real job because you'll be hearing from my lawyers the second I step beyond those gates. They'll close this place down so fast, your head will spin."

Derek smiled. "First of all, why are you yelling at me? I had nothing to do with your invites. But you're making my point perfectly. Montathena Research wanted you here. Thus, they said what was required to influence you to come. Like it or not, that is how the world works. Politicians say whatever will get your votes. News outlets report what they hope will influence your behavior. Power comes from influencing people to do what you want."

Alison stood up. "That's it. I'm going to my cabin until I'm allowed to leave. I've had it with this place." She turned around.

Derek ran after her and blocked her path. "I'll tell you what. Maybe I can arrange to let you go home early. I'll have to arrange it with Farley, but you'll have to give me one thing. Do a sleep lab tonight."

Alison's face tightened. "I couldn't care less about your stupid sleep study."

"I understand. I promise you though, if you do the study and still want to leave, I'll personally call your mother. You came all this way; we might as well get something out of it."

Alison hesitated and then shrugged. "I guess it couldn't hurt, but it won't change my mind." She marched away.

"Okay, my friends. I've got a little assignment for you as well. I want each of you to create two lists. First, come up with a hundred believable lies about yourself. Then come up with a hundred unbelievable truths. Make up lies that no one could possibly disprove. The best way to deceive people is simply to not tell them the whole truth. It's impossible to disprove a partial truth, since it's still truth.

Tomorrow you'll each choose three lies or truths and try to fool the rest of us. There'll be prizes for the cabin that succeeds the most times."

Jack thought the assignment might've been fun under other circumstances, but the very idea of lying angered him now. They'd lied to him about the 3D modeling. Who knew what else they'd lied about? What had he gotten himself into?

Jack laid back on a slatted-wood bench on the porch of his cabin with Taylor, his hands behind his head. He squinted at the reflection of the evening sun shimmering off the lake far below. Distant yelling, the splashing of water, and the clunking together of canoes told of the campers enjoying life down at the waterfront.

Tony, Carl, Jorge, Travis, and Ming rushed out of the cabin wearing their swimming trunks and flipping towels at each other. They barreled down the hill, except for Ming who stopped and gave Jack a confused stare.

"You're not going to the lake? They're having canoe races."

"We're sitting this one out," Taylor said.

Jack frowned. "They're lying to us, abusing people, and keeping us from leaving. How can everyone just go on like that's okay?"

"It's not okay," Ming said. "It's horrible. But what can we do? We're trapped here, and whenever I think about it, it just drives me crazy."

"We could look for a way to escape," Jack said.

Ming nodded. "If you can find a way out of here, I'm with you all the way. But, until then, we need to stay sane. We should try to have as much fun as we can. No matter what, it'll all be over by the end of the week. Then we can take our money, go home, and forget about this place."

"Maybe you're right," Jack said. "It's not all bad. I came here to do something about my nightmares, and I didn't have one last night. So, there's that."

"Funny you mentioned that." Ming tucked his yellow towel under his arm. "I dreamed about this camp last night even though I was only here for about four hours yesterday before going to bed. Travis, Tony, and Carl all said they dreamed about this place, too."

"Come to think of it, so did I." Jack sat up straight. "And I hadn't even seen the camp in the daylight yet. That is really weird."

Taylor said, "Makes me think they're doing something funky to our brains, dude. Can't say I remember my dream, though."

"What if it's permanent?" Ming's face became serious. He stared at the lake. "What if we never dream normally again? No payment's worth that."

Jack slid his silver lighter from his pocket and flicked the flint, then let the flame work on him like a drug. "Who knows what they're doing to our minds? We can't trust anything they say."

"This is starting to freak me out," Ming said. "Seriously, If I don't stop thinking about it, I'll give myself a panic attack. I'm going to the lake. See you at the bonfire tonight." Ming ran down the hill.

"Dude, my brain can't take this either," Taylor said. "Next time we see Derek, we need to ask him exactly what their dream tech is doing to us."

"He'll just lie about it. They're holding all the cards. Ming has a point. We need to stay calm and figure out what to do." Jack closed his eyes and tried to enjoy a subtle breeze and the tapping of a woodpecker high in the trees, but nothing could smother the foreboding he felt in his heart. The fear would not go away.

A low thud interrupted the silence. He opened his eyes and turned to a nearby cluster of low-lying pines up a steep hill to his left. He heard someone crying and glanced at Taylor.

They both stood and climbed the short hill, easing around a cluster of white spruces a few yards down the other side of the mound, near the wooden perimeter fence. Taylor brushed aside an armful of pine boughs.

Sherry jumped and a spark of terror flashed in her puffy, reddened eyes, then vanished. She wiped her face with the sleeve of her jacket, smearing eyeliner and mascara across her soaked cheeks.

"Y'all should be at the waterfront." She turned away.

"What's wrong?" Sherry's show of emotion surprised Jack. Perhaps some of the staff members were human after all.

Sherry stared at the boys for a moment, then became resolute. She marched over to Jack, lifted his I.D. lanyard over his head, and walked ten feet away and tossed it. The lanyard fluttered and landed, dangling on a low pine bough.

Jack and Taylor just stared.

"Sorry," Sherry said amid sniffles. "Your I.D. is bugged. Farley and his cronies are listening to every word you say. Taylor isn't part of the so-called research team, so his lanyard's safe."

"You sure you're okay?" Jack thought she might be losing her mind.

She forced a smile. "I'm not the one to worry about."

"Aren't we self-realizing enough?" Taylor gave a wry grin.

Sherry frowned, her lower lip quivering. "Self-realization. What a joke. Everything we've been telling you is a joke."

"You don't need to convince us of that," Jack said. "I've got the bruised ribs to prove it. Don't feel bad, though. You, at least, help people around here."

"Yes, but it's not enough!" She shook in exasperation. "Y'all have no idea what I just witnessed a few minutes ago. A sweet little darling came into the nursing station, her shoulder dripping blood from where she'd taken a knife to her neck. Why? 'Cause she had a little birthmark, no bigger than a ladybug. She tried to cut it off. All because we told her it made her ugly. That beautiful little sweetheart mutilated herself because of this self-realization garbage!"

"You can't control what people will do," Taylor said.

"Oh, but we do control them. Don't you see? That girl did exactly what Farley hoped she'd do! He wanted her to question her self-image, to destabilize her mind. He isn't interested in making good kids better, he wants to take great kids and destroy them!"

"You're blowing this out of proportion," Taylor said. "I mean, there's no excuse for what Avard did to Jack, but I thought Farley made some sense. A lot of people don't know how to survive in the real world."

"All that talk of survival is a smokescreen," Sherry said. "Nobody needs to be humiliated or embarrassed just to learn how to survive. It's all lies."

"I don't get it," Jack said. "Don't get me wrong, I'm willing to believe you, but all I've seen so far are adults telling me to be a jerk, to lie to people, and punch them in the gut when they're not looking. They're not destabilizing my mind. They're just making me mad."

"That's true, Jack, but they're making you angry on purpose, to manipulate you so you'll reevaluate your beliefs. Each session at this camp is designed to make you question right and wrong. Y'all saw how the other campers were this morning: content, friendly, self-assured."

Jack nodded. "I felt like I didn't fit in."

"That's understandable, but you'll fit in just fine by the time we're through with you. Montathena lured y'all into their web like a poisonous spider, infecting y'all with doubts about your own goodness. Once your subconscious is no longer in harmony with your conscious mind, your mind destabilizes. Them kids are already starting fights with each other, and this is only the first day of camp."

Taylor shook his head. "This still seems a bit over the top. You're telling me they invite good people here just to mess them up? It seems Montathena would have better things to do."

"It's not their goodness they care about. It's about taking away their ability to control their own dreams. Montathena is in the dream business. A destabilized mind cannot control its dreams."

"We can't do that anyway," Taylor said.

"That's what Montathena wants you to think. You're right that most people can't. Most people are already mentally conflicted because of the bad decisions they make. Bad decisions create conflicts in their minds which make it impossible for them to control what they dream. Confident, self-assured kids, like the ones at this camp, aren't like that. They've made good decisions and thus aren't hampered by mental conflicts. That means it's possible for them to control their dreams, the same way they control their lives when they're awake."

"I didn't even know it was possible to control dreams," Jack said. "And I doubt anybody else knows. So, what does Montathena Research have to gain from making it so we can't do it?"

"The mere possibility of it is enough for Farley to try to make sure it can't happen. If even one person learns to control their dreams, Montathena can't control that person and they become a threat to Montathena's profits. Their goal is to maximize their ability to manipulate you kids in your dreams. That's what this camp is really about."

"They can't manipulate us in our dreams," Taylor said.

Sherry looked around. "I've said too much. I'm putting you at risk. I'm sorry, but I can't say anything else."

"What? Dude, we deserve to know when people are messing with our brains."

"You don't understand. These people are far more dangerous than you realize. They could kill you if they found out you knew their secrets."

"Then why are you working for them?" Jack clenched his fists. "Why don't you report them and put a stop to it?"

"Because I know how powerful they are. Y'all have no idea. No one can oppose them. Honestly, Farley would kill me right now if he knew I was telling you this. But I can't stand it anymore. I can't help everyone, but maybe I can at least save you two."

"Save us?" Jack looked at Taylor and back at Sherry. "If we're in that much danger, you've got to tell us. What's their plan?"

"I want to tell you, believe me, but Farley's operatives are always watching you, even in your dreams. They're lying about y'all being a research team. You're here for a single purpose— to be observed. All they want to know is if y'all are aware of their secrets, and the more I tell them to you, the more danger you'll be in."

Jack shook his head. "We can keep secrets, come on."

Taylor stared her in the eyes. "Did you just say they're watching us in our dreams?"

Sherry turned away and shook her head, then turned back to them, looking resolute. "I shouldn't have said that. There's no point in keeping it from you now, but you both need to promise me you'll never speak of it again until you're safely home."

Jack nodded, and Taylor crossed his heart.

"We promise," Jack said.

"Okay. This is all I can tell you. We share our dreams."

"You're joking." Taylor laughed.

"I wish I were, but it's true. All people dream to the same reality. When you dreamed about this camp last night, members of our staff were there watching you. Had y'all shown the slightest evidence that you knew you were sharing dreams, y'all would've been in great danger. That's why I can't emphasize this enough. Don't give them any reason to think you know we share dreams."

"That's crazy," Taylor said. "I'd know if I was sharing dreams with people. No one's ever acted like I shared a dream with them."

"There are many reasons for that. To start with, normal dreamers forget ninety-nine percent of what they dream. More importantly, dreams are chaotic if you don't know how to control them. You might be sharing a dream with your mother, but you also might be simply dreaming up an entity to be your mother. You might even think you're dreaming about your mother, but when you wake up, you realize it was someone else. The chaotic nature of dreams is enough to keep most people from ever figuring out that we share dreams."

Jack grinned. "This is amazing. The world needs to know this."

Sherry grabbed Jack's shoulders and gave him a stern glare. "You can never do that. Montathena wouldn't hesitate to kill you and your whole family to protect their secrets."

Jack could only stare at her. He couldn't fathom such a threat being true.

"Seriously?" Taylor's eyes showed his doubt. "They'd literally murder people for knowing they can share dreams? Why? How does it hurt them for us to know that?"

"Money," Sherry said. "Power. They profit from your ignorance, a common business practice if you think about it. Think what y'all could do if you had access to every mind on earth. Y'all could ask someone their deepest secrets, tell them anything, influence their decisions. They'd wake up the next morning never realizing they gave you their bank account number or you influenced them to buy a specific stock. Accessing other people's dreams is the most lucrative business in existence."

"This is unbelievable," Jack said. "I can hardly wrap my mind around it. Why'd they want to observe me? Why'd they think I was a threat?"

"They're concerned you might already know their secrets. All the other kids on the research team have relatives with connections to Montathena or one of its affiliates. According to your file, an old woman found Farley in his dreams and asked him to enlighten you. Instead, he lured you here to be watched."

"Old woman?" Memories of repeated nightmares flooded Jack's mind. He turned to Taylor, his face ashen. "She's real! That old woman I kept dreaming about, she's a real person! And she sent me to this freakin' camp!"

"What do you know about that old hag?" Taylor placed a hand on Jack's shoulder.

"Not much. Farley thinks she heads a dream cult in South Korea. I'm sorry she got you mixed up in this, but there's nothing you can do about it now. It's critical now that y'all just act ignorant. If Farley or anyone else finds out you know about any of this, they'll either force you to work for them or they'll kill you. I'm dead serious."

"They can't force us to do anything," Taylor said.

"Why do you think I'm here?" Sherry's voice cracked. "I hate Montathena to the depths of my soul. But they found out I stumbled across their secret and now my survival depends on me helping them to protect it. There are quite a few of us on staff that don't want to be here. I can hardly live with myself anymore." Her hands flew to her face, tears streaming between her fingers.

"What're you going to do?" Jack felt his pockets, wishing he had a handkerchief to offer.

"Don't worry about me. I'm not alone. I have something planned. Just protect yourselves. I'm hoping y'all won't remember any of this while you're dreaming, but if you do, play dumb. Act like you don't know you're dreaming. When you record your dreams in the computers, be honest. Play their little game and you'll make it out of here free and alive. Promise me you'll just play dumb."

Jack looked at Taylor. He shrugged and then nodded.

"I'm pretty much an expert at playing dumb," Taylor said.

"One more thing. Don't do their sleep lab. You do that, they will own you. Make any excuse you can think of, but don't let them hook anything up to you in that lab."

Sherry looked at Jack's lanyard, still dangling from a pine branch. "Keep that lanyard on in public, and don't ever talk about their secrets, or even dreams, if you can avoid it."

"You keep saying 'their secrets,'" Taylor said. "Are there more secrets?"

Sherry sighed. "I've already said too much."

"What about after we leave camp?" Jack gave her a hopeful look.

"I suppose y'all could benefit from some lucid dreaming tips. I'll tell you what…" She pulled a small, yellowing book with frayed pages out of her purse and handed it to Jack. "Y'all can have this, but only if you keep it hidden and you open it only when you get home from camp. Can you promise me that?"

Both boys nodded, and Sherry handed it to Jack.

He shoved the book under his arm.

"That book's a training manual, but you'll notice some of the pages are torn out. There are secrets that even I am not allowed to know. It'll still tell you what you'll need to know to stay safe from people like Farley."

"So, what are you going to do?" Taylor asked.

"I'm serious when I say I can't take it anymore. Don't get your hopes up, but if things go as planned, I might be able to cut this camp short for y'all. Now get on back to your cabin and keep that book out of sight." She smiled, then walked away.

Jack and Taylor watched her disappear through the trees. Jack stared in silence, replaying her words in his mind. He turned to Taylor. "We've got to get out of here."

"I'm with you, dude, but how? This place is a prison yard."

"I don't know, but I can't just sit here and watch Farley's bullies destroy all those innocent people. And what'll happen if they decide one of us knows too much? I'm not going to be their slave for the rest of my life. We need to find a way out of here and bring these people to justice."

"We can start by warning everyone. We outnumber the staff."

Jack shook his head. "Sherry said we'll be in danger if they think we know too much. We'll be putting everyone at risk. And who knows how many cameras and listening devices they have scattered around camp?"

"We at least need to tell Ming."

"We shouldn't put anyone else at risk until we come up with an escape plan. I'm sure I can come up with something while I'm trying to sleep tonight. I doubt I'll be sleeping again until I do."

A lull fell over the campground after campers took to their cabins to change into warm clothes and prepare for the night's event. The sun hovered between the jagged peaks of a mountain range far across a sea of trees. Ever-darkening pines framed the deep blue sky and invited cool breezes and the chirrups of crickets.

Jack closed the door of the cabin and ran to join Taylor and Ming, fighting the steep trail down to the amphitheater. He tucked the end of his lanyard into his shirt pocket so no one would be able to tell that he'd removed the bugged ID badge, then checked to make sure Ming had done the same. He didn't want to risk saying something that would make the camp staff suspicious.

"Why'd you have to tell me all that?" Ming breathed faster than usual and kept darting looks in various directions. "I think I'm having an anxiety attack. You sure Sherry wasn't pranking you? I don't dare even fall asleep tonight."

"Dude, I didn't mean to trigger you," Taylor said. "I just felt you deserved to know."

"It's not your fault," Ming said. "I've always had anxiety issues, but it isn't every day that I find out people are spying on me and will kill me if they don't like what they see."

"I knew we should've waited to tell you until I came up with an escape plan," Jack said.

"I promise I won't tell anyone else until we do," Taylor said.

"How can we possibly escape?" Ming stopped and turned to Jack. "Think about it. We have no access to our car keys or our cars. The gates are guarded. We can't climb the walls. Apparently, there are cameras and bugs everywhere, and we have no way to communicate with the outside world. Even if we could escape, I'm no outdoorsman. I'd die out there in the woods."

"I didn't say it'd be easy," Jack said. "Maybe we don't all have to go."

"What if we pay someone to create a diversion," Taylor said. "Start another fire or something. With the guards distracted, Jack and I can sneak out the front gate and run to the nearest town for help."

"Even if that works, who'd believe you?" Ming started walking again and Jack and Taylor followed him. "If you try to tell the police that Montathena Research is trying to control people's dreams, they'll just send you to a psychiatrist. Besides, Farley's been bullying kids for years without anyone stopping him. I don't see any hope in fighting them unless we can come up with some real evidence."

Jack pursed his lips. "I'll find something. I have that book Sherry gave me. Maybe there's something in there."

"I say we sleep on it," Taylor said. "For now, let's try to calm down. Maybe our minds will be clearer in the morning."

"I agree." Jack hugged himself against the cold. "Let's just hope they haven't figured out a way to ruin the bonfire." Jack took a deep breath, attempting to start creating a spiritual connection with nature.

The camp exploded with bright unnatural light and sharp black shadows.

"So much for that hope, dude." Taylor said.

"Farley took care of the lighting problem alright," Ming said. "At least I won't be the only one unable to sleep tonight."

A short young woman with golden brown hair stepped past Jack and he nodded to greet her. She smiled at him with her mouth pursed shut. Jack knew why. She had a chipped tooth, making her a victim of the infamous "self-image" session. He expected he'd be seeing a lot of self-conscious kids wandering around camp.

"Hey." Jack stepped up to the girl. "Don't listen to those idiots on staff. Your smile is adorable."

The girl's eyes lit up and she walked away. She still kept her mouth pressed shut, but Jack noticed a little more of a skip in her step.

"Speaking of pretty girls, when are you going to talk to Katie?" Ming stared at Jack with an exaggerated glare of interest. "We'll know Sherry told you the truth if Katie admits she had the same dreams you did."

"I know, but there's nothing I can do about it. She's always with Damien."

"Don't worry about him," Ming said. "Next time you see her, just walk right up and ask her straight out."

"Good plan, but what would I say? 'Hi Katie, I dream about you every night. How about you?' She'd put out a restraining order against me."

"Maybe you can talk to Clara," Ming said. "Although, she's a little ditzy."

"No, she isn't," Taylor said. "I think she's hilarious. I know she pretty much wrote an entire fantasy novel and claimed she dreamed it, but I think it's just her way of rebelling."

"She doesn't look like a rebel to me," Ming said.

"Dude, you need to realize, those computers don't just tell you what's going on in your head. They also tell Montathena Research what's in your head." Taylor's face lit up. "In fact, tomorrow I'm going to do what she's doing. I'm going to start making things up. They're going to think I'm freaking Mephistopheles when they read my dream."

"You're forgetting that they're watching our dreams," Jack said. "They already know what we're dreaming, and that it's about this camp. Sherry warned us about it."

"I guess you're right," Taylor said.

"That means those computer assessments are a complete waste of our time," Ming said. "That bites. I was actually looking forward to those dream assessments."

✄

KATIE EASED PAST JORGE, Tony, and Carl, then noticed Damien standing on the back step of the amphitheater, waving at her. She waved back and pushed Clara along at a quicker pace. Clara stared up at one of the stadium lights, then lost her balance and grabbed onto Carl's head.

"Watch it!" Carl untangled himself from her arms and shoved her away, then snarled at her and rubbed his right foot.

"Sorry," Clara said.

"Haven't you seen a light bulb before? Watch where you're going!"

Katie grabbed Clara's hand and pulled her away from him. "Don't listen to that dweeb. Those lights are pretty bright. I don't blame you for looking at them."

"Actually, I was watching the bats. There's a whole bunch of them up there."

Katie looked up and saw five bats circling the fixtures, snatching up moths. Moments later, she and Clara took seats on the cool concrete next to Damien, and again they gazed up at the flying creatures.

Damien looked up for a second, then turned to Katie. "Would you save my place? Someone needs to do something about those lights. It's like daytime here." He skipped down the steps and disappeared behind a crowd of campers standing in front of the stage.

Marina walked up behind Katie, with Alison and Barbara at her side. "I'm glad I caught you, Katie," Marina said. "I hear you and Alison are both planning on doing that sleep lab tonight."

"Good thing, too," Alison said. "It'll be nice and dark in that lab. No one else will get any sleep tonight."

"Listen," Marina said. "Don't you think it's odd how desperately they want you to do that lab? I wouldn't do it if I were you. I don't trust them."

"It's nothing to worry about," Katie said. "Damien did it years ago and he's just fine. My dad runs labs like that in my basement all the time. I'm not worried." In truth, she knew the dangers existed, but she'd made her decision and preferred not to have to defend it.

Marina started to say more when Travis jumped down from the step above them. The lights at the amphitheater went dark.

"That's good timing," Travis said. He turned to Katie. "I've been trying to meet you all day. We're practically neighbors, you know. My uncle works for a Montathena affiliate in Jersey, just up the road from Boston." He moved within inches of Katie and she backed away.

"Sorry, but Damien and I are already, you know, an item." Katie looked around to make sure Damien wasn't around to expose her lie.

Travis frowned and turned to Clara. His smile returned.

"She's got a boyfriend, too," Katie said. She stepped between him and Clara.

"I do?" Clara gazed at Katie with a look of shock.

Marina squeezed onto the seat next to Clara. Travis gave her a dark look and shook his head, then walked away to sit with his cabin mates.

Katie then noticed Jack, Taylor, and Ming working their way around Travis.

"I wish Damien would hurry." She searched the fire pit below and saw him squatting down next to Derek, helping him start the flames.

"I love this," Clara said. "I've always wanted to go to a bonfire! I hope it's fifteen feet tall."

The blood rushed to Katie's face when Jack arrived with his friends. She couldn't understand her own feelings. She felt drawn to him, but it only angered her. It didn't feel natural. Only her father's company could've caused her to dream about him so often, and she couldn't bear the thought of them having manipulated her. She gave Jack an angry stare, hoping he'd get the hint and stay away.

Ming nodded at Katie as he passed her, then Taylor halted next to Clara, forcing Jack to stop. Taylor observed the empty seat next to Katie and turned to Clara. "Hi Clara." He waved at her.

Clara waved back. "Hi. It's Taylor, isn't it?"

"Yeah. I've heard about the stories you've been writing about your dreams. I think it's awesome. I want to hear more about it tomorrow."

Clara's eyes lit up. "Okay. Most people just say I'm lying, but I'm not."

Taylor navigated past Katie, all the time keeping an eye on the empty seat next to her. With both Jack and Katie watching Clara, he kicked behind Jack's knees and shoved him onto the concrete step next to Katie. Jack tried to stand up, but Taylor held him down.

"Didn't you say you needed to talk to Katie?" Taylor said. "That's alright, I can wait." He stood and blocked Jack's attempt to escape.

"I was saving that spot for—"

"Damien, I know," Jack said. "I'll move. I don't want to get between you two. I was just hoping you'd let me ask you something."

Katie nodded, her heart racing.

"Look," Jack said. "I know it sounds weird, but when I first saw you this morning, I totally recognized you. I just wanted to ask, have you ever been to Los Angeles, or maybe, South Korea?"

"Korea?" Unprepared for his sincerity, she let out a nervous laugh. Either he was ignorant of their having shared dreams or he was a convincing liar. Her fear persuaded her of the latter and she frowned and looked away. She couldn't hide the hint of anger in her voice. "I've never been to Korea. I've been to Disneyland in L.A. before, but that was ages ago."

"Okay then." Jack rubbed the back of his neck. "I can tell I stirred up some bad memories. I'm sorry."

Jack glanced up at Taylor and stood up. Katie grabbed his arm and stared at her hand, wondering what had driven her to do it. Jack turned to her and gazed at her fingers wrapped tight around his wrist. The euphoric look on his face made her uncomfortable and she yanked her hand away, then turned her gaze downward.

"You have nothing to be sorry about," she said. "My whole life is bad memories. I didn't mean to sound so angry."

"That's okay." Jack took a step back and tripped over his own foot. He blushed and then nodded and gave her a weak smile. He turned and took one step before colliding with Damien.

Damien pushed him away and gave him a wide grin. "Geez, Katie. Replaced me already? I'm hurt." Damien staggered back, overplaying a dramatic bullet wound to the chest.

"I was just asking a question," Jack said.

Damien laughed. "Just razzin' you. Actually, I'm glad to see you showing a little backbone, going after a CEO's daughter and all."

Jack shook his head. "I wasn't trying to go after her. I just—"

"Calm down. I wasn't serious. You'd be wasting your time anyway. She's heading back home tomorrow, after the sleep lab."

"That soon?" Jack turned to Taylor, his eyes wide with concern.

"Looks like Derek's ready," Damien said.

Jack nodded and stepped down one level and walked with Taylor to sit next to Ming.

Damien's conversation with Jack confused Katie. She'd assumed Damien had lied about not knowing Jack was spying on her; but their performances were too convincing. They didn't seem to know each other at all. Maybe she'd had it all wrong and Jack really didn't know anything about her dad's work. But if that was true, why had he shared so many dreams with her? Perhaps her father was using him, fooling him into spying on her without him even knowing he was doing it.

Damien sat next to Katie and the two of them watched ashes float up to a backdrop of starry sky. "Much better with those stupid lights off," Damien said.

"Won't Farley blow a gasket?" Katie pulled her sweater tighter around her shoulders.

"He's already tucked away in bed at the research facility. He'll never know, as long as Sherry remembers to turn the lights back on, like I asked her to."

Derek stood near the six-foot flames of a roaring fire, holding a microphone to his lips. "Tonight's your night, folks." He scanned the crowd. "If any of you wish to share a favorite joke, a skit, or a fun story, this is your chance. Please keep it clean. Otherwise, relax and enjoy the fire." He set the microphone on the stage platform and walked to the front row of seating and sat down.

Katie stared at Jack, wondering what to think of him. He wasn't the kind of person that usually worked for her father. She thought it odd how he stared at the bonfire, like he wanted to swallow it.

Everyone watched the crackling flames for several minutes in silence, then Barbara stood up. Marina and Clara clapped as she skipped down the steps, until she reached the timber stage. She grabbed the microphone and walked in front of the bright blaze.

"Just thought someone had to tell the famous Camp Farley ghost story."

Derek stood, rushed over to Barbara, and whispered something in her ear, all the time looking up at Katie.

Katie leaned toward Damien. "What's that all about?"

Damien shook his head and shrugged.

"Okay, my sister told me 'bout this story when she came here a few years ago," Barbara said. "She don't lie, so I can swear this is totally true.

"It all started a long time ago, like maybe like ten years ago. There was this girl who lived in an old house in one of the old mining towns near these woods. This girl had everything she could ever want. Rich parents. Hot boyfriend. Let me tell you, her life was good. Her boyfriend liked to take her to their favorite spot up in these mountains."

She pointed at the mountain behind the amphitheater. Katie joined many other campers and turned around to look.

"It was an old abandoned silver mine everyone called 'the Museum,' 'cause there was a ton of old, rusted mining tools and crap lying around.

"Then, one dark, windy night, the girl was sauntering home from her job at the drug store when she stumbled across a crumpled note that was tumbling along the ground. She stared at it for a sec and she recognized the handwriting. It was her boyfriend's handwriting. She figured the note must've blown off her own porch.

"The note said, 'Meet me at the Museum, eight o'clock sharp. I have a surprise for you, my love.' Well, that girl got so excited she could hardly move. She had a good idea what the surprise was going to be, so she ran on home and begged her dad to drive her up to the mine—which wasn't easy. Nobody's dad wants to take his daughter to some old mine after dark. But she kept begging and he finally gave in.

"She was late, of course. The sun had already gone down before her dad drove away. She could see the glowing of a campfire in the mine. She was all smiles when she strolled inside. But her joy didn't last. They say her heart melted from her soul that night. There they were—her next-door neighbor and very best friend—snuggling in the arms of the boy she thought was going to be her fiancé."

The hum of dozens of disapproving voices moved through the crowd. Barbara smiled, glad that she had won their attention.

"The girl charged out of the mine, her tears flowing like a river. She wished she could just die. Her so-called boyfriend and her so-called best friend ran out after her. Her boyfriend saw his note in her hand and searched for an explanation. He said he only brought her best friend along to witness his surprise. He swore he'd never hurt her. He begged her to go back into the mine to wait for his surprise.

"The girl's eyes dried up a bit. She hoped so much that it was all just a misunderstanding. The trusting girl reentered the mine and stood there waiting. She grabbed a burning stick from the campfire and poked at the embers.

"She thought, 'Maybe I've been too quick to judge him. He wouldn't never be so cruel.' But then she heard it—the revving of a car's engine. She dropped the stick and ran out of the mine just in time to see her boyfriend's car speeding away down the hill. She was all alone now. In the dark. In the middle of the forest. She didn't have no phone. She didn't have nothing.

"Pain and anguish consumed her. She could barely walk. She staggered into the mine, swearing that her boyfriend would pay for what he'd done to her. As if that wasn't enough, she stumbled over a wooden box lying on the ground and scraped her leg. She didn't notice the words 'dynamite' printed on its side. She just lifted her leg up and kicked that stupid box into the fire. Then there was a loud BOOM!"

The audience jumped when Barbara shouted that last word. Everyone laughed. Barbara waited for the audience to quiet down before solemnly continuing with her story.

"No one knew what happened to that poor girl. She never returned home. But dozens of people have reported seeing a young woman wandering through these mountains at night. Within a week of the explosion, a miner found the girl's boyfriend, pierced through the heart with a flaming firebrand. A week after that, a fisherman found the girl's best friend drowned in this very lake. They say that the same end comes to all who cheat on a girl in these woods.'

"So," Barbara said, "if you ever, ever consider being unfaithful to someone, you had better think twice about it. You had better be prepared to face the wrath of the ghost of Abigail Frost."

A moment passed before Katie internalized that Barbara had used her sister's name. Abby had died in an explosion, but she didn't have a boyfriend, or live in the nearby town. Her eyes welled up. It seemed impossible that anyone could've tarnished Abby's memory by twisting her tragic death into some ridiculous ghost story. Yet, they had.

Derek stood up and ran to Barbara. "I told you not to use the name!"

Barbara's hands flew to her mouth. "I forgot. I'm sorry." She looked up at Katie, her eyes wide with regret.

"It's just a story." Damien started to slide his arm around Katie. She shoved it away and stood up, her mind muddled. She barreled past Clara and charged past the legs and feet of everyone sitting along her row, her fists clenched tight and her lungs compressed and fighting for air.

Damien stood and tried to follow her, but campers now standing in the aisle hampered his progress.

Katie felt wounded to the core. How could anyone defile her sister's name? Free from the throngs at the amphitheater, she headed straight for her cabin, shoving aside pine boughs and stumbling on small rocks and clumps of grass concealed in the darkness.

Then someone to her right, half hidden behind a pine tree, caught her attention. A short person stepped into the open, dressed in robes so black they melded with the night. The stranger pulled back her hood and revealed a subtle smile and glistening brown eyes. She turned and faded from Katie's view.

Katie thought she'd finally gone mad. Her own scream didn't register to her. Everything went black.

When Katie regained consciousness, she opened her eyes to find Damien looking down at her. He kneeled over her and placed a hand on her back, then lifted her to a sitting position. Other campers surrounded her, including Jack and the rest of the research team. She heard Barbara's voice repeat sincere apologies over and over.

"What happened?" Damien wrapped his arm around her waist and pulled her to her feet. "Why'd you scream?"

Katie trembled and pointed at a nearby pine tree. "Abby. She's here. I saw Abby."

Gray sky deadened the colors of cabins, trees, and hillsides around Camp Farley, and the air hung eerily still. Jack stood on a wooden dock near a line of canoes tipped on their sides, scanning the abandoned lake. A flash of bright blue drew his eyes to the distant rocky shore and he turned and spied Katie, tossing pebbles into the water. He next found himself standing twenty feet from her, unaware he'd just traveled at the speed of thought.

He hopped from rock to rock, his eyes glued to her smiling face.

"Jack!" Her voice was music. She navigated a stony path to him, then stumbled and let herself fall into his embrace.

Jack could've held her forever.

"I'm so glad I found you." She released him, took a step back, and stared into his eyes. Moist tears glistened off her soft cheeks. "I thought you were dead. You were so brave. I don't know how you survived."

"Why? What did I do?"

"Don't be modest. We both know how hard you fought that flying lion with the sharp teeth. It terrified me. I never could've faced it. I owe you so much."

The image of a massive manticore blasted into Jack's memories, followed by thoughts of an old Asian woman and her sadistic minions pressing in around him. He remembered a huge snake, a dragon, and a pack of wolves. Jack stumbled backward, then caught himself on a tall, jagged stone. He whipped around in several directions and searched the trees and rocks behind him, then the surface of the lake. He saw no gang of cultists, only clusters of pines and the motionless water.

He turned back to Katie, then looked away from her wry smile and look of deep concern. A nervous laugh escaped him. "That was embarrassing. I can't even think about that old woman and her monsters without freaking out."

"Don't feel bad. I'd have been afraid to leave my house after what you went through. You should be proud of yourself."

"To be honest, I thought I'd dreamed it all until you brought it up. Now I'm half expecting them to come flying at me out of the trees." He sat on a nearby boulder and again scanned the trees.

"I can't imagine what you must be going through. I wouldn't worry about them, though. That old woman only ever found me walking in the gardens at my house. I doubt she'd know I'm here."

"I want to know why she came at all!" Jack leaned down and snatched two small rocks and tossed them into the lake. "I know they're obsessed about making me fight something, but why were they bringing you into it? You must have been terrified."

"I was afraid, which bothered me afterward, because I always knew somehow the monsters never actually intended to attack me. It made me crazy not being able to do anything to help you."

"You always did what you could," Jack said. "You should've stayed out of your garden, so they couldn't find you."

Katie's cheeks reddened, and she shook her head. "I always tell myself that, too, but I never seem to remember. The only thing on my mind is collecting roses for my mother. I don't know what's wrong with my memory."

"It's the same with me. I've never gone to meet that old woman. I never even remember she exists. I blink my eyes and suddenly I'm with her and she's forcing me to fight things."

Katie took hold of Jack's hands and her gentle touch melted away his fears. He looked at her face and found a loving gaze that warmed him in spite of the sunless sky. He glanced over her shoulder and gasped. Damien stood behind her, leering at him.

"It's true then," Damien said. "You do know each other."

"Damien!" Katie turned around and smiled. She walked to him and gave him a brisk hug. "What's going on?"

"Everyone's wondering where you've been. My dad and Mr. Lynch are here to check out the camp while Derek interviews everyone on the research team. They've already talked to most of you." He took Katie's hand and led her along the rocky shore in the direction of the lodge.

A half minute passed, then Katie stopped and turned around. She dropped Damien's hand and motioned for Jack to follow her. "Come on, Jack. They want to talk to you, too." She again took Damien's hand and turned away.

Jack clenched his chest against the pain of seeing someone else hold her hand. He couldn't understand her sudden change of demeanor, her sudden lack of interest in him. He worked his way along the shore, past rows of canoes and the dock. He passed the staff cabins and observed how similar they were to his cabin, except they had two-stories and demanded twice the footprint.

"Tell me, Jack," Damien said. "What do you think is happening right now?"

Jack frowned and assumed he was taunting him about Katie's having chosen him over Jack. He wasn't going to give him the satisfaction. "We're walking to the lodge. Why?"

"Yes, but doesn't something seem different to you?"

Jack looked around and realized the campground did seem unusually desolate. He counted five boys climbing on the amphitheater steps. Three girls sat on the ground by a gray canopy, talking. The girl with the chipped tooth chased a butterfly in the clearing by the main office.

"Seems like a normal day to me," Jack said. "But where is everybody?"

"Is that normal?" Damien pointed up at the balcony of the lodge. Tony stood there, leaning on the wooden railing, the butt of an M16 rifle set against his right shoulder and his eye focusing on the scope of his gun. Jack followed the line of the gun barrel and his eyebrows creased. He was aiming at one of the boys at the amphitheater.

"What's he doing?" Jack ran forward, then stopped when the gunshot rang. He turned and saw that one of the boys had disappeared. The other four didn't notice, however, and continued to chase each other around the amphitheater steps.

Tony laughed.

Carl came into view from behind him and grabbed the gun from him. "It's my turn. This is awesome."

Jack couldn't speak for several seconds. He turned to Damien, who stood there smiling.

Katie's eyes showed her fear and confusion. She pressed a hand over her mouth.

"What is happening?" Jack said. "Stop him!"

No sooner had Jack said this when two men in black suits stepped up behind Tony and Carl. They carried smug expressions on their faces. One of them was thin and wrinkled with age. He reached out and set a hand on each of the boys' shoulders. The boys disappeared. Jack could only stare and wonder what he was seeing.

The bigger of the two men reached his hands forward, palms up, and raised them slowly. He fixed his eyes on Katie while he and his elderly companion rose into the air, floated over the balcony railing, and lowered to the dusty ground in front of the lodge.

Katie turned to Damien. "That's your dad and that old grouch, Mr. Lynch!"

"I told you they were here," Damien said.

"They were flying. What's happening?" Katie's voice broke.

Fenton Murdock and Mr. Lynch walked up to her.

"Look at her, Dad," Damien said. "She has no idea what's happening. Neither does Jack. I think we can skip Derek's interview. These two are Sleepers if I ever saw them."

"I wouldn't be so sure," Mr. Lynch said. He walked over to Jack and stared him in the eyes. "Jack Park, is it? What do you have to say? You just watched one of your friends shoot a boy. You saw the boy disappear. Then you watched me and my associate fly through the air. Tell me. How is any of this possible?"

Jack gave a nervous laugh. He looked to each man, hoping they'd give him a hint, then he shook his head. "Is this a magic trick? This has to be some kind of illusion."

Lynch turned to Katie. "How about you? Explain it to him."

Katie shook her head, her eyebrows raised. "I'm with Jack. I mean, I know Montathena does dream research, but I never knew they could make me hallucinate."

"You're not hallucinating," Damien said. "This is important. Do either of you have any idea what is happening right now?"

Jack and Katie shrugged their shoulders.

Lynch turned to Fenton. "We'll see how things go during the week."

"You got to admit this looks good for Katie," Damien said. "Her dad was right; she doesn't know anything."

"You are too trusting," Lynch said. "I've known people who faked their ignorance for decades. Katie's father would do anything to keep his daughter out of the business. I don't trust him; thus, we must keep watching her."

Katie looked at Jack and her smile returned. "Are you as confused as I am?"

Jack nodded, distracted by the chopping of an approaching helicopter. He searched the gray sky and watched it fade to the cold blackness of night. The camp vanished, taking Katie and everyone else with it. Only the sound of rotors remained, which then slowed and stopped. Jack looked at his alarm clock and read that it was three in the morning.

"What's a helicopter doing here in the middle of the night?" Travis dashed to the window.

"I was about to ask the same thing," Ming said. He sat up.

Travis ran and opened the door, inviting in the echoing of a woman's screams.

"Get out of my head! Get out! Get out of my head! Don't touch me. Get out!"

The cabin's floorboards rattled with the clomping of feet. Carl and Tony followed Travis out the door.

Jack turned to Taylor but found only a wadded blanket in a heap on the floor next to the couch he used as his bed.

"Where's Taylor?" Jack stood and wrapped a blanket around himself. He pressed past Ming on his way out the door and a gust of cool air assaulted his face. He charged past the other boys, ignoring the small rocks bruising the soles of his bare feet. He brushed past shadowy leaves and trees until he collided with a warm body enveloped in flowered comforters.

Barbara stepped backward to regain her balance, falling into Marina's arms.

"What's wrong with you?" Barbara took the stance of a street fighter.

"Someone's screaming! It sounds like Alison," Jack said.

The screams had become muffled and unintelligible.

"It is Alison," Barbara said.

Jack started to move, but Barbara took hold of his arm. "Don't bother. Security's forcing everyone back to their cabins. But don't think that'll stop me from finding out who hurt Alison. Someone's head's going to roll."

Jack turned to Marina. "They didn't say what happened?"

"Farley claimed Alison had an allergic reaction to some sleeping pills, but don't believe it. I know what allergic reactions look like. They did something to her. It's just like I feared. We need to avoid that lab, whatever it takes."

Taylor stepped up behind Barbara. Two men in black uniforms stood behind him.

"Keep walking," the shortest of the two men said. "Farley wants everybody in their cabins." The guards stood still and waited.

The group turned and climbed back up the hill.

Taylor sidled up next to Jack. "Sorry I didn't wake you, dude, but you looked like you were having a great dream."

"I wasn't. It was weirder than ever. I'll tell you about it tomorrow. I'm surprised I was able to fall to sleep at all. What did you see?"

"I woke up to something scraping on concrete and then heard something pounding on metal. It was so dark, I thought I'd gone blind. So much for all them lights Farley installed. Then I heard people yelling. I swear the noise went on for like, ten minutes. I couldn't believe all you guys were sleeping through it."

"I wish I hadn't."

"Dude, I started thinking an axe murderer was out there slaughtering people. Then some of the lights came on and a helicopter showed up. A bunch of security guards dragged Alison to a helicopter. She looked like a wild animal, screaming about something in her head."

"I heard that part."

"Look over here." Taylor led him to a break in the trees where he could see the research facility below. Ming and Travis joined them and peered over Jack's shoulder, along with Barbara and Marina.

Someone had written *Farley Must Die* in huge red letters along the entire stone-clad face of the structure. The building, however, had been built much stronger than the main offices. Deep dents and scratches adorned the metal doors but hadn't broken through them. A stone-clad planter lay on its side, black soil and green plantings scattered across the ground.

"You know, it makes me feel warm all over knowing someone else out there understands that Farley is the Devil," Taylor said.

Jack and Taylor worked their way to their cabin with the rest of the boys. Jack glanced up and found Katie and Clara in front of the girl's cabin, both wrapped in a single comforter. Katie stared at Jack with a face serious and reserved. Warm feelings overcame him until her look vanished, replaced with an expression of rage. She turned and marched inside her cabin, bumping Clara aside as she went.

"That girl may have dodged a bullet, man," Taylor said. "Damien didn't make her do the sleep lab tonight because of what happened after the bonfire. It could've been her on the helicopter, along with Alison."

"Jorge did the sleep lab, too," Ming said. "I hope he's alright."

The boys gathered on the edges of their beds, anxious to discuss what they'd seen. Jack, however, dropped onto his bed and closed his eyes.

A brilliant yellow sunrise played through wispy clouds above the pines of the rising hills beyond the east palisade. Campers crowded around the breakfast buffet and loaded their paper plates and bowls with cereal, homemade granola, plain yogurt, cinnamon toast, sausages, and apple slices.

Jack nodded to Marina and Barbara, then dropped onto a nearby plastic chair to sit with Taylor, Ming, and Travis. Clara walked past him carrying two cups of orange juice and balancing two full plates of food in her arms.

"Somebody's hungry today," Taylor said.

"Hi, Taylor." Clara turned to him. "This isn't just for me. I thought Katie might get out of bed if I waved some sausages under her nose."

"You're a better friend than I am," Taylor said.

"Why does she get to sleep in?" Ming finished off a cup of orange juice. "Derek practically dragged us out of bed."

"Sherry was supposed to wake us up," Clara said, "but she quit this morning."

A lump formed in Jack's throat and he gave Taylor a knowing glance. He worried that Farley had found out about their conversation.

"It's true," Barbara said. "Marina and I talked to Derek about all the uproar last night. He said Sherry helped someone vandalize the research facility."

"Tamera's going to take her place," Marina said.

"Did Derek say what happened to Alison?" Jack took a bite of an apple slice.

"He said she's at the hospital in Kalispell," Marina said. "They're still claiming she had an allergic reaction."

"Jorge left on the helicopter, too," Carl said. Jack moved his orange juice aside to make room for Carl and Tony. They set their heaping plates on the table and sat down. "But he wasn't sick. Montathena Research hired him on. He's only like seventeen-years-old and he's already got a high-paying job. And get this, Tony and I just came back from an interview with Mr. Farley. He offered both of us jobs at Baxson Financial, where our dads work. It's an affiliate of Monta-thena. We leave tomorrow." He turned and gave Tony a high five.

"Dude, Tony isn't even fifteen-years-old," Taylor said. "They can't hire him."

"Tell that to Mr. Farley." Carl gave a shrug and shoved a whole sausage in his mouth.

Taylor tossed his plastic fork on the table. "It's always dorks like you two that get all the breaks. At least I'll get to sleep in Jorge's bed now."

"Working for Montathena is no break," Jack said. "I'd turn him down if I were you."

"You're just jealous," Tony said.

"Katie's food's getting cold," Clara said. "I'll see you later." She headed up the hill.

"How would it be to have a friend that brings you breakfast in bed?" Taylor said.

Jack motioned for Taylor to move with him away from the tables and any bugged lanyards. "I doubt Katie's still asleep. You should've seen the way she leered at me last night. I think she hates me, and I don't know why."

"You're overthinking it, dude. She could be angry about anything."

"That's true, but it still hurts. You should've seen how different she was in the dream last night. And if Sherry was right about sharing dreams, Katie knows how different she's acting. I don't understand it."

"We'll figure it out, bro. We'll find a way for you to talk to her. Maybe she'll be at Farley's lecture."

Jack shook his head. "I can't handle any more lectures. Now that Sherry's gone, I'm going to find some time to read the book she gave us. We need evidence. I'll see you later."

Jack tossed all but a green apple into the trash and headed for his cabin.

KATIE STOOD behind the amphitheater seating, next to Damien. She heard Farley speaking, but she wasn't listening. She spotted Clara four levels down, sitting by Taylor. Travis sat on the other side of her, massaging her shoulders. Clara paid him little attention; instead, she laughed and talked with Taylor.

"I'm going to beat that Travis kid over the head if he doesn't stop ogling my cousin," Katie said.

Damien grinned and nodded.

"Listen closely," Farley said into the microphone, "and if you know anyone who didn't show up this morning, make sure they hear this too, because the punishment for not completing this assignment will apply to everybody."

A buzz of whispers washed through the crowd. All eyes turned to Farley.

"Now is the time to break from your cultural shackles and seize control of your lives. From this moment forward, every camper within these grounds will perform at least three offensive actions against other people at this camp, per day.

Whispers erupted again.

"We will collect a report from each of you every evening at six-o'clock, right before evening meal. If you don't have the report, or your offensive actions are deemed too weak, don't even bother coming to dinner. You shall not be fed again until you provide an acceptable report."

The whispers grew to angry chatter.

"Anyone found lying on their report will lose a full day's meals and will clean our outhouses every day for the rest of the week. I know this sounds cruel, but your empowerment is too important. The only path to real glory is to awaken the demon inside us."

"That's enough!" A tall, muscular boy stood up in the middle of the audience and pointed at Farley. "I'd rather starve than go around offending people! I'm out of here."

At least thirty other campers arose throughout the crowd and eased past the ones that remained. Farley watched them, his expression flat and unconcerned.

Katie looked at the ground and shook her head, then turned to Damien. "This place is an insane asylum. I'm not giving any reports to that creep."

"I doubt he'd dare ask you for one," Damien said, "and I'm not just saying that because your father owns the place. Come on. Let's go check out Farley's office. I heard someone trashed it last night."

Katie nodded and ran down a grassy hill near the amphitheater. Damien chased after her. They made their way across the dusty clearing and stopped to rest in front of the main office. The exterior of the building looked undamaged this time.

Damien jiggled the door lever. "It's locked. Let's go around back."

Katie followed Damien and they made their way to the window of Farley's office. She found broken glass, shards of white wooden trim, and twisted window framing scattered in the flower beds.

Damien picked a few stray shards of glass off the windowsill before stepping over it, then turned and reached out a hand to Katie. She climbed in, wincing at the sound of glass cracking beneath her mesh slip-on shoes.

Farley's wide oaken desk lay cracked down the middle. Insect display cases lay in crumpled heaps, the dried bodies of scorpions and spiders scattered all over the wood plank floor amidst shards of glass and twisted wood.

"Could the man be any creepier?" Katie nearly flattened a large hairy spider and shrieked before skittering to the nearest corner of the room.

Damien laughed, though his sharp movements showed he was just as skittish.

"They're claiming Sherry did this?" Katie wagged her head. "That's nonsense. She was the nicest person on the whole staff."

Group photos of staff members from years past lay scattered and broken on the floor. A poorly doctored portrait of Francis Farley rested crumpled in a trashcan with the words *Death to Farley* written across it in black spray paint.

Katie zeroed in on a bronze plaque that remained untouched on the wall. It featured the original founders of the camp, half a dozen years ago. An inscription told how they'd all died in an explosion. A lump caught in her throat and her eyes grew blurry. She studied her sister Abby's face at the top of a circle of photos. It occurred to Katie that Abby was the same age in the photo that Katie was now.

"I felt like I lost a sister too when she died," Damien said.

Katie saw his moistened eyes and took hold of his arm. She surveyed the room again and let go of him, frowning. "It's clear to me that whoever's out to get Farley blames him for that explosion. Why else would they smash everything in the room but this plaque?"

"It's weirder than you think. Before last night, that plaque was hanging out in the lobby."

**K**atie sat with Damien in the lobby of the main office, looking into Damien's eyes. "You know, I was furious at first when you decided to come along, but now I'm glad you did. I was determined to be miserable the whole time, but you've made it endurable."

"I don't see why you were mad at me. I've never done anything to hurt you."

"Never done anything? You just stood there when Lynch demanded that I join Montathena. And I heard him say, 'they almost always survive assimilation.' You knew it was dangerous and you didn't come to my defense. That's what clinched it for me. I've always counted you as one of my best friends. But if you don't even care if I die, why should I?"

Damien took her hands in his, but she yanked them away.

"I've done everything I can. I don't want you to join, or to do the sleep lab. My dad is right, though; Lynch is too dangerous."

"Some of the girls think something hurt Alison during the sleep study."

"I wouldn't allow anyone to hurt you."

Helicopter rotors became increasingly loud. Damien ran to the window and peeked through the blinds.

"Speak of the devil," he said.

Katie rushed to another window blind and looked outside.

The helicopter's rotors slowed and three muscular men in dark suits exited the aircraft, taking tactical positions around it. Fenton Murdock climbed out, adjusted his black suit coat, and lent Lynch a hand to help him out of the helicopter. The two men surveyed the camp before walking toward the main offices.

Avard, Derek, and Tamera ran from the lodge and joined them.

"My dad'll freak out if he sees you in here with me," Damien said. "I better go."

"I think we're surrounded." Damien turned to the window in Farley's office. "In there." He took Katie's hand and pulled her back into Farley's office. "Hope you don't mind climbing out the window."

Katie tiptoed around bits of glass and exotic arachnids. A key rattled at the front door.

"I have to go." Damien released her hand and partially shut the door behind him.

Whatever this was about, Katie didn't want to miss it. Instead of escaping, she tiptoed back and peeked around the door edge.

"Damien," Fenton Murdock said. "Just the boy I wanted to see."

"Hey, Dad. What brings you here?"

"Where's Farley?" Lynch's raspy voice demanded attention. "What's going on at this camp? This is outrageous!"

Damien didn't need to answer. Farley had just come in from the back door. "I just finished my morning lecture. We're having a few problems with the locals, but I think we're doing just fine."

Derek sat on a desk and Tamera settled herself on an office chair, with her usual elegance. Damien made himself comfortable on a countertop. Fenton and Lynch stood facing Avard and Farley.

"I want the attacks stopped tonight," Lynch said. "We don't finance this facility so you can obsess about your own pathetic problems. I want results."

"The attacks will stop. I'm restoring the lighting as we speak."

"Not good enough! I've already assembled a task force. We'll wait them out and destroy them. I don't want to hear more excuses for failing to harvest quality recruits. You cannot accomplish anything with all these distractions!"

"You're not being fair," Farley said. "We've had great results with this crop. In just two nights, most of our targets have begun dreaming strong Archetypes. Many are showing signs of mental conflict. And we've already recruited three members of our research team. We assimilated one boy successfully. None of the others have shown signs of dream awareness. I'd say we've done well so far."

"My associates don't share your optimism," Lynch said. "I agree that the crop looks good, but the research team members are worse than I've seen in years. Yes, you assimilated a boy, but you lost a girl. The Barnes girl is a clear security risk, still not dreaming about camp. You've allowed a boy to traipse right into the assimilation facility just because he claimed to be a friend of the Park boy. And now, one of your most-trusted staff members has turned traitor. There's no telling what she's told the campers."

"We've been rolling back security tapes," Farley said. "We'll know where she spent her time."

"You know nothing!" Lynch pounded a desktop. "Mentalists like her can resist our interrogation techniques, but we know she wasn't working alone. At least one of the research team members colluded with her. I want every one of them assimilated—tonight."

"No!" Avard grabbed a nearby stapler and threw it across the room. "There are too many kids on the team. Media can't assimilate them all. Her mind can't take it. You gotta give her a night's rest."

"The assimilations will take place tonight." Lynch glared at Avard. The old man glared back for a few seconds, then looked away and stormed out of the building. Katie wondered what kind of power Lynch had, that even a bully like Avard could be cowed by it.

"There's still the issue of Katie Frost," Farley said. "Her father has forbidden us to assimilate her without proof that she's been enlightened."

"That," Fenton said, "is why we came here without him. No one questions Vance's loyalty, but recent events have blinded him. He knows Katie's destiny was settled the day her uncle joined the executive board."

"It's not worth the risk," Damien said. "We all know what happened to Alison. If Katie isn't enlightened, there's no reason to risk assimilating her."

"Katie must be assimilated tonight," Lynch said. "Now, if the rest of you will excuse us, Fenton and I need to speak privately with Mr. Farley."

The three men headed for Farley's office. Katie danced around the glass shards and dead insects until she arrived at the window. She stepped onto the sill and jumped to the flowerbed below. She ran around the corner of the building and came across Taylor and Clara standing and talking. She bulleted straight for them.

"Taylor wants to watch me write about my dream." Clara looked at Katie and her eyes widened. "You're upset. What's wrong?"

Katie took hold of Clara's arm and tried to compose herself.

"I'll see you at the research facility." Taylor smiled at Clara, turned and walked up the hill.

Katie pulled Clara into a line of trees. "I don't know what's going on here," she said.

"What do you mean?"

She looked into Clara's eyes. "I honestly don't know what I just heard. Some of my dad's partners are here. They were talking about the campers here as if we were all some kind of crop to be harvested. They don't sound like they care about anybody."

"Your dad wouldn't have sent us here if something bad was going to happen."

"That's just it, I don't know if that's true. They kept talking about an assimilation process that sounds really dangerous. Damien told me it was safe, but he didn't sound that way just now. You should've seen how Avard reacted when Mr. Lynch brought it up. He went ballistic. He said they lost a girl during assimilation. It must've been Alison. I just don't know what to think anymore."

"Don't be afraid. I won't let them hurt you." She wrapped her arms around Katie. "You're everything to me."

"Thanks Clara, but I'm not the only one I'm worried about. They were also angry at you because you haven't been dreaming about this stupid camp."

"Angry? At me?" Clara's eyes watered up and her lips quivered.

Katie smiled and patted her cousin's hand. "I shouldn't have said that. I think they're angry at Farley more than anything. It's just that creepy Lynch guy. He thinks Sherry's some kind of traitor who's been spying on them. That's what gets me. Why would anyone want to spy on a stupid summer camp? It's the same way it is at home with my dad. Constant paranoia."

"So, what're we going to do?"

Katie shook her head. "I don't know what I was trying to prove by coming here. What was I thinking? I'm such an idiot."

XVI

Two gray squirrels chattered at each other and circled the trunk of a tall pine tree. Jack lay on his back on a secluded hill near his cabin, suspending Sherry's book above his face. He figured the surveillance cameras couldn't see him since Sherry had gone to this location to be alone. He glanced at his cellphone and found he'd been reading for nearly three hours. He slammed the book shut and stood up.

Over the low hill, he saw Ming, Taylor, and Travis walking down the trail from the cabin, carrying towels.

Taylor turned and saw him. "Dude! Where you been, man? We got tired of typing. We're going to do some canoeing before lunch."

Jack nodded absent-mindedly, stuffed the book under his arm, and walked down the hill to join his friends. He saw Clara and Katie walking a few hundred yards ahead of them.

"If y'all don't mind," Travis said. "I think I'll head down to the lake with the better-looking company." He winked at Ming and charged down the hill to join the girls.

"Travis is hitting on your girl again." Ming punched Taylor's arm.

"I'm not worried. Travis is about as charming as a slug." Taylor handed Jack a towel. "Here you go. I hoped I'd find you before we got to the lake. Have you come up with a plan?"

Jack checked for Ming's ID and saw that he wasn't wearing it. "I walked the perimeter earlier, but there's no way through the fence. The front gate is guarded and the back one is locked and has a camera aimed at it. I've been reading the book Sherry gave me. It's as dry as a rock, but I couldn't put it down. Things are even worse than I thought. I can hardly believe it."

"Like what?" Taylor stopped at a covered pavilion to enjoy some shade and evade any curious ears.

"It tells you how to control your dreams. You need three things: dream awareness, control of your subconscious, and enlightenment. It doesn't explain enlightenment. That's the part someone tore out of the book."

"It's worthless then," Ming said. "There's no point only knowing two of the three requirements."

"Actually, those two requirements are still pretty cool," Jack said. "I don't even see what a third one would add. Dream awareness is the most important thing. You can control most of what you do in a dream just by being aware you're dreaming. It's called lucid dreaming."

"I've heard of that," Ming said.

"It seems easy. You choose an object that you use often—the book calls it a prime token—then you think about that object as you fall asleep, so you'll remember it in your dream. The second you dream about it, you trigger awareness of the dream."

"No way!" Taylor sat on a plastic chair and put his feet up on the table. "If it's really that easy, I can't wait for lights out. I'd love to control my dreams."

"Me too." Jack pulled a lighter from his pocket. "I already picked my prime token. I never go anywhere without this. What's cool is, once you know you're dreaming, you can literally do anything you want. You can even fly."

Taylor's eyes widened. "It'd be like living the ultimate video game. That's so cool."

"Don't get too excited" Jack said. "Dream awareness lets you do what you want, but your conscious mind is just reacting to whatever dreamscape your subconscious creates. Your subconscious ultimately controls everything in your dreams."

"So, in other words, we can't really control what we dream." Taylor dropped his feet back to the ground and put his hands up in surrender.

"I didn't say that. I'm saying we have to control both our conscious and subconscious minds. Lucid dreaming takes care of our conscious mind. The book called control over the subconscious 'Shadow Control.'"

Taylor huffed. "Why would you call it that? Who wrote this?"

"Some dude named Curtis Lynch. He calls the subconscious our 'Shadow' because it's always there, just out of view, like a shadow. Our Shadow creates situations and shapes events in our dreams. So, if you really want total control of your dreams, you have to know you're dreaming, and then your conscious mind has to overpower your subconscious shadow."

"That's weird," Taylor said. "Makes sense I guess, but how are you supposed to overpower your own mind? Sounds schizophrenic."

Jack laughed. "This could all be virtually impossible to do, for all I know. Lynch says the way to control your subconscious is to force yourself to be the same person consciously that you are subconsciously."

"What?" Taylor looked at Ming, whose furrowed brow revealed his confusion.

"It means you have to be at peace with who you are. You have to live free of guilt and regret. They call it 'Embracing Your Shadow.'"

"That sounds like what you said Sherry was talking about," Ming said.

"That's what I was thinking," Jack said. "The other campers were at peace with who they were before they came here. That means they could've easily embraced their Shadow and controlled their dreams."

"That explains perfectly what's going on here," Ming said.

"Exactly," Jack said. "Those campers were already in a position to embrace their Shadow. They only needed to be made aware that it's possible to control our dreams."

"Man, that totally explains why they didn't invite me here," Taylor said. "I'm already the poster boy for mental conflict. I doubt I'll ever be able to embrace my Shadow."

"Actually, the book said it's that way for most people. Lynch described a second way to control your dreams. He called it 'Subduing Your Shadow'. With that method, your conscious mind just has to conquer and subdue your subconscious."

"Sounds even harder," Taylor said.

"Not really. Only the best of people can embrace their Shadow, but even the worst monster can subdue it. But you have to work at it both when awake and while asleep. It means learning to accept yourself exactly as you are, no matter how awful you are. If you're the scum of the earth, you have to be okay with that. You have to convince yourself that you want to be the scum of the earth."

Taylor stood up. "That's bad news for me. I'm always mad at myself for one reason or another. What else do you have to do?"

"It sounds kind of weird, but you literally have to overpower a dreamed-up being in your dreams. It's a specific being that your subconscious mind creates to represent itself. Lynch calls that symbolic being a Jungian Archetype. It's a human-like manifestation of your subconscious; a dreamed personage that represents your Shadow."

Ming scratched his head. "Are you saying everybody has some kind of Archetype being hanging around in their dreams?"

"Yes, but only if your mind is conflicted in some way. Your Shadow automatically creates that Archetype personage to represent mental conflict in your dreams."

"What if I have loads of conflicts in my head?" Taylor grinned.

"Your subconscious picks the strongest conflict."

"Wow," Taylor said. "And all I have to do is find that archetype and tackle it?"

"I think so, yeah."

"How do you know which person is your Archetype?" Ming looked at Jack.

"The book says you first have to figure out what bothers you most. Archetypes are different for everyone. It could be a demon trying to control you, a witch trying to put you down, or maybe some hero trying to save you."

Taylor shook his head. "This sounds insane, dude."

"I know. I'd never have believed it if I hadn't seen what's going on at this camp. Montathena doesn't just keep people from embracing their Shadow, they weaken them, so they can't subdue it either. Your Archetype becomes too strong to subdue when the conflicts in your mind are too strong. The bigger the conflicts, the harder it is to subdue."

"So, the staff tells everyone to steal, cheat, and lie just to make us hate ourselves."

Jack nodded. "Sad thing is, the conflict occurs even if the staff fails to destroy your self-esteem. Either they make you feel worthless or they get you to overreact and become proud. Both responses create mental conflict, which then creates powerful Archetypes that our minds can't subdue."

Taylor's mouth hung open and he turned to stare at the nearby lake.

"It's all spelled out right here," Jack turned to a page where Sherry had scribbled in names of camp staff. He handed it to Taylor, who read it aloud:

"Avard's team—bullying and abuse. Shadow/Hero Conflict Enhancement: Targets must..."

He took on a look of disgust. "He calls us 'targets?' What a jerk." He turned back to the book.

"Targets must be compelled to feel shame for not standing up to abuse. Aroused fear and feelings of inadequacy are essential. Resultant dreams will include manifestations of the Hero Archetype as the dreamer feels a subconscious need to be rescued by someone. If target instead rises up against oppressors, the mind will enhance the equally acceptable Shadow Archetype—an unseen presence that the now arrogant dreamer feels he must rescue.

"Media's team—criticism and belittling. Senex/Wise Man Conflict Enhancement: The easiest Archetype to enhance, the Senex (or old witch) is emboldened in a target's dreams by creating self-doubt and low self-esteem. Targets who instead look inward, overestimating their own personal value, become proud. They will thusly project their exaggerated self-image into the dreamed form of a Wise Man Archetype.'

"Derek's team—guilt and deception. Trickster/Child Conflict Enhancement: Guilt aroused via deceptive behavior encourages the Trickster Archetype. Targets who refuse to deceive others may enhance the opposing Child Archetype, a symbolic personage that is excessively honest, denying the target dreamer his or her personal privacy and exposing secrets the dreamer does not want exposed.

"Farley's team—controlling and enslaving. Demon/Animus Conflict Enhancement: The Demon, as understood here, is an Archetype obsessed with controlling others. The Animus, on the other hand, is reflective of one whose appetites and emotions are uncontrolled, like an animal. Encourage animal-like carnality, selfishness, and unkindness to enhance the Animus Archetype. Targets who react obsessively to these behaviors in others will instead enhance their need to control others—a fascist behavior that manifests in the form of a Demon Archetype."

XVII

Jack, Taylor, and Ming didn't know how long they'd been standing there below the canopy staring at the lake, pondering the words Taylor had just read. The staff's behavior now made total sense to Jack, and the book verified everything Sherry had told him.

"It's all real," Ming said. "I kept telling myself we were over-thinking it, that Sherry was just being paranoid, assuming things, blowing them out of proportion. But if there's a shred of truth to that book, it's all true. We need to get out of here."

"That book sounds like good enough evidence to me," Taylor said. "I say we go with my plan. Tonight, Ming can set something on fire down here by the lake. Jack and I will wait for the guards to be distracted and then we'll sneak out the front gate."

"What if they catch me?" Ming started breathing fast. "They'll figure out I know too much. We have to get someone else to do it. I don't know if that book will help us, anyway. Who's going to read it? The police aren't going to listen to a couple of teenagers with a weird book about dream control."

"All we can do is try." Jack said. "It won't matter if they catch you.

Farley tells everyone to do bad things. If you're caught, just tell them you were obeying Farley."

"I don't know." Ming looked away. "I'm not brave like you guys. I feel like I'm about to pass out. I just can't do it."

"You're stressing yourself out again," Taylor said. "We don't have to commit to it right now. We can think about it for a few hours. Maybe we can tell Travis everything, and he'll do it. For now, let's just relax and join the others at the lake."

"Good plan," Jack said. "I see Katie down there. I still want to talk to her before we go."

"Let's go then." Taylor headed for the lake with Ming and Jack following a few steps behind them.

Ming caught up with Travis and climbed into a boat with him. Jack stared across the water and spotted Marina and Barbara in a canoe on the far side of the lake. He groaned when he noticed Damien jogging to the docks in black swimming trunks, showing off his chiseled hairy chest. Katie and Clara rowed their canoe to shore and Clara climbed out.

Clara ran to meet Taylor. "Hey. You want to canoe with me? This is so fun."

Taylor smiled and nodded. He looked at Jack, who stood strapping on a life preserver.

"Go ahead," Jack said.

Taylor looked at Jack and then Katie. "I definitely want to canoe with you, Clara, but I need to do something first. Hey, Damien!"

Damien had one foot in Katie's canoe when he looked over at Taylor.

"Rumor has it you think you're pretty quick with a canoe." Taylor fastened a sun-bleached orange life preserver around his ribs.

Damien's eyes lit up. "Are you really challenging us to a race? You must be coming down with something."

Taylor shook his head. "Just you and me, dude. Two times to the farthest buoy and back."

Damien stepped out of Katie's boat. "I'll be back before your paddle hits the water." He winked at her before abandoning her and rushing into another canoe.

Clara sat on the dock to watch the race, dangling her feet over the water.

Taylor shoved a canoe into the water and climbed in. Jack wondered what had brought on this sudden urge to race Damien, then became aware of Taylor eyeing him and tilting his head toward Katie. Jack looked at Katie and realized she was sitting by herself.

"You want to start the race?" Taylor dipped his paddles in the water.

Jack nodded. "Three, two, one, go!"

Damien and Taylor paddled away with all their strength.

Jack took a deep breath and sauntered over to Katie's canoe. "No sense in us just sitting here." He pushed her canoe farther into the water and climbed in. He grabbed a paddle and asked Katie for her lanyard.

"We're not supposed to take these off," she said.

"It might get wet."

She handed it to him, and he tossed it on the dock and paddled away, careful to isolate his canoe from the other campers.

"They're bugged," he said.

"What?"

"The lanyards. Sherry told me they have listening devices in them. Your father's company is spying on us."

"I wish I could say that surprised me."

"Listen, Katie, I've heard you're planning to sleep in the lab tonight. I want you to know that Sherry warned me against it before she left."

Katie nodded. "I'm having second thoughts about it anyway, after what happened to Alison. You and Taylor went to a lot of trouble to get Damien out of the way so you could warn me. For what it's worth, thanks."

Jack nodded. "You still don't think I look familiar to you at all?"

Katie looked at the dock. "I hate to leave Clara over there alone. We better get back."

"Please, Katie. Sherry told me other things about Montathena. We share dreams. I recognized you from my dreams the moment I saw you. Are you sure you've never dreamt about me?"

"Dreams are just dreams. Shouldn't we..."

"There was an old woman, a Korean. She was with a gang of her followers. They kept tying you up and forcing me to fight things to save you. There was a manticore one time. A pack of wolves another time. Then there was a gang of thugs. And one time..."

"Okay. Okay." Katie glared at him. "Do you work for the Intershroud?"

"What? I don't even know what that is."

"Don't play dumb. It's the parent company that calls the shots at Montathena Research, Baxson Financial, and dozens of other phony companies. My dad's company is just one of their faces. I know you don't work for my dad because Damien doesn't know you, but you must belong to one of their other companies. You couldn't have entered so many of my dreams without knowing their secrets."

Jack dropped his paddles on the floor of the boat and looked around. He tried to find the right words. "So, you admit that we shared those dreams?"

"I'm not saying another word until you tell me who you work for and why you're here."

"Everything I know about your dad's company I learned in the last two days. I have no idea why we shared those dreams. Do you know those people? Or that old Korean woman?"

Katie stared at him, waiting for the slightest hint of insincerity, then shook her head. "I assumed you knew them."

"I never met any of them until I started dreaming about them months ago. I came here hoping someone could make it stop, and next thing I know, I see you. Can't you tell me anything about what's going on?"

Katie shook her head. "This one has me stumped, too. I know it sounds strange, but even though I've always known my dad was experimenting with dreams, I only started finding out the truth a few weeks ago, from my housekeeper."

"What did she say?"

"Mind-blowing stuff. She told me about the Intershroud and how it destroys lives. She belonged to a group that opposed them until someone at my house discovered her. She was preparing to run away when she told me there were hidden cameras all around my house and that my dad's employees were watching me in my dreams."

"Why would they do that to you?"

Katie shrugged and furrowed her brow. "They're looking for my mother. She took something from them, and they hoped she'd contact me—as if she cared one bit about me."

"If they were watching you all the time, how could we have shared dreams without them knowing about it?"

She put a finger on her nose. "Ding, ding, ding, that's the million-dollar question. Damien's one of the people the Intershroud sent to spy on me, but it scared me how angry and surprised he looked when I told him I'd dreamed about you."

"So, you have no idea how you ended up in my dreams?"

She scrunched her mouth as she thought about it. "Now that I think about it, there was a Korean man that guarded me sometimes. That must be it! He must've found me alone in my dream and then made me dream to that old woman. Maybe he belonged to her gang."

Jack leaned back, smiling wide. "That has to be it. Thank you. I don't know if it fixes anything, but it's great to finally have a workable theory."

Katie waved at Damien who was completing his first return to the dock. He slowed his pace and glared at Jack, having no reason to worry about Taylor half a lap behind him.

"Why did you even come here?" Jack lifted his hands. "Your dad owns this camp. Your sister founded it. I wouldn't have stepped foot here if I knew what your housekeeper told you."

Katie's face reddened, and she stared at her feet. She shook her head and frowned. "I hardly know myself. I guess I just didn't care anymore. After the company found out about my housekeeper, Stephani, one of my dad's associates demanded that I join Montathena and I refused. But no one cared what I wanted, not even Damien. I guess I just gave up."

"It surprises me to hear you say that. You were such a fighter in those dreams. I never imagined you as someone who gives up."

Katie gave a weak smile. "I didn't know what I was getting into. I'm really scared now. My dad's partners arrived a few hours ago and one of them wants all of us assimilated."

"Assimilated?"

"I think that is what they do in the sleep lab. Damien keeps telling me it's safe, but I think he's only saying that because he's scared of that old geezer, Mr. Lynch."

"You mean, Curtis Lynch? Sherry gave me a book he wrote. He's here?"

"Him and Damien's father. Even Avard and Farley are afraid of them. There's no chance we'll be able to avoid the sleep lab."

"You'll have to escape with me and Taylor then. We'll all have to. I've been trying to come up with an escape plan, but you must have connections. Maybe you can find where they're keeping our car keys and my car."

Katie frowned. "No one here cares what I want. They don't care about anybody. You can't run away from them. I know, I tried. I ran away from home once, but they found me within hours and started watching me ten times as much."

"There's got to be something we can do. There's a south gate that's always locked. They only use it for access to a trail that runs along the mountainside east of here."

"I told you, I can't—wait a minute." Katie looked down at the pocket of her jeans and shoved her hand inside. She pulled out a torn fragment of yellowed newspaper, unfolded it, and held it out to Jack.

"Please tell me you didn't leave this under my pillow during Farley's speech this morning."

"I didn't give you this." Jack unfolded the weatherworn paper and read the words scribbled diagonally across its crinkled surface in dull black charcoal:

*KATIE*
    *DANGER*
    *TRAILHEAD*
    *DUSK*

"It's got to be a joke. Maybe Damien wrote it."

"He wouldn't do something that creepy. It had to be someone from your cabin, probably Travis."

Jack nodded. "I can see him thinking he could fool you into meeting him alone at night."

"Whoever wrote it, tell him to get a life. It's disturbing finding something like that shoved under my pillow."

Jack folded the note and tucked it in the pocket of his tee-shirt, then stared at her glistening eyes. "If it helps. I already told Travis he didn't have a chance with you, what with a guy like Damien as a boyfriend."

Katie glared at him, her lips pinched tight. "He's not my boyfriend! Things have changed since we came here though, and I like where it's going. I don't want anything to mess it up."

"I wasn't trying to make you mad."

"It's not you. It's them and their constant meddling with my life. Yes, I felt the same things you felt. The Intershroud gets into my head and messes with my mind, but I refuse to give in to my feelings toward you. They aren't real! I won't accept them, and I won't allow you, or anybody else, to manipulate my thoughts and feelings."

"Katie, I'm sorry, I don't know what to say."

"Then don't say anything." She stared at him wide-eyed and resolute, though her lower lip twitched slightly. "I refuse to have feelings for someone just because some jerk planted them in my dreams. Dreams are just dreams. I care about Damien. He's real. I've liked him since we were kids. I have to live my life in the real world, and you should do the same."

Jack tensed up, desperate to hide the knots twisting within his heart.

Katie looked away.

"I see what you're saying, Katie, but who's to say what's real and what isn't? You can't just—"

Katie screamed. The canoe twisted to one side and Jack scrambled to grip the gunwales, water swallowing him up. Laughter assaulted his ears. Confused and alarmed, he and Katie gurgled and flapped their arms and legs in the cold water. Jack stared daggers at Damien when he saw him. The young man grinned and patted the sides of his canoe. He'd rammed and tipped Jack's boat.

"Rookie mistake, not paying attention to superior canoeists," Damien forced his laughter and directed Katie to take a firm grasp of his muscular right arm. He grabbed the opposite gunwale with his other arm and heaved her into his canoe.

As soon as she settled herself on a seat, Katie shoved Damien hard in the chest, knocking him to the floor of his canoe. She hugged herself, shivering and frowning, turning away from Damien and treating Jack to a brief show of empathy with her eyes. Damien climbed back onto his seat, grabbed the paddles, and dipped them in the water before rowing away.

Taylor arrived seconds later, breathing heavily and glistening with sweat. He gave Jack his hand, but the canoe nearly tipped him out when he attempted to pull Jack in.

"I'll just swim to the dock. It's not far." Jack dived forward and swam, putting all his anger into each stroke.

Taylor rowed alongside him. "What a jerk! Not cool."

Clara waited for them at the dock and ran to Taylor when he arrived.

Jack pulled himself up onto the dock and sat freezing, frowning, and staring into the murky water.

"You still want to canoe with me?" Clara wrung her hands together and stared at Taylor.

He shook his head and pointed at Jack.

"Go ahead, Taylor," Jack said. "I'm not going to be good company for a while. Go have fun."

Taylor nodded, took Clara's hand, and helped her into his canoe. "Okay, but if Damien comes within ten feet of me, he's going into the water, even if I have to dive on top of him." He sat down and paddled away.

Jack shivered and watched them row away, then turned to stare at Katie. He grinned at the thought that she was fighting feelings for him, but the smile quickly went away. It was too late. He'd lost the battle for her affection. She'd never trust her feelings for him. One thing, however, was certain. He wouldn't let the Intershroud assimilate him. He'd find a way out of this fortress no matter what it took.

XVIII

Wood timbers held a sloped wood-slat canopy over the outdoor dining area, shading campers from the hot noonday sun. Katie shared a white plastic table with Marina, Barbara, and Clara while the boys of their neighboring cabin huddled around an adjacent table.

Katie poked at her sandwich and pretended not to notice Jack at the far side of his table, staring at his plate of untouched turkey pita and sliced cantaloupe. She regretted what she'd said to him at the lake, but she knew it had to be done. Jack needed to understand that nothing she dreamed with him could be trusted. She didn't understand why the Intershroud wanted to connect her with Jack. She only knew it had to be stopped, even if it hurt.

The clatter of a chair flying to the ground captured Katie's attention. A stocky Hispanic boy tackled a smaller red-headed boy and wrestled him to the concrete floor, knocking a large cookie out of his hand. The Hispanic boy stood up and kicked the other boy before heading to get another cookie.

Farley watched from the lodge balcony, smiling.

Taylor, Ming, and Travis had stood up to make room for the fight. They grabbed their chairs and carried them to Katie's table. Taylor waved Jack over, but he shook his head and turned back to his plate of food.

"We've started on Derek's assignment," Taylor squeezed his chair next to Clara's.

"Three lies or truths about yourself that will fool everyone," Travis said. "The cabin whose members can fool the most people gets a prize."

Ming thought for a few seconds, then shook his head. "This is impossible. I totally suck at lying."

"Liar," Marina said.

Taylor laughed. "No, he actually does suck at it."

"I'd say our cabin has that prize in the bag," Barbara said. "No one's beating Clara. You've seen what she writes in her dream journal. Go ahead Clara. Try to fool us."

Clara's eyes gleamed and she smiled. "Let's see. I have an uncle that died, but my mom says he's alive again. My other uncle, on my dad's side, used to be a ghostwriter for a famous author. I lived in a cabin in the woods with my mom for eight years. I never watched TV all that time. And, I'll someday free the Great Sprite from captivity."

"You only need three, Clara." Katie sensed her face turning bright pink. "Please don't include your dreams on your list. It makes you sound crazy."

"They were all lies," Barbara said.

"Nope." Clara giggled. "Only one was a lie."

"You're amazing," Taylor said. "Which one was the lie?"

"You'll have to figure that out in Derek's session," Clara said.

Taylor laughed and shook his head.

Derek step up behind Taylor, his face somber. He tossed a lanyard across the adjacent table to Jack, then handed another one to Ming. "Don't leave your cabin without these anymore," he said. "People will be arriving this afternoon to put a stop to these attacks on Farley. You don't want to find out what'll happen if they think you don't belong here."

Jack and Ming slid their lanyards over their heads. Derek stepped aside to make room for Damien, his father, and Mr. Lynch.

Damien looked around the tables and, raising one hand, counted the faces in the immediate area with his index finger. "Looks like the whole research team is here. We have the honor of a visit from two of the top executives at Montathena Research. This is my father, Fenton Murdock, and this man over here is Curtis Lynch. If you'll give him your attention, he has an exciting offer for you."

Jack's eyebrows rose, and he looked at Taylor.

"It's good to see young people taking an interest in cutting edge technology," Lynch leaned on his octopus handle cane. His forced smile revealed crooked yellow teeth. "The data you've provided us will not only serve you well but will help us to improve our technology. I'm sure you've heard we already recruited your friend, Jorge, and we'll soon bring on Tony and Carl."

Tony and Carl each sat up straight. Carl nodded his head.

"As a reward for your cooperation, we're proposing to offer each of you an additional two-thousand dollars."

"Dude," Taylor smiled and looked around. The others grinned at each other.

"To earn the bonus money, however, we're asking each of you to sleep in the research lab tonight. We gain enormous amounts of data from the lab readings, and you'll find it quite comfortable."

"What about Alison?" Barbara folded her arms and glared at Lynch.

Fenton stepped forward and stared her in the face. "There's no need to worry about that. We've discontinued use of the sleep medication that caused her allergic reaction."

"It didn't sound like an allergic reaction to me," Marina said. Everyone turned to her and showed surprise at hearing such a bold statement from the shy girl. "She kept screaming about something happening in her head. I don't think you're telling us the whole story."

"It's not our wish to hide anything from you," Fenton said. "Alison didn't want us to tell you this, but the attacks on the camp caused her a great deal of anxiety. She had a panic attack, which her allergic reaction amplified. That's why we've ordered additional security for tonight, in hopes of ending these attacks. I assure you the sleep lab will be perfectly safe."

"I say we think about it and give you our answers later," Marina said.

Lynch sneered at her and then smiled. "Fine. Think on it, but I want your answers before the evening meal. Any longer than that and I'll have to rethink the two-thousand-dollar bonus." He jabbed his cane at the ground and walked away. Fenton and Derek followed a few paces behind him.

Damien grabbed a chair and sat by Katie. "Now you won't have to go alone. The whole team will be there."

✖

DAMIEN AND KATIE moved to a table on the far side of the eating area. Jack couldn't stop watching them. Katie laughed at something Damien said and Jack looked away and stood up, suddenly realizing only Taylor and Ming remained with him. Jack tucked his I.D. badge into his pocket and motioned them to follow him.

Ming stuffed his I.D. in his pocket and followed Taylor and Jack to the open area in front of the lodge.

"It starts," Jack said. He kept his voice quiet. "Lynch is desperate to assimilate us tonight. We need to commit to the escape plan—right now."

"We need a new plan," Ming said. "We can't just abandon everyone here to be assimilated."

"Or to die in the process," Taylor said. "Ming's right. We're going to have to tell the others what's going on. We all need to be out of here before the sun sets."

"I'm with you," Jack said, "but how are we going to do that with everyone wearing a bugged lanyard?" Jack looked over at Katie. "And I doubt we'll have a chance to talk to Katie again today, with that doofus ogling over her every second."

"Don't ask me what she sees in that phony," Taylor said. "The dude practically oozes with insincerity."

"Maybe we can write up some notes," Ming said.

"Perfect," Taylor said. "We can write something concise and make sure they read it somewhere private and out of camera view. I'm not much of a wordsmith, though."

"I can write the notes," Ming said. "You guys just need to help me pass them around."

"Just make sure no one else sees it," Jack said. "And, to be honest, I think we need to steer clear of Tony and Carl. I don't think we can trust them."

"I agree," Taylor said. "They both seem too happy with Montathena Research."

"Let's get to it then" Ming waved for Taylor and Jack to follow him. and started marching toward the cabin.

"You guys go ahead," Jack said. "I want to check something out, first."

Taylor gave him a nod. "Don't be long."

J ack walked past the main offices but stopped when he found himself surrounded by at least twenty strangers, each clad in camouflage and carrying rifles. He looked around for familiar faces, but didn't find any until he noticed Lynch, Derek, and Mr. Murdock standing on the bridge in front of the entrance gates, welcoming the troops. The serious expressions on everyone's faces did nothing to curb his anxiety. They were preparing for an all-out military conflict.

Jack zigzagged through the troops until he reached the tree line at the head of the trail leading down to the research facility. He'd always suspected that Farley had hidden his car keys somewhere there. The newcomers were paying no attention to him, which increased his hope that he might be able to search the building without anyone asking questions. He hiked down the trail.

He'd expected to find the usual security guards stationed in the lobby, but he saw no one. He walked farther into the building and found nobody in the computer room, then, peering down the blue stairs, saw no one there, either.

His mood brightened. Even if he didn't locate his keys, perhaps he'd finally uncover a little evidence. He speed-walked down the corridor and tried every door, finding them all locked, except for the computer room and a small break room with a well-stocked refrigerator. He helped himself to an éclair.

Doubling back, he charged down the stairs and passed the lounge fireplace before entering one of the sleep labs. Judging by the stuffed bunnies, unicorns, and puppies—the posters of male pop stars and shelves stocked with cosmetic products—this was the girl's lab. He guessed the boy's lab was beyond the gray door on the far side of the girl's sleep quarters.

Six queen-sized beds lined the beige carpeted floor, with intermittent warm, wooden nightstands. The homey décor, however, couldn't quell the uneasiness Jack felt. Dozens of wires and inch-diameter black tubes coiled down to each bed from openings high on the back wall. A wide, mirrored-glass observation window dominated the wall opposite the beds.

"Nothing makes for a great night's sleep like knowing some unseen stranger is staring at you all night," Jack muttered to himself.

He pressed his face against the cool reflective glass and strained to see if anyone was watching him within the darkened observation room. His heart jumped when a door swung open behind him. A tall, slender woman in a white lab coat stepped in from a back room—Tamera, if he remembered right. She paid no attention to him as she crossed the sleep lab and lounge and dashed up the stairs in her black high-heeled shoes. Jack slid across the room and slammed his shoe against the edge of the back-room door before it could latch.

He winced, sensing the door edge slip from his foot and close. He yanked the door lever with his left hand, then clenched his right fist in victory when he learned that the lock hadn't latched. He pulled open the door and slipped inside, then waited for his eyes to adjust to the dim light of a long, concrete-walled hallway. He stared for several seconds, surprised at how far the building extended into the hillside.

Jack approached an open oak door and glanced inside someone's luxury bedroom, complete with a king-sized bed, mahogany night table and dresser, ornate flowered lamps, and a flat-screen TV. The same black tubes he'd seen in the sleep lab converged in this room. They snaked down to several black plastic barrels from which emanated a throbbing, pumping wheeze.

He entered the room, unable to take his eyes off three glowing orange tubes, each as thick as his wrist. The tubes climbed down the wall behind the bed from an opening near the ceiling and glowing, reddish globs oozed up and down them, like long, narrow lava lamps. They converged on a headset resting on the nightstand. Other black tubes twisted from the headset to the barrels.

At first, Jack thought the bedclothes had been left in a pile along the center of the bed. Then he saw the woman lying there with her eyes closed tight, breathing erratically.

*That's Media*, Jack thought. *This must be her bedroom! What's she got to do with these assimilations?*

His stomach turned, thinking of her wearing that headset at night, with orange fluids flowing through it. Media tossed back and forth, wheezed, and began moaning. Jack backed out of the room and rushed down the hall and around a corner.

He entered a spacious, concrete-walled room with a prominent two-level black, metal staircase at its center. Electrical equipment dangled from the high, coffered-concrete ceiling. Jack wanted to find out where the orange tubes were coming from, so he opened the metal door of the adjacent room and found a cylindrical white electrical generator dominating the small rectangular space. He entered and eased past the generator, then unlocked a door on the far wall.

He peeked behind it and saw what he'd expected to see—the girl's sleep lab. He closed the door without relocking it, thinking that if Lynch or Farley did force him to take the sleep lab, this door might be a means of escape. He looked up and saw the orange tubes drooping across the ceiling into sealed cylindrical sleeves that led into yet another room.

He ran to the next room but didn't have to enter it. A wide window afforded a hazy view through thick, cold glass. Frost clung to the corners of the glass and smothered metal items within the room. The orange tubes sloped to three long, blue metal boxes that resembled caskets, except for long, narrow windows that ran along the sides.

Jack gasped and stepped back two steps with his heart beating double time. Human bodies lay inside the boxes. They couldn't have been alive at the subzero temperatures, unless this was some kind of cryogenic chamber. Each orange tube penetrated a box and attached to a black sleeve directly against the inhabitant's head. Or, were they passing *through* their heads?

Jack staggered back and nearly toppled an old computer resting on a wheeled metal stand. Nausea welled up inside him. He didn't care what those sleep studies were now. This was far beyond creepy. He suddenly remembered why he was there, rescued his otherwise useless cellphone from his pocket, and began taking videos of everything he'd seen so far.

Voices sounded nearby and he negotiated a maze of scattered tables and electronic equipment, then ducked behind the wire mesh guard rails of the black iron grating stairs. When the voices grew quiet, he decided to find out where the stairs led. If there was an exit up there, it had to be somewhere close to his cabin.

He rushed up the stairs, two steps at a time, and just evaded Damien and his father passing through the room below. Jack hugged the railing and held his breath until the men left the room, then dashed up the remaining steps. At the top, he encountered a narrow concrete passage, eight-feet-tall and lined with three metal ladders on each wall. He detected another line of ladders a few hundred yards down the hallway to his right. Name plaques affixed to the rough concrete next to each ladder read: Katie, Clara, Barbara, Alison, and Marina.

A sickly yellowish glow emanated from a ledge above him. He chose Katie's ladder and climbed the eight feet, before peering over the ledge. A glowing yellow jar at the far end of a deep plywood compartment mesmerized him. Wires pierced the sides and top of the glass jar.

Jack stared into the dim casket-like space, his throat contracting, his breathing quickening, and his palms sweating. Half a minute passed before he forced himself into the shaft, determined not to give into his claustrophobia. A piano hinge that ran along the bottom of the panel at his right gave him some comfort, assuring him he could open the panel if his phobia became too intense.

The closer he inched toward the canister, the more it shook. A tube pumped thick yellow fluid into and out of the jar. Two hissing metal nozzles protruded from the lid. Jack arrived within inches of the jar when two large, glossy black eyes blinked out at him through transparent eyelids.

Jack gasped and slammed his head into the plywood ceiling. Some kind of bulbous, gelatinous creature flopped around within the yellow goo. Jack rubbed his head and fumbled for a latch at the top of the side panel. The board dropped, and cool air brushed against his face. He rolled out from the compartment and stood, looking around the girls' cabin.

He'd emerged from below Katie's mattress. Nozzles on top of the canisters sprayed something invisible directly at her pillow. He knew he'd have found the same thing below the other beds—below his own bed.

The canister rocked violently back and forth, and Jack figured the creature in the jar didn't appreciate the light. Coming back to his senses, Jack filmed the jar, confident now that he had all the evidence he'd ever need. He turned to march out the door until he spied Derek talking with several newcomers outside. He couldn't risk them catching him. He needed to hurry back to the research facility lounge.

Jack slid back under the bed, closed the side panel, and scooted out of the chamber. He climbed down the ladder, rushed along the concrete passage, and skipped down the stairs, all the time watching for staff members below. He intended to head down the hallway back to the lounge; Tamera, however, now stood talking to Media in her doorway. Jack ducked behind some computer equipment and headed in another direction, past the cryogenic room to another concrete corridor.

The soft rhythm of pop music echoed from a low-lit room at the end of the hallway. Jack entered it on the tips of his toes. Computer stations, tables, filing cabinets, and dozens of monitors filled the surveillance room. The extent of the spying exceeded Jack's expectations. Specific beds in the north cabins had whole monitor screens dedicated to them. Even the restrooms were on screen. Other monitors indicated *Heart (bpm)*, *Eyes*, *Body*, and *Brain*.

*They're already studying us as we sleep,* Jack thought. *Those labs have nothing to do with monitoring our sleep.*

He filmed everything in the room but stopped when the monitor of Katie's bed caught his eye. It occurred to him that her monitor had probably recorded him entering her cabin from under her bed. This was his chance to erase it. Jack ran to the mouse in front of Katie's monitor and clicked on a box at the bottom left of the computer screen. He scrolled through a list of app icons until he found one that looked like a camcorder. He clicked on it and then meant to select a triangular arrow pointing left, that he expected would rewind the video. But in his haste, he clicked a square icon next to it and skipped a whole day.

He cursed and clicked the double right-pointing triangles, fast-forwarding the tape. He slowed it down a little when he spotted Katie entering her cabin with Marina and Clara, and then leaving with them moments later. He slowed it down again when he saw someone else enter the cabin.

*What is that?* His jaw dropped.

The four-foot-tall intruder hobbled like an ape and kept itself covered entirely below a dirty green tarp. Something on the stranger's back created creases in the fabric along two long, thin ridges. The visitor shoved something under Katie's pillow, briefly revealing its black, hairy hands, then it ran out the door.

Jack remembered the weird note Katie had given him. He could only imagine how terrified Katie would be if she knew what had actually left the message. He hardly believed it himself. He continued fast-forwarding the video until he saw Katie again returning to her cabin.

He slowed the film and watched her reaction to the odd visitor's message.

Approaching voices snapped Jack to action. He sped up the video to where he saw himself rolling out from under Katie's bed, then Damien's voice echoed from the hallway.

"We can review the tapes in here," he said.

Jack searched the room. There was nowhere to hide.

J ack ducked behind a wooden table that left the lower half of his body exposed to view, then he stood and tried to squeeze next to a tall filing cabinet. His arms fell limp and he stepped forward and braced himself for a scolding. Then he noticed the ajar door to an adjacent room.

"I just wish you'd try harder to protect her!" Damien said. He shoved open the surveillance room door.

Jack dashed inside the darkened room and stooped down next to a wide wooden desk. He clenched his teeth when he realized he'd left the door half open.

"Do you think I like risking the life of my best friend's daughter?" Fenton sat down. "The council has made its decision. It's out of our hands."

"I know that!" Damien pounded on a table. "I just don't think they're aware of the sway I have over her. She doesn't need assimilating. She trusts me. I can convince her to join the Intershroud and train her myself."

"I'm sure you could, but the council says she's a risk. End of story."

"What about the risk she'll be taking? Are you prepared to tell Vance how you allowed his daughter to be killed?"

"She won't be killed."

"You don't know that. Alison died less than an hour after her brain rejected the mind fogging."

Jack gulped. His knees weakened, and he almost dropped his cellphone. He hoped it had enough battery left to record the rest of this conversation.

"Enough!" Fenton said. "Alison's willpower was too strong. Farley never should've used the procedure on her. Our technology isn't magic, I don't care how powerful Media is. Katie will be fine. She doesn't have Alison's willpower. Vance and I have been breaking down her self-confidence for years."

"It's still too dangerous."

"Which is why I sent you here to observe."

Jack watched the men through the half-open door. He glimpsed the monitor to Katie's cabin and his heart stopped. Over Damien's shoulder, the screen showed Jack standing in Katie's room videoing the canister under her bed, in slow motion. Damien's father had only to notice it. Damien turned his head and Jack stifled a gasp.

"What are you doing in here?" Curtis Lynch thumped his cane on the vinyl floor and hobbled into the control room. "Is this how Farley runs his security? That imbecile is useless. Where is he?" Lynch leaned on a desk and shook his head.

"He's sleeping," Damien said. "He wanted to stay up for all the action tonight. Should I wake him? He's in the office over there."

Damien walked toward the room in which Jack was hiding. Jack looked to his right. Sure enough, Farley lay sprawled out on a cot only ten feet away. Had his eyes been open, he would've been staring directly at Jack. Jack held his breath and kneeled behind the desk. Damien stepped in and patted the wall in search of the light switch.

"Ah, let him sleep," Lynch said. "He's idiot enough when he's not drowsy. Last thing we need is to give him excuses when he starts messing things up."

Damien returned to the control room. "What did you need him for anyway?" He pulled up a chair and straddled it backwards.

"Mm, just wanted to inform him that his pathetic obsession with ghosts has riled everyone on the board. His activities tonight cannot interfere with the assimilations. Without exception, all members of the research team must be assimilated tonight."

"We can't do that!" Damien stood up. "That many people will overwhelm Media's mind. Avard won't allow it."

"You are both to keep this from Avard and Media." Lynch raised his cane and pointed it at Damien. "We failed to discover Sherry's accomplice. We have no choice but to assume that any one of the team members could be guilty. We must immediately secure their loyalty to the Intershroud."

"This is crazy," Damien said. "We know Katie's no spy, and Clara isn't even all there in the head. I don't know how she's been resisting the dream inducers, but it's clear that she's stuck in some fantasy realm. Marina, Barbara, Ming, and Jack are clueless. We successfully controlled Jorge's mind. Carl and Tony have already signed on. Taylor doesn't even belong in the risk group. He's no threat. You can't tell me that these people are worth driving Media into total mindlessness."

"You'd better watch yourself, boy!" Lynch stepped closer to Damien and sneered. "Learn from Miss Sherry what happens to defectors in this business. For your information, the threats are far worse than you're willing to admit. I don't buy Clara's act for one second. We want the essence fogging increased on her until she dreams about this camp or dies resisting it."

"Unbelievable!" Damien shoved his chair, letting it roll across the room and slam against a waste basket.

"You're right about the Bowman boy, I've already instructed my forces to eliminate him."

A lump formed in Jack's throat. He needed to warn Taylor immediately, but how? There was no way out of the room without getting caught.

"Still, we all know that Katie is no threat," Damien said.

"She's the biggest threat of all! Open your eyes. Her father kept a housekeeper for three years before discovering she was a spy. She was communicating with the girl's mother! How she managed to circumvent your constant surveillance of Katie, I'll never know. Who can guess what she told her? Had she not blown her cover stopping Katie from overdosing on pills, we'd probably never have known she was a spy. I'm sorry that it's so inconvenient for you, but the girl's mind must be adjusted."

Fenton gave Damien a sympathetic glance and turned to Lynch. "How are you planning to get them into the lab without Avard finding out?"

"Avard will be busy guarding the south grounds tonight. If we cannot convince the kids to come voluntarily, we'll have to release the sleep-inducing agents into their cabins."

Fenton nodded. "They'll wake up not even knowing why they're singing praises to the Intershroud."

Jack cringed. He looked down and discovered a familiar newspaper lying next to him in a trashcan. *The Essential Expositor.* Whoever had placed the warning note under Katie' pillow had used that same newspaper. The headline read, *Camp Farley—Intershroud Recruiting Station Poses as Innocent Summer Camp!*

*Whoever wrote that is an ally*, Jack thought. He slid the paper from the trashcan, gently folded it up, and slowly tucked it into his pants pocket.

Lynch looked at Farley's office door. "Incidentally, why is Farley so certain another attack is possible? Nightmares won't attack the camp with the lights working. The transformer Sherry damaged was repaired and is much less accessible."

"There are other ways to cut the power," Fenton said. "The power lines used to short out all the time when the camp first opened. The lines running over the research facility touched every time a strong wind blew. There were blackouts every other month until someone tied something between the lines to keep them separated."

"We'll need guards on the roof then," Lynch said. "I don't want the power going out during the assimilations."

"You don't have to worry about that," Fenton said. "The building's generator will kick in. Besides, I don't see how anyone could get to the roof."

"I suppose I should be discussing this with Avard," Lynch said.

"Why don't one of you do Farley's job and find someone to watch these monitors." Lynch left the room.

Fenton started to pat Damien's shoulder, but Damien shoved his hand away.

"If anything happens to Katie, I'll never forgive any of you." He stormed out.

Fenton watched his son leave and took a deep breath. He glanced at the monitors, just missing the footage of Jack pulling the trap door closed under Katie's bed. Fenton pulled a tin of mints from his coat pocket and popped one into his mouth before sauntering out the door.

Jack darted to Katie's monitor and grabbed the mouse. He set the video to overwrite the footage of his escapade into Katie's room, then searched for a way to change the time code. He couldn't figure out how to do that, however, and decided just to be grateful that no one would know who messed with their footage.

His mind spun. He left the room, rushed down a hallway and passed through a door that led into the boys' sleep lab. He charged through the lab and slipped through the door into the lounge. The game had changed now. Jack had all the proof he needed to convince the outside world what was happening here. Tonight, they were escaping Camp Farley, no matter what it took.

Below an overcast sky, Jack leaned forward against a short spruce tree with his foot pressed against the tall gray posts of the palisade. He'd found the highest point from which to observe the campground. He peered over a multitude of spruce boughs to study the green metal roof of the research facility. Two power lines sagged low from one end of the roof to the other, held apart only by a thick stub of wood wrapped with green nylon rope.

He slapped at one of the mosquitos buzzing around his ears, shoved himself away from the pine tree, and started working his way through a maze of low-lying scrub oaks that covered the northern hillside. He crossed a narrow trail that led to Katie's cabin and spotted Taylor climbing it toward him.

"Dude, where've you been? You missed Derek's lying competition. Clara's cabin won. You wouldn't believe how good she is at lying."

"Sorry I missed it," Jack said.

"You've had way more important things to worry about, dude. That video you took is creeping everyone out."

"So, you passed my phone around to everyone? And Ming's note?" Jack hiked down the trail and Taylor followed him.

Taylor slid Jack's phone from his back pocket and handed it to Jack.

"Dude, just touching that phone makes me feel sick now. I showed the notes and video to everyone I could. They were as freaked out as I was. Barbara almost threw you phone on the concrete when she saw that weird thing in the glass container, but I grabbed it from her. The yellow blob freakin looked like nausea in a jar. What was that?"

Jack frowned. "All I know is it was spraying something at our heads at night. It makes me want to take out my brain and scrub it off. At least we finally have the proof we needed. They all agreed to escape with us tonight, didn't they?"

"Definitely. No money on earth could've bribed them to stay once they saw them dead dudes in the freezer. Ming almost fainted. Travis looked pale, too. Marina thinks they control people's thoughts by sending something from those dead people's heads into ours. How gross is that? Don't worry, dude, everybody's on board now. We're all going to need therapy after seeing that."

"What did Katie say about it?"

Taylor shook his head. "Couldn't catch her or Clara alone. Katie seems to think I'm trying to send her messages from you."

"We have to get it to her. We can't just leave her here. Are you sure no one saw you?"

"I located a lot of surveillance cameras this afternoon, so I'm pretty sure I stayed out of view. Carl and Tony don't know anything. They think I stole your phone and showed the others embarrassing videos of you. So, what've you been up to?"

"I've been trying to plan our escape. I hoped there'd be a way to short out the power on the roof of the research facility, but it's impossible. There's a retaining wall on the north side, but we'd have to jump more than twenty feet. This is so aggravating."

"You're getting too worked up, bro. It's dinner time. Let's get some food. You'll think better with something in your gut."

"You're right. Also, we need to sneak as much food as we can. Who knows how long we'll be hiking through the woods?"

"How are we going to do this? Guards are everywhere now, and they're armed."

Jack shook his head. "It does seem impossible, but that doesn't matter anymore. We have to find a way."

"I think our best hope is the south gate. It's shorter than the rest of the fence, and no one's guarding it directly. If we can take the power out, the camera there won't be a problem."

The clearing across from the lodge came into view and Jack turned toward the eating area. He searched for Katie and found her sitting at a table between Damien and Clara. The approaching thumping of feet warned him someone was running up to him from behind. He turned and found Marina and Barbara. Marina looked serious and Barbara's eyes were wild with fear. Neither girl wore their I.D. lanyard around their neck.

"I'm totally freaked out right now!" Barbara grabbed Jack's arm. "What was that? Frozen old dead people! What was that thing under our beds? I almost threw up."

"Don't forget that Alison died, and they lied about it," Marina said.

"You find a way out of here, we're in," Barbara said. "I won't be able to sleep tonight anyway. I'm not sleeping another night with that gooey yellow monster under my pillow."

"I don't see what we can do," Marina said. "The camp's as bright as daylight at night and there are guards everywhere."

Jack shook his head. "You heard Lynch. He'll force us to do the labs if he has to. We're in danger no matter what we do."

Jack slid his hand into his pocket to search for his lighter and brushed against a wrinkled piece of paper, still moist from when Damien dunked him in the lake. He pulled it out and read the words again: *KATIE, DANGER, TRAILHEAD, DUSK.*

"That's it!" Jack grinned and dangled the note in front of Taylor and the girls.

They each returned blank stares.

"Don't you see? Somebody left this note on Katie's bed! They're trying to help her escape! We have help from the outside! The trail-head starts at the south gate. We just need to get there by sundown."

"That's the only hope we have right now, dude," Taylor said. "It's really overcast, though. I'm not sure we'll know when dusk arrives."

"Let's just plan on being at the south gate around nine o'clock," Jack said.

"I don't know," Barbara said. "Whoever wrote that note is probably behind all the attacks against Farley. Lynch's people will be looking for them."

"She's right," Marina said. "It's too dangerous."

"You all can do what you want," Jack said, "but I'm going to be at the foot of Mount Farley Trail at sundown, whatever it takes." Jack headed for the buffet table. Taylor, Barbara, and Marina followed him.

Jack and the others loaded their plates with hot-baked chicken, rice and gravy, peas and carrots, rolls, and peach cobbler. Taylor piled rolls onto a second plate and when Jack noticed what he was doing, he did the same. Jack found Ming and Travis at a table, then led everyone to sit with them, but he couldn't take his eyes of Katie. She sat across the floor, laughing with Clara at something Damien had said.

"Don't worry about her, man." Taylor took a seat next to Travis. "Even if you can't warn her, her dad will protect her."

"We don't know that." Jack sat down and flattened out a napkin on the table. "Does anyone have a pen?"

Ming pulled one from his shirt pocket and handed it to him.

Jack scribbled a long note.

"What's that, dude?" Taylor grabbed at the napkin, but Jack slammed his hand over it.

"It's for Katie. I told her if they force her to do the lab, I'd try to take the power out so she can escape out the door to the generator room. I told her about the stairs to the compartments below our beds and to join us at Farley Trail."

"How are you going to give it to her without Damien seeing it?"

Before Jack could answer, Derek climbed onto a table near Katie and pressed a microphone to his face. "Everyone listen up. I've got some bad news. The dance scheduled for tonight has been cancelled. I'm sure you've noticed the increase in security around camp. We've learned that the attacks on Mr. Farley have been coming from outside the camp and we're expecting another one tonight. For your safety, everyone will be confined to their cabins for the rest of the day."

The sounds of disappointed campers coursed through the area.

"We deserve a refund," someone yelled.

"It won't be that bad," Derek said. "Think of it as an opportunity to play some cards or board games and get to know your cabin mates better. We just want to make sure no one is underfoot while we prepare for tonight. If you need to leave your cabin for any reason, we'll have escorts for you."

Derek jumped down from the table and looked around. No one was leaving.

Avard stepped forward. "Weren't you listening? The man said get to yer cabins!" He kicked a rear leg of a chair from under an unsuspecting boy, pitching him onto his back with a thump. Everyone watched in silence as the boy pushed himself up from the concrete.

"This place is ridiculous," Barbara stood and walked over to gather two handfuls of rolls. Grumbling campers gathered into groups and made their way to their lodgings.

Jack pulled his cellphone from his pocket and searched for the video of his experience in the research facility. He wrapped his napkin message around it, his eyes fixed on Katie, Clara, and Damien.

Taylor grabbed his hand. "Dude, what are doing? It's too risky. That phone's our only evidence."

"I won't leave her here. I know she'll come with us."

"Dude"

The moment Katie stood to leave, Jack shook his hand away from Taylor, rushed behind her chair, and slipped his phone into her bag.

Bright lights flickered on below a sea of dark clouds, causing the beige curtains of Jack's cabin to glow like lanterns. Jack sat on his bed reading the single-page newspaper he'd found in Farley's wastebasket, shaking his head. He folded the paper and tucked it into his pants pocket. Taylor leaned cross-legged against the backboard of a bed across the room, in a circle with Travis, Carl, Ming, and Tony, cards in their hands.

"I'm out," Ming said.

Taylor grinned at the whining of the other boys and Ming pushed a small pile of butterscotch candies toward him.

"You cheat." Carl tossed his cards on the bed, then stood and dropped on his own bed across the aisle from Jack. "We can't leave the cabin, so we might as well go to sleep. If you guys had any brains, you'd go do the sleep lab."

"We're not doing the sleep lab." Jack walked to window and brushed aside the drape. Through the trees, he made out three men in army fatigues standing guard on the roof of the research facility. Nine o'clock had passed fifteen minutes ago, but armed guards were everywhere, and the grounds looked like daylight below the new stadium lights. There was no way to get to the south gate unseen.

Jack dug his fingernails into the wooden windowsill, gritted his teeth, and glanced up at a light fixture in the corner of the ceiling where he knew the Intershroud had concealed a camera and microphone. He'd endured three hours, trapped like a caged animal in this cabin, unable to discuss anything with his friends. Jack jumped when he became aware of Taylor suddenly standing next to him.

"What was that paper you were reading?" Taylor handed him a piece of yellow candy.

"I found a newsletter in the trash in Farley's room." Jack spoke quietly, hoping the microphones wouldn't detect him. He pulled the paper from his pocket and handed it to Taylor. "It's by an underground group that's trying to expose you-know-who. They must have spies here because it says a lot about the things I saw in the research facility."

Taylor read the heading. "Essential Expositor, published by Cable and Martin Rook." He handed it back to Taylor. "What did it say?"

A loud knock on the door brought all the boys to their feet. Jack rammed the paper into his pocket.

Derek walked in, brushing between two men decked in army fatigues, standing motionless outside the door. The guards faced away from the cabin and their gloved hands clasped tight around the pistol grip and hand guards of their rifles. Derek tucked a pink box under one arm and held the door open with his other hand, allowing entrance of two huge, long-haired soldiers whose bulging arms, stern faces, and thick necks were smothered in tattoos of dragons, snakes, knives, snarling wolves, and writhing chains.

Jack had never felt more intimidated or confused. He looked at Taylor who offered him a wry grin. The buxom torsos of these soldiers suggested, against all other indicators, that they might be women.

"Taylor Bowman, come with us!" The gruff voice of the bigger of the two soldiers gave no clue as to the owner's gender.

"He's staying with me!" Jack darted to his friend and grabbed his arm.

"Not tonight," Derek said.

"If he goes, I go!"

"Same here," Ming said.

The two soldiers snarled and shoved Carl and Travis aside on their way to Taylor. Derek held his hand up to stop them. He walked up close to Jack.

"I'm sorry, Jack. I really am. If it were up to me, things would be different, but I have no say against Mr. Lynch. Taylor wasn't invited to this camp and Lynch is demanding that he go."

"Then I go too."

Derek shook his head. "You signed the papers promising to complete this program."

"Sue me then. I'm going with Taylor."

Pain shot down Jack's right arm and vice-like hands twisted it behind his back. The slightest movement increased the pain. The larger soldier secured Taylor in a similar fashion and pushed him toward the door.

"Let him go! Where are you taking him?"

"He'll be fine," Derek said. "They're taking him to the airport where they'll put him on a plane and send him home, probably first class. I don't know why you're so worked up. From what I've seen, you hate it here." He motioned for the soldier to release Jack's arms. Jack yanked his arm down and massaged his aching shoulder.

Jack's eyes brightened. "Why can't he drive home in his car? You can fly me home later."

Taylor stared at Jack for a second, then smiled. "Yeah, man, why can't I drive home in my own car?"

Derek shrugged. "It makes no difference to me. I thought it was Jack's car. Go grab his keys from Farley's office and escort him to the satellite parking area. Make sure he leaves."

The larger soldier gave Derek a grin that made Jack shudder. Jack feared they had no intention of taking Taylor to the car. They were going to kill him. The guard let Taylor go, nodded, and opened the door for him. The shorter soldier winked at Jack before joining the larger one by the door.

Taylor stopped and turned to Jack. "See you back home, dude. I'll try to take a picture of that road south of the camp before I leave." He winked at Jack.

"No pictures," the shorter soldier said.

"If you can't take pictures there," Jack said, "take one of that old house we passed on the way here. You know, the one with the leaning porch columns?" Jack wanted to warn him that his life was in danger, but there was nothing he could say that would help.

Taylor smiled and nodded, then the two soldiers shoved him out the door and left.

Derek faced the boys, the pink box still tucked under his arm.

"Guys," Derek's voice sounded way too friendly. "I know it's been inconvenient being stuck in your cabins all evening, but there's a real threat out there and I think Lynch and Farley are right to take it seriously. You guys are lucky, though. You're all invited to sleep in the lab tonight. It's much nicer than this cabin."

"Forget it," Jack said. "We're not doing it." He couldn't hold back the venom in his words.

Derek looked at Ming and Travis and found them both standing resolute with their arms folded. Tony and Carl looked at each other with raised eyebrows, then shook their heads. "Really? Wow. I wasn't expecting this. It's just a sleep study. Why are you so worried? Montathena Research really needs those lab results and they're paying you top dollar for them. You'll never make easier money. We're literally not asking you to do anything but sleep. I assume you're planning to sleep tonight anyway, aren't you?"

"Actually, I've been having trouble sleeping. We all have." Jack folded his arms.

Derek opened his mouth then shut it and furrowed his brow. Jack knew Derek couldn't admit he knew the boys weren't having trouble sleeping.

"I guess that's it then." Derek shook his head. "I thought we were friends, Jack. I promised Lynch I'd bring you all to the lab tonight. I didn't imagine you'd turn it down. He's not going to be happy." Derek shoved the pink cardboard box into Carl's hands. "I even snagged these brownies to make up for your troubles."

"I'll bet you did," Jack said.

Derek glared at Jack then yanked open the door before storming from the cabin.

Ming walked over to Jack. "Isn't it your car?"

Jack grinned and nodded. "There's a road that runs along the south wall of the camp. If we can get away from here, Taylor will be waiting for us on that road. If they make him leave, he'll wait for us near an old house we saw in Silverton."

Carl set the brownies on a nearby nightstand and grabbed three of them. Tony rushed over to take four more and Travis took one. Ming picked up a few and handed one to Jack, but he tossed it on a table and looked out the window along with Ming. They watched Avard standing in a Jeep near the main offices, talking to a dozen armed soldiers. Four other troops marched toward the front gate. Two guards were standing at the doors of every building in their view.

"We don't have a chance," Ming said. "There are people every- where and they all have guns. There's just no way."

Travis walked up behind them. "Remember to keep your voices down."

"It doesn't matter anymore!" Jack pounded on the windowsill. "We've lost."

"What are you guys talking about?" Tony shoved a whole brownie in his mouth and sat on edge of his bed.

Ming nibbled his brownie. "All I can say is, nobody's forcing me into that lab. I'd rather be shot dead than let them mess with my mind."

Travis nodded and placed a brownie in his mouth when Jack grabbed his arm and pointed at Carl, laying at an awkward angle across his bed, his eyes closed. Tony laid down and closed his eyes, too, then drifted off.

Jack slapped the brownie from Travis' hand and slammed the box to the ground, sending mangled brownies scattering across the floor. Ming let his dessert drop to his feet.

"That crazy old geezer!" Jack stomped on the brownie box. "Lynch said they'd do something to force us to sleep."

"I thought he said they'd release some kind of gas into the room!" Travis brushed crumbs from his hands.

"They're not taking any chances," Jack said.

Ming ran to the sink, flipped the faucet handle, and scooped water into his mouth. He gurgled and rinsed out his mouth three times, but when he looked at Jack, the drooping of his eyelids told him that he'd been too late.

"That's it! I don't care who sees me. I'm out of here." Jack tore open the door. The two guards turned around and faced him, their huge bodies forming an impenetrable wall.

"Nobody leaves!" the man on the right said. He shoved Jack back into the room, but his actions were not what held Jack's attention. Beyond his shoulders, Jack spotted Katie and Clara, in their flowery nightclothes, walking down the path to the research facility. Damien escorted them. The guard slammed the door and Jack stood motionless, staring at it.

Perhaps he only imagined it, but he thought he heard the soft hiss of sleeping agents releasing into the room.

K atie stood with her arms folded, watching her reflection in the lab's observation window. She shivered at the discomforting thought that Farley might be ogling her and Clara at that very moment, on the other side of the glass. Brass sconces washed the corners of the room with light that cast a web of shadows from the black rubber tubes and wires hanging above the row of six inviting beds. The air temperature didn't account for the chill she felt.

Clara stood next to her and pretended to be brave, but her tight grasp on Katie's wrist told another story. The door opened, and Farley walked in, his hands clasped together. He approached so close to Katie she had to take two steps back.

"You're here," Farley's face twitched when he smiled. "I'm glad I could at least count on you two to cooperate. Pick any bed you like. Make yourselves at home."

Clara glanced at the beds and sat on the nearest one, still clinging to Katie's arm.

"I need to speak to Damien." Katie didn't budge.

"Why so nervous? You remind me of your sister; always so skittish. Would you like something to drink?"

Katie's face flushed. *How dare he talk about Abby like that?* "Who wouldn't be afraid around someone like you?" She pulled Clara's hand from her arm and tossed her bag on the bed next to her. "Let me talk to Damien!"

Farley laughed and pulled a radio from his lab coat pocket. "Damien, you back there? Mm hmm. Yes. She wants to talk to you." He looked her up and down. "He'll be here in a minute. Can I get you anything else?"

Katie just stared at him.

Farley rolled his eyes, then turned and left the room.

"Seems like a comfy room." Clara set her backpack on the bed and pulled out a gray stuffed elephant.

The door opened, and Damien walked in. "Hey, Farley said you wanted to talk to me. I heard the others opted out for some reason. Tomorrow, you'll be able to show them how irrational they were."

Katie just stared at him, struggling to speak without releasing a flood of emotion. Damien stopped talking and looked away. She had one question for him, and she felt that her whole future—her whole life—hung on his answer to it.

Damien looked at Clara, then back at Katie. "What's wrong? You okay?"

Katie briskly shook her head, then looked into his eyes, tears blurring her vision.

"Come on," Damien said. "What's wrong?"

Katie wiped her eyes and took a deep breath. "Damien, I want to ask you something, and I want you to be honest with me. I've been lied to so many times. I need you to tell me the truth."

"Of course. I have no reason to lie to you."

"You know how I feel about you?"

He nodded. "I care about you, too."

"Okay then, tell me. Is this sleep study dangerous?"

Damien looked down and then to the left. "That's a strange question, I mean, I told you before. I'm fine, aren't I? I did this same sleep lab in this same building."

"Answer my question!"

"I did. I mean, I'm not going to say that some kind of freak accident couldn't—"

"Damien, stop skirting the question! I want to hear it from you. Is this safe?"

"Yes!" Damien glanced up at her for only a second before returning his gaze to the floor. "It's perfectly safe. You'll see. Tomorrow morning, you'll be thanking me. Stop worrying about it. Why can't you just trust me?"

Katie felt her insides melting away. She felt his hands take hold of hers and she jerked them away. She had nothing more to say. She walked to the bed next to Clara's, moving more like a robot than a person, and pulled aside the comforter. She climbed into her bed and lay there staring at the ceiling.

"Katie, why are you acting like this?" Damien rushed to her side.

She pretended not to hear him.

He shook his head. "I don't know what the problem is, but you need to know that I'm here for you no matter what you think. I'll be on the other side of that window every second, making sure nothing happens to you." He marched out of the room.

Tamera entered, her heels clacking on the vinyl floor. "Good Evening, girls. Please, lie down, Clara, while I attach these sensors to you. It will feel a little cold, but it is perfectly harmless."

Katie hardly knew what was happening. She heard the bed springs complain as Clara laid back on her bed. She heard Tamera prepping her for the sleep study. She just felt numb—not sad or angry or afraid —just devoid of feeling. Jack's note and cellphone recordings kept running through her mind. Was this procedure going to wipe out her mind? It didn't matter. She wasn't so sure she cared about her current mind anyway.

"I assume you heard what I said to Clara." Tamera stood at Katie's side and squeezed blue gel onto a wired, disk-shaped sensor before attaching it to her left forearm. She circled the bed and applied sensors to each of Katie's legs, three places on her forehead, and a few on her stomach.

"There you are." Tamera closed the gel tube and placed it in her pocket. "Place this headgear over your face and you will fall right to sleep." She handed Katie a clear plastic mask with elastic blue straps.

Katie stretched the bands and pulled the mask over her face.

"Perfect. Sleep tight." Tamera strutted to the light switch by the door and dimmed the lights before leaving the room.

Air coursed through one of the tubes attached to Katie's facemask and she tore the mask from her face.

"You need to keep the mask on," Tamera said over a speaker.

"I will. I just need to get used to it first."

"Take all the time you need." This time Damien spoke.

Katie stared at the mask and again pondered her relationship with Damien. She was so sure he'd tell her the truth. She wanted him to be her hero, the one to rescue her from the clutches of the Intershroud. Instead, he'd betrayed her again. She'd aligned her whole future with him, but now she saw no future. Nothing mattered. She slid on the mask and tried not to think about what was about to happen to her mind.

A sickly glow radiated from a translucent tube above her head. She glanced at Clara. Her cousin's eyes were wide open, only rarely blinking, and she clutched her comforter like she was descending the downhill slope of a roller coaster. A gaseous yellow substance flowed from a box by her bed and into her mask.

Katie's troubles evaporated. She wanted to kick herself. Her poor cousin was terrified, and Katie hadn't even informed her that her life was in peril. She'd been thinking only of herself. She grabbed her mask and started to yank it off but realized it would make no difference. She searched the wall for the generator room door and wondered if Jack really would take out the power.

*What have I done?* she thought. *Don't let us down, Jack. Please don't let us down.*

She watched Clara's eyelids drop, then Katie did something she hadn't done since her mother left her that dreadful night three years earlier. She prayed.

✠

JACK PACED the cabin like a caged animal. There was no way to get to Taylor. He'd failed to warn Katie and lost his evidence in the process. Ming sat on his bed, struggling to stay upright, yet he'd only nibbled a brownie. Tony and Carl lay comatose and Jack suspected Marina and Barbara were out, too. He couldn't leave the cabin. Gunmen were everywhere. Time had run out. He'd run out of hope.

Travis yanked at the edge of a panel below Ming's bed, then stood up and kicked it. It wouldn't budge. "They've won, guys. We might as well have enjoyed those brownies."

"They can't do this to us!" Jack kicked the crumpled pink box across the room. "It's supposed to be a free country!"

"They've got guns," Ming said.

"Then they'll have to shoot me." Jack ran to the door and yanked it open.

"Get back inside!" One of the guards gripped his rifle tight.

Jack froze. He couldn't think. Something crossed his line of sight that caused him to question his own eyes. Four shadowy forms dashed through the pine trees just beyond the guards. They looked like small bears until they sprouted wings and lifted into the air. They glided toward the roof of the research facility.

"What was that?" One of the guards fixed his rifle on one of the creatures and fired five shots. The creature didn't even slow down. A dozen other gunshots pierced the silence from locations throughout the camp.

Jack, Ming, and Travis darted to the window. Two guards already lay prostrate on the roof of the research facility. The third man rolled off the roof edge and clung to it for a few seconds before falling to the ground.

Five hairy, winged, dwarfish creatures scrambled around on the roof. Six soldiers gathered around the building and fired at them non-stop. Two of the winged beings disappeared in clouds of black smoke, and Jack wondered if sleep agents were making him hallucinate. The remaining three dark entities surrounded the block of wood tied to the power lines. They grabbed the wood and pulled and twisted at it until one of them lit up like a candle and fizzled into another black cloud.

A roof hatch swung open and another soldier brought out a rifle and started shooting. Another manlike creature turned to smoke. The last creature held the green cord in its hands and the block of wood dropped and slid down the metal roof.

Indistinguishable voices shouted. An alarm sounded. More shots reported. Other flying beasts dived from the trees and slammed into gunmen on the ground, knocking them to the earth. The last creature on the roof laughed like a mad gorilla and yanked the power lines tight with all its strength. Sparks bathed the roof in electric light.

Then there was inky blackness.

✠

KATIE SMILED when darkness enveloped the sleep lab. A generator buzzed on a half-minute later and the lights flickered back on.

"Katie?" Damien spoke over the loudspeaker. "Very funny. Get back in bed. Clara?"

Katie took a deep breath and gently pressed a finger over Clara's mouth. She twisted the thumb-turn on the generator room door. Damien called her name several times before shaking the locked door lever to the generator room.

"What's going on here? What're you doing?" It was Farley's voice.

"Don't ask me," Damien said. "They're gone, but all the doors are locked."

"I don't care about them! Can't you see we're under attack? Get outside! I want these attacks stopped!"

A key scratched against the door lock and Katie turned to the generator. Clara leaned on a nearby wall, her eyes half shut.

"If you're awake enough, help me disable this thing." Katie felt a little drowsy, but Clara was much worse off. Katie searched the large metal box but found nothing easy to destroy. Clara picked up the connector plug. Katie dug into her bag and brushed aside combs, a mirror, a small purse, and a make-up kit before finding her pocketknife. She pulled the plug and plunged the room into darkness again, then cut the thick three-pronged plug from the wire. She grabbed Clara's hand and led her out the back door of the room.

JACK GRASPED the window curtain in his hand. The camp had gone dark below the thick cloudy sky. Gunshots and unintelligible shouts railed from the left and right, all over camp.

One of the guards outside the door let out a loud "Oof," and metal clanged against the cabin's wooden porch deck.

"What in the—" the second guard didn't finish his sentence. Jack heard the crack of a wood railing.

"This is our chance!" Jack felt for his backpack in the near darkness and ran to the door. He opened it and stepped over a lit flashlight spinning on the porch. Ming rushed up behind him, grabbed the light, and shined it on the two guards. One lay curled up on the porch, his arms around his stomach and breathing with forced effort. The other man lay passed out in the dirt amidst parts of the former railing.

"Let's go!" Jack said.

Ming tripped on the sling of a rifle and kicked it aside. Travis leaned down, grabbed it, and joined Ming and Jack.

The gunshots and shouting never stopped, and headlights now pierced the blackness. Motors revved, and the chopping of helicopters echoed through the mountains.

The boys ran for the trees.

XXIV

Katie held tight to Clara's hand, fearing who or what she might bump into in the lightless rooms of the facility. She waved her free hand in front of her and wiggled her foot in the air before each step, but her precautions didn't save her from slamming her right shin into the metal leg of a table. She winced and stopped, leaning over to massage her leg.

"Where are we going?" Clara's words came out slow and slurred.

"We're leaving." Katie stood up, hitting her head on an unseen shelf, and massaged the painful welt near her left ear.

"Is the sleep study over? Why's it so dark?"

"Shush. They'll hear us." Katie moved with slow, careful steps. She searched for the stairwell and stopped at a square concrete column, sliding her hand over its surface. She felt a computer monitor and then bounced her hand along a row of them. Moments later, her left knee found the armrest of a leather-clad office chair and she froze at the loudness of it crashing into a metal desk.

Then she remembered her cellphone had a light. She dug around in her bag but stopped when the beam of a flashlight swung through the room. The light revealed to her that she'd just missed the stairwell. She pulled Clara behind a column next to it.

"Katie?" It was Damien. "You back here? What're you doing? This isn't a good time for games."

Katie hushed Clara and pulled her down behind the metal stringer of the stairs.

"Ouch!" a woman said. The slow drawl could only be Media. "Watch where you're going! What's going on?"

"Media?" Damien flashed a light on her.

"'Course it's me. Who's messing with the lights?"

"Have you bumped into anyone back here?"

"I haven't seen anyone. I'm sure they'd have headed straight for the exit. That's where I'm going. My head is killing me."

Katie peeked through the wire-mesh guardrails, then ducked when a flashlight beam again passed over her head.

"You're right. Let's head out," Damien said. "The girls are probably out there anyway."

Damien and Media left for the sleep lab, and the light faded with them. A door slammed and the room again went dark. Katie pulled her cellphone from her bag. She lit up the stairwell and urged Clara to follow her up.

"Why're we hiding from Damien?" Clara grasped hard to the handrail, lacking the energy to climb stairs.

"Hurry Clara, I'll explain later. We need to move fast, before the lights turn back on." Katie found the rows of ladders at the top of the stairs and ran to the one next to her name plaque, the one nearest her cabin's front door. She waited for Clara to climb up the ladder and followed her into the chamber below her bed. Neither she nor Clara could take their eyes off the glowing jar wiggling at the head of the compartment. The bulbous yellow mass made her feel sick and she had to look away.

She found the release hook, let the panel fall open into her cabin, and rolled out of the chamber, followed by Clara. They pulled their selves to their feet and Katie scanned the room, finding only Marina remaining, lying motionless on her bed, with her feet on the floor. Katie hefted her legs onto the bed and shook her a few times.

"Marina! Wake up! We need to get away from here." The girl didn't stir.

Clara stepped up to Katie, her eyes wide with fear. "What is that thing below your bed? Is Marina alright?"

"She just sleeping. We're going on a hike, Clara. Put everything you can into your backpack." Katie grabbed her backpack and scrambled to stuff warm clothes and toiletries into it. Shadows danced around the room from flashlights outside, amidst the eerie glow of the pulsing yellow jar below the bed.

"How'd you know about that secret compartment?" Clara tossed her pack over her shoulder and rubbed her eyes.

"I'll explain later. We need to run." Katie cracked open the door. The men she'd seen guarding the cabin earlier were no longer there. Three helicopters hovered over the camp, their searchlights scanning the terrain around the lake, the lodge, and the research facility. Guns popped and people shouted, their words muffled by motors and distance. Katie found a shadowy area on the hill to her left and waited for a searchlight to pass.

"Now, Clara!" She charged up the short hill and ducked into a grove of trees. Clara left the door open and ran up behind her. They heard footsteps to their left, then the slamming of their cabin door to their right. Katie saw shadows moving around inside the cabin but didn't wait to find out who it was. She urged Clara to follow her and charged southward, in the direction of the south gate.

✖

JACK HUNCHED low and kept his hands in front of him to catch the branches of low shrubs. He froze when shots fired within a hundred yards of him. Other guns reported from distant locations beyond the lake and back at the research facility. Jack turned to make sure Ming and Travis were still behind him, then flattened himself against a tree trunk to dodge the headlights of two vehicles speeding along the path towards the lake.

Ming and Travis dived to the ground and rolled into a row of ferns for cover. After the trucks passed by, Jack started off, but stopped again to avoid a flashlight courtesy of someone down by the main offices. A helicopter hovered above him, its searchlights playing through the leaves for several seconds before it flew away.

Ming and Travis stood and ran to Jack.

"Did you see that?" Travis pointed at the trees ahead of them.

"I know. There are people everywhere. This place is in chaos," Jack said.

"I don't mean that," Travis said. "In those trees ahead. I saw something jump between those branches. It didn't look human."

"I saw it, too," Ming said. "I thought I was seeing things."

"I've never been this scared in my life." Travis held up the rifle he'd taken and presented it to Jack.

"Don't give it me," Jack said. "I've never used a gun."

"Me neither," Travis said.

"Don't look at me," Ming said.

Shots sounded from somewhere near the lake. Travis ducked and slapped a hand to the side of his head. He looked up at Jack, terror in his eyes. "A bullet just whizzed by my head!" He took off at a dead run.

Jack charged after him, slapping aside branches and tripping over tree roots. He ran past one of the cabins and around a low hill behind the amphitheater, nothing on his mind but the fear that someone could be behind them with a gun aimed at his back. He slammed into Travis who'd stopped to ease around three guards lying on the ground, groaning in fetal position. Whatever the attacking creatures were, they had a knack for pounding people hard in the gut.

Ming caught up with them moments later. Jack motioned them to follow him behind three pine trees and leaned over to catch his breath. His throat burned from the overexertion.

"You know we're going to die, don't you?" Travis's lip quivered and he looked away.

Ming nodded. "He may be right, Jack. This can't possibly be any better than what they were going to do to us in that lab. Those are real bullets. I'm so scared, I'm shaking." He held out a trembling hand.

Jack looked away and tried to think, to weigh the risks. Maybe it was too late; the cards had already been dealt. Then he remembered Alison. "Alison died in that lab. The risk is the same no matter what we do. I doubt they mean to shoot at us. They're after those creatures we've been seeing. We just need to stay calm and get to the south gate."

Travis began to speak when Ming put up a hand and motioned for Jack and Travis to move into the pines. They heard the cracking of twigs and approaching footfalls. Barbara stepped into the small clearing in front of them. She started when Jack stepped out of the shadows.

"Oh man, I thought I'd never catch up to you guys." Barbara breathed heavily and looked at Jack, then frowned. "This is Twilight Zone stuff. I swear I saw flying ape people on the roof of the research facility. People are shooting at us. I could just keel over right now, I'm so scared."

"You're not alone," Jack said. "Where's Marina?"

Barbara shook her head. "I couldn't wake her. Derek must've drugged the brownies he gave us. I've never been so glad I was on a diet. I thought they said they were going to pipe sleeping gas into our cabins?"

"Who knows what these maniacs are going to do from minute to the next," Ming said.

"They piped in enough gas to tire me out," Barbara said. "I'm already exhausted."

"We all are. We'd better keep moving." Jack waved the others to follow him and wove through the trees along the palisade wall. He passed the last grove of trees and the south gate came into view. A meadow of low yellow grass stood between him and the gate, and he saw no place to hide other than a smattering of low scrub oaks and a wooden sign nailed between two white posts that displayed information about Farley Trail.

Jack squinted in the dark and smiled.

XXV

Katie pulled Clara around the corner of a cabin near the lake and pressed back against the cedar logs. Three guards stood along the amphitheater seats, and she hoped they couldn't see her and Clara standing in the shadows.

"There's one over there," a guard said. She leveled her M16 and fired four shots into the trees far away from Katie. The other two guards stood ready to fire. "Come on," the woman said. The three guards ran within twenty yards of Katie before disappearing into the trees.

Katie turned to Clara and found her frowning, her eyes wide with fear.

"Katie, tell me what's going on! Who are they shooting at?" Clara wiped her eyes with the sleeve of her flannel pajamas.

"I don't know, but we can't stop to talk about it yet. I promise I'll explain everything when we're safe." Katie scanned the area and searched for the shadiest path. She figured they'd be safest close to the cabins of other campers. She tightened her grip on Clara's hand and pulled her along as fast as she dared move. She squinted at the ground to watch for tripping hazards, but the absence of moonlight blinded her to a short clump of grass and she fell, pulling Clara with her. She'd barely pulled herself up again when she stepped on a gnarled stick and scratched her leg on a low branch. She breathed hard in relief when she arrived at the outer wall of the next cabin.

Katie caught sight of two soldiers keeping watch at the south end of the amphitheater seating. She turned and headed deeper up an incline and into the cover of the trees. She hadn't gone far when an eerie chill crept up her left arm. The darkness played with her mind. She could've sworn someone was there, breathing next to her ear.

"Avoid the clearing."

Katie jumped at the airy voice, but when she looked behind her, she found only Clara. "I don't know what was in those tubes, but it's messing with my head." Katie led her cousin to an area where the density of trees tapered off and a wide, cloudy sky opened to her eyes.

"This way." Katie grabbed Clara's arm, determined to avoid the clearing. She hiked amidst the trees, and the tips of the palisade wall came into view. She'd not gone fifty yards before she saw an all-terrain vehicle crouching on a low hill between two clusters of pine trees. She squinted and recognized Avard, with his cropped military haircut, sitting on the hood between two other men, each with guns at the ready and aimed into the clearing.

Blood rushed from Katie's face and she fought an urge to faint. She realized those men might've shot her if she'd not listened to that voice. Then it happened again, a frosty sensation, this time brushing past her right shoulder.

"Run! Straight ahead."

Katie looked back and then turned to Clara. "Did you hear that?"

"What?" Clara shook her head.

"Never mind. Come on. We need to run. Lift your feet so you don't trip." Katie rushed forward and brushed past pine trees, concentrating on her footfalls. She looked back to make sure Clara was still behind her. More footfalls joined theirs.

"Someone's chasing us." Clara's voice trembled. Katie picked up her pace.

"Turn left."

"We need to go left." Katie pulled Clara's along to the left, up a shallow hill.

"I heard the voice that time," Clara said.

They ran to a long row of pine trees and Katie squeezed between the boughs, pulling Clara in with her. The stomping of feet passed by her and moved on, but someone stopped and began shining a flashlight in random directions. The light stopped abruptly, and the flashlight thudded against the ground. A man cried out and Katie heard him rolling down a nearby hill, the trees quaking as he passed them.

"Can we rest now? I'm so tired." Clara took a deep breath.

"You must keep moving."

Katie tensed up at the ethereal voice and emerged from the trees with Clara. "Who are you? I can't see you." She looked all around but saw nobody. A cold sensation spread around the right side of her neck and she turned and put out her hand. "Why won't you show yourself?"

"Do not fear. Leave now. The pathway to your friends is cleared for you."

Katie perceived a faint shadow moving among the trees and then there was silence. "Come on. Let's find the others." Katie eased down the hill to level ground and spotted a flashlight and two rifles among the pine needles. Clara took the flashlight and aimed it forward. A meadow stretched through the remaining trees and beyond that, four people stood by a broken gate hanging in an opening in the palisade wall.

✖

JACK STARED at the demolished gate, wondering what could've torn it from its hinges and tossed it so forcefully against the palisade wall. "This is our chance, guys." He rushed out the gate, grinning at their good luck.

Travis, Barbara, and Ming ran up behind him.

"Wait here a minute, I'll see if Taylor's here." Jack ran a hundred yards to the corner of the south palisade wall and peered around it. Ming ran up to him and shone his flashlight down the narrow asphalt path that ran along the south fence, and they each searched for any sign of Taylor or Jack's car.

"You sure you understood him, right?" Ming flicked off the flashlight. "His message was pretty cryptic."

"I've known Taylor a long time. We understand each other without speaking half the time. He'd have been here if he could have. I guarantee you; he'll be waiting for us by that old house in Silverton."

A searchlight from the main road brightened a swath of meadow grass south of camp. Jack waved for Ming to follow him back to Travis and the others.

"He wasn't there?" Travis chewed on a blade of meadow grass.

Jack shook his head.

"We might as well start walking," Barbara said.

"The note said to be here at dusk," Travis said. "I can't tell if it's dusk, with all these clouds, but my watch says it's almost ten o'clock."

"We're too late," Ming said.

"Someone's coming!" Barbara ducked into a cluster of pines.

Jack squeezed behind the boulders next to Ming and Travis, and ducked down. The lights in the camp flickered on and bathed the treetops in light, casting spike-tipped shadows from the palisade wall against the forest trees. The thumping of footfalls grew louder, and two human shadows imprinted on the ground.

Jack grabbed two rocks and handed one to Ming, then looked up. His jaw dropped at the sight of two familiar faces staring down at him. He looked to see if they were alone, then smiled and let the rock drop from his hand. "You're here."

Everyone stood up.

"Katie! Clara!" Barbara ran from the trees, shoved the boys aside, and wrapped her arms around the girls.

"Wait. I saw you go to the lab with Damien," Jack said.

"How do we know they didn't assimilate you?" Ming still gripped his rock.

Katie at first looked hurt by the accusation, then pursed her lips and searched for something in her bag. She pulled out a cellphone wrapped in a paper napkin and slapped it in Jack's hand.

"You really think I'd be here, in my pajamas, if I'd been brain-washed? I watched Jack's video."

"Then why did you go to the lab?" Jack slid the phone into his pocket, ecstatic to have his evidence back.

Katie looked away. "What does it matter? We're here now and I want to get as far away from this place as possible."

"My thoughts exactly," Travis said.

Jack nodded and panned the area. "If everyone agrees, I say we head up Farley Trail until we're out of view of the camp, then cut across the mountain and make our way toward Silverton."

"Maybe we should wait for whoever tore down that gate for us," Barbara said.

"I'm not waiting," Travis said. "Somebody shot at me. Jack has a good plan. Whoever's helping us should know where to find us."

"They're already here," Clara said.

"What do you mean?" Ming stared at her.

"Someone helped Katie and me escape, but we couldn't see them."

"Are you saying they're invisible?" Travis grinned and shook his head.

"They just didn't *want* us to see them," Katie said.

The chopping of a helicopter sounded nearby.

"We need to move." Barbara watched the sky and walked toward the trailhead. Travis and Ming ran to catch up to her.

Clara leaned against a boulder and shut her eyes.

Jack leaned toward Katie, his eyes fixed on Clara. "Will she be able to keep up? I've heard parts of the trail get steep."

"She'll have to." Katie put an arm around Clara and urged her to stand up. They headed up the trail, Jack following behind them.

XXVI

The trail narrowed and became sandwiched between a low embankment on Jack's left and a sharp drop off on his right. A searchlight leaped through the treetops, followed by the sound of rotors.

"Find cover!" Jack lifted himself up, rolled over the embankment, and dived below a pine tree. The aircraft breached the trees and hovered over the trail for half a minute before moving on up the trail. Jack laid still until he could hear crickets chirruping again. He rolled back down onto the trail. Ming jumped down from the embankment ahead of him, and they rushed to catch up with the others.

They soon found Travis and the girls standing in a clearing around a demolished light post at their feet, its bulbs crushed into the dust.

"It's one of the perimeter lights Farley installed," Travis said. "I thought he was nuts installing those, but now I know why he did it. He was trying to scare away those flying things we saw."

"What were those things?" Barbara pulled a stick of gum from her pack.

No one answered for several seconds, then Jack spoke. "Whatever they were, they helped us. I think one of them put that note in Katie's room."

Katie looked ill. "Just one more reason we need to find the quickest way out of these woods."

"Silverton is north of here, straight past camp," Jack said. "Farley trail won't take us there. I don't remember seeing any cliffs, so our best bet would be to cut through the woods and head straight north."

The sound of a distant helicopter echoed in the trees.

"We'll be safer off the trail anyway." Travis climbed up on the embankment and everyone else followed his lead. Jack slid his hand along the prickly lichen of a rock on the embankment, pulled himself up, and walked up behind Ming. They hiked in single file, Travis at the front and Jack at the back.

"Won't we be in view of the camp if we go this way?" Barbara pointed forward. "We'll be crossing the mountainside above camp."

"It'll be better hiking above the camp," Ming said. "I can hardly see a thing. Maybe the light from the camp will help us see where we're going."

"We just need to stay in the shadows." Jack stared at the dark ground. Each of them took turns, at random intervals, slipping on pine needles, moist ferns or loose soil.

Jack thought about Taylor and wondered what was happening to him. He wished he was here. He thought about the things Sherry had said and what he'd seen in the research facility. He looked forward to breaking the greatest news story ever told.

Jack walked into Ming, not having noticed his companions had stopped to rest. A wide expanse of rocks covered the hillside and provided places to sit and watch the campground far below.

"Let's hope this is the last time we ever have to look at that travesty," Ming said.

Jack gazed down at the metal rooftops and pines, surrounded by a palisade protruding amidst a sea of pine trees and aspens. A helicopter searched the mountains beyond the camp.

Clara sat on a rock, took a deep breath, and turned to Katie. "Is someone going to tell me why on earth we're running away from camp?"

Jack climbed onto a boulder and sat facing the group. "Actually, there's a lot more you all need to know."

✠

KATIE GRINNED at the blank expressions on her companions' faces, then realized she'd had the same look on her own face. She could hardly process the information Jack had shared with them from what he'd learned from Sherry and read in Lynch's Intershroud training manual.

He'd answered so many of her questions about her father's business—all people dream to the same dream world every night. Montathena Research destabilizes people's minds and takes advantage of them in their dreams. People can control their own dreams by being aware they are dreaming and establishing a prime token, then subduing their subconscious.

"This changes everything." Ming broke the silence. "Think about it, we can't run away from them. We'd have to hide from them in our sleep, too."

The boulder Katie sat on suddenly shook and an apocalyptic noise ripped through the trees. Rocks rattled, loosened, shifted and rolled down the mountain around her. One slammed into her left hand and she groaned in pain. She stood up and raised her hands, squinting at the bright orange light filling the sky from the direction of Camp Farley. Tiny objects floated and fell from the sky amidst vast plumes of dark smoke.

Katie couldn't accept what she was seeing, and she turned to the stunned faces of her companions, all of whom stood, staring. Clara ran and hugged Katie, staring at the sky with terrified eyes.

"What just happened?" Barbara looked back and forth at the camp several times, then at Jack.

Jack could only stare with everyone else at the debris falling in apparent slow-motion, some pieces landing and shaking the trees only a few hundred yards down from them.

The smoke started to clear, and Katie watched campers, staff, and guards emerge from cabins and other buildings, now lit only by the burning remains of the gaping hole that minutes earlier had been the research facility. Jack's cabin had disappeared, along with Katie's.

"Impossible," Travis said. "No one could've penetrated that building. It had walls a foot thick!"

Barbara shoved him. "Who cares about walls? Marina was down there! Someone just blew her to bits and all you want to talk about is a stupid building!" She slumped onto a pile of stones, her face contorted in her effort not to cry.

"Even Tony and Carl didn't deserve to go like that," Ming said.

Travis grabbed a rock and hurled it down the hill.

"We've got to go back!" Barbara said. She stood up, resolute, looking Jack in the eye.

"Maybe she's right," Ming said. "If we keep running, people will think we did it."

Jack frowned and looked at his friends. "That's why they did it. I wouldn't put it past them. We escaped, so they destroyed all the evidence."

"And they can claim we did it," Ming said.

"No," Katie said. "Even Lynch wouldn't go that far. They're still looking for us."

"Like I said, we have to go back," Barbara said. "They can't claim we did it if we go back."

"No one's going to believe what we say, no matter what we do." Jack pulled his cellphone out of his pocket. "This video is our only hope. We have to get this to the police."

"They just blew up a building and killed a friend of mine!" Barbara stepped up close to Jack. "People who'll do that won't sit back while we hand evidence to the cops. We don't have any options. We never did."

"Then all we can do is stand up for what we believe in," Katie said. "Lynch didn't blow up that building. Whoever attacked the camp wanted Farley dead and it looks like they got what they wanted. But they did kill Alison. Maybe we can't beat them, but I'm willing to try— for Alison's sake."

Barbara stared at Katie and nodded. "You're right. We're doing this for Alison, and Marina, and anyone else they've hurt." She yanked a branch off a nearby dead tree and dug the end of it into the soil. She started walking, and Katie and the others followed behind her.

A blanket of thin clouds immersed the forest in a kaleidoscope of ghostly gray shapes. Katie stared at the crescent moon and grinned. "I feel a lot safer now that I can see where I'm going."

Rotors echoed off the hills of the gulley in which they hiked, and Katie ran for cover in a thick grove of pines. Jack squeezed into the pine branches near her and they waited for the sound to go away before running to find Travis and Barbara.

"We better wait for Clara and Ming," Katie said.

"They need to keep up," Travis said.

"Give 'em a break," Jack said. "We're all dead tired, but Ming took in a pretty good bite of that brownie. There were a few times back there when I thought he was going to trip and roll down the mountainside."

"Clara breathed in a good dose in the sleep lab, too." Katie said. "It seems to be wearing off a little, but I still have to keep holding her up."

"We're totally lost out here," Barbara said. "Maybe we should've stayed by that gate until someone showed up."

"I told you," Katie said, "they never intended to meet us there. I think they just wanted to protect me."

"Why'd they single you out?" Barbara leaned on her walking stick.

Katie shrugged. "I can't even image." She didn't dare bring up her sister's ghost. She knew, however, that she hadn't hallucinated. She believed Abby wrote the note and had guided her and Clara to the gate, but she knew the others would call her crazy.

"Barbara's right," Jack said. "We can't afford to get lost. We need to head more to the west until we find the stream, or the road."

"There you are," Clara trudged over to Katie, Ming hanging on her shoulder, and her face contorted from struggling to hold him up. Katie put an arm around her, glad Clara was still able to hold herself up. "Lucky I heard your voices. I almost went the wrong way."

Clara pulled Ming's arm off her shoulder and gasped when he slumped down on his knees in a patch of dry pine needles. He rolled onto his side in a fetal position.

Travis walked up and gave him a shove with his foot. Ming didn't stir.

"You know," Travis said, "we all should get some sleep, unless one of you wants to carry Ming. I doubt we'll find better cover than this area."

"We can't sleep," Jack said. "Weren't you listening? They can find us in our dreams."

Katie shook her head. "We can't stay awake forever. Clara's exhausted. Ming's comatose."

"We'll get caught," Jack said.

"We'll get caught anyway if we're so dead tired we can't think straight," Katie said.

"We have to try, at least until we get to Silverton," Jack said. "I don't even know if we'll be able to resist dreaming about camp. This whole escape will be for nothing."

"We'll just have to find each other in our dreams," Katie said. "We can help each other stay away from Farley and his people."

"One of us can stay awake and wake us up every hour or so, make sure we're alright," Barbara said.

Jack shook his head, but he knew they were right. Ming was already asleep. There was no point in fighting the inevitable.

"Clara and I can take first watch," Travis said.

"She needs sleep." Katie smiled at Clara and waved her over to a heap of pine needles below a cluster of tall pine trees.

Travis turned to Barbara.

"As if," she said.

"Whatever." Travis tossed the sling of the M16 over his shoulder.

"You don't even know how to shoot that thing." Jack pointed at the rifle.

"No. But if anyone shoots at me again, you can bet your life I'll figure it out. I'll go find a good lookout spot and wake one of you in an hour or so." He looked for a path through the ferns and wildflower beds, then started up the mountain and disappeared beyond the trees.

"I'll stay with Ming," Jack said. He took Ming's hands and dragged him below a pine bough.

Katie nodded. "Wake us if anything happens. Come on, Clara."

Moonlight illuminated the ferns, bear grass, and flower beds, but not enough to ease Katie's fears of what might be skulking in the shadows.

"That looks like a good spot," Barbara said. She pointed at a cluster of lodgepoles with a wide-open space at the lower part of their trunks.

Katie plowed through a field of moist purple wildflowers to a bed of pine needles, then dug three thick sweaters from her bag. She intended to use them as a blanket, pillow, and mattress, but then she became aware of both Clara and Barbara hugging themselves against the cold. She handed a sweater to each of them.

"Looks like pine needle mattresses tonight," Katie said. "I should've grabbed some comforters; it's going to be cold."

"You saved my life. I was freezing." Barbara wrapped the sweater around her shoulders and dropped to her knees, then pulled a thin nightgown from her backpack and rolled it up to use as a pillow. She laid down and pulled Katie's oversize sweater over herself.

Katie turned to Clara and found she'd already fallen asleep, snuggling her stuffed elephant. Katie tucked her sweater over Clara and laid down near her. She stretched her hands behind her head and closed her eyes, discovering the pine needles to be surprisingly comfortable.

JACK STARED into the thick branches above him, tucked his felt blanket around himself, and scratched his neck where the pine needles were tickling him. Hours had passed, and he hadn't slept. He couldn't stop his mind from churning.

"We should've tried to save Marina," he said to Ming, though he knew he was sound asleep. "She was small enough, any of us could've carried her. I should've tried to convince Tony and Carl, too. We didn't even give them a chance." Images of the explosion ran on a loop in his thoughts.

Then he remembered the flying creatures that had attacked the camp guards with no concern for their own survival. "What were those things? Intershroud experiments? Was Farley combining human DNA with chimps and bats? It's all so unbelievable."

He frowned, and a tear rolled down his cheek. "I know I should be glad they blew up that research facility, but Marina didn't deserve to die."

He turned and stared at Ming whose only response was a light, steady snore.

"I need Taylor. This is making my mind spin." He wiped his blurry eyes. "Who am I kidding? Lynch and his army will find us. Even if they don't, we'll get lost out here, or starve to death. Why didn't I just listen to Sherry and act dumb? We're all going to die because I never listen."

Jack started at a sudden thumping noise to his left and he clenched his fists.

"You couldn't sleep either, huh?" Katie laid down next to him and tucked a thick gray sweater around herself. "I never thanked you for trying to warn me. I feel so stupid."

"I'm the stupid one. I should've found a better way to tell you. I just hope we don't die out here because you all listened to me."

"I almost died because I *didn't* listen to you. Clara and I would've been sleeping in that building when it blew up. You saved our lives."

Jack grinned and watched her stare up into the trees, her dark eyes sparkling in the moonlight. "Thanks, but all I did was show you what I found out. You're the one that escaped the lab. You saved Clara."

"We escaped because you told me about the generator room door. Don't try to deny yourself credit. If I hadn't watched your video, I'd be dead now."

"I'm glad you watched it, then."

"I just wish I knew what I was looking at. It still creeps me out thinking about it."

Jack sat up. "I can help you there. I never had a chance to tell anyone. I found a newspaper in Farley's office, written by enemies of the Intershroud. They must have spies among Farley's staff because the articles explain the whole process."

"What did it say?"

"Intershroud found a way to capture creatures from our dreams and transfer them into the real world. They create the creatures in a dream about Camp Farley. They know about nothing but Camp Farley. They call them 'dream inducers.' They put them in specially designed jars and hid them below our beds, where they gradually dissipate. They were releasing fine essence particles directly into our heads, where they penetrated our brains, forcing us to dream about the camp."

"My dad has a research lab in my basement," Katie said. "He probably created those creatures. But it doesn't explain what was going on with Media and those frozen dead people."

"Media is what they call a 'Mentalist.' She was an orphan when Avard discovered her in a dream in India. She has an ability to leave part of her mind in the minds of other dreamers, where she can then influence their thoughts. People wake up with unexplained desires to give her food or money. Avard adopted her and used her to serve Intershroud."

"The way Media talks so slow, it must be taking a toll on her."

"Definitely. She's done it so often, she's literally losing her mind.

The article said Intershroud operatives watch dreamers everywhere, searching for other Mentalists. They monitor hospitals to find out when Mentalists are on their death bed, then they put them into a coma state.

"Intershroud bribes doctors to keep the mentalist coma victims alive after pronouncing them dead. Then, after the pretended burial, the bodies are stolen and placed in cryogenic chambers like the one I saw. The tubes we saw were designed to mix Media's mind with the minds of those comatose Mentalists, allowing her to leave less of her own mind in other people and reduce her own mental deterioration."

Katie shook her head slowly. "So, that's their idea of 'assimilation,' using the minds of creepy brain-dead people to allow Media to manipulate our minds? That's what they must have done to turn Damien into a Montathena Research fanboy. I can't believe my father was going to let them do that to me!" She clenched her teeth.

"Why'd you even go to that lab?"

Katie looked away. Jack felt more awkward with every second of her silence.

"I wanted to give Damien a chance," Katie finally said. She faced Jack and wiped a tear from her lip. "I was sure if I asked him to his face, he'd tell me the truth. The worst part is, I didn't give a moment's thought to Clara. I was so sure Damien would be there for me. I thought he cared about me."

"Some hero he turned out to be," Jack said.

Katie gave a slight nod, then laid her head back and closed her eyes. Jack worried that he'd said too much, bringing up her decision to go to the lab. He couldn't force his eyes off her glowing, moon-lit face. Katie's hand gently slid over his and an electric warmth radiated through his body. She showed no sign that she was aware of it, but Jack had never known such happiness. He dared not move for fear she might move her hand away. He shut his eyes and held on to the moment.

XXVIII

Jack's thoughts drifted until he found himself standing amidst a wide crater, surrounded by jagged slabs of concrete, twisted steel bars, and smoldering wood panels. The singed blue carpet on a nearby stairway informed him he was seeing the remains of the research facility.

The gray sky welcomed wisps of smoke from smoldering couches and crushed cabinets. Jack looked around, fearful he might find casualties. He remembered his lighter and pulled it from his pocket. A sudden thought came to his mind.

"I'm dreaming." He grinned and shoved the lighter back into his pocket. "Let's see how awesome lucid dreaming really is." He looked up the stairs and jumped, then laughed at himself flying twelve feet into the air. He landed on an exposed steel beam and turned toward the front door. Where marble floors had once been, he found only chunks of twisted concrete dangling from mangled floor joists. Jack leaped up again and glided over the demolished hallway and lobby, then landed on a concrete slab near the exit doors, which now stood alone like a gravestone.

"Now, let's try some super strength." Jack gripped the door lever and yanked it back. The double doors cracked and flew with their frame back across the lobby, crashing into a floor joist. Jack laughed and strutted onto the gravel path outside. He strolled at a slow pace, forgetting all about the real world. He stared at the cracked concrete foundation wall that had once supported his cabin. His elation faded to sadness and a dull pain formed in his throat.

He moved on and entered the clearing, turning toward the outdoor eating area, and stopped. Damien stood there, talking to his father. The only guards in view ushered campers toward the amphitheater on the opposite side of the clearing. Jack walked at a brisk pace toward the main offices where he knew he'd be out of Damien's view. Once there, he changed course, ran around the back of the building, and darted to the redwood slat fence next to the outdoor eating area. He peeked through a gap between the slats and gasped when he saw Travis and Barbara sitting on a row of white plastic chairs with Carl, Tony, and Marina—each staring at the nearby lodge with blank expressions on their faces. Jack's chest tightened. He feared Lynch had already gained control over his friends.

Then he saw Ming standing next to another plastic chair, facing away from Jack, with Lynch standing behind him. Tamera stood behind Media who sat in a second chair, facing Ming with her eyes closed. Blood stained the cheeks of her normally beautiful Indian face, now contorted beyond what would be possible for an awake human being. Tamera clenched her fingers tight on both sides of Media's head.

"Sit, my boy," Lynch said.

Ming looked at him, nodded, and sat down.

"No one gives massages like our Media," Lynch said. "You'll think you're in heaven." The old man nodded to Tamera.

*He doesn't know he's dreaming!* Jack thought. *Lynch is lying to him.* Jack saw a wider gap at the far end of the wood screen, near Damien and his father, and ran to it, searching for a way to rescue Ming.

"There are only three left?" Fenton Murdock said.

Damien nodded. "Jack thought he was clever running off, but he and Katie will be here as soon as they fall asleep. I don't know if Clara's able to dream here."

"After an emotional experience like that explosion, even Clara might dream about this place."

A scream rang through the air and Jack turned to Media.

"No more! Please! It's too much. It hurts! Let me go!" Chairs and tables became visible through Media's shaking, semitransparent body.

Ming stared forward and smiled.

*He can't hear her or see her,* Jack thought. *What's she doing?*

"We better stop," Tamera said. Her voice trembled.

"We have no choice!" Lynch grabbed Media's arm, looked her in the eye and squeezed hard. "Our entire organization is at risk. Do your duty if you want to survive this night."

Media's face twisted in agony and she reached for Ming's head with shaking hands. Ming looked down at the floor and tapped his fingers on the armrests. Media's fingers disappeared inside his head and she moaned.

Jack froze, a knot squeezing his stomach.

"You've always wanted to join Montathena Research," Media's sobbing made her shaky words even slower than when she was awake. The words rolled out too loud and then too quiet. "Montathena Research only wants to help people. Lynch, Murdock, Farley—these are your heroes. You'd do anything for them. You'd die for them. You'd die for Intershroud. You'd die to protect its secrets. Its enemies are your enemies."

"Tell him to return to the camp," Lynch said.

"You want to come back to camp. You never wanted to leave. Come back and the company will reward you. You—"

Media's body faded nearly to invisible and a black mist formed around her head and rolled along her arms. The mist engulfed Ming's head before shrinking and penetrating his skin.

Ming lifted his chin and stared forward with the same blank expression as the others.

Media convulsed, her head rolled from side to side, then a black liquid trickled from her mouth. She cried out and fell forward, but Tamera caught her before she could hit the concrete. She kneeled next to Media and held her head up.

"She can't handle any more of this!" Tamera glared at Lynch. "We have to get another Mentalist for the others."

Lynch pursed his lips. "I suppose you're right. There's nothing left in her. Go see if anyone is available from one of the other camps."

"What are they doing?" A female voice spoke from behind Jack.

He turned and looked up, finding Katie standing next to him, peeking through another gap in the redwood fence, her forehead creased with concern.

Jack stood up and placed his hand lightly in front of her mouth. "They did something to Ming and the others. We've got to wake ourselves up somehow and try to help them." He saw a shovel and grabbed it, then handed it to Katie and closed his eyes.

"Hit me with this. If it wakes me up, I'll hurry and wake you up."

Katie glared at him then set the shovel aside and crossed her arms. "Have you lost your mind? We're not dreaming."

The redwood screen suddenly vanished, and Jack fell backwards onto the concrete at the feet of Fenton Murdock.

"Hey," Damien extended a hand to help up Jack. "I wondered when you'd show up. Everyone's getting massages over here." He waved for Jack and Katie to follow him to Ming.

"We don't want a massage," Jack said.

"Speak for yourself," Katie said. "I could really use one."

"Tamera and Lynch went to get the masseuse." Damien gestured at Ming to go sit next to Travis, and he did.

Jack turned to Katie and leaned into her ear. "Can't you see they're lying? It isn't a massage. We need to run while they still think we don't know we're dreaming."

"Would you stop?" Katie turned and slapped Jack's arm. "I think I'd know if I was dreaming. I'm not dumb."

Jack shook his head and turned to Ming. "Would you tell her this wasn't a massage? Tell her what Media did to you."

Ming stood and clenched his teeth, fury in his eyes. He shoved Jack in the chest so hard, he fell back onto the cold pavement.

"Why do you always overreact?" Ming tightened his fists. "Just stop it! This camp is the best thing that's ever happened to me. Just calm down and wait for Tamera!"

Jack turned to Travis and Barbara and found them both sneering at him and nodding.

"You got to admit, you're always judging people," Barbara said. "You don't know how much good this company does for people. You only want to criticize it."

Jack turned around and saw that Lynch had returned. He stood talking to Damien and his father. Jack pulled himself to his feet, his heart aching, and turned to look for Katie. His eyebrows rose at seeing her moistened eyes and a face that showed she'd seen the change in her friends. She understood something was wrong.

Tamera appeared out of nowhere near the lodge, standing next to a short bald man. Everyone turned to face them except Katie. She yanked on Jack's sleeve and leaned into his ear.

"Run!" Katie stepped back slowly and darted behind a trash bin. Jack did the same, watching for any eyes looking his way. He rounded the trash bin and charged across the clearing, out of everyone's view. He barreled after Katie toward a section of collapsed perimeter fence and disappeared into the low hills beyond his demolished cabin. Katie looked back at him only once, then ran at a speed only possible in dreams.

They didn't stop running for what seemed like hours, though he couldn't really tell how much time passed. Katie finally slowed down at a stream bank and stopped and leaned against the trunk of lodge-pole pine, pounding on it with the side of her fist. Jack walked up next to her.

"Did they see us leave?" Katie lowered her hands.

Jack shook his head. "We made it to the fence before anyone noticed we were gone."

"Did you see their faces?" Katie wiped her eyes with her hand.

Jack nodded. "They were like different people. I'm hoping we can snap them out of it after we wake up."

Katie smiled. "You still think this is a dream? I hope you're right."

"Well, what do you know?" Avard emerged from the trees carrying a shotgun in each hand. "I thought I'd seen you two running around the forest like a couple o' bunny rabbits."

"What're you doing out here?" Derek stepped up next to him and laughed. "Did you get lost?"

"I could ask you the same thing," Jack said.

"Don't get smart." Avard leveled his shotguns at the faces of Jack and Katie.

"We know this is just a dream," Jack said. "You can't hurt us."

"I couldn't care less if I hurt you or not." Avard laughed and lowered his weapons. "Ol' Lynch sent us out to kill the culprits that blew up our research facility, but I'm fixin' to thank 'em. That infernal camp is finally closing down. I get to retire, and Farley won't be harming my Media no more."

"Media didn't seem too happy to me," Jack said. "She was screaming her head off back at camp."

"If Media hurt my friends, I don't feel one bit sorry for her," Katie said.

Derek went pale and turned to Avard. "They're just trying to get your goat."

Avard leered at Derek, his eyes bulging, and his mouth pressed into a tight line. His aged knuckles tightened around the triggers of his guns. "So, that's what this goose chase's all about! You lured me out here so's I couldn't stop 'em from hurting my daughter! Do you have any idea what this'll do to her?"

"I had nothing to do with it. It was Lynch's orders."

"I'll kill him! I'll kill all of you!" He raised his guns and blasted Derek in the face. He disappeared. Avard turned a shotgun on Katie. Jack heard the gunfire, but didn't see her vanish, having closed his eyes tight when Avard shot Derek. He opened his eyes long enough to stare down the barrels of one of Avard's shotguns and listen to a loud boom.

# XXIX

Jack slapped his face and chest, searching for bullet wounds, his heart pounding. He opened his eyes and turned to Katie, who'd already sat up, hugging her sweater.

"Please tell me you didn't just dream about Avard shooting us in the face." Jack sat up and brushed pine needles out of his hair with his hand.

Katie stared straight ahead and said nothing.

Warblers sang beneath a blue morning sky and sunlight bathed the western mountaintops. It would've been a pleasant morning were it not for the darkness Jack felt inside. Every detail of the dream stood vivid in his mind. How much of it was real, he couldn't tell. He glanced over at Ming who slept nearby, curled in a ball, then looked around the glade.

"I don't see Travis. I hope he didn't get lost," Jack said.

"He was in our dream. He must've fallen asleep."

"Let's not make any assumptions. We could've dreamed up all of that without them."

Katie gave a brief nod but didn't look convinced.

"Tony and Carl were there," Jack said. "They couldn't have been dreaming. They were in the cabin when it blew up."

Katie perked up a little. "I saw Marina, too. Maybe we did dream it all up."

Jack nodded. "Sun's coming up. You better wake up Barbara and Clara. We should get moving while the weather's good."

Katie stood and weaved around the trees to the area where the girls were sleeping. Jack turned to Ming and gave him a shove.

"Knock it off!" Ming swatted Jack's hand.

"I don't blame you for being grumpy, but we need to go."

"I'm not being grumpy. You're being bossy. I'll get up when I feel like it."

Clara came around a clump of scrub oaks, her hair poking up and full of pine needles. "Barbara won't get up either. Do you have anything to drink?"

Jack nodded, stood, and rolled up his blanket and tied it onto his backpack. He pulled three cartons of apple juice from his pack. "I managed to sneak these off the table yesterday." He handed one to Clara and pulled a bundled-up paper towel out of his backpack and unfolded it, revealing a pile of dinner rolls. He grabbed a few and handed one to Clara.

"I'm glad one of us was thinking ahead," Clara said. "I thought I was going to starve."

Katie emerged from the shrubs, shook her head, and took a roll and a juice carton Jack handed her. "Thanks. Barbara won't budge." She eyed Ming for a second and gave Jack a serious look.

Jack bent over Ming and shook him three times. "We need to go. Lynch's people could show up any minute!"

Ming bolted upright and glared at Jack, his mouth fixed in an angry sneer. "I don't care about Lynch! Their lab blew up. They couldn't hurt us now if they wanted to, and I'm starting to wonder if they ever did want to. You got us all worked up over nothing. It's cold. All I want now is a warm bed."

A knot formed in Jack's stomach. This angry person wasn't the Ming he knew. He looked at Katie and she looked away. "I better find out what's up with Travis." Jack handed his backpack to Clara. "Give

Ming and Barbara something to eat. I'll be back in a minute. I smell smoke. Do you?"

Before Clara could reply, Jack raced up a narrow deer trail that wound up a gradual slope along rows of pine trees and dewy ferns. He came out of a thicket to the edge of a narrow clearing and found Travis in the center of a glen, fanning a fire that sent a column of black smoke into the lodgepole tops.

Jack charged across the clearing. "What are you thinking? That'll be visible for miles!"

"It's freezing."

"They're going to find us." He kicked dirt into the fire and seconds later found himself on his back, violet wildflowers around his head.

Travis stared him in the face and clamped his powerful hands against Jack's shoulders. "You listen to me!" Travis released Jack with a shove and stood up. "We've been going about this all wrong. We don't really know what we saw in that video you took. We should've talked to Farley, let him have a chance to explain it."

"They shot at you!"

"They were shooting at those creatures. The guards didn't know we were out there, running off like a bunch of idiots. They must've thought we were some of those ape-things."

Jack pulled himself up and wiped dirt off his arms. Hearing someone behind him, he turned around. Ming emerged from the trees, followed by Barbara, Katie, and Clara.

"What's all the yelling about?" Ming said, his tone serious. He walked over to Travis and the girls followed him. "Are you fighting?"

Jack pointed at Travis. "He knocked me down. I was trying to put out that fire."

"He won't listen to reason," Travis said. "We need to go back."

"Reason?" Jack pulled his own hair. "We talked about this. They want to control our minds! They killed Alison!"

"It was an accident," Travis said.

"They covered it up!"

"Of course they did! They didn't want everyone running home, telling stories."

"Dude, help me out here." Jack looked at Ming. "Last night you said you'd never let anyone control you. Tell Travis we can't just waltz back there and surrender."

"I'm with Travis," Ming said.

"What?" Jack took his backpack from Clara.

"Hear me out." Ming looked down and squinted, then placed his hand against the side of his head. He relaxed a moment later and looked up again. "To be honest, there's something about Montathena Research that really impresses me. I know I complained about them before, but I actually like the way Lynch and Farley run things. They want to help people."

Jack's mouth dropped. He turned to Katie, who stared back at him with the same knowing expression. "Those are not your words," Jack said. "Media said those things to you in our dream! Don't you remember? You, Travis, and Barbara were all there. Media did something to you. She told you things that weren't true. You have to remember!"

"This is what you always do," Ming said. "You keep saying crazy things like this and freaking me out. I want to go back. I don't think I ever wanted to leave."

Barbara stepped up to Jack and shook her head. "He's right, you know. You sound seriously crazy. Even if I had dreamt about Media, it was just a dream, right? We need to go back and maybe get you some counseling."

Jack didn't know what else to say. He looked to Katie, but she only stared back at him, frowning. Jack shook his head and scoffed. He threw the strap of his backpack over his shoulder. "Suit yourselves." Jack's voice wavered with emotion. "I didn't force you to come with me. I guess I'm on my own. Good luck slaving for Intershroud."

Travis raised his rifle. "You're coming with us. You'll get lost out here."

"Really? You're going to shoot me? You don't even know how to use that thing."

Travis hesitated a few seconds before dropping his arm and letting the gun fall into the wildflowers. "Dude. Just come back with us!"

Jack marched down a narrow trail into a ravine. He couldn't bear to look at his friends anymore. He walked only a few steps before he heard a thump behind him.

J ack turned around and found Travis laying in the dirt, rubbing
his head. Clara stood next to him clenching a jagged rock in her
hand. Her eyes widened, and the rock dropped from her hand.
"He was going to hit you with his flashlight." She looked down at
Travis. "I'm so sorry." She kneeled next to him and tried to look at the
wound, but Travis glared at her and shoved her hand away.

Katie screamed. Barbara braced herself behind Katie, her right arm
wrapped tight around Katie's neck and her other arm latched behind
her head. Katie's face reddened, and she struggled to pull down on
Barbara's arm.

Ming arrived at Travis' side. "See what Jack drove us to?" Ming
shoved Clara aside and picked up Travis's flashlight. The chop of a
helicopter echoed from a nearby mountainside. Before Jack could
think what to do next, Ming grabbed his left arm and circled around
him, pushing up on his arm and forcing him to double over. Travis
grabbed hold of Jack's legs and held them tight.

"You're making us do this, Jack," Travis said. "Your paranoia is out
of control. We just want to get you the help you need."

Jack wiggled his legs but could hardly move them.

"Let him go! Why are you doing this?" Clara tried to pull Ming's arm away.

Jack looked over Clara's shoulder and saw Katie turn her head and grasp Barbara's arm with both her hands. She raised her shoulders, tucked her chin down, and bent her knees before stepping back and locking her right foot behind Barbara's foot. Katie curved forward, stepped around 180 degrees, and pulled Barbara's arm across her body before tripping her and throwing her to the ground with a thud. She kicked Barbara in the ribs before turning and running to help Clara.

"Run for it!" Jack freed one of his knees enough to pound it hard into Travis's face, making his nose bleed and causing him to let go. Katie pulled Clara away and both girls ran across the glen and disappeared down a hill, behind a line of tall shrubs. Barbara pulled herself up and charged after them.

"Just let us help you," Ming said.

Jack wished he knew how to escape a headlock the way he'd just seen Katie do it. With Travis sitting in the dirt, tending his bloody nose, he knew this was his best chance to free himself. He leaned diagonally against a tree behind him and shoved with all the strength in that direction. Ming's right leg found a branch and he lost his balance long enough for Jack to twist around and slide his head under Ming's arm. He stepped over an old toppled tree nearby and swung his backpack at Ming's head, causing him to duck and tumble over the log.

Jack charged down a steep hill into thick pines, not looking back. The helicopter grew louder, and he feared the pilot had already seen him. Not wanting to lose Katie and Clara, he turned in their direction and scurried like a deer. He leaped over logs and shrubs and dived below low branches, running until his lungs burned.

A minute later, he stopped and squeezed between two pine trees, breathing heavy and searching for his pursuers. After a few seconds, he found Travis emerging from the trees on a nearby hilltop. A low-flying helicopter arose from the other side of the hill and hovered above him. He put up his hands and shook his head, then pointed toward a line of short pine trees. Jack breathed a little easier knowing Travis had no idea where he was.

Jack had often felt a burning in his chest when he ran too hard for too long, and this was no exception. He waited for the pain to subside before moving on. The aircraft hovered near Travis, which made it easier for Jack to avoid him. He didn't know, however, where Ming or Barbara had gone.

At the sound of rustling leaves, Jack dashed to a wide decaying tree and ducked behind it. He snatched up a nearby broken branch, yanked off the twigs, and held it up like a baseball bat and held his breath. An elk emerged from around a hill and scampered away at the sight of him. Jack took a deep breath and let his arm drop, but became alarmed again when Ming and Travis appeared and ran in the same direction.

*They must have thought that was me.* Jack marched on, worried he'd never find Katie and Clara again. He hadn't walked far before he heard a woman groaning. He rushed through a thicket, fearing the worst, and found Barbara sitting alone on a fallen log, rocking back and forth and rubbing her head. Jack stepped back slowly, hoping she hadn't seen him.

"Jack!" Barbara turned toward him. "Don't go. Help me. I don't know what got into me. I'm sorry. I want to go with you."

Jack stared at her for a few seconds. "I'll send help." He turned and ran away.

"No, Jack, Come back! You idiot! Don't you see? Something's wrong with your mind. You're being paranoid!"

Her cries faded in the distance.

THE SUN LOWERED over the western mountains and Jack stopped to listen for Katie and Clara. The day had snailed by so slowly, it felt like a week had passed. The low buzz of a hummingbird's wings surprised him. He watched the tiny green bird zip past him and disappear into the forest.

He frowned. "The town has to be close. Katie and Clara are probably there already, waiting for me." He sniffed and kicked a small stick in his path. "Who am I kidding? I probably passed the town hours ago. I'll never find my way out of here. The girls were probably caught, or even killed. I don't know what I'm doing."

He dropped to his knees and looked up to the heavens. "Someone help me! Please."

A faint whisper startled him. "Turn south. Follow the crows."

"Katie? Is that you?" He looked around but saw no one. He thought he'd hallucinated until a cawing sound reached his ears and he turned and discovered three black crows soaring from a treetop and alighting on a low branch at the mouth of a narrow ravine.

"Did that just happen?" He had no other plan to guide him, so he turned south and followed the birds. Whenever he approached within a few yards of them, they'd fly off and glide to a rock or shrub another forty yards away. After a half hour of this, the crows flew to a distant thicket by the base of a cliff and disappeared in its leaves. Jack heard another helicopter approaching, darted to the scrub oaks, and dived under them. The aircraft hovered nearby for a few seconds, then flew off.

The crows emerged from the leaves and flew along the cliffside before landing on the ground by a pile of branches. Jack stared at them and shook his head. "Either I'm delusional, or those birds just helped me hide from a helicopter. Maybe I *am* losing my mind."

Jack trailed the crows to their next stop and watched them disappear behind a copse of stones at the base of a steep cliff. When he arrived, he couldn't see the birds anywhere. He climbed onto one of the larger boulders, looked around, and sat down and leaned his back against another rock to enjoy the warmth the stones had soaked up all day.

He froze at the sound of footsteps, then jumped down from the rocks and peeked around the boulders, ready to strike someone with his makeshift walking stick.

"It's Jack!" Clara ran to him and hugged him, squealing in delight.

Katie then emerged from a cavity within a large pile of boulders, her cheeks red from tears.

"I thought they killed you," Katie said. She almost hugged him but stopped herself. "This is a nightmare."

Jack nodded and frowned. "I know. I keep wishing I'd wake up."

"Did you see Barbara's face? She looked possessed. Ming, too."

Jack nodded and pounded his walking stick against a boulder. "It's like that newsletter said. Media's in their heads, controlling them."

Clara gave Jack a blank stare. "I must be the only one that missed that dream."

"That's why you're the sanest one here," Jack said. "I still can't believe you hit Travis with that rock."

Her eyes widened. "I only meant to knock him down. He was going to hurt you. I need to tell him I'm sorry." She looked back as if to search for Travis.

"You didn't do anything wrong," Jack said. "You had to stop him. If anyone's to blame, it's Lynch. He forced Media to control their minds."

"What are we going to do?" Katie stared at Jack. "We can't stay here forever, and we can't stay awake forever. What can we do?"

Jack looked around. "We have to get to Silverton."

"Don't you get it, Jack? They know our plans. Ming and the others will tell them everything. We can't go anywhere—not even in our dreams."

XXXI

"A bby told us to go to a cave down this ravine," Clara pointed into a narrow passage sandwiched between a steep mountain and thick forest trees.

"Clara!" Katie looked at Jack, her face red. "I never said I was sure it was Abby. I just thought I heard a voice."

"The stress is making us hallucinate," Jack said.

"I didn't just imagine it!" Katie had a hint of anger in her voice. "Someone put that note under my pillow. Someone protected me last night. Clara and I heard someone tell us to go to a cave near here. If they can't help us, I don't know what we can do. We might as well turn ourselves in."

Jack nodded. "Maybe you're right. I admit, something led me here, too. Thing is, we can't just ignore that Farley was messing with our minds. We may be hearing and seeing things that aren't real. I'm just saying, we shouldn't trust ourselves."

"Clara and I both heard the voice. It wasn't an illusion."

Jack gave a nod and began working around fallen rocks in the narrow ravine. Katie and Clara lined up behind him, each watching their steps as they navigated the hundreds of loose, wobbly stones. Tall boulders hugged both sides of the gulley, adding further darkness to the blackening clouds now filling the sky. A chill wind piped up and raindrops peppered Jack's shirt.

"We better find shelter soon," Jack said.

Clara skipped from rock to rock, making a game of the hike. She passed Jack and smiled, then started whistling a song he didn't recognize. Jack grinned and watched her stop to admire a crow bouncing along the tips of a row of loose branches leaning against the mountainside. The bird fluttered into a thin gap between the sticks, then flew back out again and landed on a crooked branch of a dead tree across the narrows.

Katie ran past Jack to the row of sticks and pulled them aside, revealing a rounded opening bordered by worn gray timbers. "It's a cave!" Katie's eyes widened, and she clasped her hands.

Jack ran to join her and gazed inside. "It looks like an old mine." He entered only far enough to kick a loose timber and send a clump of dirt exploding at his feet. "Seems dangerous. We better find someplace else."

Katie pushed past him and looked around inside. "It appears safe to me. It's been here for decades. We just need to watch our step."

Jack nodded and gave a nervous laugh, trying to underplay the tightness in his chest and his suspicion that the cave was inevitably destined to collapse and bury him alive. He took a deep breath and entered at a slow pace, his hands in front of him, and watched every shadow for snakes, spiders, cougars, bears, and shrinking walls.

Jack felt Katie's breath on his neck. She locked her step behind him, using him as a shield from whatever might be lurking in the dark. Light suddenly flooded the cavern and Jack turned to see Clara holding her flashlight. The light bounced around the many cracks and niches in the cave walls and ceiling, where gray and black spiders lurked amidst their webs. A rusty pipe hung from the rounded ceiling, parts of it drooping down to the ground thirty feet ahead. Jack's feet found the narrow set of tracks that ran along the tunnel floor.

"I don't see any bats," Clara said. "Oh well."

Thunder pealed, and the pattering of rain transformed into a torrent. Jack rushed out of the cave and grabbed the moistened branches, setting them back in front of the entrance to block the cold wind. He walked over to join Katie and Clara who'd found a more open area that had ragged stone ledges jutting along its sides, ideal for seating.

"Looks like we found this place just in time," Jack sat on a flat part of one of the ledges. "We should be safe here for a while."

Clara placed her flashlight next to him, aimed up at the ten-foot-high ceiling, and sat on the ledge across from him. She pulled a sweater from her backpack and wrapped it around her shoulders, then set down her pack to use as a pillow. She laid down. "If it's alright with you guys, I need a rest."

Katie dug an off-white sweater from her own bag and sat next to Jack. "You think it's safe for us to sleep?"

"Maybe we can take turns. We can wake each other every hour or so. I've heard it takes a few hours of sleeping before dream cycles start."

"I've heard that, too. I wish I knew how Clara does it. Tell me something, Clara. Have you ever dreamed about the camp? This isn't time for stories. Tell the truth."

Clara leaned up on her elbow and shook her head. "I don't know why it happens. No matter what I do, I only dream about my kingdom. I tell myself to dream about other things, but I never do."

"It's nothing to worry about." Katie draped her sweater around herself. "Dreaming about your own little world is the best thing you could do right now. At least you have a chance at a good night's sleep. I think it's happening because your mom kept you so secluded."

"I wondered if that was it, too. She hardly ever let me leave our cabin. She read me tons of books about fairies and dwarves and trolls, then I couldn't help dreaming about them. Now that I look back, it's strange she was so obsessed about those stories."

"Not strange for our family," Katie said. "Your parents used to work at Montathena with my parents. They talked about dreams all the time. It wouldn't surprise me if your mother did something on purpose to make you dream that way, to keep you safe."

"And maybe that's what Abby's doing, too. She's keeping us safe." Clara laid down and closed her eyes.

Katie glanced at Jack and he looked away. He didn't want to let on that he didn't believe they were being helped by the ghost of Katie's sister. He knew she only believed that because it was so hard for her to stay at the same camp where her sister died.

Jack shivered from the cold, humid air and put an arm around Katie, surprised by his own audacity. He'd never been this forward with a girl. He pulled her close, exhilarated that she didn't push him away. He snagged a rolled cotton blanket from his backpack, then unrolled it and flung it over Katie and himself.

"You looked cold."

Katie closed her eyes and snuggled her shoulder against Jack's chest. He couldn't remember ever having felt so happy.

"Abby was the last flicker of sanity in my life," Katie said. "My baby sister, Marcy, hardly even got to know her."

"You have a little sister?"

"She's gone, too. After Abby's accident, my parents started arguing all the time. Then my mom took off one night with Marcy. Didn't even say goodbye. I never heard from her again. She didn't...she didn't care about me enough to take me with her."

Jack sensed the tenseness in Katie's muscles. A tear rolled down her cheek.

"That can't be true. Don't think that. She probably didn't have a choice. She probably had to get out of there too fast. Knowing Intershroud, they probably forced her to run away, just like they did with us."

Katie perked up and looked at Jack. She wiped her eyes with her sleeve, a smile forming on her face. "I never thought of that. She could be on the run. Our housekeeper told me my mom went into hiding, but I thought she was making up stories to make me feel better. It makes perfect sense now. Oh, I feel so much better now. I just need to find her."

XXXII

Jack wanted this moment to last forever, Katie leaning against his chest, her soft hair brushing against his cheek. She became animated when she spoke of vacations she'd taken with her family but grew somber when she related how her creepy Uncle Marlin lured her parents into the dream research business.

How much time had passed, Jack didn't know, but he was starting to feel it. He'd only slept a few hours the previous night and had hiked all day. His mind began to drift. The pattering of rain, the warmth of Katie's body, and the melody of her soft voice—it all conspired to lull him to sleep. He imagined himself exploring the lower level of a building. Smoke hurt his eyes and the heat of flames wafted through the demolished room.

*I don't even need my lighter to tell me I'm dreaming this time,* Jack thought.

He stumbled upon a long gray board someone had positioned to serve as a ramp out of the wreckage. He rushed up it and arrived at the same doorway where he'd dreamt the night before, except the doors were gone and someone had set the frame on fire.

"I predicted you'd dream to the flame—like a mindless little moth." Curtis Lynch's crooked teeth stretched in a grin. Fenton Murdock stood to his left and a tall, heavyset man glared at him from Lynch's right. The flames died out.

"Your dream profile noted your obsession with fire," Lynch said. "I always tell my cohorts that dreams are our greatest asset, yet they insist on wasting resources searching all over the forest for you all day in their little machines. Alas, here you are."

The tall, heavyset man barreled over to Jack, his face red and contorted with anger. "How dare you!" He shook his clenched fist in Jack's face. "I've made sacrifices you can hardly imagine, making a decent future for my daughter. If she has been harmed in the slightest, I'll see to it that this is the last dream you ever have."

"You're the ones harming her!" Jack surmised the man was Katie's father. "She wants nothing to do with your company."

"Don't presume to know my daughter better than I do," Vance Frost said.

"Mr. Park," Lynch said, "this discussion is pointless. Clearly, you've been enlightened about dreams and therefore must be assimilated. Let's get on with this, Mr. Frost."

Jack stepped back. "I know you can't hurt me. This is a dream." Jack leaped up, but only rose a few inches off the ground before dropping back down. He turned to run, but found his legs moving in place, his feet no longer touching the ground.

Mr. Murdock stood with one arm outstretched, holding him in the air with his thoughts. Jack stopped fighting him, is body going limp and hanging in the air.

"You've much to learn about Somnolic Powers, my friend." Lynch circled him and studied his face, his fingers pressed together in front of his chin, reminding Jack of an art connoisseur admiring his latest purchase. "You're a Free Dreamer now, among other Free Dreamers. There's no point in resisting us. You won't be able to dream anything extraordinary among us, since you no doubt have yet to discover your dream powers."

Jack flailed around, glaring at Lynch. "I just need to wake up." He slapped himself twice, then closed his eyes. "Wake up. Wake up! Katie, wake me up!"

Fenton laughed. "I know you're not that stupid. An atomic bomb could go off in a dream and Katie wouldn't hear it. Relax. You'll find Intershroud will give you a great life if you just embrace it." He nodded to Vance.

Mr. Frost held his hands up with fingers vertical and tight together, then moved a palm to each side of Jack's head. Jack wriggled with all his might, swinging his feet three times at Mr. Frost, but each time met the invisible wall of Murdock's mental power.

Vance said, "I'm sure you know it's impossible to avoid thinking of something once the suggestion of it is in your head."

"Leave me alone!"

Vance clamped his hands against Jack's cheeks. "Think about the place where you're sleeping right now."

Jack tried to outwit him by focusing on other thoughts: his cabin, the lodge, the lake. Still, for a split second, the image of the mineshaft flickered inside his head. The moment he thought it, the dark cave materialized around him. He felt himself dropping from Vance's hands onto the solid ground.

Vance smirked and stepped back, studying the cave. "It's one of the mines." He rubbed a hand along a plank of wood shoring.

"Impossible," Murdock said. "Farley demolished the mines years ago."

"The fool missed one," Lynch said. "This explains the Nightmares showing up at camp. This is a secondary entrance to a mine that imbecile failed to fully destroy."

"Do we have any choppers in the air?" Vance looked at Fenton.

"Staff members took off in one right before I went to sleep. Jack's friend ditched his escorts in Kalispell and they're looking for him."

"Taylor got away!" Jack smiled.

"Not for long," Lynch said. "Fenton, run outside and find our bearings, then wake yourself and contact that pilot before he lands."

"Got it." Mr. Murdock walked to the cave opening and tossed the branches aside with a flick of his wrist. Once outside, a circular clump of earth arose from the ground below his feet and he ascended out of Jack's view, into the sky.

"I think we're done here," Mr. Frost said. "You ready to wake up, Mr. Lynch?"

"One moment." Lynch approached Jack and looked him in the eye. "Do you see now, Mr. Park? You're but the tiniest of little gnats—not even the slightest threat to this organization. We'll soon teach you your proper place in this world. Let's go, Mr. Frost."

Vance Frost nodded, pulled a hand grenade from the pocket of his black suit coat and threw away the pin. He waved and tossed the grenade to Jack. "See you shortly."

A split-second noise preceded a blinding white light.

JACK BOLTED UPRIGHT, breathing heavily, and blinded by pitch darkness. He felt around the cold stone ledge searching for the flashlight. The realization hit him that Katie wasn't where she'd been when he'd fallen asleep. He shoved his hand into his pocket, grabbed his lighter, and lit it. He looked around for Katie, shadows playing on the walls wherever he swung the flame. He saw only Clara, curled up and sleeping soundly.

He shook her. "Clara, wake up. Where's Katie?"

She sat up and rubbed her eyes, shivering and pulling her sweater tighter around herself. "She took the flashlight. Maybe she, you know, when Mother Nature calls…"

Jack's face reddened. "I didn't think of that. I just had a nightmare that Lynch and his partners found us, and it freaked me out. I thought Lynch got to her in her sleep."

The rain had stopped, its patter replaced by the chopping of an approaching helicopter. Jack struggled to accept that something in his dream could've had any relevance to his awake life, but he knew that helicopter couldn't be a coincidence. The branches at the entrance remained bunched tightly together. Katie hadn't gone outside.

"We need to get out of here." Jack stood and searched the dark interior of the mine. "Katie! Lynch knows where we are! Where are you?"

He waited ten seconds and called her name again, every second feeling like an eternity. Katie didn't come.

A searchlight brightened the branches at the cave entrance. Jack grabbed Clara's arm.

"Don't be afraid." Damien's voice bellowed from a megaphone. "We know you're in the cave. Come on out. No one's going to hurt you."

XXXIII

"Should we go out?" Clara picked up her backpack.

Jack shook his head. "He's lying. At least it doesn't sound like they have Katie."

"Why'd Katie go into the tunnels by herself?"

"I don't know. It's dangerous in there, too. Let's hope we can find someplace to hide. Maybe Damien will think we left."

Jack tied his blanket onto his backpack and shoved the strap over his shoulder. He grabbed Katie's bag and pushed Clara on in front of him. Shadows from the rocky walls created an eerie feeling that someone was lurking around every protrusion. The dirt and stone walls curved to their right, held aloft by old wood timbers connected with bent steel plates.

They rushed down a gradual slope which then curved upward, then they ducked below wooden posts that crisscrossed over their heads. Jack tripped over another that had long ago fallen on the ground. About a hundred yards inside, the path narrowed, and the walls wedged inward from fallen rocks and soil.

"Jack." Damien's loudspeaker now echoed from inside the cave, far behind them. "There's no point to this. We know you're in here.

There's nothing to be afraid of. No one's blaming you for anything. We're going to send you all back home."

Jack marched on, shoving Clara ahead of him and keeping his eye on the ground for stray rocks and broken timbers visible in the dim light of his lighter. "What could've possessed Katie to wander this far into the tunnels by herself?"

Clara shrugged.

Avard's gravelly voice now sounded on the loudspeaker. "Park! What do you durned fools think yer doing? Come back here before this place collapses. Yer gunna get us all killed."

Clara stopped and looked at Jack, but he shook his head and pushed her onward. He began to perspire and breathe harder, imagining the walls growing narrower with every step. He searched every niche for any kind of outlet. He sweated and his body felt tense. He needed fresh air. A girl's body came into view, kneeling motionless against a pile of fallen timbers. He stopped, petrified.

"It's Katie!" Clara ran to her and bent down to hug her.

Katie looked up at Clara, then at Jack. She handed him the flashlight and he pocketed his lighter.

"What happened?" Jack held her bag out to her.

She took it and set it in her lap. "I'm alright." She pulled herself to her feet and rubbed her eyes. "I was just resting."

"Resting? I thought they'd taken you in your sleep. Why'd you run off?"

"There was a bluish light. You fell asleep and I turned off the flashlight, but I still saw light. I was scared at first, but then I recognized a voice. It was so faint I almost missed it."

"Why didn't you wake me?"

"Because it was her. Don't you see? I saw Abby. I knew she was the one helping us escape. She said not to be afraid. I had to go to her."

Jack looked down. He couldn't tell her she was hallucinating, experiencing some side effect of Farley's camp. "We need to keep moving. They've found us. We need to find another exit." He walked forward and waved for them to follow him. Katie stood and followed him, with Clara at her side.

"I would've screamed like a crazy girl if I'd seen her," Clara said. "Did she look all ghostly and scary?"

"I didn't really see her, exactly, but I knew it was her. She told me she'd been visiting our reality too long and couldn't make herself visible anymore. I know it sounds crazy."

"What else did she say?" Clara ducked below a fallen timber.

Katie frowned. "She wasn't herself. She was so angry and only wanted to know if Farley survived the explosion. She admitted she led the attacks at camp."

"Stop it!" Jack halted and turned to Katie. He grabbed her forearms and looked in her eyes. "You have to snap out of this. Don't you see? They did something to your mind. I've been hallucinating, too. There is no such thing as ghosts. Your sister died. I'm sorry. I wish it hadn't happened, but it did. She isn't coming back. You have to accept it."

Katie wiggled out of Jack's arms and glared at him. She folded her arms and set her feet rigid on the hard soil.

"Guys!" Damien's voice echoed from the megaphone. "There's no other way out. The mine is unstable. People died in here. Come on out. I give you my word no harm will come to you."

Katie shook her head, took hold of Clara's hand, and walked past Jack at a slow pace, looking away from him.

"Don't be mad," Jack said.

Katie kept walking, pretending Jack wasn't there. They hiked up and down the varying slopes of rough ground for fifteen minutes and Jack started wondering if this labyrinth had an end. Katie stopped in front of an eight-foot drop-off. Jack climbed down first, holding tight to a thick strand of worn rope, then he helped each of the girls down in turn.

They found no side tunnels in which to hide.

A cold liquid spattered on Jack's face and he looked up and found water dripping from cracks in the rock ceiling. Clara screamed. Katie grabbed the strap of Clara's backpack, holding her back from a deep fissure. Clara's flashlight slipped from her hand and disappeared into the abyss, basking the tunnel in darkness.

Jack fumbled for his lighter and struck the flint. By its light, they found two boards that formed a rickety bridge across the six-foot-wide chasm. Katie stepped across with elegant balance and Clara followed her with much less speed. Jack imagined himself slipping off with every step. When he reached the other side, Katie leaned down and dragged the boards far from the shaft.

"That ought to slow them down," she said. "We need to pick up our step. There's got to be a place to hide in here somewhere." She quickened her pace and Jack pushed Clara along to keep up with her. After another ten-minute hike, Katie stopped at a wide-open space strewn with dozens of boulders and scores of broken timbers. Splintered boards, piles of dirt, and rocks of all sizes littered the ground and filled the cave in front of them.

"We're trapped." Clara pushed on a diagonal beam and a clump of dirt dropped on the ground next to her, releasing dust into the air.

"We needed a rest, anyway," Jack said. He breathed fast and held a hand over his burning throat. "There's air flowing through this rubble. Try to find a pathway." He worked loose a board of rough timber and pulled it aside, but found only more boards.

Unintelligible male voices bounced off the walls, growing louder every second. Brief flashes of light illuminated the rock ceiling.

"They're catching up," Clara said.

Jack looked around at a dozen dark boulders that had turned the area into a miniature maze.

"Maybe we can hide in one of these holes and hope they don't see us," said Katie, pointing to a deep niche between two boulders. "A soon as they pass us, we can run the other way. Wait. What's that?" She stepped out of Jack's view into the niche between the boulders.

"Careful Katie, it's dark in there."

"This board seems loose," Clara said.

Jack ran to Clara and helped her work a wide board away from a pile of rocks in her path. A long, narrow tunnel came into view along the top of the stones and Jack raised his lighter. He frowned when he saw that it came to an end about ten feet in. He waved the lighter around and grew worried when he realized Katie wasn't in sight.

"Katie," Jack said. "You okay? We found a dead end over here, but if we work together, we might find one we can squeeze through. Katie?" He turned to Clara, wide-eyed.

"Katie?" Clara darted to the boulders where Katie had gone and disappeared into the cavity.

Jack followed her. "Did you find an exit?" His shoulders brushed against coarse stone and he stretched his lighter high over Clara's head. He stopped abruptly upon pressing against Clara's back. "Sorry, Clara."

"I saw a crow fly back here," Katie leaned over Clara's shoulder, "but I can't find it now. Careful with the fire!" She placed her hand between Jack's lighter and the stone wall. Piles of black powder caked the rock ledges, stuffed into every crevasse. Red sticks of TNT lay scattered on the ground amidst long coils of fuse and a bundle of long incense-like sticks meant for lighting them.

"There are plastic containers all around here," Katie said. "They might be explosives."

"I think you're right." Jack grabbed a fist-sized container of cloudy white fluid off a fallen timber and pried the lid off, then coughed at the scent of detergent and gasoline. He replaced the lid and set it down. "Let's keep moving. Did you see where the crow went?"

"It's too dark, but I know it went this way."

Jack tried to walk forward, but Clara continued to block him.

"You're pushing me into Katie," Clara turned and pushed Jack back a step.

"We have to hurry. They'll be here any second."

"You finally got something right," Damien said.

Jack turned around, squinted at the blinding glare of three powerful flashlights.

"Watch your lighter," Katie said.

He felt her fingers push his hand away from one of the containers and it triggered an idea. "Let us go or I'll blow this place sky high!" He swung his lighter inches from a container.

"That's napalm," Avard said. "There's gunpowder everywhere, too. And TNT."

"Are you serious, Jack?" Damien lowered his flashlight. "You'd kill us all just to keep from going back to Camp Farley? What about Katie and Clara? You willing to kill them, too? Think about what you're doing. This mine is unstable and full of explosives. If it was just you, I'd say go ahead and kill yourself, but I won't let you take Katie with you. You need therapy, Jack. Put away the lighter."

Jack grabbed one of the incense-like sticks and lit its round tip, then lowered the flame half an inch from one of the napalm containers.

"You're a fool," Avard said. "Haven't you done enough damage already?"

"He's bluffing," Damien said, "but just do what he says. There's only one way out of this mine. He can't stay in here forever. Katie, I'm sorry I lied to you, but I wasn't lying when I said I wouldn't let anyone hurt you. My dad made me keep everything a secret, but that's all history now. Come with me and I'll tell you anything you want to know."

Jack glanced back and saw Katie peering over Clara's shoulder. Her hesitation created a knot in his stomach. He resisted an urge to beg her to stay, but he knew he'd already asked too much.

"I gave you your chance." Katie turned away from him.

Damien shook his head and squeezed past Avard.

"You can wait outside, but I know a bluff when I see one," Avard blinded Jack with his flashlight. "Yer gunna pay for what happened to my Media."

"I didn't do anything to her! I never even met her!"

"You ran away! She could've dealt with you in the lab, but you ran off. Because of that, Lynch forced her to visit you in yer dreams, and it ruined her! She can barely speak!"

"I didn't force Lynch to do it!"

Avard pounced at Jack, his powerful left arm pressing around Jack's chest and forcing air from his lungs. Jack pulled down on Avard's arm and reached forward, keeping Avard's free hand away from the flaming stick.

"Give me that stick!" Avard slammed all his weight into Jack, causing Katie and Clara to groan under the pressure. Jack lifted his feet and pushed hard against the sides of the two boulders, shoving Avard back and slamming his head against one of the rocks. The man loosened his grip on Jack and his eyes closed. He fell backward, knocking four canisters of napalm off the ledges before he hit the ground with a thud.

The bald man from Avard's self-defense team came into view behind Avard. He set his flashlight on a timber and knelt next to his friend, light reflecting from his tattoo-covered head. He placed two fingers on Avard's neck, then looked up and sneered. "Proud of yourself, kid? You hurt his daughter, now you knocked him out. How many more people you gonna hurt?"

Jack tightened his fists, his lighter in one and the fuse-lighting stick in the other. "You had no right to mess with our minds!"

The bald man looked to the side, then jumped over Avard and grabbed Jack's hands so fast Jack couldn't respond. He pried the lighter from Jack's fist, at the same time breaking the stick and letting the flaming end dropped into the dirt next to Jack's lighter.

Jack backed into Clara, his fists raised, wondered what was keeping Katie from moving beyond the boulders. "Leave us alone! You have no right to treat us like this! You have no right!"

At that moment, Katie fell forward beyond the rocks and Clara collapsed over her. Jack rolled backward over Clara. They looked back at the approaching bald man, the snarling features of his face exaggerated by the flashlight resting on the timbers behind him.

The man took two steps and his body flattened against an invisible wall. He studied the invisible wall with confused eyes, not noticing his feet kicking the still-flaming stick laying on the ground. The stick bounced up against one of the boulders and landed in a puddle of milky white gelatin.

The space between the boulders filled with blinding fire and light.

# PART 2

# DREAM
# RUNNING

XXXIV

Katie lay on her side, staring at the empty passageway where the bald man had been standing seconds earlier. He was gone. No ruins. No smoke. No rubble. Just an open path between two boulders. No flashlights or flames accounted for the dim, yellowish glow illuminating the cavern around her.

"Are you okay, Katie?" Clara pushed Jack off her stomach and rolled over to her right.

"I think so. What just happened?"

"The explosives." Jack propped himself up on his elbows to see over Clara. "Avard spilled that napalm all over. I think that bald guy kicked the flame into it."

"Then why aren't we dead?" Katie stared at Jack. "Why didn't this place collapse?"

Jack only stared back at her.

Katie forced herself upright and looked around the beehive-shaped space, its bumpy, curved walls rising into a conical ceiling carved from rough stone. A rounded tunnel entrance punctured the wall fifteen feet behind her and another tunnel cut into the wall twenty-five feet beyond Jack.

A cawing sound turned her attention to a black bird perched on a protruding rock near the ceiling. It soared to a ledge on the opposite side of the cavern. She gave Clara a hand and helped her up.

Jack stood and rubbed his eyes, then massaged his ribs. He took three steps toward Katie, his eyebrows rising, and looked down at his feet. "The ground looks solid, but my feet keep sinking into it."

"Mine too," Clara said. "And your voices sound muffled. And where is that weird light coming from?"

"Nothing's making sense." Katie shook her head and wiped dust out of her hair. "One minute, you two were shoving me against a rock wall, and the next, the wall disappeared and you both were falling on top of me."

"What wall? You told me that crow flew through the passage." Jack pointed at the bird.

"It flew between the boulders, but the passage was dark. I followed it and ran into a wall. Couldn't you tell I couldn't move? You pushed me against the wall so hard I couldn't breathe."

"I'm sorry. I assumed you stopped to move rubble out of the way, or something."

Clara shook her said. "So, you're saying a rock wall just disappeared into nothing?"

"I don't know what I'm saying," Katie said. "All I know is there was a wall right there and now it's gone. That bald guy was following us, but he stopped all of a sudden, like he'd run into a window. He kicked that fire stick and everything went really bright for a second."

"That's how it looked to me, too." Jack walked between the boulders, looked around, and shook his head. "Now it looks like no one ever passed through here. It's got to be an illusion. They did something to our minds."

"This does feel like a bad dream." Katie heard a scraping noise and turned to a tunnel behind her. She gasped when a wall of solid rock appeared in its place. A new tunnel appeared in a wall to her right and she turned to Jack, eyes wide.

The crow dived from its perch and glided down the new tunnel.

Jack ran to the wall where the tunnel had vanished and pushed against the stone. His hands sunk three inches into the wall and the ground rumbled below their feet. He pulled his hands back and observed the imprint he'd formed in the rock. He placed his hands on his head and walked in a circle. "The rock feels like dry clay. Our minds are gone. It's the only explanation. I don't know what to do."

"We should follow that crow," Clara said. "It led us here."

Jack shook his head. "What if the new tunnel disappears while we're inside?"

"Abby sent that crow," Katie said. "I saw it with her. I think she sent it to guide us to safety."

"Don't you get it?" Jack frowned. "None of this is real! The flying creatures, the crows, this cave, the disappearing tunnels, your sister's ghost—it's all in our minds. It can't be real. It's those things that were below our pillows, shooting stuff into our brains. Our dreams are mixing with reality. We're seeing things that don't exist."

Katie folded her arms and shook her head. "They couldn't have made all three of us hallucinate the same things."

"Who knows what Intershroud is capable of? I can't take this. I want out of here!" Jack charged to the passage between the boulders, then paused and stared at one of them. He sunk his hand into it and the cavern rumbled. "These rocks weren't soft like this when we came through here before. And the napalm is gone. Maybe all that fallen rubble's gone, too. I'm going to see how it looks on the other side."

"You might be walking back into their hands," Katie said.

Jack stared down the passage, then turned to Katie. "If I'm not back in thirty seconds, follow that crow."

✖

JACK MOVED FAST. His right shoulder rubbed against a boulder, carving a slice of it off and knocking it to the ground with a thump. He entered the tunnel beyond the passage and smiled. The collapsed wooden shoring now stood erect, supporting the stone walls and ceiling. No fallen earth or stone obstructed the ground and a bright light glowed a few hundred yards forward, promising Jack access to the forest around the distant corner.

"The rubble we saw before must've been an illusion." He turned and cupped his hand beside his mouth. "Katie, Clara, come here! There's a way out!"

The stone walls absorbed too much of the sound. He walked between the boulders but stopped when a large stone brushed past his nose and crashed into a nearby wall with a loud crack. Jack stared at the bowling-ball-sized stone near his foot, then looked to see who'd launched it.

Avard stood twenty feet away, breathing heavily through clenched teeth and leering at him with bloodthirsty eyes. "You murdered me!" He found another rock five feet away, grabbed it and launched it at Jack.

Jack ducked, the stone brushing through his hair before crashing against a boulder. "You're crazy! You're not dead. You're standing right in front of me!"

"Always the know-it-all, aren't you, Park? You blew up the mine, fool! You knocked me out, then blew me up! I'll end you if it's the last thing I do!" He hunted around for another rock.

"Nothing blew up. We're hallucinating!"

Avard charged at Jack and wrapped his hands around his neck, his face contorting in his thirst to strangle him. His hands sometimes passed into Jack's head, but he didn't feel it.

Jack yelled and gave Avard a push. The man flew back ten feet and rolled on the ground.

"So, that's your power." Avard pulled himself up and brushed dirt from his torn brown shirt. "Super strength. Don't think for one second it'll save you. If there is any justice in this world, I'll get my revenge."

"I didn't do anything to you!"

"You murdered me!" He looked around again. His eyes lit up and he sneered. "What am I doing? I'm a ghost. I have my own powers!" He focused his gaze on his arms and his clothes moved and changed colors. He laughed at his camouflaged army battle gear. A combat helmet appeared on his head and black assault rifles formed in his hands. He raised the guns and pointed them at Jack.

"Let's see how yer super strength handles this."

Jack didn't wait to find out. He dived between the boulders and ran as fast as he could move his legs. The cavern shook and rumbled, chunks of stone collapsing from the walls whenever Jack pushed off them or rubbed against them. Gunfire peppered the stone behind him, mixed with Avard's laughter.

"Katie, get to the tunnel!"

Jack entered the cavern but found no one there. Solid walls now replaced the tunnel where the crow had escaped. He turned and saw Avard stepping over fallen chunks of stone and realized what he had to do. He charged at the boulders and began shaving large chunks of it into the passageway. The cavern shook violently, and Jack struggled to keep his footing, but he didn't stop until he'd filled the passageway with rubble.

Avard groaned, trying to heave rocks as big as his chest out of his way. "Don't think you've stopped me, Park! I'll never stop! I'll get my revenge!"

**XXXV**

Jack didn't stop shaking when the cavern did. He stumbled to the wall where the tunnel had been and trembled at the thought of Katie and Clara entombed in solid stone. He clenched his teeth and tightened his fists, pounding them six inches into the wall. The cavern quaked.

"Katie, are you there? The rock is soft, like clay! Try to dig through it!" He pounded again and again, yanking a cubic foot of stone off the wall with each swipe. After a dozen hits, the earthquake stopped, and the tunnel reopened.

Katie and Clara ran out and hugged Jack, then stepped back from him.

"I swear this cave is alive," Katie said. "We heard you yelling and thought you'd catch up to us, but the entrance closed off."

"We heard shooting," Clara said. "Are you okay?"

A rock tumbled down the pile of stone in front of Avard and a gun barrel poked through a gap, pivoting toward Jack.

"Run!" Jack waved for the girls to move back into the tunnel, scooped up two rocks, and darted to the barrier in front of Avard. He planted the stones into Avard's gun—a bullet ricocheted into the ceiling—then ignored Avard's groaning and pushed the entire pile deeper into the crevasse, sealing him in. The earth didn't stop rumbling.

Katie shouted, warning Jack to look out. He glanced back at her and shrugged, unsure why she was yelling. His knees buckled, and a four-foot-diameter section of earth lifted him into the air. Approaching the ceiling at a high speed, he raised his hands, ducked, and bent his knees, preparing to jump. Before he could do anything, however, the platform stopped six feet in the air and tilted slightly before rocketing down a new tunnel.

Jack dug his fingers into the platform of soil, holding on for his life. He whipped down the mine shaft, breezing past scores of timbers which sometimes broke against his head, chest, or shoulders. Why they didn't hurt him more severely, he couldn't guess. At last, the dim light brightened at an opening to the outside, and yellowish daylight assaulted his eyes. The slab of earth flung him ten feet into the air, then crumbled into dust all around him.

Jack flew between two tall pine trees, screaming and flailing his arms, then dropped flat on his stomach and sunk deep into the rocky surface of a mountain trail.

KATIE FROZE and stared into the now-empty cavern until a rock wall appeared and blocked her view.

Clara ran and pressed her hands against it, but it only expanded, shoving her backward two steps. "This mine seems to be alive."

"We've got to find Jack!" Katie carved a deep gouge in the stone with her hands then shook with the rumbling ground. Stone scraped against stone and a bright light suddenly cast shadows on the wall before her. She and Clara turned around to a new opening in the side wall of the tunnel twenty feet away. Katie rushed to the opening, peered down the fifty-foot-long cross tunnel, and smiled at the sight of pine trees and daylight.

"The mine wants us to leave." Clara placed a hand on Katie's shoulder.

"We can't abandon Jack."

"The mine isn't letting us get to him."

Katie glanced at the blocked entrance to the cavern. "Abby sent that crow. We should find her. Maybe she can tell us what to do."

Clara nodded and they walked to the exit together. Once outside, Katie squinted from the brightness of the gray-yellow, cloud-covered sky. It rendered everything with a sepia glow. They stood on a narrow trail by a low hill rising to their left, overlooking a shallow valley of dark green pines.

Katie leaned toward Clara. "I need to tell you something and I hope it won't upset you. I don't think we're hallucinating. I don't think all this is just in our minds."

Clara nodded. "It seems too real to me, too."

"It isn't just that. You see, I watched that bald man. He ran into some kind of invisible barrier before he kicked that stick. I saw the explosion and couldn't understand why I wasn't hearing or feeling it."

"So, you're saying the invisible barrier saved us?"

"No. I'm saying there's a reason we didn't hear or feel it. Clara, I think we died in that explosion." Katie's voice cracked.

Clara's eyes widened. "But we're standing here. My feet hurt. We can't be dead."

"I know. It's not what I expected either. But I watched that man disappear. Everything changed after that explosion."

"Do you think Abby led us here on purpose, that she wanted us to die, to be with her?"

Katie shook her head. "She wouldn't do that. She always protected me. I don't think she meant for us to die."

Clara frowned and pointed at something up the hill. "There's someone up there!"

Katie looked up and her jaw dropped. Dark riders, donned in sinuous black robes, floated on ghostly black steeds enveloped in a billowing murky mist that rolled along the ridge. Blackened medieval armor covered their heads, hands, and feet, and they held lances tucked under their arms. Their bodies had the appearance of unsolid, narrow, waving rolls of tenuous black cloth. The apparitions disappeared over the ridge, without a sound.

"What were they?" Clara looked at Katie, her eyebrows raised. "Medieval knights in the middle of Montana?"

"They looked like cosplay actors, but who knows what's going on." She clenched her mouth tight and leaned her hand against an aspen. The tree leaned and made a cracking sound. Katie pulled her hand away and observed the imprint she'd left in the trunk, her mouth agape. She looked at her hand, frowned, and shook her head.

Clara wrapped an arm around her. "We'll figure this out. If this is the World of the Dead, we'll find Abby. But I'm not so convinced we're dead. Something's just not right. This place seems familiar to me somehow."

Katie took Clara's hand. "You may be right. Everyone tells me I always assume the worst."

"Let's find Abby, she'll be able to explain everything. I just don't know where to start."

"Abby had crows with her, so maybe if we can find any crows, we'll find her."

Three gunshots reported behind Katie and she turned around. Avard stood behind her, leaning against a boulder, clothed in military combat armor and dangling an assault rifle from his right arm. "You two ain't going nowhere 'til you find me yer buddy, Mr. Park."

XXXVI

Jack lifted his head from the ten-inch-deep imprint he'd left in the earth, sucking in the dusty air and wheezing with each breath. He stared down for five seconds before shaking dirt from his face and hair and pushing himself up. He winced at every movement of his aching arms and legs.

"How did I survive that?" He dragged himself from the body-shaped impression on wobbly arms, rolled over and sat cross-legged, then looked around to find his bearings. A high, pine-covered mountain stood behind him, running along the trail on which he sat. Loose rocks smothered the lower twenty feet of the mountainside. The dense white trunks of thousands of aspens dominated his view along the other side of the trail, except for a fifty-foot-wide rolling meadow of yellow grass a few hundred feet down the trail.

Jack started to stand when movement caught his eye among the trees. A green, slimy blob crawled toward him through the low grass. The creature snagged a nearby twig for a walking stick, stood up on its spindly hind legs, and placed a felt hat on its head. Jack gasped and rubbed his eyes. Before him stood a rather large, human-like bullfrog.

"My, you aren't the normal fare, are you?" The animal had a deep English accent.

"What the…?" Jack scrambled to his feet and stepped back.

"Bit daft, aren't you?" The frog hobbled two paces closer and rolled his bugged-out eyes. "What do you mean, 'what the?' I'm a frog-who-walks-and-talks—obviously. You seem to be on a journey. You don't mind if I join you, do you?"

"Wow." Jack laughed. "This tops them all. I've gone insane."

"I'm not inclined to argue with you."

"You wouldn't happen to know what's going on here, would you? I need to find a way back into this mine. My friends are trapped in there." He searched the stony hillside for an entrance and located a five-foot, circular opening, twelve feet up, through which the cave had spewed him out.

"What is occurring here presently is, I introduced myself and you asked me a question. I'd have thought it was fairly obvious."

"Very funny." Jack was in no mood for bad jokes. "What's obvious is that you're a figment of my imagination and I'm wasting my time talking to you. I'm going to see if I can climb back in through that hole up there."

Jack charged up the mountainside, watching his step as he hopped from rock to rock. He soon realized however, the gravel below the rocks was sloughing off with his every step. He couldn't make any progress up the mountainside. He put all his strength into it and raced up the slope until he reached the opening, but the entrance collapsed and filled with rocks, showering him with dust. Jack stopped and the rocks slid him back down to the foot the mountain.

"It's like the mountain is alive!" Jack kicked a rock and sent it bouncing down the trail.

"The cave has collapsed," the frog said. "If you don't mind my saying so, caves aren't my preference for journeying. Let us henceforth proceed with our walking and talking along this delightful mountain trail."

"My friends might suffocate in there!" Jack bent down and shoved an armful of stones aside, amazed that they weighed less than loaves of bread. He smiled and shoved aside larger piles of them, until he realized new stones were popping up out of nowhere. He gritted his teeth and pounded swathes of stones aside, but the mountain reacted. He held his arms up to block hundreds of stones now flying at him, hurled by an unseen force. Despite the jagged appearance of the rocks, they felt to him like mere jets of air. The combined force, however, threw him backward and sent him rolling on his back across the trail and into the aspens.

"Why are you doing this? Let me in! My friends are in there!"

The rocks rolled from the trail, flew up the mountainside, and came to rest.

"The cave rejects you," the frog said.

Jack charged after it and the frog hopped away, screaming. A moment later, Jack stopped and dropped to his knees, rolled on his back against the rocky slope and placed his hands over his face. He wanted to melt into the rocks and disappear.

"What am I going to do?" Jack peeked between his fingers and spotted two vultures circling, riding the updrafts high in the gray-yellow clouds. "What've I done? Katie would've been just fine if I'd left her alone. She had money. She was beautiful. Her father is a CEO. Then I came along and ruined her life. She trusted me, and I've probably killed her."

The frog poked its head up from behind a rock, then stood and walked to Jack. It pushed aside a fern with its little walking stick and stared at Jack with a bewildered expression on its face.

"I'm sorry, Katie!" Jack sat up and yelled as loud as he could, hoping she could hear him within the mountain. "I'm sorry! I didn't mean to hurt you. I shouldn't have talked you into coming with me. I'm sorry for everything."

"Screaming is not pleasant," the frog said.

"Get out of here!" Jack grabbed the nearest rock and hurled it at him.

The bullfrog squealed and leapt out of the stone's path, then dived into a clump of ferns next to a wide tree stump.

"Your density is far more than physical, my friend. You want to know why birds-who-eat-dead-animals circle in the sky above us? Clearly, they're waiting for us to die of old age, sitting here talking to

Katies who aren't there. I beseech you to becalm yourself such that we may recommence our journey in a more civilized manner."

Jack nabbed a nearby rock and threw it at the frog, but it ricocheted off the tree stump and crashed against an aspen.

"It's no surprise to me that this mountain abhors you," the frog said. "Is this Katie of yours this irritating?"

Jack reached for another rock, but thought for a moment, and dropped it.

He grinned and jumped to his feet. "You could be right. Maybe the mountain doesn't like her." He hiked down the trail at a brisk pace.

The bullfrog leaped after him from its hiding place, hopping to keep up. "Is this hasty pace necessary?"

"I have to hurry. If the mountain doesn't like my friends, it might've pushed them out somewhere, same as it did with me. Look for impressions in the ground."

Jack scurried along the mountainside trail, the frog leaping behind him. He scanned the mountain for openings and the ground for depressions. He rushed past a cluster of young aspens and wondered at some of the leaves floating in the air, taking their assigned places on the trees without actually being connected to them.

"I beg you to please slow down, if you don't mind." The frog took a heavy breath between every few words. "Running is not conducive to conversation."

"Just answer me one thing." Jack stopped and stared at the frog. "Are you an illusion? Am I just imagining you're here?"

The frog rolled his eyes. "What nonsense is this? I assure you, my friend, I existed long before you came along." He looked down at one of Jack's footprints. "Your tracks are deep. You eat too much."

Jack shook his head and began jogging at an even faster pace but slowed to a brisk step a few hundred feet later. His chest ached, and he couldn't muster the energy to keep running.

The frog grinned with contentment at the slower pace. "This is a short shrub. I could easily leap over it, but I choose to go around it. Leaping is very distracting when one is talking, you know. Those bushes are not short; thus, the leaping option is not applicable. Ah, this is a rock. This is another rock. Rock. Rock. Another rock. I find there are numerous rocks on my walks. That rhymes, you know—rocks and walks. I'd not advise you to look below rocks. Snakes, you know."

"Do you ever stop talking?"

"Doy. In what world does a frog-who-walks-and-talks stop talking?"

They didn't tread much farther before Jack came across two sets of footprints that matched the depth of his own. He darted to them and bent down for a closer look.

"Ha ha! They're okay! They escaped." The tracks led off the trail into a meadow and then over the crest of a nearby hill, into the thick lodgepole pine forest.

"Your friends didn't care to wait for you, I see. I don't recommend wandering off the trail as your friends have. Mountain lions, you know. Shall we continue on the trail?"

"They're alive. That's all that matters."

Jack fixed his eyes on the girls' footprints and turned off the trail, his legs brushing against tall meadow grass. "I don't know why they chose to wander off the trail. They must not have known where to look for me."

"Surely they assumed you dissipated. Happens every day, you know. As for myself, I only leave the trail when there's danger in my path."

XXXVII

Katie stopped at an embankment that overlooked a narrow, gurgling stream sandwiched between rocky soil dotted with tufts of green grass. She searched for crows on the pine-filled horizon, glancing up at the yellowish-gray sky and noting how depressed it made her feel.

"Keep moving," Avard said.

Katie winced at the jab of Avard's gun between her shoulder blades. "Stop it! We're doing what you asked!" She waited for Clara to hop down from the embankment, then stepped down herself and reached for the bare branch of a fallen lodgepole. She gasped when the branch crumbled in her hand, forcing her to grab onto Clara to regain her balance. Her feet splashed in the stream and she laughed with Clara at the unexpected airy sensation.

"The water feels like cold fog from a dry ice machine," Katie said.

"But it looks just like normal water!" Clara bent down and filled her cupped hands with water, letting it trickle through her fingers.

"I said keep moving!" Avard jumped from the bank and shoved Clara, forcing her to stand up. He then turned to Katie. "Don't think I won't shoot you."

"It won't matter if you shoot us," Katie said. "You can't hurt us here."

"You don't know a thing about this place! Let me assure you, miss, bullets still hurt like a bear, and if you be ghosts, I know exactly how to obliterate you. You uppity kids think you know everything, but yer father didn't tell you nothing. He was always one of the few Intershroud big shots I could stand, but I'm dead now and I won't let nothing stand between me and my revenge. So, you best just stop protectin' yer little buddy and tell me where he went. Then I'll let you go."

"I told you, we don't know what happened to him! He's probably hurt. The ground just lifted him up and took him away. I kept expecting it to do the same to us."

"The mountain took him away cause he's a durned fool! He kept breaking chunks of stone off its walls until it had enough and spit him out. But that don't mean he's dead. I won't rest 'til I see his rotting body. I'll hold on 'til the end of time if that's what it takes. It's just a matter of time, so you might as well tell me where he is!"

"We don't know!" Katie shouted.

"Then keep moving. I figure them Ghost Knights'll help me if you can't." He waved his gun, signaling her and Clara to continue forward. Katie crossed the stream and helped Clara climb up the embankment on the other side. Together, they climbed up a low hill covered in tall green grass.

Clara looked at Avard. "Why are there medieval knights riding around in the middle of Montana?"

"Good gravy kid, would you want to stay in one location for five centuries? Some of them Ghost Knights is five hundred, maybe even a thousand years old. They's ghosts who lost their chance for revenge. They was robbed of the opportunity in their own day, so they been roaming the world for centuries, helping other ghosts get their revenge. That's what I'm gonna ask them to do for me."

"They looked so terrifying," Clara said.

"They look how they choose to look, a form that inspires fear and matches the darkness of their hearts."

Katie altered her path around a low cluster of scrub oak and stopped to wait for Clara to catch up. "What's the point in wasting away centuries of time, fixated on something someone did to them centuries ago? They're stupid to be so obsessed with revenge."

"What do you know about it? It's easy fer you to criticize them when nobody's robbed you of yer life! Imagine if you was me, just following orders, chasing down foolish teenagers hiding in a dangerous old mine, and one of them starts waving fire next to some explosives. You try to steal it away from the durn fool, and he shoves yer head against a rock and knocks you out cold. You find yerself dreamin', wondering what just happened, 'til you sense yer life draining away. Yer standing there terrified, knowing yer livin' body ain't there no more. It's gone. You feel the desperation of yer soul, struggling to pass on to the next life.

"Except, then you remember the explosives. You remember the little punk with the fire. You realize he set off them explosives. He killed you! He killed you in cold blood! It fills yer whole being with rage. How dare he kill me! How dare he take my life! I mustered up all the force of my being to yank my soul into this world, to keep myself alive long enough to get my revenge.

"That's what it was like for them Ghost Knights. Vengeance is their only reason for existing. They lived too long to satisfy their hunger, but it ain't too late for me. I'll have justice!"

Katie trembled at the hatred in his eyes. "How do know all this? You act like you've been here before, like you've died before."

"Course I ain't never died before! You don't gotta die to come here. What do you think the Intershroud's all about? They teach you all you need to know about this place. Can't say I like their methods, but Intershroud done learned me things most people never imagined could be true. Had you stuck with the program, you'd be knowing how to deal with ghosts and nightmares, too."

Katie felt too confused to seek anymore answers. She continued up the hill, tall lodgepoles rising into her view with each step. She soon reached the top and surveyed a shallow valley of pines interspersed with open, yellow meadows. Three deer bowed their heads in a distant field, feeding amidst the trees.

"I don't see anyone," Katie said. "This is pointless. We have no idea where Jack went, and you don't need us to find him. We're all ghosts anyway. What does it matter? You can't kill people who are already dead."

Avard stepped up to the hilltop and searched the valley, then looked at Katie. "I'm not so sure you is dead. You sure don't seem bent on vengeance."

Clara looked at Avard. "But, there was an explosion. We couldn't have survived."

Avard shook his head. "I admit, I'm confused myself. Most ghosts don't never go far from their haunts. When they pull their soul into this world, they create a door between this place and the material world. I know a lot about it, on account of Intershroud sent me on a lot of missions to make deals with them, back in the day. Lynch was always experimenting with their haunts, trying to transfer things into the material world.

"It got easier when we came across some of them Ghost Knights. Them guys found ways to abandon their haunts, and they teach their tricks to other ghosts. So, we was able to use their abandoned haunts. I don't think I made a haunt when I died, though. My guess is, it's 'cause there was already a ghost haunting there."

"What do you mean?" Katie looked Avard in the eyes. "What ghost?"

He looked at her with a confused expression on his face. "You don't know? That rubble back in the mine, it was caused by an explosion years ago, a few weeks before Camp Farley opened. That rubble is where yer sister died."

## xxxviii

A cool breeze brushed through the evergreens, carrying a subtle, but pleasant, scent.

"Ah, the aroma of pine. Delightful, don't you think?" The frog stood in Jack's path and stared up at him.

"Sure. Whatever." Jack barely heard what the frog had said. "That's strange."

"What? Pine? I cannot say I agree with you, my friend. The scent of pine is common in these parts. Nothing strange about it."

"No, I mean the tracks. Look at them."

The frog hopped to a set of impressions in a patch of dirt on the path and squatted, his bulging eyes hovering an inch from the ground. "I see what you mean. They're wearing shoes." The frog looked up and grinned. "Why anyone would do that is beyond me."

"No, dummy, don't you see? There're three sets of tracks and two of them are a lot deeper than the other. Someone's with them."

"Or perhaps the light-footed one was chasing them. Happens to me all the time."

"The lighter ones overlap the others, and they're a man's shoes. We need to find them, fast." Jack eased around the frog and walked at a quick pace, the frog either walking or hopping beside him.

"Now this is a nice round stone." The frog hopped over it. "Whoa, almost walked into this sapling here. Fine tree that will make some day. Ah, here is a twig. Rather resembles my walking stick, don't you think?"

"You don't have to talk every single second of the day, in case you don't know."

"Yes, but why confine one's adventures to the prison of one's own mind when one could so easily share them and bring delight to one's companions? Whoops! Must mind my feet. Almost collided with that clump of grass."

"'Bringing delight,' so that's what you're doing?"

"No need to thank me. Goes straight to my head, you know."

Jack wagged his head. He stopped at the peak of a low hill to observe the undulating pine tree forest. A yellow warbler darted from a nearby tree and hovered in front of his face, like a hummingbird. Wherever Jack moved his gaze, the bird darted back into view. "Knock it off!" He swiped at it several times, but it always fluttered out of the way.

"It wants you to look at it," the frog said. He leaned his flimsy hand against Jack's leg and panted. "It's an attention hog, if you ask me."

"Not if I can help it."

The little bird chanced a brief glance at the frog just as Jack made a final effort to swat it away. He hardly felt its fragile body disappear against his swinging palm. Jack frowned and looked at his empty hand, then took a step back to avoid a sudden swarm of yellow birds scattering from the pines all around him. The frog moved in front of Jack and slowly shook his head, his arms folded.

"I wasn't trying to hurt it," Jack said.

The frog rolled his eyes. "Of course not. One never means to hurt something when one crushes it to oblivion with a swipe of one's fast-moving fist."

Jack looked away and attempted to rest against the white trunk of an already-leaning ash tree, but instead it tipped over and its roots ripped from the ground, tossing clods of wet soil everywhere. Jack jumped aside and stared at the toppled tree, confused and afraid. He turned his gaze toward the frog. "Tell me what is going on! Why am I having all these hallucinations? None of this is real. Frogs don't talk. Birds don't vanish, and I'm not strong enough to topple a tree. I feel like I'm dreaming, but I know I'm awake. What's happening?"

The frog just stared at Jack, its eyes bulging and its wide mouth hanging open.

"Oh, I see. Now that I actually want you to tell me something, you're speechless."

The little frog frowned. "No need to insult me. If I understand you correctly, you're saying nothing that is happening is really happening. By your most-unique mode of reasoning, therefore, what's happening is nothing. Am I right?"

Jack shook his head. "You're worthless. Let's get going." He started off again and the frog hopped after him. He glanced down at the frog. "Can't you tell me anything?"

"Indeed, I can. I'm most adept at telling people things. You're here. This is mountain-with-many-trees."

"And you're frog-with-no-clue. You aren't getting it. Here's a few theories I've worked out. Someone transported me to another planet, and you're some weird alien sent to test me."

The frog nodded. "Ah, yes, that makes sense to me. That's it."

"I don't know." Jack shook his head. "Another planet wouldn't look just like Flathead Forest. I recognize Ingalls Mountain over there to the west, and Ashley Mountain south of it. Maybe I slipped through a portal into a parallel dimension."

"Definitely." The frog nodded. "No doubt in my mind, that's the only sensible explanation."

Jack ducked below a low branch, then shook his head. "Nah, I'm not convinced. I don't care what science says, there can't be a dimension where frogs walk around talking. This doesn't even qualify as science fiction."

"True, true. 'Tisn't wise to lend much credence to scientific mumbo jumbo. Parallel dimensions, indeed. Pure blather, preposterous drivel."

Jack took a deep breath. He could no longer ignore the only explanation that made any sense. He stopped and sat on a toppled tree trunk, tensing at the sound of the rotted wood cracking and sinking a little under his weight.

"Tell me the truth, Frog. I died, didn't I? I don't feel like I'm dead. I'm starving. I'm tired. My feet hurt. But there's no other explanation." He slapped his pocket, hoping he'd find his lighter there, but there would be no flickering flame to comfort him today.

The frog stood in front of him and leaned on his walking stick, a contemplative expression on his moist amphibious face. He nodded his head. "Yes, I believe you've hit the nail on the head this time, my friend. You're most certainly dead. Dreadfully unfortunate, to be sure. But what can you do? So, it goes, as they say."

Jack stared down at the yellow wildflowers around his feet and frowned. "It's not me I'm worried about. I shouldn't have lit that fire around those explosives. I'm paying the price for my stupidity. And I took Clara and Katie with me. I killed them. They'll never forgive me." He pressed his face into his hands and surrendered to his emotions.

After a few moments of silence from the frog, it spoke. "We must run. Something is coming."

Jack waved him off. "Go ahead. I don't care anymore. I'm dead. They can't do anything to me now."

"Gah! You humans have no survival instincts. No wonder you're dead. I must go." The frog dropped its stick and hopped away at lightning speed, making for the shadows among nearby scrub oaks.

Jack looked up, then stood and stretched. A clicking noise sounded behind him.

"Don't move," said a baritone voice.

T all, yellow grass blanketed the steep hillside, sweeping through the shallow basin in front of Katie and up the low hill on the other side. She struggled to slow her descent, and Clara passed her by at an even quicker pace. They both fell against three boulders at the foot of the hill, turned, and plopped down, taking heavy breaths. The stone depressed half an inch where they sat. Avard arrived moments later, showing no signs of fatigue.

"You know you don't have to be tired, don't you?" He stood in front of the girls. "Yer not in Materia no more. All this tiredness is in yer mind. If you think you have the energy, you'll have it."

"That may be true for you," Katie said. "But I've never felt more exhausted in my life."

Avard stared at Katie and wagged his head. "I'll give you one minute, then we're off. Them knights ain't taking no rests, that's for sure."

Katie closed her eyes and took several deep breaths, then she looked at Avard. "Tell me something. You said my sister died in the mine. Is she here? Do you know where she is?"

"It ain't likely she's still around, since she got her revenge. Ghosts can't hold on to their soul once they've eliminated their whole reason for holding on to it."

"It was Abby then, wasn't it? Abby was the ghost attacking the camp."

"'Course it was. She durn blew up the research facility, too. Why you think them Ghost Knights is here? She's been trying to kill Farley since the day she died. She forced him away from his own camp the last four or five years. He only come back when he heard you was coming. He hoped you'd distract her, weaken her obsession with him. Fool thought he'd finally put a stop to her hauntings. Didn't count on her making arrangements with the Ghost Knights."

"You're saying she moved on, but it's not true. I saw her. I saw her in the mine before it exploded."

"Can't say it ain't possible she hung on fer a day or two, but I doubt them Ghost Knights would be heading out right now if they wasn't done avenging her. No, you'd do yerself a favor forgetting all about that girl. You wouldn't've liked what you saw anyhow. After all these years, she'd gone plumb crazy with hatred. She'd have done anything to kill Farley. Never thought she'd blow up a whole building, though."

"She killed Marina, then." Clara frowned at Avard.

"Nope. She didn't kill no one."

"No one?" Clara's gleeful face showed intense happiness. Katie closed her eyes and reveled in the good news.

"Farley was the only one in the facility when it blew up. Last I heard, he was in a coma. May die any minute. Yer friend, Marina, and them boys, Carl and Tony, they was found sleeping on the ground more'n a hundred feet from their cabins. We all thought they'd died, but someone carried them to safety afore the explosion."

"Who do they think saved them?" Clara couldn't hide the excitement in her voice.

"I reckon the same person who let them ghosts into the building. Somebody invited them into the restricted areas where they tore up a gas main and lit it up. Could've been anybody done it. Farley ain't got no friends."

"Was Abby right about him?" Katie looked away, scowling. "Did

Farley kill my sister?"

Avard shrugged. "It was before my time. Farley denies it. He claims she only blames him 'cause he was the only survivor. He's got the burns on his face to show fer it. He claims he loved yer sister."

"I can't believe Abby would've wanted to start a camp that tries to control people's minds," Clara said.

Avard laughed. "Yer sister never wanted that. That was all Farley's doing. Abigail was like lots of kids whose parents work for Intershroud. She learned too many secrets, so the bosses demanded her absolute allegiance. She came up with the plan to create a retreat, an isolated mountain resort where young people could live without joining Montathena Research or other Intershroud affiliates, a place where they could live in peace and not be a threat by Intershroud. Yer father talked Lynch into letting her do it."

"But Farley had different plans," Katie said.

Avard nodded and his eyes bulged in anger. "He wanted to use innocent Mentalists to visit the kids in their sleep, to alter their minds so they'd think they always wanted to join Intershroud. I wanted nothing to do with it, no matter how much they offered me, but Farley claimed he'd come up with a way to use Media's mentalist power without using up her mind. I shouldn't have believed him. It slowed down the process, but he used her so often, she went from a valedictorian to a simpleton in just five years. I should've killed Farley myself. Everyone knew he killed yer sister. It was way too convenient that he ended up with full control of the camp."

Avard's expression soured. An assault rifle formed in his hand and he leveled it at the girls. "Enough wasting time! Get up! Them knights'll be in Idaho by the time we catch up with 'em."

Katie stood and put an arm around Clara. "This is pointless. They have horses. We'll never catch up. We might as well go back and look for Jack."

"Them knights ain't in no rush. We'll find 'em. 'Sides, I saw the impressions you just made in that rock. Yer as strong as yer pal, Jack. I'm going to need them knights if I'm going to kill him. Now, keep moving."

Katie shook her head and took care to watch her footing in the tall grass of the gulley.

Clara walked beside her. "So, Mr. Farley blew up Abby and the others, in cold blood."

Avard nodded and eased around a log hidden in the grass. "Frost and Murdock wanted the mountains cleared of dangerous mine shafts, so they ordered crews to find the old silver mines. Farley joined Abby's crew. One afternoon, he led her and six others to investigate that mine back there. No one but Farley knows what really happened, but people heard the explosion for miles around. They found Farley that night, unconscious and severely burnt. The others were buried in the mine. It was much too dangerous to excavate."

"So, Farley claims it just spontaneously blew up?" Katie shook her head.

"He claimed one of the kids had a cigarette that set off the natural gasses in the mine, which set off the TNT that was lying around. I ain't convinced, but that's what he claims."

"My sister's bones are still laying there in that pile of rubble?" Katie kicked away a large pinecone in her path. "It wasn't too dangerous to excavate. I know how Montathena Research works. They just didn't want to pay for it. They could've used the tunnels we entered."

"Could be, but believe me when I say nobody knew about that entrance 'til yer pal, Jack, led us to it. We all thought the mine had totally collapsed. If Farley'd known about that other tunnel, he'd have found yer sister's haunt ages ago and destroyed it. She'd have faded away, believing she'd never get her revenge."

"I don't understand," Clara said. "How could Abby fade away? If this is the World of Spirits, where does her soul go when she fades away? Don't their souls belong here?"

Avard stopped and laughed so loudly Clara's face turned red. She stopped walking and folded her arms, staring at the ground. Katie glared at Avard. He finally calmed down.

"Young lady, who told you this was the World of Spirits?"

Jack raised his hands high in the air and turned around slowly. A short young man stared back at him, a domed helmet on his head and wearing a dirty green military uniform. A bulky pack hung on his back from straps over his shoulders and his rifle sat fixed in his arms, aimed at Jack's chest. Faint male voices rolled through the underbrush and two men, equipped like the short man, emerged from around a cluster of pines. Startled by Jack, the first man, a burly black man, dropped the cowboy hat he'd been holding and fumbled for his rifle. He circled to the left of Jack, his gun leveled at his chest. The third man, an older, lanky white man, raised his gun and took a position between the other two.

"Is this the guy General Farley's looking for?" The black man made a rapid glance at the short man standing behind Jack.

"I'm not sure," the soldier said. "He kinda looks Vietnamese, but I don't see the girls General Farley said would be with him. There are three sets of tracks besides his, but only two of them are as deep as his. I don't know who the shallow tracks belong to."

"We better take him in," the black soldier said. He turned to Jack. "Sorry to bother you, sir. We're looking for three fugitives who were caught delivering intel to Viet Cong spies. I need you to tell me your name and what business you have here."

Jack glared at the man. "I'm not Vietnamese, I'm American. And this is Montana! I don't know anything about intel."

"Your name?" The black man nodded to the older man, who then lowered his gun and pulled a strand of rope from his pack. He approached Jack and made a circle motion with his index finger, signaling Jack to turn around.

"I'm Jack Park. You have no right to treat me like this."

"Park? It's him alright. Tie him up. I'll watch him while you two find the girls. They can't be far."

The short man stepped up behind Jack. "Put your hands behind your back."

Jack hesitated, prompting the man to grab his right wrist violently and yank it behind his back. Jack yanked his hand back, surprised at how easily he'd freed it from the man's grip. The other two soldiers glanced at each other and stepped back from Jack. Their eyes widened, and they gripped their rifles tighter.

"What did you do to him?" The older soldier leveled his rifle at Jack.

Jack waved his hand behind him and took a brief glance back. The short soldier was no longer there. "I didn't do anything. It's another hallucination."

Jack looked at his hands and then at the soldiers. "Wait. What am I doing? You can't kill me. We're already dead. We're spirits. You guys died in Vietnam, right?" He lowered his hands and approached the men. They fired. Jack stiffened at the gunfire, but the bullets just bounced off his chest. They felt like tiny rocks.

"Something's wrong with the ammo!" The black man tossed his rifle down. "Grab him!" The older man rushed behind Jack and wrapped his arms around his neck and chest, then placed a booted foot against his lower left leg. Jack yanked the man's arm and it disappeared. Turning his head, he could no longer see him anywhere.

The black man pounced a second later. "You're a traitor!" He took a boxer's stance and punched hard twice at Jack's face. Each blow felt like bursts of air pressure, knocking him back a step but caused no serious pain.

Jack swung back and hit the soldier's raised left arm. The man disappeared. Jack looked around and found no one else to fight, wondering if he'd imagined the whole thing. He stopped to catch his breath, stumbled back to the fallen log, and dropped onto it.

Moments later, the frog hopped out from the shadows of the scrub oaks and grabbed a new walking stick. It stood up and grinned wide. "Well, well, my friend. I'm indeed the most fortunate of amphibians to have secured the companionship of one so powerful. Shall we continue our journey?"

Jack got to his feet. "We need to catch up with the girls. I don't know what those soldiers were about, but they were taking orders from Farley. He must've died in the explosion at the camp and now he's got people looking for us. Come on!"

Jack started off again, following the girls' tracks. He tried to walk fast but didn't have the energy to maintain a brisk pace.

"This is a very tall tree," the frog stepped around the trunk of a lodgepole pine and gazed at tufts of reddish-brown needles nestled on its high branches. "I enjoy gazing up through these branches. One can never tell what might be up there. There's a clump of pine needles. I often think it could be a prickly-rodent-who-climbs-trees. They climb trees, you know."

"You mean a porcupine?"

"Yes. Yes. What else would I mean? Ah, here we come to an incline. What? Do you hear that? Somebody is moaning most obnoxiously in that thicket." The frog pointed to the gnarly branch of a fallen tree protruding from a small patch of scrub oak.

Jack stopped to look but heard nothing. He walked to the thicket and looked around.

"No, no. Let us move on, my friend. No need to involve ourselves in the distresses of others. It tends to be contagious, you know."

"Quiet! I hear something." Jack bent over.

A miniature moan whispered through the leaves, "Help me, please.

Augh. Make them stop! Have a heart? I'm sorry for what I did. Mercy!"

Jack pushed aside a clump of leafy twigs and found a black pouch hanging and wiggling, tangled on a branch. "There's something in there." He untangled the cord and peered inside, then dropped the bag and stumbled back. A fist-sized block of carved stone rolled out of the pouch, with a tiny, shirtless man chained to it by his hands and feet. The fettered man, not more than three inches tall, had a weatherworn red face and a short gray beard. Blood stained his emaciated body. He winced and writhed in agony as pea-sized magpies circled and dived at him, pecking at his hairy chest.

The frog stretched its legs to see over the branch. "Interesting. Best leave it be. Shall we move on?"

"We've got to help him." Jack reached for the little man, prompting the tiny birds to turn their attack on his hand. He swatted at them and backed away, then nursed a dozen red welts on his hand.

The little man jerked wide-eyed stares at him. "I'll do anything you ask."

"Who did this to you?"

"What? Jeb Colton created me. Please, just help me!"

"Okay, give me a second." Jack pulled his sleeve down and wrapped his hand in the gray cotton fabric of his hoodie. The birds attacked but couldn't penetrate the cloth. Jack pulled on the chains but couldn't break them.

The fettered man slapped at Jack's hand. "Just take me back to Jeb. Put me back in the pouch and take me to Jeb."

Jack shook his head. "Is that who is with Katie and Clara?"

"I don't know. Please, just take me to Jeb."

"I have no idea who that is, but I'll take you with me." Jack grabbed the stone, careful not to hurt the little fettered man, and eased it into the velvety black pouch. The tiny birds pecked a few more times at his covered hand, then flew inside the pouch. Jack tightened the cord, tied it to his belt, and stood staring into a valley of tall yellow grass. He marched on until he came across some boulders with two depressions pressed into the top of them.

"The girls were here." Jack picked up his pace, the frog hopping alongside him.

Minutes passed, and Jack dropped against a tree to catch his breath, careful this time to not tip it over. A familiar female voice reached his ears and he darted to a wall of leafy underbrush and peeked through the leaves. A man stood there, decked out in full-body armor and holding an assault rifle. He paced back and forth in a wide clearing at the base of a steep, boulder-strewn hill. Jack searched the ground and finally saw Katie and Clara resting against the rocky mountainside, surrounded by dense green foliage.

The man glanced toward Jack but showed no sign that he'd seen him.

"It's Avard," Jack whispered. He squatted in the cover of leafy shrubs and listened to Avard's words, awaiting his chance to free the girls. The frog starting to open its mouth and Jack stretched a hand in front of him.

"If you give me away, I'm having frog legs for lunch."

Avard glared at the girls and shook his head. "It ain't possible you can be this tired. I never felt so energetic. Just think you have energy. Like I said, this is Essentia."

"I heard what you said," Katie said, "but it makes no sense. How can this be the Dream World? I've dreamed thousands of times, and never felt like this. I'm exhausted. I'm awake and I'm starving. I'm not dreaming."

"Believe what you want." Avard chuckled. "You really thought this was the Material World? That ole cave back there would've kept you trapped forever if Jack hadn't started tearing it apart. I don't know how the three of you ended up with such dream power, seeing how you dented in them rocks just by sitting on 'em. With power like the that, the cave had to get rid of Park just to save itself. Then it led you and me out just to be safe."

"You talk as if it was alive," Katie said.

"It is alive. Everything here is alive. That's what I'm saying. Everything you can see is just Essence particles clinging together in response to our thoughts. Even our own bodies, our Aspects, are only held together by our mental energy."

Clara perked up. "You're saying we can create things just by thinking about them."

"Sure. Essence particles are extremely fine, they say—finer than atoms. When we sleep, our minds can't stop thinking, so they leave our bodies and come here. Our minds think about things that happened during the day and the essence obeys our thoughts. Billions of dreamers come to Essentia every day. They dream up everything, and everything exists only to be what we dreamed it to be."

"Then why does it need our attention?" Katie stretched her neck.

"It all dissipates over time. Things in Essentia need our thoughts the same way we need food. The more attention they get, the denser they become, and the longer they can exist."

Katie watched Clara reach for a dead tree limb and snap it off the trunk. Though she could barely wrap her fingers around the branch, she easily broke it in two. She laughed, her eyes twinkling. "One thing's certain. I've never been able to do that before."

"We all have our powers," Avard said. "I could think whatever I wanted if you two wasn't here thinking something else. If I were alone though, I could turn this whole forest into an ocean. I just can't over-power yer thoughts that this is a forest."

"So, let's just think ourselves to those Ghost Knights," Katie said. "We can all agree to think that together, can't we?"

"It don't work like that. If you had the confidence to think us to them knights, you'd have thought us there already. You gotta have a lot of confidence in yer thought afore you can just think something contrary to the reality yer used to."

"I must have a lot of confidence in being heavy and strong," Clara said.

"That's how it seems. Everybody has extra confidence in some ability. I always obsessed about weapons, so mine turned out to be an ability to shape military machines and weapons."

Avard looked up and raised his arms. A subtle wisp of black smoke condensed and formed into a matt-black Apache helicopter, hovering above the treetops and bending the trees, blowing the yellowed grass in waves. Katie could see the terrain beyond Avard, showing through his now-translucent body. He lowered his hands and turned solid again. The helicopter flew higher and started circling the area.

Katie glowered at him. "You mean to tell me you can create helicopters out of thin air, and you're making us walk? We'd find those Ghost Knights in two seconds from a helicopter."

"You think I don't know that? Yer getting on my nerves. You two are leaving inch-deep footprints in solid soil. I ain't getting inside a moving vehicle with you. I'm barely holding my Aspect together as it is, and I intend to keep it 'til I know Park's dead."

"Why aren't Clara and I just like you?" Katie wrung her fists. "You say we're not acting like ghosts, so what are we? This is not just a normal dream!"

"How should I know? I reckon yer in a coma. No doubt yer lying unconscious under a ton of rock. I can't imagine they'll be digging you out, neither. You might as well accept that you'll either be ghosts soon, or yer souls'll be saying sayonara for good. Thank your pal, Park, for that. He's the one who put you in a coma."

"There's got to be a way to wake ourselves." Katie slapped her face twice.

Avard laughed. "You'd have to kill your Aspect to wake yerself up, but if you do that while yer in a coma, you'll be brain dead till you die. You see? Park killed the two of you, same as me. You have as much reason to want him dead as I do."

"He didn't set off the explosives," Katie said.

"He brought the lighter! He knocked me out! My daughter's all but brain dead 'cause of him! He'll pay for what he done. He deserves to die!" Avard aimed his automatic rifles at two lodgepole pines nearby and fired at them, eyes bulging. Shredded bark and chunks of sapwood flew in every direction until the noisy spray of bullets exposed the ragged heartwood of the trees. He lowered his guns and stared out into the open fields, a deep frown on his face.

JACK LISTENED INTENTLY to Avard's conversation with the girls when he felt tiny wet fingers wrap around his left pinky finger. He looked down and found the little frog pulling at him with all his strength.

"We must go," the frog said. "That man is insane!"

Jack shook off the frog's hand, causing the creature to fall and roll into a nearby fern.

The frog stood up, scowling. "You have the fortunate advantage of being able to come back to life after being killed, but I have but one life, I'm afraid. I'll look for you later, when you come to your senses." He hopped away, into the safety of the ferns.

Jack shook his head, then turned toward the clearing.

Avard stared back at him, his eyes wide and his mouth stiff in a wicked grin.

XLII

The attack helicopter circled behind Jack, tipped forward, and dived like a bird of prey. Its chain guns fired rapidly on its chin turrets, advancing successive explosions toward him in two lines along the ground and sending plants and soil flying into the air.

Jack leaped forward, dived over leafy shrubs, and rolled on his shoulders in the tall grass near Avard. The helicopter buzzed past Jack and curved upward, circled over the trees, and returned for its next attack.

Avard laughed, his wild eyes fixed on Jack. He lifted his arms forward, his body quivering and fading. The sharp angular form of a beige M1 Abrams tank materialized ten feet from Jack, already in motion, crushing fallen branches and scraping bark from tall tree trunks. It moved toward Jack, then slowed down. Its main gun swiveled and stopped at a point aligned between Jack's eyes.

Jack froze.

"Stop it!" Katie rushed toward Jack, Clara running a few feet behind her. Avard swung an arm toward them. Rows of taut wire materialized in their path, emanating an electric buzz, and stopping them in their tracks. Circular strands of razor wire topped the fence, stretched between ten-foot-tall wooden posts. Katie searched every direction but found no way past the wire.

Jack stood but froze again when the helicopter veered behind him at high speed, firing its guns. He rolled to his left and the main gun of the tank followed him. An identical tank appeared to his left, its main guns swiveling.

"Alright! You win!" Jack raised his hands.

"You think this is a game, Park? This is justice!"

"Leave him alone!" Katie leaned down, grabbed a palm-sized rock, and hurled it over the fence. It disappeared in the tall grass twenty feet from Avard.

He ignored her and approached Jack, assault rifles nestled in each arm. "I sure hope you're a ghost, Park. It's only right I should get to end yer life!"

"I didn't do anything to you! You attacked me! Your friend caused the explosion!"

"It was your lighter and now your body'll rot forever with mine, below a pile of rocks."

Gunfire shook the air and the assault rifles rattled in Avard's hands, emptying casings into the grass at Avard's feet. Jack recoiled, raised his hands to protect his face, and turned to look at Katie, wanting her face to be the last image he'd see in this life.

He wondered, however, why death hadn't already come. Sharp bursts of pain stung his arms, hands, chest, stomach, and legs, with a few attacking his forehead and chin. He stepped backward, compelled by the force of the mass of bullets, but soon realized he could bear the pain. The gunfire felt no different than a child pelting him with pebbles. After what seemed like several minutes, he summoned the courage to peek between his fingers. Avard's maniacal expression twisted into a look of bewilderment, followed by extreme disappointment. The gunfire stopped and he hurled his guns into the grass.

Jack lowered his hands and glanced down at the spent bullets laying scattered at his feet, bullets that hadn't even torn his clothes.

"I guess we'll need the big guns!" Avard turned to his tanks.

Jack ran, but each tank swiveled its main guns to follow him. The helicopter rotors grew louder and a third tank barreled from the trees in Jack's path.

"You can't run, murderer!" Avard laughed.

Explosions rang in Jack's ears and his feet left the ground, the massive tank in front of him disappearing behind a bright ball of orange fire. Another fiery explosion went off to his left, altered his airborne course sideways. He hit the ground, rolling through tall grass and low shrubs, stopping when his back found a pine tree, which flopped to the ground with a thump.

Jack's ears rang as he lay hidden in the yellow grass, flashes of orange brightening the sky amid loud pops. Ordinance whooshed over his face and found nearby pine trees, reducing them to burning stubs. The helicopter dived into view and released two rockets before buzzing over him. Jack rolled aside, and the rockets plowed into the earth, exploding behind him. His body left the ground, flew over the grass, and landed near the fence where Katie and Clara stood trembling, terror in their eyes.

Jack used a fence post to pull himself to his feet, rushed backward, and narrowly avoided the barbed wire that slammed in front of his feet when the fence tipped over. He rubbed a dull pain in his ribs and observed the helicopter coming around for another dive, this time not pulling up. Jack dived sideways and rolled on the ground, the helicopter crashing in the grass near him and exploding in a fiery orange ball of twisted metal and shattered glass, which rained around him and across the clearing. His face and clothes blackened with dirt and his hair disheveled, Jack pulled himself up, turned to Avard and leered at him.

Avard's mouth hung open. "How?" His arms dropped to his sides. "This is impossible! No Aspect could've endured that! Not even in a coma." He stared for a moment, then placed a hand on his stubbly beard. "That's it. That has to be it. You're not in a coma. You're neither ghost nor Aspect. You're not even asleep!"

"You're insane!" Jack limped toward Avard at an increasing pace, his face contorted with rage. "I've had enough of you!" He barreled his right shoulder into Avard's chest and sent him flying twenty feet through the air, landing with a thud against the trees he'd shot at earlier. His body faded out of view for two seconds before solidifying again.

Avard straightened himself and gave a weak smile. "I know what I'm dealing with now, boy. I thought it was a myth, but here you are. Yer Dream Running—all three of you. Don't know how you did it, but you've passed into the Dream World with yer bodies intact. You ain't tough. You just ain't made of essence like everything else in this world."

"Don't care!" Jack yelled. "Just tell us how to get back!"

Avard laughed. "You think I'm a fool, don't you, Park? This is perfect. I get to kill you after all. I don't even have to do nothing. Sooner or later, Essentia will swallow you alive."

"We'll find a way out," Katie said. "My father will help us."

Jack turned to Katie and Clara and saw them stepping with slow precision between the toppled electric wires and razor-sharp barbed coils until they reached the open field.

Avard sneered and looked up at the nearby mountainside, eyeing a wide cluster of boulders resting precariously near the hilltop. "Let's see you walk away from this!"

He squinted his eyes and tilted his head, then clenched his teeth and stretched his hands out to each side. Olive-drab wheeled platforms appeared, aligned with his arms on each side of his now nearly transparent body. Each platform supported an angular rotating metal turret that held eight slender, white missiles. The turrets swiveled until the sharp-tipped rockets aligned with the base of the boulder-strewn hillside.

Jack glared at him. "What are you doing? You'll bury us all!"

Katie and Clara started to run and signaled Jack to join them, but he saw no point in running if those rockets went off.

"Say hello to sweet justice!" Avard laughed and flicked his wrists.

All sixteen missiles hissed and smoked, then lifted from the missile launchers. In midair, however, they lost momentum, flipped, and spun around. Then, somehow transforming into liquid, they splashed against the rocks, their remains dripping between the stones.

Avard's eyebrows creased. He jerked glances at his rocket launchers, now also deforming and melting into the earth in large graygreen puddles. The three tanks out in the field morphed into blobs of greenish clay and melted into the tall grass.

"What?" Avard's body solidified again and he searched every direction for an explanation. He stopped when a stranger approached him out of the shadowy thickets.

XLIII

A scraggly man with a long, grizzled beard traipsed through the
trees in ragged patchwork clothes that gave him the look of an
old nineteenth-century prospector: dingy gray coveralls, a torn straw
hat, and an old Winchester rifle strapped to his shoulder. A black
pouch hung from his belt.

Jack felt around for the pouch he'd tied to his own hip, but found it
was gone. He'd lost it sometime during Avard's attack.

Jack's frog companion peeked around the old miner's right leg and
grinned at Jack, but ducked back behind the old man upon spying
Avard's fuming face.

Avard raised his arms forward and two more assault rifles materialized in his hands. At a flick of the stranger's left wrist, however, the
guns melted into a thick goo which oozed down around Avard's arms
and plopped in small globs onto the ground at his feet.

"Mind yer business, old fool!" Avard shook the sludge from his
arms and flung globs of it into the nearby shrubs.

The old man approached Avard, focusing intensely on his face, his
feeble hands outstretched. "Methinks it durn unkindly of ye to go on
like that. I cain't allow ye to bring harm to these young'uns, that be
certain."

Avard started to fade, warning Jack that he was forming another military weapon somewhere. Sure enough, another drab green tank appeared behind the old stranger. The old man stretched an arm behind himself and the armored vehicle transformed into a gelatinous mass that dropped into the grass.

Avard scowled and wheeled his left arm to his side for another attack, but his body dropped suddenly until only his head remained visible above the grass line.

"Ye've had yer diversion, me friend." The old man waved his hands and four granite slabs shot up from the ground around Avard. A horizontal slab appeared and slammed hard on top of Avard's sunken prison cell.

"Jeb Colton!" Avard's muffled voice yelled. "Let me out of here! So help me, I'll kill you! Don't think I won't!"

"Sorry, me friend. Ye cain't convince me these younguns offered ye any harm. This here frog told me all. He told me this boy be a might simple, and it don't take a genius to see these young lasses be as innocent as babes."

"Yer taking info from a stupid dreamed-up frog?"

"Tis certain these younguns be a dreamin', if ever I seen it. Let 'em dream in peace. Save yer vengeance for the deservin'."

"Colton! Yer a ghost! You know I deserve my revenge. Let me out of here!"

"The Ghost Knights'll be returning afore long to set you free. Revenge be their line o' work."

Avard continued pleading, but Jeb ignored him. He turned to Clara and stared at her motionlessly for half a minute, his eyes softening and a subtle smile peering from behind his grizzled mustache. He turned to Katie and Jack. "Don't be afeared. I'll protect ye from the likes of this scoundrel. Follow me." He waved his hand and a stretch of tall grass vanished in a long line in front of him, creating a narrow path. He walked forward, glancing back to make sure Jack and the girls were following him. "Best o' luck to ye, sir," he said to Avard.

Katie and Clara ran to Jack with outstretched arms, but he put up his hands and pointed at his aching ribs.

Katie held Clara back from hugging him. "You must be covered in bruises."

"I can't believe you survived all that," Clara said.

Jack nodded. "I'm just glad I found you. I don't know what I'd have done if anything had happened to you."

"We thought you died." Katie's voice cracked.

Jack patted her arm. "If we don't get back to our world soon, you won't be wrong." He limped past Clara, Katie, and the frog until he arrived at Jeb's side. "Is it true, you're a ghost? Do you have a haunt? Avard said we're Dream Running. We need a haunt, so we can return home."

Jeb grinned at him. "Tis easy to be fooled in a dream, me friend. Ye can make any thought become true. Don't be listenin' to that ol' rascal. Tis certain ye're dreamin'. I'll wake ye if ye needs proof." Jeb raised the steel barrel of his rifle toward Jack and Jack pushed it back down, his heart beating fast.

"No. No. You don't understand. Avard was telling the truth. We *are* Dream Running. It's the only thing that makes sense. Look at our footprints. We're Material. We came here through a haunt, somehow. If you won't take us to one, we'll have to head back to that mine and try to force that mountain to let us in."

"Ye cain't reason with a mountain, that be certain. I ask ye to trust an old miner who's been wandering these woods for more than a century. Ye dreamed them deep tracks along with everything else. But I suppose, if it calms ye troubled mind, I can lend ye me own haunt."

✕

KATIE, Clara, and Jack followed the ghost of Jeb Colton through the forest, sharing with each other their stories of what had happened to them since they separated back at the cave. Katie soon grew impatient, not knowing when they'd arrive at the haunt. She looked ahead and smiled at the weirdness of the situation. Jack massaged his bruised ribs and limped along a few feet in front of her, leaning on an old crutch Jeb had formed for him. Clara walked in front of him, a skip in her step and chatting with a little frog that had taken residence on her shoulder, its feeble left arm holding tight to her golden hair. The two seemed meant for each other, Clara laughing at whatever the frog was saying to her, and the frog grinned wide, basking in her undivided attention.

Then there was Jeb, a century-old miner leading the way to his haunt and singing an old folk song while controlling matter around him without hardly giving it a conscious thought. He flicked his left wrist, and a large rock on the trail in front of him vanished into the dirt. He approached a depression, gouged by a long-gone creek, and waved his right hand. A thick pink slab of sandstone appeared, bridging the depression mere seconds before he arrived to walk across it. Now and then, the old man would swing a hand behind his back and the terrain behind him would return to its former shape, erasing all footprints or any other evidence he'd seen there.

Katie quickened her pace, offering Jack a smile as she passed him. He looked up, about to speak, but instead winced and looked down, then rubbed his sore side. Katie clenched her teeth to show some empathy for him, then moved on to Clara's side.

"This is what life is all about, my good friend," the frog said to Clara. "Walking and talking and staying close to someone who can encase your enemies in a box of solid rock."

Clara laughed. Katie smiled and pushed on to catch up with Jeb, whose singing continued:

> "Sellin' my soul for a vein o' silver,
> Moon shines down on the lazy river,
> Fix'n my meal and a cot for dreamin',
> Tomorrow, her heart'll be mine..."

He stopped singing when Katie stepped up to him, then came to halt and leaned toward her on his walking stick. "Good day, miss. What cain I do fer ye?"

She took a moment to catch her breath and rested her hands on her hips. "Back there, you said the Ghost Knights were coming back.

Are they coming to help Abby? Is she still here? She's my sister. You might know her as Abigail."

Jeb pursed his chapped lips and looked at her, raising an eyebrow. Jack and Clara caught up to them and stood waiting for his response.

"Aye, I know the ghost they call Abagail. Ye best let her be, miss."

"But she's my sister."

Jeb wagged his head slowly. "Breaks me heart to say it, miss, but the sister ye knew is no more. 'Tis certain what's left o' her shall bring ye not but sorrow. Her soul already was nigh at rest 'til it were rumored that the vermin, Farley, returned to these woods. The knights be returning to finish him off, then yer Abagail will be no more. As I says, let her be."

Katie smiled. "I can't just ignore her. Can you take us to her?"

Jeb shook his head. "Sorry, miss. She roams where she pleases."

"Could the Ghost Knights take us to her? That's what they're here for, isn't it?"

"Ye've much to learn 'bout ghosts, me friend. They won't be doing ye no favors. Revenge is what matters to them—and yer sister is like-minded. If we run across them, 'tis certain they'll wake ye. They won't be hindered, even fer their own kin."

"You have to take us to her."

Jeb stared at Katie for a second, then glanced down at the black pouch hanging from his belt. He grabbed it and squeezed it hard, yanked open the tie string, and pulled out the little fettered man and dangled him by his head. Jeb shook the little figure violently, his eye's dark with hate, his face reddened and contorted, and his teeth clenched.

Katie gasped and her hands flew to her face, the change in Jeb's demeanor hardly registering as possible.

"What are you doing?" Clara's eyes bulged.

The little fettered man kicked and writhed, moaning in agony, the weight of the heavy stone stretching his arms and arching his back. The tiny magpies swarmed around him and pecked at his face and bared chest without mercy.

"Stop! Please let me go," said his tiny voice. "Forgive me, please."

"That's the pouch I found." Jack pointed at it and glared at Jeb. "What's wrong with you? What is that?"

XLIV

Jeb looked at each of the teenagers in turn, his face ashen, and a kindly grin returned to his face.

"I saw that pouch fall from your belt when you leaped over a hedge," the frog said to Jack. "I came across Mr. Colton later and told him where it was. Old acquaintance of mine, you know."

"'Tain't real," Jeb said. He shook the tiny man one more time and shoved him and the stone block back into the pouch, the birds flying in on their own. "Sorry I had to show ye that, but it had to be done. Ghosts is all that be ugly in this world. Even I cain't escape what I became when I died."

"But it's so awful," Clara said.

"'Tain't more awful than what that vermin did to me little Alice. The little man in this pouch be me son-in-law, or rather, I created it to look like the ol' scoundrel. He deserves everything I can think on to torture him. He killed me little granddaughter, then killed me when I tried to make him pay fer it. I need this pouch to stay a ghost. If ever I quit a-thinkin' on what that monster did to her, 'tis certain I'll fade away. I cain't hold meself together without thinkin' on it."

"Then maybe you should move on," Clara said. "It's just too horrible."

Jeb frowned. A stone appeared behind him, at just the right height to sit on, and he sat down. "I don't expect ye to understand, miss. Ye wasn't there that night. I returned home early and heard a curious noise in me attic, a whimperin' sound. I took me rifle, went up the stairs, and there he was, the husband o' me oldest daughter, a demon if there ever was one, standin' by me little Alice. I cain't tell ye what I saw, 'tis certain to bring ye nightmares to the end o' ye days. There be me little Alice, a layin' there, nigh dead. I raised me rifle, but that devil be quicker than an old man. Never saw what he hit me with."

"And you became a ghost," Clara said.

"That be certain. I dreamed, but I had no other thought than to save me little Alice. I forced meself back to that room and saw me own body layin' there dead on the floor. That devil took one look at me and high-tailed it like a coward, leavin' me little Alice to die alone in that dreary attic. There I stayed, at me haunt, watchin' me daughter collapse over me, me Alice in despair, watchin' them take me own body away, watchin' them take her innocent little body away forever. There I waited, day after day, for the smallest hope of avenging her. Never saw that devil again."

Clara frowned and placed a hand gently on Jeb's shoulder. He held it tight.

"It's too horrible to imagine," Katie said. "It's got to be destroying you inside."

"That it has done, miss. I don't deny it. That be my point. Nary a ghost exists that hasn't been destroyed inside."

"But that happened a century ago," Jack said. "He had to have died decades ago."

"'Tis true. I suppose I could move on if I had proof he died in some horrible way, but I cain't let go o' the hope that he could still be around here somewhere, wanderin' about like me, as a ghost."

"So, you came up with that pouch, so you could look for him," Katie said.

"Them Ghost Knights taught me that trick. They heard rumors of a haunted house in these parts and paid me a visit. They taught me to shape this pouch, so I could think on me revenge anywhere, without having to stay near me haunt. Certain, 'tis nothin' to be proud of."

"We better keep moving," Jack said. "I'm not feeling too good."

"Cain't say I disagree." Jeb stood and the rock he was sitting on disappeared. The frog laid back against Clara's hair and she followed Jeb. Katie moved aside so Jack could walk in front of her.

Jeb looked back as he walked. "Perhaps I should've told ye, there's been other Aspects a searchin' fer ye."

"I know," Jack said. "I met some soldiers earlier."

"They be soldiers a dreamin'. Them scoundrels at Farley's camp find old soldiers and make 'em think they're fighting a war just to get 'em to do their work for them. There be others searchin' for ye as well. Some o' yer kin, I gathered."

"My kin?" Jack stopped walking.

"I come across some strangers. Looked to be of the orient. They were flying through the sky like a flock o' pigeons, then they landed aside o' me and said they were lookin' fer a boy by the name o' Jack Park. Do I gather rightly, that be you?"

Jack nodded and looked at Katie. They both knew who they might be. "They were looking for me?" He limped to Jeb's side.

"'Tis certain, nothin' to be concerned about, Master Park. They told me they was concerned fer ye. Cain't say where they flew off to."

Jack shook his head. "Before I came to camp, I was having nightmare about an old Oriental woman and her followers. They're not my friends."

Katie rushed to Jack's side and wrapped her arm around his back. "They won't have me tied up this time. We'll face them together if they show up."

"I'm here, too," Clara said.

"Let's just get out of here," Jack said.

"That, we can do." Jeb stared at Clara for a moment and turned.

"Why do you keep doing that?" Katie turned to Jeb. "You keep staring at Clara."

"Me apologies, miss. I meant no harm. It's just that, your Clara looks just like me little Alice. Dead ringer she is. Truth be told, 'twas her that convinced me to take ye to me haunt. I wouldn't have done it otherwise."

The frog jerked suddenly on Clara's shoulder, then stood up and stared off to their right, into the trees. "Someone's coming. I suggest we make haste for the shrubs."

Jeb turned to Katie. "'Tis good luck to have a Nightmare round when ye be on the run. They have extraordinary senses. Shall we move faster, or do ye want me to wake you up?" He half raised his rifle.

"Let's keep moving," Katie said.

They marched on for another ten minutes, everyone lost in their own thoughts except the frog, who never stopped talking. "Ah, we approach a clearing. Watch for hawks. They're carnivorous, you know."

"How about you worry about hawks!" Jack jabbed his crutch into the soil. "We'll worry about being hunted by a sadistic old woman's cult, an army of oblivious troops with guns, a revenge-obsessed squadron of Ghost Knights, and a blood-thirsty ghost that can create attack vehicles out of thin air."

Katie frowned at him.

"I'm sorry," Jack said. "I'm just so tired. I'm hungry, my ribs hurt, and I keep losing my breath. I'm stressed out, and that frog just keeps jabbering on, like we want the whole forest to know where we are."

"We're all stressed," Katie said. "Let's catch up to Jeb and see if he'll let us rest a few minutes."

"Maybe he knows where we can get something to eat." Clara skipped along the narrow trail to catch up with him.

Heavy tree growth sandwiched the pathway. Jeb stopped at the top of the inclining path where the tree line ended and leaned on his walking stick, scanning the open forest in front of him. Jack and Katie caught up to him and Clara.

They stood at a flattened ridge where they could see for miles. To their left, the receding tips of pine trees poked up from the sunken terrain of a deep ravine. Katie welcomed the peaceful gargling of an unseen river she heard rolling along the base of the ravine. Straight ahead, a thin line of chimney smoke rose beyond the distant trees before a backdrop of hazy mountains. To their right, larch trees and lodgepoles formed a ring around a vast open meadow.

A hawk glided above the waving yellow grasses, curved upward, and darted over the gulley to their left.

"Yonder be Silverton." Jeb pointed at rising smoke. "Won't be long now, if ye can stay asleep another hour."

The frog stood up and leaped from Clara's shoulder, then circled in front of Jeb. "The riders are coming!" He stared back down the trail. "They have that Avard fellow with them."

XLV

Jack stared down the trail but couldn't see anyone. He leaned over to address the little frog. "You sure it's the Ghost Knights?"

"Are you blind?" If frogs had eyebrows, he would've been raising them at him. "There's a black mist emerging from the trees. How do you dreamers survive? We need to run. There's a river down this hill. If we hurry, we can jump in it and hide under the rocks."

"We're not frogs," Jack said.

"Them Knights have no business with us. 'Tis certain Mr. Avard's bringing them. Ye may have to head to Silverton without me. I'll make ye a hideout." Jeb looked around, then focused on a low mound in the meadow ten feet to his right. "This spot'll do."

"They'll see us for miles around," Jack said.

"No one'll think to look for ye out in the open." Jeb held his arms forward and squinted his eyes. The tall grass faded away on the mound in a ten-foot-wide circle, and the exposed soil sunk four feet straight down, creating a cylindrical impression in the earth. The domed crown of a huge buried boulder, covered with patches of orange lichen, appeared over the hole, its edges digging into the surrounding terrain. No one could've guessed the boulder hadn't lain buried there since the dawn of time.

"You're good," Jack said. "Avard kept fading away when he created things. You don't do that."

"You learn a few tricks wandering Essentia nigh on to a century. That rock may look solid, but it's actually thinner than a cow's hide. Hardly took an ounce o' me essence. No more squawking now. I shaped this hideout just fer the three o' ye."

"What about you?" Clara's face showed concern.

"Avard knows I'm taking ye to me haunt. I'll have to convince them knights I have no interest in ye. You'll have to head there without me. My haunt be in the attic of the grandest house on the main street, an old clapboard home, dull blue in color. When I'm gone, head toward that smoke. The river'll lead ye to it."

"Avard will try to hurt you," Katie said.

"I can deal with him. Now make haste. Climb into the hideout."

The frog hopped onto the stone, stomped three times, and turned around frowning. "Not to put too fine a point on it, but I've found hiding on top of solid rocks to be less than effective."

"That hideout taint fer you, frog. Get on down to the river and hide. Them horses will notice the tiniest sounds, and from what I've been hearin', ye ain't nothin' if not a noisemaker."

The frog glared at Jeb for a few seconds, then nodded and gave him a wry smile. "They're almost here." He scurried down the hill in lengthy leaps.

"Alright, young'uns, be quick. I know it looks solid, but the three of ye can step right on through it. Careful now."

Jack limped to the rock and attempted to step onto it, his foot landing on nothing but air. He dropped his crutch, flailed his arms, and fell through the stone lid, landing four feet down on his hands and knees onto a hard granite floor. He rolled onto his side and found a stone ledge along the perimeter of the circular space, just right for sitting on. He slid his hand over the soft brown, black, and white rabbit furs that covered the floor. Looked up, he saw only the yellow-gray overcast sky, the lid being invisible from below.

"You alright there, Master Jack?" Jeb peered down at him, though Jack knew he saw nothing but rock.

"I'm fine." Jack stood up straight, a sheepish expression on his reddened face, his upper half protruding above the stone. Clara and Katie grinned and looked at each other, prompting Jack to look down at his chest. He smiled too, realizing how odd he looked with nothing but a legless torso sitting on a slightly domed stone.

"This is awesome," Jack said.

"Hurry now!" Jeb patted Clara and Katie on their backs. "If they see you, we're done fer. I'll have to wake ye."

Clara and Katie approached the stone lid and sat on the edge, their legs disappearing through the rock. They then jumped the remaining few feet into the cylindrical chamber, their heads still visible above the lid.

"They're here," Jeb said. "Duck down and make ye selves comfortable. Don't make a peep. If it be in the cards, I'll meet ye at me haunt."

Jack sat down on the ledge and Katie sat next to him, Clara taking a seat on the other side of Katie. Subtle protrusions along the false stone lid rose up just enough to allow them to see what was happening above ground. Clara smiled wide when Jeb stepped onto the stone above them. He seemed to be walking in the air.

Jack motioned the girls not to make a sound. A rolling black mist billowed through the trees from the trail and concealed the hooves of the black steeds that galloped noiselessly toward Jeb. A paralyzing fear enveloped Jack. He couldn't have made a sound if he wanted to.

The riders wore blackened steel helmets held aloft by the sinuous strands of their dark bodies—strands that moved, stretched, and twisted in the air. Sharp metal gauntlets encased their huge hands, their feet melding with the mist. The horses circled around Jeb, many of them hovering above the hideout before coming to a stop. The lead rider approached Jeb and turned his shadowy face toward him.

Avard rode up next to the leader and pointed at Jeb, his lower legs hidden in the dark mist. He dismounted and strutted up to Jeb, putting his face within inches of Jeb's grizzled beard. "Where are they?"

"You mean them young'uns?" Jeb shook his head. "They done woke up ages ago."

"Liar! They're Dream Running and you know it. Where're they hiding?" Avard looked around, stopping in turns to study every patch of trees where someone could be concealed.

Jeb looked up at the lead rider. "Good day to ye, Master Ezekiel. I see ye found the gift I left fer ye. I caught this feller bringin' terror down on a few young'uns a-dreamin'. He thinks he's a ghost, but he ain't got the haunt to prove it."

"I was killed at Abigail's haunt, you fool. Jack Park murdered me. Tell me where you're hiding him, or I'll tear you to pieces!"

"Ye hear that, Ezekiel? This wingnut thinks he can kill an Aspect. Tis certain he just wants to feed off their fear. Every child deserves a sweet dream."

"They're not dreamers!"

"Like I said, they done woke up, fer the love o' Pete."

Avard bolted at Jeb, wrapped his hands around his neck and shaking him. He lowered his right hand long enough to form a pistol in it. Before he could fire it, however, the Ghost Knight nearest to Ezekiel wheeled his long wooden lance toward Avard and a dark gray mist shot at him from its tip. Gray fog engulfed Avard's body and he shot ten feet into the air, his arms and legs stretched taut by chains of smoke that pulled him into the shape of an X. His pistol dropped from his outstretched fingers and clanked into the ground.

# XLVI

Jack knew no one could see through the stone lid above him, but that didn't make him feel any less anxious, staring up at a man who wanted him dead.

Avard couldn't budge. "Let me go!"

"Thou shalt not harm the old man." Ezekiel's powerful deep voice echoed throughout the clearing. "We of the Emend Delegation have need of his haunt. Destroy him and thou shalt perish."

"Fine. Fine. I'll leave him alone. I just want my revenge! You people swore to help ghosts like me. Make him tell me where them rodents ran off to!"

"Mr. Colton is a man of his word," Ezekiel said. "Thou seeketh a boy who slept and hath now awoken."

"He's a liar! They're Dream Runners. They're Material beings."

"Cease with this absurdity!" Ezekiel turned his steed toward Avard. "A Material body cannot survive in Essentia. 'Tis clear that thou art mad."

"So, what if I am? You're the Ghost Knights of the Emend Delegation—sworn to bring peace to the souls of all ghost-kind. Park killed me, and I deserve your services as much as that Abagail woman does."

Jeb chuckled. "What's wrong with ye? 'Tis certain ghosts cain't get no vengeance by wakin' little Sleepers. Material bodies cain't be a wanderin' about in Essentia. They'd die. Plumb crazy, that is."

"Idiots!" Avard shook his body. "Y'all swore an oath! Even if he is an Aspect, what's that to you? I'm telling you, I'll be at peace if I can get my revenge on him as he is right now. Let me go! Fulfill your oaths!"

"I remain inclined to believe the boy hath awoken, as testified by the honorable Mr. Colton," Ezekiel said. "Nevertheless, 'tis sooth that the Emend Delegation has vowed to bring peace to the souls of our ghosted brethren. I hereby grant thee our aid."

Ezekiel waved a hand to the knight with the smoke-emitting lance. The smoke dissipated, and the knight returned his lance to his side.

Avard cried out and dropped to the ground, landing hard on his feet before falling on his hands and knees. He groaned, pulled himself up and brushed dirt from his hands. "Let's get on with it then. What do I got to do to kill a Dream Runner? I know you know what to do."

"Think this through, Master Ezekiel" Jeb said. "Yer feedin' the delusions of a madman, 'tis certain."

Ezekiel gazed at Avard. "The delegation consents to assist thee only upon thine vow of allegiance unto me. Shall I recite the terms?"

"I couldn't care less about yer terms. Stop wasting time! Just tell me how to kill that boy before he finds his way back to Materia."

"'Tis agreed then. The Emend Delegation hereby binds itself to thee."

Ezekiel leveled his lance at Avard. A black cloak enveloped his body, melding with it, and splitting it apart into sinuous strands of ethereal cloth. Black chainmail wrapped around his arms and legs and sharp black gauntlets with spiked metal knuckles formed around his hands. A tall metal helmet encased his head, the angled visor covering his eyes. An ebony steed ascended from the dark soil below him, clouded in black vapor and raising him up on its back.

Avard yanked off his helmet and grinned with evil delight.

"Thou art now a Delegate," Ezekiel said. "Our oath binds us to avenge thee."

Avard nodded.

"Forget not, however, that thou art likewise bound to our cause."

"Goody. Now let's get moving. I know Park's nearby somewhere. Force that old specter to tell us where he went."

Jeb sighed. "They went where all Sleepers go when they wakes up, ye durn donkey's patoot."

Avard started to speak, but Ezekiel hushed him, raising a hand in front of his face. The Ghost Knights raised their lances to their sides in unison, preparing for a battle. The high-pitched whistle of a chickadee sounded through the trees behind Ezekiel. He nodded to two nearby riders who then turned their horses around and charged down the trail. Moments later, they returned with two other Ghost Knights in tow.

"Ezekiel," a female knight reported, "the situation is critical. This area will be swarming with Sleepers in minutes, mostly American soldiers, puppets of Lynch and his crew. They're searching for two girls and a boy."

"Don't mind them," Avard said. "They only care about the Frost girl. They want Park dead almost as much as I do. If they get to him first, I'll consider your vows broken."

"We shall grant thee vengeance when it best serves our purposes," Ezekiel said.

"What?!"

"We cannot avenge thee with dead ghosts. Intershroud knows nothing of honor. I shall not sacrifice my brethren by crossing them. We shall wait them out at the stronghold."

"My revenge takes priority! You're under oath!"

"We are not sworn to die for thee," Ezekiel said.

"Them puppet soldiers will leave us alone! They're just sheep. I demand we find Park."

Three lance tips leveled at Avard's chest and Ezekiel raised his own lance toward him.

"You obey me now. We shall hunt for the boy when the forest is safe." Ezekiel looked at Jeb. "As always, we offer thee our protection."

"I'll be okay."

"No, he won't," Avard said. "He don't want to follow you 'cause he wants to take them kids to his haunt the second you leave. I say we head to his haunt and wait for them."

Ezekiel stared at Jeb, waiting for a response.

Jeb shook his head. "Durn fool. If it'll ease ye minds, 'tis fine with me hiding out in ye stronghold. I ain't got no death wish neither. Give me a durn horse."

A Ghost Knight near Jeb held out a hand and a gray mare materialized next to Jeb. The old miner admired it for a few seconds before hefting himself onto its back.

"Fine ol' mare. Always wished I could shape an animal like this."

Ezekiel clicked his tongue, guiding his horse down the mountain pass into the ravine. "Giddyap," Jeb said. He and the squadron of Ghost Knights rode after Ezekiel.

"You cowards!" Avard threw his helmet and it bounced along the stone above Jack. "No wonder y'all was murdered. I ain't takin' no orders from you!"

He turned his steed in the opposite direction and kicked his feet against its sides. He'd only ridden a few paces, however, when his horse bucked up and wouldn't take another step. The strands of Avard's body twisted and pulled apart, stretching him ten feet into the air. Streaks of light and dark-red blood flashed through the tendons of his body, his arms and legs flailing around and his head sliding sideways, swallowed up by the elastic rolls of his uncontrolled body.

He shrieked in agony and kicked at the horse with wild swings of his nearly dismembered feet, finally persuading the animal to turn back around. Upon moving in the correct direction, Avard's body condensed and reassembled. He slumped over the mane of his steed and yelled out in anguish, gasping for breath, his arms hanging limp.

One Ghost Knight remained, his arms folded and facing Avard. "Thou art bound to Ezekiel now, and to the Emend Delegation," he said. "You heard the Master's command. Obey him or perish." He handed Avard his helmet, turned, and charged down the trail after his leader.

"Augh!" Avard shot his helmet to the ground a second time, letting it roll into the tall grass. "Jack Park! I know you're here somewhere.

Don't think this is over! It'll never be over! I'll find you! I'll get my revenge!" He gritted his teeth and led his steed down the path.

Jack stood still for a minute before daring to budge, not sure if he'd breathed the whole time the knights were there. He turned to Katie and Clara. "I've never been so terrified in my life. Did you hear Avard? Everyone wants me dead. First Ming and Travis turn on me, then Avard freaks out. Now the whole Intershroud can't wait to kill me. This is insane. What did I do? I didn't do anything to anybody. I just want to hide right here for the rest of my life."

"We'll find Jeb's haunt." Katie placed a hand on his shoulder.

Approaching voices caught Jack's attention and he and the girls peeked above ground level, careful to keep their heads below the domed stone lid. Jack searched the meadow for the source of the voices. Men emerged from the trees by the dozens, hiking through the tall grass in their military camouflage and searching every inch of the meadow, rifles clutched in their hands.

Jack grew anxious when two of the soldiers beelined toward the rock lid of their hideout. They marched onto the dome and stopped directly above him, taking advantage of the elevated location as an ideal spot from which to survey the area. Jack's eyes widened when he recognized Derek, panning the terrain with his binoculars, donned in the uniform of an Army Officer.

"This is sweet," said the short, younger man next to him. Katie turned to Jack, her eyebrows raised. Jack shook his head, wondering how Tony had survived the explosion. He was the last person Jack expected to see. "It's so awesome commanding real soldiers." Tony laughed and took hold of Derek's binoculars, but Derek yanked them away, glaring at him.

Tony snarled. "Why didn't you tell us about Intershroud when we first arrived at camp? It's Jack's fault, isn't it? Idiots like him always ruin things. Why would anyone not want this kind of power in their dreams? That dork totally died for nothing."

"Shut up, Tony," Derek said. "We don't know Jack's dead. And if he is, he may have been a fool, but at least he died standing for something. It's better than you or I'll ever do."

# XLVII

Jack laid on the soft bed of rabbit furs, his hands under his head, wondering when Derek and Tony would leave the roof of his hiding place. The last thirty minutes had felt like hours. The two had done little more than stand around with their hands in their pockets, watching the soldiers do all the work—searching all around rocks and logs, scanning the upper reaches of tall trees, and pulling aside the branches of bushes and pines, all in search of Katie, Clara, and himself.

No one thought to search under the vast boulder below Derek and Tony's feet. Jack understood how Jeb had survived so many years as a ghost—the old man knew how to hide.

He glanced over at Katie, who lay near him, her eyes studying every inch of the hideout walls. She clearly wanted to get moving as much as Jack did. The wait was no problem for Clara, whose mouth hung open and eyes were shut. She'd fallen asleep.

Moving shadows on the floor told Jack that two more soldiers had arrived, and he looked up and saw a black woman with her hair in a bun and an unarmed Asian boy. Katie grabbed Jack's arm, her eyes wide. Barbara and Ming stood above them.

"Our patrols have searched the other side of the ravine," Barbara said. "They're not there."

"They have to be here somewhere," Derek said. "A surveillance hawk spotted them in this exact area, talking to an old resident ghost."

"Maybe it didn't see their actual Aspects," Ming said. "In Essentia, anybody could've dreamed up a version of them. I think we're wasting our time. They couldn't have survived that explosion at the mine."

"Lynch insists it was them," Derek said. "He thinks they're ghosts, but I'm not so sure. It's way too rare to become a ghost. It takes insane levels of raw emotion. It just isn't going to happen to three people at once."

"Five, if you count Avard and that bald guy who was with him," Barbara said. "I heard another bird spotted Avard riding with a group of ghosts a quarter mile from here."

"They're all in a coma," Tony said, "dreaming until they die."

Barbara and Ming frowned and looked at each other, then Ming turned his gaze downward, his brow furrowed and eyes darting about. Jack tensed, thinking Ming could somehow see him through the stone lid, but then relaxed. Ming's expression told Jack that Media hadn't completely turned Ming and Barbara into his enemies.

"Maybe Avard or that old ghost woke them up," Barbara said.

"I hope not," Derek said. "I don't want to think what they'll suffer if they wake up, trapped below all that rubble. We need to find that old ghost and talk to him. Barbara, I want you and Ming to take your Sleepers to Silverton. The ghost's name is Jeb Colton. Find him. Tony and I'll head northwest along the river where they sighted Avard."

Barbara nodded, tapped Ming on the shoulder, and signaled him to follow her. The two of them jogged away. Derek walked away in another direction and Tony ran to catch up with him.

Jack lay still for another five minutes, wanting to be sure the soldiers were long gone before trying anything. Katie rolled on her side and faced Jack, her head resting on her arm. She dangled a gold, heart-shaped locket in front of her face and followed its swing with her sparkling brown eyes half-closed.

"Have you given any thought to a prime token?" Jack broke the silence.

Katie let the locket drop into her hand, then looked into Jack's eyes. "I think I have enough to think about right now."

"We'll need to be able to control our dreams when we get back. You need a prime token, like that locket, so when you dream about it, you'll remember you're dreaming."

"I've never dreamt about my locket, that I can remember. Maybe my cellphone would work better."

"That should work." Jack laid back and stared at the sky. "I never imagined ghosts live in the same world where we dream. I wonder if everyone comes here when they die."

Katie shook her head. "Avard said only the ones who are dreaming when they die come here, and then, only if they are emotionally distraught."

Katie spent the next few minutes explaining everything Avard had told her: who the Ghost Knights were; how a haunt was created; how obsession with vengeance kept ghosts alive; how Marina, Carl, and Tony had survived the explosion; and how Farley had murdered her sister, Abby.

Jack watched her the whole time with admiring eyes. When she finished, she lay back and closed her eyes. He kept staring at her, wishing he could spend forever with her like this, but he knew better. He knew she'd disappear from his life forever once they made it back to Materia. She and Clara would return home to the protection of her father and he'd be left to face Intershroud alone.

Katie's hand dropped on the rabbit furs. She'd fallen asleep. Jack yawned and considered waking her but changed his mind. They wouldn't find a safer place than this to take a nap. He wondered what she might be dreaming, if it was even possible to dream while sleeping in the dream world.

*What if the minds of dreamers in Essentia escape to some other dream world when they slept?* Whatever the case, he resolved to stay awake in case something weird happened.

# XLVIII

Jack stood in the tall grass near the hideout, scanning the meadow of the verdant ravine for any sign of Intershroud. Two chipmunks chattered and skittered along a half-rotted log, then darted up a dead pine tree. Three crows glided over him, one cawing at him as it flew southward after the other two. Movement a hundred feet down the mountainside startled him, and he eased down the slope for a better look.

*Katie? How'd she slip past me?*

She stood next to a spruce tree, her head down and a frown on her face. A wrinkled old woman stood before her, dressed in tattered, dirty rags. The old woman stood with her back bent over and her disheveled gray hair hanging down to her knees. She shook her head at Katie and ogled her with sallow, sunken, half-closed eyes. Jack figured she was some ghost relative of hers.

"You'll get yourself killed." The women snarled, exposing her long yellow teeth. She shoved a gnarled finger in Katie's face. "Who do you think you are—trying to be a hero? You're weak. Stupid, stupid child. You know I speak the truth!"

Katie nodded.

"What are you thinking, traipsing around these woods without your father? Tell me you'll contact him as soon as you can."

Katie nodded briskly.

Jack jogged down a shallow hill next to her. "Who is this?" He glared at the old woman.

Katie jerked her head and flinched, then smiled. "Jack, you startled me."

He started to repeat the question, but the woman had vanished. "What? Where'd she go?"

"Who? Come on. We need to hurry." Katie ran to him. "We must've slept for hours. I feel so much better."

Jack realized he also felt much lighter and full of energy. "Huh. I don't remember sleeping. But you're right. I feel pretty good, too."

"Let's get moving then. Jeb said to go this way, toward Silverton." She skipped down the hill through the tall grass.

"Wait up! What about Clara?" Jack hurried after her, surprised at how fast she could skip. "Are you sure you weren't speaking to an old woman just now?"

"Keep an eye out for Derek and his Sleeper soldiers!" Katie started to run, then she stopped cold.

Jack stopped, too, his mind so muddled by fear, he could hardly accept what he saw approaching through the trees. Dozens, if not hundreds, of dark, gorilla-like creatures grunted and growled, leaping across the ground or gliding through the air on leathery bat-like wings. Others swung through the trees, grasping branches with precision with their feet or hands. Crows soared among them, sometimes landing on their shoulders. More creatures arrived by the minute, surrounding Jack and Katie on every side, in every tree and every shrub, pounding the earth with their massive fists. Their long ears stretched back when they flashed their canine fangs. Jack shuddered at their malevolent faces. They looked more human than ape.

"Stay away!" Katie stretched her hands in front of her and screamed, then backed toward Jack.

"They can't hurt us! We're Dream Running. Kick them and they'll disappear."

Katie nodded, but screamed again when two of the winged ape-men pounced at her. The first one wrapped an arm around her waist and tossed her over the right shoulder of the other. The creature held her tight, ran three steps, and launched into the air with a few flaps of its massive wings. It was then that Jack recognized the beasts. They were the same creatures that had appeared at Camp Farley.

Jack flinched when a beast landed in front of him with a loud thud. Jack gave it a swift kick in the chest, but rather than disappearing, it merely snarled and gnashed its teeth. Two more creatures took to the air and landed near Jack, their feet kicking dust into the air.

Before Jack could respond, a man with a long white beard jumped in front of him and jabbed a thick brown stick into the ground, using it to propel himself into the air. His feet made contact with the two nearest ape-men, knocking them ten feet backward. The man jumped again, spinning around and landing in front of Jack, facing away from him.

The ape-men slowed down, their eyes fixed on the stranger.

The man glanced back at Jack and winked at him, his hairless crown reflecting the yellowish light.

Jack's jaw dropped. He recognized him! Though he had no memory of having met him while awake; he remembered well the many dreams he'd had about the olive-skinned old man. In those dreams, the man was always coming to his rescue, the same as he was doing now. He'd dreamt about him often until the old witch woman had started dominating his nightmares.

"It's you!" Jack said. "I can't believe I'm finally meeting you, for real. Are you a relative of mine—a ghost?"

The old man wore the same thin rags he'd always worn in those dreams—an old loose mesh fabric that revealed a gray tank top and a thin white baggy shirt. Jack waited for him to say something, but he just stood there, waiting for the ape-men to make their move. Then Jack remembered—he'd never said a word in those dreams.

The ape-men surrounded Jack and his protector in ever-increasing numbers. The one closest to the old man jumped at him, its teeth flashing, triggering the rest of the mob to attack. The old man spun around and kicked the first attacker, then ducked and kicked another beast with his other foot, while at the same time cracking his walking stick over the head of a third beast.

Within ten seconds, however, so many creatures had piled on him that Jack couldn't see him. Two of the winged demons snuck up behind Jack, grabbed his arms, and twisted them behind his back. Two more hefted him into the air and slung him between the wings of another ape already in flight. Jack looked back and saw the beasts dispersing, but the old man was nowhere in sight.

Jack's captor darted low, gliding among the tops of shrubs and low pines, leaves brushing his shins. The creature dodged a tree, landed on a branch, and jumped twenty feet to grab another one. It swung over that branch and tossed Jack through the air, where another flying creature, darting below him, secured him on its back. Jack held on for his life.

At least forty other flying beasts glided nearby on all sides of him, some scurrying below him, fists to the ground. Others leaped from branch to branch through the trees. Jack searched in every direction but saw no sign of Katie.

Jack's knuckles turned white from his grip on his captor's long black fur, but the fear of falling vanished when he found himself closing in on a 50-foot-tall wall of solid granite. The demons showed no sign of slowing down.

Jack screamed and closed his eyes, cringing as he collided with the solid stone. Five seconds passed before he realized he wasn't hurt. The rock wall had been an illusion. His transport soared along a cold, narrow crevice, now and then jutting to the right or left without warning. Finally, he entered a circular, open-air clearing at the center of the mountain and the creature dropped him on the ground like a sack of wheat. He rolled sideways, stopping at Katie's feet. She reached out a hand to him and pulled him to his feet.

Crows flew off or roosted on roots or shrubs protruding from the rocks. Jack's and Katie's abductors bounded to ledges or disappeared into the dozens of caves and crevasses randomly situated along the high stone walls. None of them showed any further interest in their prisoners.

The space resembled the maw of a dormant volcano, only deeper. Jack couldn't stop shaking.

Katie pressed herself against him. "What do you think they want with us?" She stared at two eight-foot-tall ape-men standing guard at a large opening at the foot of a rock wall.

Jack shook his head. "They're the same creatures that attacked our camp. One of them left that note under your pillow."

## XLIX

A familiar dark mist flowed from the large split in the rock, smelling of wet soil. Sinuous Ghost Knights emerged, mounted on their black steeds. Jack spotted Jeb, who stood out as the only ghost not covered in black armor and sinewy cloth. He dismounted and hobbled up to one of the large ape-men, removed his hat, and whacked the demon with it. The beast cowered and guarded its face with its hairy hands.

"Durn foolish imps! 'Tis certain I told ye to leave the young ladies alone. They only summoned the boy."

Jeb turned to Katie. "No offense, miss. 'Tain't that it ain't good to see ye again. Where's ye little friend, Clara?"

Katie's eyes went wide, and she turned to Jack. "We forgot about Clara!"

"At least she's safe." Jack shook his head, wondering how she could've so completely forgotten about her.

"'Tis likely she done woke up," Jeb said. "Did I tell ye how she reminds me o' me little Alice? Never mind. 'Tis best a young'un like her never thinks on nightmares like these."

"Jeb," Katie said. "I'm sure you mean well, but we don't have time for this. We need to get to your haunt."

Jeb looked away.

"Thou art free to leave," boomed Ezekiel's voice. He rode forward, peering down at Katie through the visor of his dark helmet. "The boy shall remain to face his challenger."

A chill raced through Jack's bones.

"He's leaving with me," Katie said.

"I'm truly sorry, miss," Jeb said.

"No." Katie hugged Jack. "You knights claim you help the innocent. Well, Jack's innocent!"

Cool air from the flapping wings of two imps brushed past Jack's face and the imps landed on both sides of Katie. They each grabbed an arm and dragged her toward the nearest wall, her boots dragging in the dirt. They held her against the stone.

"Let me go!" She twisted and kicked at them but couldn't budge their powerful arms.

"Leave her alone!" Jack ran toward her, but only slammed against the dark hairy chest of another imp that had dived to intercept him. Jack turned to Jeb and glared at him. "You traitor!"

The old miner shook his head vigorously. "No, no. Ye misunderstand, me friend. 'Tis certain this be the best I could do fer ye. Ye'll agree with me when ye wakes up."

"I wouldn't bet on it," said a gruff, too-familiar voice.

Jack stiffened and turned around. Avard stood before him, helmetless and clad in Ghost Knight armor, his eyes bulging with malicious anticipation.

Ezekiel rode forward and faced Avard. "Is this the boy from whom thou hast demanded justice?"

"You know he is."

Jack shook his head. "He's lying!"

Ezekiel turned to him. "Thou art accused of igniting the explosives that took this man's life. Dost thou deny it?"

Jack pointed at Avard. "His friend knocked the fire stick into the explosives!"

"Jack didn't kill him!" Katie kicked hard at one of the imps, but it didn't seem to notice.

"Didst thou not bash tis man's head against a rock, rendering him unconscious?"

"I kicked to get away from him. I didn't know he'd hit his head."

"Didst thou protect him from the explosives after having rendered him unconscious?"

"I didn't know he was unconscious."

Ezekiel stared at Jack for five seconds, then turned to Avard. "The accused didst fail to protect thee. I judge thine accusation valid. 'Tis my duty to inform thee, however, that the accused is neither ghost nor Material being. He is merely an Aspect, a dreamed entity. He shall not truly die."

Avard laughed. "Oh, he's Material all right. He's Dream Running. He'll die. He's a living, breathing Material being. Nothing'll bring me peace like crushing his skull."

Ezekiel started to dispute him when Jeb stepped in front of him. "Now hold on here, Ezekiel. The Emend Delegation ain't about telling the ghostly folk how to find their rest. The man says he'll be satisfied wakin' the boy. I say, let him have his rest his way!"

"Yes, Ezekiel, let me wake him up." Avard laughed.

Ezekiel stared at Jeb for a moment, then glanced at each of four other knights. They nodded their heads in turn.

"So be it. Commence with the execution." He backed his steed to the perimeter wall.

Jack stumbled backward and looked at Jeb, who winked at him.

"Don't be a scared, son. Ye'll be fine."

"Jack didn't kill him," Katie yelled. "Leave him alone!"

Jack garnered no illusions. His life was about to end.

Avard grinned wide and faced him. "It's time to die."

KATIE FELT USELESS. Powerless. She used all her weight and strength to wrench her arms free but couldn't budge the vice-like grips of these imps. The one on her left grinned at her. She saw no malice in its eyes, just the loyal obedience she'd seen in her dogs back home.

They were just faithfully obeying their beloved masters, the Ghost Knights.

The twenty-plus Ghost Knights in the cavern dismounted and stationed themselves in a wide circle around Jack and Avard. Imps descended from their ledges to tend to the shadowy warhorses. A tall knight stepped forward and swished his right hand through the air. Every opening in the surrounding walls faded and became solid stone. Ethereal, heavy, rhythmic drums and trumpets echoed within the chamber in unison with a chorus of unseen alto voices.

Avard beamed with malicious delight. Imps shook with excitement, grunting and dancing in rapturous ecstasy. Exhilaration permeated the air. Clearly, the Emend Delegation lived for exacting revenge.

A short, pudgy knight posted herself near Avard and faced him, clenching her fists. "Think on thine preferred weapon of execution and it shall be granted thee."

"I can shape my own essence weapons. You got something that'll kill a Material being?"

The woman nodded once, slowly.

Avard glanced at his hands and smiled at a gray cloud condensing and solidifying until it transformed into a shotgun in his hands. He squinted, and the gun faded and expanded into another foggy mass before reshaping and stretching into a rocket launcher, nestled on his shoulder. The same process repeated, and two Uzis formed in his hands. He laughed aloud and glared at Jack.

"Leave him alone!" Katie threw her weight forward and the imp to her right slammed its hairy palm over her mouth.

Avard's Uzi expanded into a fog and reformed into a sphere which then condensed into a basketball-sized orb that radiated dozens of six-inch spikes, a type of morning star. The heavy ball hung from a thick black metal chain.

"I can feel the density in these weapons," Avard said. "This'll take out a Material being." He leered at Jack and swirled the massive ball over his own head.

"You know I didn't kill you," Jack said.

He hadn't finished his sentence before the razor-sharp spikes of the morning star slashed diagonally, inches from his face. Half of the pointed ball disappeared into the solid soil with an earth-shaking thump. Rather than lifting it again, Avard let it decompress into a cloud of dust and took hold of a new one forming in the air behind his back. With a grunt, he swung it high over his head and dropped it straight down between Jack's feet.

Jack fell backward. Imps clapped and grunted with glee. jumping up and down.

Katie turned her head, terrified of what she might see. She gritted her teeth when she found Jeb easing over to her.

"That be no way to treat a lady," Jeb waved a pistol in front of the imp and yanked its hand from Katie's mouth. "Don't be afeared o' these imps, miss. They's got no minds o' they own. They exist to serve the Delegation."

"I don't care about them! You're letting Avard kill Jack!" Katie screamed when Jack barely jumped aside from a heavy blow.

"Your friend set off the explosives!" Jack said. "He's the murderer."

Avard laughed louder.

# 1

Katie pulled again to free her arms, but she could do nothing but watch.

Avard swung the spiked ball horizontally and Jack leaned back, out of its path. Avard snarled and the morning star expanded into a mist, stretching and condensed into the form of a two-headed battleax. Jack ducked, and the ax brushed through his spiky hair.

Avard's eyes bulged. "Hold still so I can cut out that noisy voice box of yours."

"Let him defend himself," Katie yelled. "Give him a weapon!"

A cloud of dust formed around Avard's free hand and condensed into another morning star, half the size of the others he'd been using. He swung it sideways and let it go, sending it directly at Katie's face. It dissipated into a cloud of dust only inches from her eyes, blurring her vision for several seconds. She nodded her appreciation to the short knight who held her hand outstretched in Katie's direction. She'd saved her life.

"You coward!" Jack leaped up and swung his right leg in the air, landing a solid kick on Avard's right cheek. The old man staggered back and faded from view for a few seconds.

"Give him a weapon!" Katie screamed.

"Fine!" Avard glanced at Jack's hand and a cloud of dust formed into a short steel dagger. A larger mist became a long sword in Avard's hands.

"You're just playing with me!" Jack feigned a jab with his dagger, instead ducking low and swinging his leg out wide, meeting Avard's right leg at the kneecap. Avard bent sideways and fell, caught himself with his right hand against the ground, and pushed himself back up, regaining his balance.

Jack stood up straight and took two steps back. "Just shoot me and get it over with!"

"I think I like this sword better. Don't want you dying too fast. It's too much fun watching you squirm. You don't deserve no quick 'n easy death." Avard raised his sword, his face creased with fury, and swung it hard past Jack's neck, then took two steps and swung at Jack's left arm. Jack stepped back from each blow, knights and imps moving out of his way and allowing him to work his way backward around the perimeter of the cavern.

The blows kept coming. Jack's hand flew to a nick on his right shoulder. Blood soaked his left side after Avard's next strike. The man lacked the finesse of a practiced fencer, but he made up for it with his relentless, constant attacks, one after another. Jack dodged another swing at his head and jumped back from a blow to his right arm.

Katie clenched her teeth, infuriated that Avard had only allowed Jack a useless dagger.

Jack stayed about five feet away from Avard's sword. He ducked another swing to his head, spun around, and jumped forward, thrusting his dagger at Avard's chest. Jack's victorious grin faded when the blade curled sideways against Avard's breast. The dagger was only a rubber child's toy.

Avard doubled over in laughter, the tip of his sword clanking on the rocks near his feet.

Red-faced, Jack tossed the useless toy aside and kicked his opponent in the forehead, spun around, and kicked him in his left arm. "You don't fight fair!" Jack clenched his fists and shook with anger. "You don't care what's right! This is not right!"

A long sword formed in Jack's hand. There'd been no condensing cloud. No transforming form. It just appeared out of thin air. Katie didn't know what kind of power Jack had in Essentia, but his words reminded her of what Jack had said when they first entered the haunt into the dream world. When something wasn't right, he could make it right.

The smirk on Avard's face turned to an expression of shock. He focused on Jack's sword and a thin fog enveloped it, but then dispersed. He glared at the pudgy knight who'd been providing his densified weaponry.

She wheeled her clenched fists toward Jack and squinted hard, but the sword remained.

Jack wasted no time laying into Avard with all his strength. He swung the sword across Avard's chest, and this time, Avard stepped back with fear in his eyes.

Ezekiel lifted his lance and pointed it at Jack's sword. A thunderous bolt of purple lightning exploded from the lance's tip. Sparks of light bounced from Jack's silver blade. The ancient ghost shook his head when the sword remained unaffected in Jack's hand.

The fury in Jack's eyes increased and he charged Avard with renewed energy, knocking Avard's sword from his hand with his next blow, and forcing him back, cutting his right arm.

Avard slapped the blood trickling down his arm and his eyes bulged.

"So, this is how you want it, Park? So be it." A dark cloud formed around Avard's arms and quickly condensed into a two-barrel shotgun. He started to lift it, but Jack swung at it with his sword and knocked it clattering against the nearby rock wall.

Katie grew hopeful and bit her lip. Avard formed another sword in his hand and parleyed with Jack for ten seconds before sliding sideways from a blow, twisting around, and thrusting his sword deep into Jack's chest.

Katie trembled, too overcome to scream. Jack's sword fell from his hand and clanged against the rocky soil. He dropped to his knees and glanced at Katie, apologizing with his eyes before dropping lifeless onto the dirt. The drums and trumpets faded away.

Katie stared in mute shock and disbelief, Avard's loud laughter filling her with pain.

He kicked Jack and rolled him on his back. Jack's lifeless eyes stared out. He was dead. Avard looked around, a smug grin on his face, and stared at his hands. Katie knew he was trying to produce another weapon, but nothing appeared.

"Aw, don't I get to kill his accomplice?" He grinned and gestured at Katie.

"Justice has been served," Ezekiel said.

The imps flew up to the high ledges and the two that were holding Katie relaxed their grip. Katie shoved them aside and darted to Jack's limp body, her muscles tense and aching with stress and fear.

Jeb stepped up behind her, keeping his eyes focused on Jack with such intensity that Katie found it creepy.

"This is all your fault!" Katie punched him in the chest. "Stay away from him!"

"Ye don't understand, miss. Everything'll be all right. Ye'll see."

"You're insane!" She pointed at Jack's body. "You're staring right at him. Can't you see him? He's dead!"

She didn't know why she could see the rock wall through Avard's increasingly transparent body, and she didn't care. "You murderer!" She charged at Jeb, stopping when two knights grabbed her arms.

"Let me go! You got what you wanted! Take your hands off me!"

Ezekiel approached Avard, paying no attention to Katie. "Brother Avard, thou hast achieved the purpose of thine essential existence. The Emend Delegation envies thy triumph even as we rejoice in your victory. Thou shalt now have thy rest. May God have mercy on thy soul."

Avard glanced down at his fading arms, then darted looks around the cavern. "Wait a minute. What's happening? This ain't right. I won the fight. How do I stop this?" He charged at the nearest Ghost Knight but passed through him, his body now barely visible. "Was this some kind of trick? Tell me how to stop this!" His voice faded with every word until it went silent and he disappeared.

"Whew, I thought that vermin'd never go," Jeb took his eyes off Jack's dead body and it disappeared, leaving only his sword laying on the ground.

"Where'd he go?" Katie ran to Jeb. "What'd you do to him? I hate you! I hate all of you! You knew he was innocent. He didn't kill that monster! I hate all of you!" She pounded on Jeb's shoulders.

"Miss," Jeb patiently enduring her strikes. "Ye don't understand. That vermin woulda pursued yer friend fer the rest o' his life. It's a win-win situation. We gave him his rest so he'd go away. Jack'll be thankin' us. Tis certain. Ye'll see."

"He's dead!" Katie dropped to her knees. "Can't you see, you crazy old loon! You're all crazy. You helped that man murder him!"

"No, miss. Here, I'll show ye." Jeb lifted his pistol to Katie's head and pulled the trigger.

**LI**

Katie bolted upright, shaking and holding her breath. She felt the side of her head for a bullet wound. Jack stared at the wall of their hideout, taking deep breaths.

"We fell sleep," Katie said. "Those imps, your execution, Avard's moving on—it was all just a dream."

Jack nodded.

"It seemed so real, I thought you died," Katie said.

"I know. I keep looking for a hole in my chest."

Katie smiled. "You think that's dumb, I woke up looking for a hole in my head."

Jack laughed for a second, but then frowned. "Thing is, it was real. Somewhere out there, the Ghost Knights think they executed me, and Jeb helped them."

"I didn't think of that. Our dreams aren't just dreams anymore. Jeb actually shot me in the head. We're in a world where nightmares really happen." She shivered at the thought.

"Katie, I can't do it. I don't want help from Jeb or any other ghost anymore. Avard thinks I'm dead and I want to keep it that way."

"Avard's gone. He faded away when he thought he killed you."

"Wow. He's really gone. I can't believe it. But still, I can't…"

"I know. I'm sure we can make it to Jeb's haunt without him. I wish I could find my sister. She'd help us." She turned to look for Clara, then started. "Clara! She's gone!"

Jack stood and searched the hideout, then climbed through the invisible ceiling and out of the pit. Katie climbed after him and scanned the meadows but found only a trio of swallows skimming the tall grass for insects.

She searched the tree-filled ravine. "You don't think she went down there by herself?"

Jack's eyebrows rose. "She might have gone searching for that frog."

"Wait. Do you hear that?" Katie cupped a hand behind her right ear and detected faint voices filtered through the trees to the southwest.

"She's down there." Jack waved for Katie to follow him and she sprinted after him to the edge of the ravine. They curved around three boulders and past dozens of pine trees dotting the sloped terrain. She watched every direction for soldiers and camp staff, finally arriving at a cluster of low spruces. She peered between two pines and gasped at the dozens of Sleeper soldiers swarming around Clara in a clearing, some relaxing on dead logs, others sitting cross-legged in the dirt, smoking, or sipping water from their canteens.

"They got to Marina." Katie bent a branch aside so Jack could see Marina, donning a camouflage military uniform and sitting on a log next to Clara.

"I figured they'd get her sooner or later," Jack said.

"What should we do?" Katie moved behind the trees out of view of the soldiers. "Should we turn ourselves in? We can't leave without Clara. As bad as Intershroud is, I don't see another option."

Jack stared at her for five seconds, then started when a jet-black crow alit on the ground near their feet, hopping and pecking at the ground. It tilted its head and studied Jack and Katie for a few seconds before stretching out its wings and fluttering away.

Jack nodded his head. "You're right. We can't abandon Clara. We'll have to try to rescue her, and if we fail, we'll have to try to escape again when we get back to Materia."

"Let's see your hands," a voice sounded behind them.

Katie turned around and faced six soldiers, each staring at her, their high-powered rifles fixed on her and Jack.

"We were just about to surrender." Jack raised his hands.

"Good job, men." Carl pushed between the troops, who sneered at him when he wasn't looking their direction. Carl folded his arms, stuck his chin out, and looked Katie and Jack up and down. "March these two over to Marina. General Farley will be pleased."

"You heard him," said a heavyset soldier in front of the group. He motioned Katie and Jack to follow him with a jerk of his rifle. Katie followed Jack around the pines and marched to the clearing.

Clara glanced at her, jumped up, and ran to her with her arms outstretched and eyes brimming with gleeful tears. "I was so confused; I didn't know what to do." Clara held Katie tight.

"You shouldn't have left the hideout. You were safe there." Katie said.

"I know. I'm sorry but I heard the scariest grunting sounds and it woke me up. It sounded like people fighting. I thought I heard Jack's voice, but he was lying on the rabbit furs, sleeping right next to you. I was so scared, I couldn't move. After a few minutes, that frog showed up and told me it was safe to come out, so I climbed out to look around. He said a bunch of flying monkey people took you and Jack away, which didn't make any sense."

"He was right. They did take us away," Katie said. "But they only took our dream selves."

"I wondered if that was what happened, but that frog kept arguing with me. Then he ran off to hide again when the soldiers showed up with Carl and Marina. I couldn't get back to the hideout without them seeing me, so I ran after that frog, but they caught me."

Katie hugged her tight one more time.

"They were bound to catch us sooner or later," Jack said. "We just saw one their crows spying on us."

"We don't use crows." Carl faced the nearby soldiers. "Don't take your guns off these three."

"We're not going to run, you idiot!" Katie glared at him. "We need you to help us get to a haunt."

"Why would you need a haunt? Dreamers don't need haunts. And if you were ghosts, you'd already have a haunt. If you hadn't run off, Derek would've filled you in on all this, like he did for the rest of us yesterday. Face it, you're just a couple of Sleepers dreaming about the woods."

"We're not sleeping. We're Dream Running," Clara said.

"What's that supposed to mean?"

"Carl," Marina said, "you're just agitating them. Let me talk to them, alone."

"Fine," Carl said. "But hurry up. I'll send a bird to alert the other patrols. Can't wait to see Tony's face when he finds out I captured them." He whistled, and a bluebird dived from a treetop fifty feet away, landing on his arm and tilting its head. Carl whispered something to it and it darted away, gliding high over the ravine. Katie watched it in the distance, then spotted a white hawk shoot out of a tree and slam into the bird, sending blue and white feathers drifting in the breeze.

No one seemed to notice except Marina, who afterwards turned and winked at Katie. She shuffled Katie, Jack, and Clara twenty yards down the hill, away from Carl and the troops, and huddled with them. "Listen. First, Clara says she saw you two sleeping and then heard one of your voices somewhere else. Then, if I'm hearing her right, your dream selves were doing things while your bodies were sleeping next to Clara. And now Clara mentioned Dream Running. Who told you about that?"

"Avard told us," Katie said. "And you're right. We fell asleep in our hideout, then Jack and I dreamed the Ghost Knights captured us. Then we woke up in our hideout."

Marina stared at Katie for several seconds, then looked around. "This is incredible. I don't know how it's possible, but Avard may have been right. It's important that you don't tell anyone. Who else knows?"

"No one but Avard, and he's apparently moved on," Jack said. "We told Jeb and the Ghost Knights, but they refused to believe us."

"That's good." Marina looked around the hillside. The ground rumbled. "What's going on?"

The rumbling intensified and the ground quaked with such force Katie had to stretch her arms out to keep her balance.

"It's an earthquake!" a soldier yelled.

"Everyone get out of the path of those rocks!" yelled another.

Hundreds of boulders, large and small, shook from their resting places and plummeted down the slope above them, cracking against each other and filling the air with thick dust. A dozen small gray sparrows darted from the tall grass. Soldiers slid behind trees only to find them lifting from the earth by their roots and crashing over them. Carl tumbled to the ground in a plume of dust, disappearing below a cascade of tumbling rocks.

The earth below Katie's feet gave way and she found herself weightless, dropping straight down. Jack fell alongside her, his arm wrapped around Clara. Marina was gone. Katie prepared to slam into the floor of the sinkhole, but instead found only a spongy, shock-absorbent surface that forced her forward onto her knees. The earth folded over the top of her and her companions, casting the world into inky darkness.

LII

J ack lost all sense of distance, imagining himself falling dozens of
feet before being buried in an inescapable, lightless tomb. He
charged across the bouncy floor blindly before slamming into a
hard, earthen wall. Clods of soil rolled down his cheeks as he clawed
at the wall, dirt crumbling between his fingers. His shoulder brushed
against an adjacent wall and he moved his hands over to it. He yanked
dirt to the ground by the handful. He turned around and stumbled in
the dark, making his way to another wall ten paces away, paying no
attention to the complaints of Katie and Clara over whose legs he'd
tripped.

"Jack, calm down!" Katie's voice echoed.

"I've got to get out of here! Help me climb out!"

The earthen walls began to brighten, and Jack stopped to look
around the roughly twenty-foot square pit, desperate to find an
escape route. He found only Katie and Clara, pulling themselves up
off the floor, which now started shifting along with the walls.

Katie hugged Clara and they sidled closer to Jack, staring at the
walls of earth above and around them. It reformed into smooth, white
wall planes and a high ceiling. Jack shifted to keep his balance and
stared at the dirt below his feet, now flattening into a plush, beige

carpeted floor. Two soft brown sofas and a blue armchair melded up from the carpet along with a wooden side table, a coffee table, two tall turquoise lamps, a stocked bookcase, and a wooden armoire. Light-blue curtained windows appeared on two of the walls, diffusing warm daylight into the cozy room.

Clara smiled and rushed to flop onto one of the sofas, bouncing a few times on its airy leather cushions. An ornate wooden door creaked open and revealed a similarly furnished adjacent room and a young blue-haired woman Jack hadn't expected to see.

"Sorry," Marina rushed into the room without closing the door. "I had to make sure my rockslide woke up everyone. Hope I didn't scare you. Hungry? You must be starving." She held out her right hand, palm up, and a white china plate appeared in it, holding six triangular-cut turkey and cheese sandwiches and a stack of thinly sliced carrots. She handed it to Katie.

Dumbstruck, but starving, Jack grabbed a sandwich and shoved it in his mouth, then grabbed another. Katie and Clara each did the same.

"What just happened?" Jack took another bite. "I seriously thought I was going to die."

Marina winced. "Sorry. I forgot you were claustrophobic. In my defense, I had to act fast when you started talking about Dream Running. Believe me, you don't want Intershroud to know you're Dream Running."

"I'm just glad you're alive," Clara said. "We thought you died in that explosion until Avard said someone carried you out of the cabin."

Marina laughed and pointed at the coffee table. A plate of choco-late chip cookies and three tall glasses of water appeared.

"Actually, I saved myself. I pretended I was asleep when you entered the cabin. I came to investigate the Camp—not to run from it. After you left the cabin, a ghost discovered you'd left open the panel below one of the beds. I kept my eyes shut, but I know at least four of them entered the research facility through that opening. They bragged about how they were going to break a gas main and blow up the place. So, I ran to the other cabin and dragged Carl and Tony a safe distance away, then laid down near them and pretended I was asleep again."

"How do we know you're not working for them?" Jack grabbed a glass of water and chugged it down, ecstatic at the feeling of cool liquid rolling down his parched throat.

"You don't, but that's the right kind of question to ask. Truth be told, I'm risking my life for you right now. Lynch'll want to know why I didn't wake up in that rockslide."

"Why were you helping him at all?" Jack set his glass on the table harder than he'd intended.

Marina glanced back at the open door. "Look, I can tell you what you want to know, but right now, we need to get away from here. Now that you know dreams are real, Lynch sees you as a huge threat." She rushed to the exit and waved for Jack and the girls to follow her. Katie and Clara each took another sip of water, then ran after her.

Jack grabbed a few cookies and followed them from the room, entering an identical room—an exact copy, right down to the three empty glasses on the coffee table. He looked ahead at an endless succession of identical rooms with identical open doors.

"Pick up the pace, guys. I doubt Intershroud will find us down here, but we can't take any chances. We'll be safer far away from here."

Jack glanced over his shoulder in time to see the room behind him grow dark and fill with solid earth, the door fading until it turned to soil along with the wall. He faced forward again and scrambled into the next room and the same thing repeated, with Marina guiding them from room to identical room. She stopped for a second and flickered in and out of view.

"What's happening?" Katie placed a hand on Marina's shoulder.

"I was worried about this. Someone's trying to wake me up. I saved some of Farley's drugged brownies for tonight, so I could stay asleep, but I don't know how much longer they'll work. We need to hurry. I won't be able to help you if I wake up." She quickened her pace, abruptly turning to her right, and guiding them in that direction through another succession of identical rooms.

"So, how about it? Why were you helping them?" Jack pushed past Katie and Clara and locked step next to Marina.

"After the gas main blew, Lynch and his stooges gave us the option to serve Intershroud for life or become belated casualties of the explosion. Let's just say the first option had its appeal. They gave us a crash course on controlling dreams, then they forced poor Media to visit us in our sleep to secure our loyalty with mind control. You witnessed some of that, if I'm not mistaken."

"How did you resist her powers?" Katie asked.

"Media's so mentally drained, it wasn't hard to fool her into thinking she had me under her control. The others could've resisted her too, if they'd known what was happening."

"She still must've had some affect on you," Jack said. "You're not acting like the Marina I know."

"I'm not the Marina you think you knew. I'm a lot older than I look. I belong to a rebellion that's been fighting Intershroud for decades. We call ourselves Purites. Sherry came to us, begging us to help her escape from Intershroud. She helped me infiltrate the camp. You provided some priceless info on your cell phone, by the way."

"So, you're the one Lynch said was helping Sherry," Katie said.

Marina nodded. "Now I need to figure out how to help you three. Dream Running isn't just rare, it's dangerous. Essentia is unpredictable. I'm surprised you've survived this long."

"How did this happen?" Katie asked. "How can we be Dream Running?"

"Wish I knew. I hate to say it, but until now, I thought Dream Running was a myth."

"It feels like a myth," Jack said. "None of this seems real to me. If dreams are real, why doesn't anybody know it?"

"Intershroud works tirelessly to keep the world shrouded. The reality of dreams makes sense if you think about it. There are three basic components to existence: physical material, laws of nature, and the power of thought. Those three components of reality are constant and eternal. Physical things never cease to exist in one form or another. Laws of nature, likewise, always exist. Why, then, would 'thought' be any different? Thought can never stop functioning."

"I think I get it," Clara said. "When your brain sleeps, it doesn't let you continue to think, so your thoughts are forced to leave your brain and go somewhere else. They come to this world where they can keep thinking."

"Exactly. Your mind goes to Essentia and takes you wherever you think yourself to be, at the speed of thought."

"But, I have nights when I don't dream at all," Katie said.

"Not true."

"Scientists have been studying dreams for ages," Jack said. "We don't always dream."

"You assume you remember all your dreams, but you don't." Marina turned to her left and led them through another line of rooms. She flickered from view again for a split second.

"Are you waking up again?" Clara grabbed Marina's arm.

Marina nodded. "Don't worry. If I do wake up, I'll do whatever it takes to fall back asleep. Lynch should have a hard time finding us. Now, what was I saying?"

"You said we don't remember all our dreams," Clara said.

"Yes. Intershroud falsifies dream studies before they're made public. Trust me, you dream all night long. Scientists can only observe physical brain activity. They can't measure what the mind is doing in another dimension."

"Then how are we going to keep Intershroud from finding us here?" Katie winced when her shoulder bumped against a doorframe.

"When we return you to Materia, I'll teach you how to embrace your Shadow, so you can control your dreams as Free Dreamers. The side benefit to that is that you'll be able to remember every moment of your dreams."

"That's if we can survive this one," Katie said.

# LIII

J ack tripped on a wooden threshold and fell against a doorframe.

"Let's rest for a minute," Marina said.

Jack leaned against the frame. "Sherry's book told me a lot about controlling dreams. I can lucid dream, but I have no idea how to control my Shadow. How do I find out who my Shadow Archetype is?"

"You said you recently awoke from a dream," Marina said. "Did you meet anyone that was out of place? Unexpected?"

Jack thought for a moment, then smiled. "There was an old woman talking to Katie right before the imps showed up. She said all kinds of rude things and Katie just nodded her head."

Marina pursed her lips and looked at Katie. "That would've been Katie's Shadow. The old woman is a Senex Archetype. She's an old hag on whom you project your feelings of low self-worth. I suggest that you don't embrace her. Subdue her instead. Defy her. Your worth is far greater than she tells you it is. Next time you dream about her, confront her and tell her she's wrong. Don't be afraid of her. She can't hurt you."

Katie nodded. "I've dreamed of that woman a lot, now that I think about it."

Marina turned to Jack. "So, how about you? Did anyone else unusual show up?"

Jack took a deep breath, surprised at how tired he felt. He thought about the dream and shook his head, but then he remembered. "There was an old Korean monk. He showed up and fought off some of the imps, until they overpowered him. I recognized him from other dreams. I assumed he was the ghost of some old relative of mine."

"Sounds like a Hero Archetype," Marina said. "I should've guessed it, judging from your personality. Hero Archetypes follow you around, waiting in the shadows for an opportunity to come out and protect you from enemies in your dreams."

"You make me sound like a wimpy little kid." Jack reddened and frowned.

Marina grinned. "He probably started showing up many years ago, when you *were* a wimpy little kid. He's the hero your subconscious believed you needed. Evidently, you don't see yourself as a hero. Be that hero, Jack. Embrace him."

"What about me?" Clara looked at Marina. "I dream about so many things, I can't imagine which one would be my Archetype."

"I have to admit, you're a complete mystery to me, Clara. You dream to the same location night after night—even with Intershroud tech trying to force you not to. Either something very unusual happened to you or someone else is manipulating your dreams."

"Someone else?" Katie's eyes widened. "Clara lived alone with her mother for years. There was no one else."

"You can never know who might be sharing your dreams," Marina said. "Some people can dream in the form of other people. Some can dream without being seen. Agents of Intershroud aren't the only ones manipulating people in their dreams."

"Like those soldiers." Jack said. "They seemed to think they were fighting in some war."

Marina nodded. "Exactly. Those soldiers are just ordinary Sleepers, unsuspecting veterans or war buffs that Lynch fools into dreaming they're serving in a real war, searching for three kids behind enemy lines."

"Speaking of enemy lines, we better get moving," Katie said.

Marina shook her head. "You three look exhausted. I think we've come far enough."

"What do we do now?" Clara asked.

Marina took a quick breath. "I've noticed your minds aren't affecting the dream world as much as they would if you were actually asleep. That gives me a little more power to do things I normally wouldn't be able to do in the presence of other dreamers. I may be able to verge to another location where I have friends that can help us. They might be able to verge all of you to a haunt far from here."

"What do you mean 'verge' us?" Jack scratched behind his left ear.

"Some Free Dreamers have a power to transport people. They're called 'Vergers.' Damien's one. He can disappear from one dream location and reappear in another. That's what we'll need if we're going to get you out of here."

"What? So, every dreamer has some special power?" Jack smiled.

"Before you were enlightened, your mind had every power imaginable. But Free Dreamers can't come to terms with doing the impossible. From now on, you'll be limited to the power in which you have the most confidence. I'm a Shaper, for example."

A baseball appeared in Marina's hand and stretched into a baseball bat, then shrunk and turned dark brown until it took the form of a small chocolate muffin. She popped it in her mouth.

"Derek's also a Shaper. Mr. Lynch is a Shade, which means he can dream invisibly." Marina flickered out of view for several seconds.

"We can talk about this later," Katie said. "You need to go get your friends. I need to get out of this place before I lose my mind."

Jack's legs gave out and the ground swelled up below his feet. He fell back against a window and held the walls that now rattled and flowed like liquid waves. Katie and Clara held on to each other, then collided with Marina.

Marina grabbed the door frame and pulled herself out of the room. "They found us! Run!"

Jack felt like a ball in a bingo cage, flinging against one wall, then stumbling against Clara and spinning sideways before slamming his shoulder against a door frame. The floor undulated, robbing him of his sense of balance. He reached for Clara's hand and steadied himself before following Marina into the next identical, undulating room. Jack bit his lip upon seeing Katie holding her breath and pushing as hard as she could to loosen herself from between door jambs that had bulged in on her from both sides. The wooden jambs spread out and she stumbled into Jack's arms.

Columns of blinding light sprung through new cracks in the paneled ceiling, forcing Jack to look away. Marina glanced back at him, stopped, and closed her eyes tight. She leaned her head back, fists clenched. The room grew dim and a thin gray mist blocked the view all around the four of them, slowly densifying into new shapes: a white concave ceiling, a long row of square windows to each side of them, and two rows of blue cushioned benches. Jack's leg brushed against the soft upholstery now running along both rows of windows.

"This looks like one of those old mining trains," Clara said.

Marina, her eyes still clamped shut, put up an index finger to silence her, then squinted and tightened her fists so hard she began to shake. Jack fell backward into Clara and Katie, who both slammed with him against a locked door. The subterranean train lurched forward, curving nearly straight down with such speed, Jack felt light-headed and feared the bile rising in his throat would soon find its way out of his mouth. He slid sideways, dropped onto a side bench, and gripped its armrest tight. Katie and Clara did the same, taking seats across the aisle. Marina remained standing, shaking so hard Jack couldn't understand how she was staying asleep. He imagined they were a mile deep by the time the train finally slowed and stopped.

The train dissipated instantly, rendering Jack weightless for a few seconds before his knees and hands found the cool surface of a solid concrete floor. Marina fell to her knees and rolled onto her back, staring upward, her eyes closed.

Clara pulled herself up and ran to her. "Marina! You okay?" She shook Marina's shoulders.

Marina lay still for several seconds before rolling her head to face Clara. "Now, that's the kind of concentration that hurts."

Jack took a deep breath, pulled himself up, and looked around the vast open room. Curved wooden beams supported an ornate vaulted ceiling at least thirty feet over their heads, divided by beige plaster panels and stained-glass skylight windows. Balconies with black wrought-iron railings ran along the side walls, ending at giant round windows at both ends of the long hallway. A row of arched openings, rimmed with flowery ornamentation, ran along both walls for hundreds of yards.

"This place is amazing," Katie said. "It looks like an old railway station."

"It's an old Union Railway Station I saw once in Indiana, to be exact. Best I could do under these conditions."

"When can we get out of here?" Jack wiped away sweat and paced back and forth. "I can't take much more of this."

Marina sat up. "Each of you look away from me. Stare at that rose window. I'll try to verge out of here. When I do, you need to stay here so I can dream back to you again. It's extremely important that you remain in this exact location."

"We'll do it," Jack said, nodding.

Jack joined the girls, turning around. A few pigeons fluttered around the sill of the round window. The ceiling and walls started to close in.

## LIV

The room continued shrinking and Katie wondered if it had anything to do with Marina's attempt to verge away.

"It's no use," Marina said.

Everyone turned to her.

"It looks like your thoughts are still strong enough to keep me from dreaming out of here. Jack's claustrophobia is making the room shrink. I created a large room to combat that, but it isn't enough. You'll need to learn how to overcome phobias like that, Jack. Fear has a way of transforming your dreams into something you don't want."

"Why don't we just go to sleep right here?" Clara's eyes brightened. "It worked against the Ghost Knights. We can go to sleep, then Jack and Katie can go find Mr. Farley and the others from camp. Then, when they wake up, Farley will think we're gone, and we'll be able to go to the haunt."

Marina shook her head. "Not a bad plan, but I'm afraid Farley and Lynch won't give up so easily. If they believe you're ghosts, or in a coma, they'll know you won't wake up easily. Since you'll actually be easy to wake up, they'll know you're still alive somewhere and you'll eventually dream back to Essentia. They won't stop looking for you."

"So, we're toast," Katie said.

"No. I'm just going to have to wake up and fall back asleep so I can start my dream in another location. It's risky, but I don't see another way."

"How's it risky? Lynch will want you to go back asleep anyway," Jack said.

"True, but he's already wondering why I didn't wake up in that landslide. If I go to sleep again and don't immediately show up with his crew, he'll be suspicious."

"Then we need another plan," Katie said.

"Actually, I think I can still make it work. When I wake up, I'll tell them one of you caused the landslide, but I dodged it. I'll say I spied on you. I'll come up with some story and convince them I need to leave camp. There are a few guards at the camp who are sympathetic with the resistance. With any luck, I'll convince Lynch to let them drive me to Kalispell. I'll sleep in the car and Lynch'll never know it."

Jack grinned wide. "Well let's get on with it then. How do you wake up?"

Marina slid a black metal handgun from her waist and handed it to Katie. "A shot to my face ought to do the trick."

Katie cringed and forced the gun into Jack's hand. "I can't shoot you in the head."

Marina turned to Jack. "You're not killing me. You're just shocking my mind out of its sleep state."

Jack hesitated for a few seconds, then raised the gun to Marina's forehead. He closed his eyes and pulled the trigger. Marina's body fell limp, disappearing within seconds. Jack opened his eyes, his face registering relief upon glancing at the empty floor.

"All we can do now is wait," There was a hint of fear in Clara's eyes.

The walls creaked, and the room decrease slightly in volume. Katie looked at Jack but stopped herself from saying anything. His sheepish expression told her he knew he needed to control his fear.

A shuffling sound turned Katie's gaze upward. White dust drifted from a small round hole in one of the ceiling panels. A small rodent poked its forepaws and buck-toothed head from the hole, gazed down at her, and scurried back into its hole.

Katie gave Jack a smile, but it faded when the floor lurched up below her and her knees buckled, forcing her to the concrete floor, along with her companions. She rolled onto her back, feeling like she weighed five hundred pounds as the entire structure rocketed upward, the glass skylights rattling and loosening from their frames before crashing to the ground in thousands of pieces. The balconies twisted and creaked, and plaster dust swirled in the air.

When the movement finally stopped, Katie pulled herself up. Jack stood, massaged his left elbow, and helped Clara to her feet. A cool breeze brushed against Katie's face, flowing in from one of the arched openings, and a stream of black smoke snaked from the arch and gushed across the concrete floor.

"No, no, no! Not now!" Jack looked at Katie, his eyes wide with fear.

The Ghost Knights emerged from the archway and surrounded the three Dream Runners, their obsidian black steeds stamping their silent airborne hooves.

Ezekiel lifted a hand to his side, informing his cohorts to stay back. He raised his lance and a deafening violet bolt of lightning blasted from its metal tip, slammed into Jack's chest and sending him flying backward. He crashed against a pilaster, sinking a half inch into the Venetian plaster, which now cracked and sloughed off the wall and slid, in hundreds of powdery pieces, across the polished concrete floor.

Clara's scream had hardly finished before Jack pushed himself away from the wall unharmed. He glared at the Ghost Knight leader, brushed plaster dust from his arms, and stepped forward.

Ezekiel looked at each of his five companions in turn, nodded his head, and faced Jack. "The rumor is true, then," Ezekiel said. "Thou art truly awake in a world of dreams?"

"You didn't have to blast me across the room to figure that out!" Jack clenched his fists. "Move this room back where it was. Marina needs to meet us there."

"Regrettably, we cannot return thee to the exact location," Ezekiel said. "Our spies determined your friend to be in the service of Intershroud. It was our intention to rescue thee from her grasp."

"You might as well get revenge on yourselves then," Jack said. "You've as good as killed us. Marina was our only hope of escaping this nightmare."

"Now, now, don't be so sure o' ye self." Jeb's voice echoed from behind the six mounted knights. He stepped around Ezekiel, faced Katie with a twinkle in his eye, and pulled the reins of three misty black steeds. On his right shoulder sat a familiar frog, its flimsy left arm hugging the old miner's sunburnt neck. It grinned, enjoying the attention.

"A crow done showed us how ye awakened ye selves right here in Essentia," Jeb said. "'Tis certain I couldn't believe me own eyes. That ol' varmint, Avard, was telling the truth. Ye truly are Dream Runners."

"Yes," Jack said, "and now we're going to die here because you made it so Marina won't be able to find us."

"No worries, me friend. We came here to rescue ye. I's gonna lend ye me own haunt, see."

"Why would we trust you?" Katie scowled at the old man and marched up to him. "You shot me in the head!"

Jeb stepped back, frowning and furrowing his brow. "No, no, miss. I apologize, but I had to awaken ye. 'Tis certain I had to show ye that Jack weren't dead."

"You could've just told me." Katie folded her arms.

"I tried, but ye was convinced the boy was dead."

"You didn't have to force me to fight at all!" Jack said.

Jeb shook his head. "'Tis most certain that I did. That rascal got it into his head that the three of ye were Material beings and that ye murdered him. I was certain he'd lost his mind. I was certain ye was just a few young Aspects off a dreamin'.

"That's when I done convinced Ezekiel to let the ole rascal wake ye, thinking he killed ye. Ye must know that ol' Avard would've followed ye for the rest o' yer days if we didn't give him his revenge. So, we let him fight ye. I made sure yer Essence body remained, looking all stone cold and dead. It worked. We fooled him. Once avenged, ol' Avard hadn't no thoughts left to hold onto his soul. He dissipated, and he'll never bother ye again."

Katie let her arms drop and she cracked a half smile at Jack.

"We were thousands of feet below ground," Clara said. "How'd you find us?"

"I helped them," the frog said. He stood up on Jeb's shoulder, folded his arms, and looked Clara in the eyes. "We frogs are most adept at detecting subterranean vibrations, if you must know. Your efforts to abandon me were neither successful nor appreciated, but don't worry about me. My adventures with the three of you have been nothing but peril. It's most frustrating attempting to walk and talk with people who feel inclined to run and hide every five seconds. I'll be confining my walking and talking to Mr. Colton from now on."

Clara smiled at him and held out a hand, but the frog stepped back and looked away.

Jeb rolled his eyes. "Don't ye be listenin' to this feckless little toad. 'Tweren't him who found ye. A crow showed us the blue-haired lady steelin' ye below ground. This here frog set us in the right direction, but it were our gophers that sniffed ye out. I was frankly surprised we was able to bring ye back up."

"I just want to know how we're going to make it past Lynch's troops without being seen. They're everywhere," Jack said.

"Don't ye be worryin'. These Ghost Knights know all the tricks. Intershroud certain don't want to get on their bad side. We'll make it to me haunt. You'll see."

"I thought the Ghost Knights only cared about revenge," Jack said.

"'Tis true, fer certain, but the knights'll make allies with the livin' when it serves them. Miss Abigail convinced me to lend ye me haunt 'cause she needs your help to seal Farley's fate." Jeb held his hand toward a rider next to Ezekiel and, upon noticing it, quickly dropped his hand. Everyone turned to the rider who now stared down at Jeb.

The knight dismounted and marched over to Jeb, reached out a muscular right arm, and hefted him into the air by his throat. The old man wheezed and grasped at the unmoving hand, his legs kicking at nothing.

"I should awaken you forever for this," the knight said. The voice was female.

Katie inched closer to the woman.

"Abby?"

LV

The Ghost Knight released her steel grip on Jeb's neck, and he dropped on his feeble feet, staggering backward until he fell against a pilaster. The tendinous black strands of Abby's body collected into a solid bulbous mass, which then retracted and reformed with a rumble into the shape of an athletic-looking young woman in a black leather jacket, tall black boots, and black gloves. She slid the helmet from her head and revealed her short blonde hair and a face that resembled Katie's, except that her bloodshot brown eyes rarely blinked and the lines of her cheeks and mouth were frozen into a perpetual frown.

She stared at Katie for several seconds but turned her head when a loud creaking sound distracted her. The multi-colored glass of a white-framed skylight drop from the vaulted ceiling far behind her and crash against the concrete floor, dispersing into a thousand shards.

Katie grew anxious, having watched it hit the floor through Abby's now semi-transparent body. "Abby!" Katie sprang forward, her arms stretched in front of her.

"Stop!" Abby backed away and slid behind her horse. The animal stamped its leg, lowered its head at Katie, and snorted at her.

Katie stopped and stared at Abby, her eyebrows furrowed.

A twitch of a smile crossed Abby's lips, accompanied by an increase in her transparency. "You can't touch me, Katie. Your Material body might crush and destroy me. When a ghost wakes up, they cease to exist." She looked away and her body became more solid in appearance. "If I die, I'll be robbed of my justice. I cannot let that happen."

Katie nodded and let her arms fall to her sides. "I'm sorry. I understand. I'm just so happy. And to think you were here the whole time! Why were you hiding from me?"

The ceiling creaked again, and Katie looked up. A four-inch-wide crack snake across four plaster panels on the ceiling. White dust rained from the fissure.

Abby glanced at a knight to her left, and the man lifted his hands upward. A light gray fog appeared and hid the entire ceiling from view before densifying into an identical ceiling, but without cracked plaster or missing skylights. Abby stepped through the black mist around her mount and approached within a few yards of Katie. Her lip quivered, and she started to fade.

She looked away and solidified again. "Your sister is dead. Don't be fooled by the illusion you see before you. I'm only her hatred, her anger, her loathing for the dog who devoured everything she valued. I think of nothing else. I am nothing else."

"That's not true!" Katie's eyes welled up. "You're just choosing to be that way. I know you. You were always stubborn."

"You know nothing!" Abby glanced at Katie for only a second, then looked away again. "You want to know why I hid from you? I hid from you because I couldn't bear for you to see me like this—miserable and hopeless. I wanted you to remember me as I was—not this. Now, Farley has taken even that from me."

"But he hasn't. You're here now. And when I get out of here, I'll be able to visit you in my dreams whenever I want."

Abby's face tightened, her teeth clenched, and she glared at Katie and shook her fists. "Listen to me, little sister. I'm not the girl who used to ride bikes with you on sunny mornings along the docks.

Abigail Frost is dead! Accept what I am! What I've become! I feel nothing but hate. I think about nothing but killing Farley."

Katie tried to speak but couldn't find her voice. Her lip trembled.

Clara rushed to her side and hugged her. "We don't believe you! Abby is still in there somewhere. Why else would you be helping us? You still care about Katie. I know you do."

Abby turned and stared at Katie, he face holding back emotion. The dark steeds behind her became visible through her fading body and Katie wasn't sure want she wanted more: to have her sister back, fading into nothing, or this hate-filled stranger who'd somehow taken over her body.

Abby's form solidified again, and her eyes bulged in fury. "It doesn't matter who I once was!" Her screaming voice startled Jack and sent Clara and Katie cowering and stepping back from her. "Look at me! I'm a ghost! I didn't come here to be your sister again! That woman is dead. I help you only because I need your help. Farley is in a coma. I can't kill him, but if we can find him, I can destroy his Aspect and turn his Material body to brain-dead mush, a living corpse. That will be enough to satisfy my hunger."

"What's that got to do with Katie?" Jack ran to her side.

"If I can't find Farley, I'll need you to return to Materia and make sure he dies. You must kill him for me. If you won't do this, your feelings for me are meaningless!"

Katie's lower lip stiffened, and she shook away from Clara, her fists clenched. "How dare you yell at me. I don't like Farley any more than you do, but I'm no murderer. I won't kill for you!"

"Murderer?" Abby's face stretched into a wicked, hideous grin. "That worthless insect murdered your sister in cold blood, and you call killing him 'murder'? Killing that demon is no more murderous than poisoning a rabid rat! To let him live is to condone murder. Kill him or don't call yourself my sister!"

Katie knew this wasn't Abby speaking. The pain, the injustice, the long years of suffering, had poisoned and warped her mind. But that didn't make it hurt any less. It took all her strength to endure it.

Clara held her tight and scowled at Abby. "Now you're just being mean."

"Get used to it." Abby placed a foot in a stirrup, and with a small spring, jumped up and swung her leg over the horse's back. She settled in the saddle, looked down at Clara, and placed her helmet back on her head. "Be grateful I was able to persuade these few knights to accompany you to the haunt. To them, it's foolishness for a ghost to risk his life to spar with Aspects. Their purpose in life is to help their ghost brothers find peace, not to help kids get to a haunt."

"Then maybe you should just leave," Jack said. "We'll find out own way."

"It's in our interest to make sure you return to Materia." Abby squeezed a black pouch tied to her waste and something writhed around inside—the miniature voice of Francis Farley wailing in pain.

Katie frowned and stared at the floor.

"Mount your horses!" Abby grabbed the reins of a nearby steed and led it to Katie.

"Leave her alone," Jack said. "She doesn't want anything to do with you. We're not going to help you."

"She's already helped me. She left a panel open below a bed in her cabin. All it took after that was a broken gas line and an electric spark. I'd have been at peace already had I not learned that the insect survived. I'm only asking her to help me finish the job."

"You're as much of a monster as Mr. Farley." Clara hugged Katie tighter.

Katie looked up and saw shadows of an archway through Abby's fading body.

"I'm sorry, Katie. I can't control what I've become. I take no pleasure in the fact that I can't be the sister you once knew." She looked away and her body rumbled and stretched into the tendinous form of a Ghost Knight. She led her mount toward a nearby archway and disappeared beyond it.

Jeb pursed his lips, shook his head slowly and placed the reins of three horses into the palms of Clara, Katie, and Jack. "Can't say 'tis certain these ol' steeds'll support the likes o' the three o' ye. Them knights focused all the thought they could muster on these critters. They be as densified as we could dream 'em. Mount up and we'll be on our way."

Jeb took the reins of his dappled gray mare, stepped into a stirrup, and swung a leg over its back. He settled in the saddle and patted his horse on the neck. The frog leapt to the horse's back and wrapped its tiny fingers into its hairy mane.

Ezekiel turned his steed and rode a few steps toward Jack. "The forces of Intershroud have increased since the rockslide. We must make haste. They are desperate to find thee." He looked around the room before putting a gloved hand to his mouth. "Onward ho! Let us make for Mr. Colton's haunt!"

More than a dozen imps glided into the great hall from the shadows of every archway. Two landed to each side of Katie and clamped their hairy hands around her arms. She pulled back, trying to free her arms, her eyes wide with fear, but soon realized their intentions were friendly. Gusts of air from the wings of passing imps blew her hair into her face; she turned and saw them hovering in pairs, hefting Clara and Jack onto the backs of their mounts.

Katie's feet left the ground and her legs dangled in the air while the imps positioned her over her steed and lowered her onto a warm leather saddle. The stallion felt like a horse-shaped cushion of air. It bothered her not being able to see her own legs through the thick black mist below them.

LVI

Ezekiel aimed his sword at the archway through which Abby had gone and clicked his tongue. His companions lined up behind him and disappeared through the archway, the imps leaping and gliding after them.

Jack was surprised when Clara smiled wide and pulled the reins to one side, leading her horse in a circle. Anyone could see she'd spent a lot of time with horses. Jack, however, hardly dared move and kept staring down at his steed.

"You've never ridden before, have you?" Katie sidled next to him.

Jack shook his head.

"Don't ye be afeared, me friend," Jeb said. "The best thing about a dreamed-up horse is they does what they was dreamed up to do. He'll get ye where ye's going, that be certain. Now, let's be off." Jeb steered his mount next to Clara's and waved a hand to urge the three teens on.

Katie waited for Jack to muster courage to click his tongue and give his mount a timid kick. The steed lurched forward through the archway and Jack leaned back, his knuckles white from holding onto the reins. Katie followed him. Jeb trotted next to Clara and the two galloped through the arch.

Jack pulled himself up straight and smiled now that he knew that he could slow his horse using only his thoughts. In his mind, he told his horse to follow close behind the Ghost Knights. He chuckled at how they paid no heed to the landscape as they rode. The knights approached a thick cluster of pines rooted in their path, and a short female rider to his right flipped her left wrist and sent the trees shifting to either side of the trail. He liked the way she held the sinewy stands of her ghostly body inward, giving an attractiveness to her figure that the other knights lacked. Her brown hair hung from the back of her helmet in a single twined braid.

Jack looked back and watched the trees return to their original location behind them. He nodded a 'thank you' to the woman, but soon questioned the wisdom of showing her gratitude. From that point on, he caught her looking away every time he glanced at her. He hoped no one else had noticed, but the next time he turned to Katie, she smiled wryly and gave him an encouraging wink. Jack's face reddened, and he looked away, shaking his head.

A few minutes later, a hefty knight riding next to Ezekiel leveled his lance at a low pile of loose logs and blasted them with a narrow beam of silent silver light. The knight's left eye glowed red and tele-scoped from his face plate, improving his aim. Jack threw a hand up to shield his eyes, and when the brightness diminished, the logs had dissipated with it. The same knight then took aim and blasted a hawk circling in the sky, high in front of them to their left. Jack surmised it was an Intershroud spy, but that didn't explain why the man ignored a second hawk when it darted out of a tree and dashed away to their right. Perhaps his mechanical eye told him when a bird was just a bird.

A tall hill ascended into view in front of them, and the heavy-set rider next to Katie placed his hands to each side of his head. The central ten feet of the mound melted away, trees and soil abruptly sinking into an unseen void and carving a narrow passageway straight through the mount.

Jack envied their power. Nothing could stand in their way. He joined the band of riders passing through the divide and enjoyed watching the exposed soil and severed roots and rocks rising high to each side. They exited the other side of the hill and rode through tall, dense aspens for five minutes before the view opened to a wide field of grass and a tall mountain to their right.

A solitary crow dived from around the bend ahead of them and Ezekiel raised a hand to halt the riders. The bird landed in Ezekiel's lap, out of Jack's line of sight. The leader of the Ghost Knights gazed down at the bird for ten seconds before holding it out on his hand and watching it take flight the way it had come. He turned to a large knight to his left. Jack shivered at the sight of him. Five-inch tusks ran down from his visor on both sides of his mouth.

"Intershroud troops have gathered beyond the next bend," the tusked knight said. "We shall need to descend below ground."

The tusked ghost gripped his lance with both hands and aimed its tip at the terrain in front of Ezekiel. Jack saw, through the knight's fading body, a reddish cloud emerge around the rocks and grass in a ten-foot circle before dissipating, revealing a new subterranean tunnel. A brown cobblestone ramp led through the round tunnel, constructed of rough-textured red bricks with lamps burning on wrought iron sconces situated along the walls.

Ezekiel motioned for everyone to follow him. The steeds made no sound against the cobblestones, making it obvious to Jack why the Ghost Knights could travel so easily undetected. The only sounds were an occasional grunt from a horse and the regular screams from miniature voices every time a knight squeezed the pouch tied to their belt.

Even the frog sat unnaturally quiet.

Jack turned to Abby. "Why don't we just go all the way to Silverton below ground?"

"Takes too much mental power, me friend," Jeb answered for her. "Ghosts fade fast, shaping things like this. 'Tis certain, we'll need to come above ground shortly."

"I'm glad you came back to help us." Clara sidled next to Jeb.

"'Tis certain ye are an expert with a horse, Miss Clara. Yet another thing ye have in common with me little Alice. Ye could be her twin, ye could. Ride a lot, do ye?"

"Every night when I dream," Clara said. "I never rode a horse while I was awake."

Jeb chuckled to himself. "Me Alice used to say she dreamed about horses."

"I'm sorry for what happened to her. It must've been horrible." Clara's eyes teared up.

"'Tis certain a man never could o' felt worse than I felt then. Never saw the face again o' the villain's what took her from me. Far's I know, he got his due ages ago. Don't make no difference to me. It might as well o' happened yesterday."

Clara forced a smile. "So, now you live in a real live haunted house?"

Jeb laughed. "I'd give me toe knuckles to give ye a ripe big hug. Truth is, I've not much need for me haunt no more. But it warms me old heart to think that it may save the life of as fine a young lady as ye. It's like I truly is saving me own little Alice."

Elongated shadows of the leading riders played along the curves of the tunnel's brick walls, and Jack squinted at the daylight now emanating from the round exit at the top of the sloped path ahead. Jack galloped up the ramp behind the Ghost Knights and out into a shallow, grassy ravine sandwiched between hills thickly smothered with pines. The last two riders, Clara and Jeb, barley arrived in the gulley behind Jack before tall green grass appeared behind them, replacing the tunnel's opening.

The tusked knight, who'd been maintaining the subterranean passageway, now appeared only as a faint gray mist. He slumped forward on his steed and his features started to regain color and opacity. The hefty knight behind him placed a hand on his back to hold him steady. Ezekiel waved his hand around and the already-thick forest grew three times denser with tall lodgepole pines. He made another motion with his hand, signaling the party to move forward with caution.

The horses traveled only a few hundred feet before Ezekiel held up a palm, warning his posse to stop. A rumbling noise grew louder, and the ground shook with increasing intensity.

Jack's jaw dropped. A vast herd of bison lumbered across their path, tearing through the high grass and kicking up clouds of dust in their wake. Jack looked at Katie, and they smiled.

Jack gazed beyond the hundreds of hefty beasts and spotted a tall church spire peeking above the trees on the far side of the open field. He turned to Katie and Clara, pointed at it, and yelled over the roar of the stampede, "That must be Silverton! We're almost there!"

# LVII

Katie shielded her eyes from the dust storm the lumbering bison kicked up, turned and found Clara staring at Abby's frightening form.

"I'm sorry about what Farley did to you," Clara said.

"Save it." Abby kept her gaze forward. "Your pity won't give me back my life."

"Killing Farley won't either," Clara said.

"No, but it'll give me peace. You don't know what I suffered. I created that camp to be a place where I could live without fear of Intershroud. It should've borne my name. Then Farley came along, harassing me. Pestering me. I should've killed him then!" She turned to Katie. "You could've killed him! Why didn't you? What kind of woman lets a man live who murdered her own sister? You owe it to me to kill him!"

Katie looked down. "Dad said your death was an accident."

"That coward! He knew how I died. He was always too scared to stand up to the Mighty Intershroud."

"How do you know it wasn't an accident?" Jack rode up between Abby and Clara. "Farley wasn't in the cave when it exploded."

"It was no accident!" Abby leaned in toward Jack, and he stared back with fear in his eyes. "Farley guided us into that mine to seal it off, then he claimed he felt sick and ran outside. Next thing I knew, I was dreaming, unconscious, and yet aware I was dying. I remembered subtle hints Farley had given us before the explosion and my soul writhed in agony. I felt the fabric between Materia and Essentia wrench apart and form a haunt. My ghost body entered Materia and found that soulless wretch sitting there admiring his work, a smirk on his bloody and burnt face. I refused to die. I still refuse. I won't rest until I see his twisted rotting corpse!"

"Can't you see what this is doing to you?" Katie's eyes welled up. "Why can't you let it go?"

Abby didn't respond. The last few bison lumbered by and Abby started forward, leading the party onward to Silverton.

Jack galloped next to Katie. "I know this is hard for you. We just need to get away from this nightmare before we all go crazy."

Katie nodded and rode on.

They'd ridden only a few hundred yards when Clara gasped and pointed at a black heap lying in the dirt, a yellow-shafted arrow protruding from its motionless body. Katie moved closer and realized it was a crow, and it wasn't alone. Four others lay scattered in the yellow grass, each with a feathered arrow through its heart.

"That one's moving!" Clara rode over to it.

Abby sped past Katie and halted her steed, then jumped down and wrapped her hands around the bird. She turned and rushed it over to Ezekiel. The Ghost Knight leader cradled the bird in his right arm and waited for it to roll on its side to face him. It opened its large black beak and a clear iridescent bubble emerged from its mouth. The bubble grew steadily until it reached the size of a beach ball. Katie pushed her steed closer and Jack and Clara crowded in with her.

A miniature scene appeared within the bubble, seen from a bird's eye view. A large company of American soldiers marched with staff members and campers from Camp Farley. Travis, Ming, and Barbara each carried assault rifles and Derek and Tamera stood in the back, talking to each other. Katie couldn't see Marina anywhere and hoped it was because her plan to go to Kalispell had worked.

She detected something else in the image, lurking in the shadows of trees. It hid behind a massive boulder, its long black legs barely visible, emerging from the undergrowth. Katie looked up and her stomach lurched when she realized she was looking at the same boulder the monster had been hiding behind in the crow's message.

"Incoming!" The tusked knight spun his horse and pointed to a cluster of trees to their right. The other knights rallied at the cry and searched for the attackers.

Three missiles crashed through the treetops and exploded in the dirt in front of them. Gunfire sounded from five or six locations all around them. Katie became confused and disoriented. Scores of soldiers emerged from behind pine trees and bulky rocks, many falling on one knee and steadying their assault rifles at Ezekiel's company.

Two camouflaged military vehicles appeared from nowhere, already in motion, swerving around the Ghost Knights. Travis, Ming, Barbara, Carl, and Tony hopped from the back of the vehicles and took positions in a row, leveling their M16 rifles at Katie, Clara, and Jack.

Derek and Damien climbed from the front of one of the transport trucks, and Tamara emerged from the other. They walked behind the soldiers, no weapons in their hands, and turned to face their captives. Damien frowned and glared at Jack. Gone was the syrupy smile that had always adorned his face before.

Two tanks rumbled into the clearing from the underbrush in three directions, and their main guns swiveled at the Ghost Knights. Two Blackhawk helicopters dived from behind the trees, chopping overhead.

Jack glared at Ming. Ming frowned and glanced back and forth at his rifle and at Jack, then he looked around at the soldiers. Katie could see the cogs in his head starting to question what was happening.

Jack seized the moment. "What are you doing, Ming? We're friends. A few days ago you said you wanted to be a veterinarian. Now, you want to shoot us? Can't you see that Media messed with your mind? This isn't you." Jack turned to Travis. "This isn't any of you."

Ming stared at his rifle, lifted it, and aimed it at Jack's face, his arms shaking. Five seconds passed, and he let the gun drop from his hands and clatter in the dirt at his feet. He pressed his right hand against his head and winced. Barbara looked at him and flung her gun on the ground near Ming's. She trembled and lifted her hands to the sides of her head.

Carl shook his head and snarled, then lowered his rifle and marched over to Ming. He gave him a shove. "Don't listen to this imbecile. You and Barbara, go back with Derek!"

Ming nodded, turned around, and weaved his way through the battalion of soldiers back to Damien and Derek. Barbara followed him. Katie knew they weren't obeying Carl. They just didn't want to participate anymore.

Movement behind the boulder startled Katie and she gasped. The creature she'd partly seen in the crow's bubble message emerged from a greenish haze. It descended a low craggy incline, four of its eight thin, spidery legs jabbing at the ground with each step, while four other appendages reached outward, their clawed ends snapping at the air. Two crab-like pedipalps reached forward at the ends of human arms.

The creature's human hands became visible whenever its massive claws scraped together. Its barbed and segmented tail swayed back and forth over its serpentine back and two pouches lined both sides of its yellowish, snakelike underbelly, each harboring a curved scimitar. Atop the scorpion's long segmented neck sat a face that would've frightened Katie in its normal human form.

It was the face of Francis Farley.

# LVIII

The intensity of Jack's feelings muddled his thoughts. His vision blurred, and he felt faint. He saw no hope of surviving hundreds of readied M16 rifles; two sleek M1 Abrams tanks swiveling their main guns toward him; two Blackhawk helicopters hovering low, their machine guns and rocket launchers ready to fire; and a monstrous beast tossing divots of earth with every step, making its way through the troops—a monster with the face of another monster.

Jack turned to the Ghosts Knights and wondered why they weren't reaching for their weapons. They had the power to uproot trees and toss them like matchsticks, to form massive boulders out of thin air, to create chasms in the earth that could swallow up everyone in this clearing. Yet they just sat on their dark steeds, their gloved hands resting in their laps.

At least the frog behaved according to expectations. It bounced around Jeb's head and clung to his ears and beard, searching high and low for a pathway to safety. It finally stopped in front of Jeb's face and clamped its wiry arms and legs around his head. "Shape an escape route for me, you nitwit! Guns make short work of frogs who walk and talk. We're not particularly bulletproof, you know."

Jeb's muffled response was unintelligible until he succeeded, with much yanking, pinching, and shoving, to twist the frog's body around to the left side of his head. "What in tarnation's wrong with ye? I cain't help ye with yer confarned belly in me face."

A loud electronic resonance permeated the air and a foot-wide, bright orange beam of light struck the center of a sparsely-branched lodgepole pine twenty feet beyond Jeb. The top half of the tree swung back and dropped with a thud, toppled away from Jack, and flopped into the ground with a loud swoosh. Jack turned to the source of the light beam and found the creature with Farley's face standing amid the troops and grinning. The glowing orange barb of his scorpion tail dimmed and went dark.

"Do I have your attention now?" Farley puffed out his segmented chest and danced two steps to the left and back again. "When you put as much work into a magnificent limn like this, you expect people to pay attention."

"You're just a murderer!" Katie clenched her teeth.

Farley's shoulders lowered. "Is that what these ghost folks have been telling you? Don't listen to them. Your sister's been spreading lies about me ever since she died. She assumes that just because I survived the explosion, I must have caused it. She was so obsessed with revenge, she taught herself how to link to me whenever I dreamed. I had to develop this scorpion limn just to keep her from dreaming about me. It wasn't easy, either."

"No one cares!" Katie gripped the reins of her horse so hard her knuckles whitened. "How dare you call her a liar! She saw you outside the mine after it blew. You were laughing. There isn't a word low enough to describe what you are!"

"So, you've had words with your deluded sibling, I see. I was hoping she'd be here with you. I may have enough power to destroy her, now that I'm in a coma. But, since I can't take care of her, I'll have to settle for ridding my life of you and your foolish friends."

Farley's tail stiffened, and Jack squinted at the increasing orange glow. The female Ghost Knight next to Jack took her lance in hand and charged in front of him, aiming at the scorpion man. Abby and

Ezekiel turned their heads toward her with speed that told of their intense disapproval.

"You cannot interfere with the rites of the Ghost Knights," she said. "The Treaty of Phantasmagoria forbids it."

Farley sneered. "That treaty also forbids ghosts from interfering with Intershroud business. You demolished my lab and forced the closure of my camp. The treaty is void."

"What about Uncle Vance?" Clara rode up next to Katie. "He's your boss. He wouldn't approve of this."

"Don't think for a minute you won't pay for hurting his daughter," Jack said.

Farley gave a wry smile and Katie turned her gaze downward to evade the brightness increasing at the end of his barbed tail. "You seem to forget that the three of you are currently unconscious, trapped below tons of rubble in a mine that you blew up, Mr. Park. I'm only going to disperse your minds, so you'll never have to be conscious of your hopeless situation."

"Katie's father isn't dumb," Jack said. "He'll know you attacked us out of revenge."

"Then I'll have to make sure there's no one around to inform him." Orange light exploded from Farley's tail, its electric resonance muffling screams from Katie and Clara.

Abby and the Ghost Knights reached for their lances. Jeb stretched his arms forward and a six-foot-wide boulder formed out of nowhere, hurtling through the air toward Farley and intercepting his light beam.

The scorpion man jumped sideways on his thin, agile legs, and the massive rock rumbled through the grass behind him before disappearing over a low hill.

The tusked knight motioned upward with his hands and the earth trembled. A bastion of thick stone arose from the earth in front of Jack and his companions, but it didn't come fast enough. Farley's light beam had dropped low when he dodged the boulder. It carved a long, deep rut in the ground heading toward Jack and Katie. Three soldiers in its path disappeared instantly on contact with the beam. Jack held tight to his horse's reins and leaned back, the course hair of his steed's mane flying up and smothering his face. The bucking animal grunted and hopped backward three steps on its hind legs. Jack winced at the hot breeze of the orange beam passing below his legs. His stomach clenched—the shaft of light had passed through the body of his mount.

He sunk through the liquefying flank of the animal, a sensation not unlike diving backwards into a bath of warm gelatin. He flinched at the sudden jolt of his backside slamming against sharp rocks. The horse's torso sunk and disappeared within a rising black mist that dropped and flowed outward, then dispersed through the meadow grass. Jack turned and saw Katie horseless and squatting low on one knee amidst a similar fluid mass of blackness.

Jack stood, motioned for Katie to follow him, and darted behind the steeds of Abby and Ezekiel, holding his head low and using the black mist for cover. Katie started to push herself up, but froze, a grimace of pain on her face.

Clara swung from her steed, ducked down, and ran to her cousin and kneeled by her side. "You okay?" She reached out a hand and Katie grabbed it, nodding her head.

"It's my back. I'll be fine."

Clara helped her up, then they ducked low and edged over to Jack.

"Tamera and Derek are both Shapers," Jack said. "I saw them waving their arms around. They're creating all these tanks and helicopters." Jack grew anxious at remembering the tanks and he turned to look for them over the rampart. He breathed easy when he found one tank already flattened into a mass of mangled steel below a giant boulder near Farley. Another lay upside down, thirty feet away, sunken four feet into the earth with an eight-foot wide tree trunk planted into its underside. He grinned. The Ghost Knights had been busy while he was falling through his horse.

Beyond the upturned tank at the far side of the battlefield, Derek frantically waved his arms out to his sides and descended slowly into a trench with his companions. A sloped embankment arose in front of him. Tony, Carl, and Travis worked their way through the ranks of soldiers, darted up the ridge, and jumped, disappearing into the trench to join Ming, Barbara, Damien, Derek, and Tamera.

Farley stood, surrounded by his soldiers, and grinned at Katie. She stood paralyzed, her gaze riveted on Farley's quivering, glowing scorpion tail.

A shadow flowed over the terrain, dancing through the grass and trees. Farley's lopsided grin vanished, and he looked up, his eyes wide with terror. His barbed tail jolted upward and fired far above Katie's head, the orange blast carving a long wavy line through the sky.

Gunfire sounded from everywhere, trees on all sides shaking with the masses of bullets. Every soldier emptied his magazine into the sky, then reloaded, walking backward with baby steps. Jack looked up over his shoulder and shivered. Hundreds of winged ape-men soared over the treetops or leaped from pine branch to pine branch. They grunted, whooped, and howled, their faces contorted with frenzied glee.

LIX

Dozens of imps dropped from the trees and sky, riddled with scores of bullet holes. Others dropped from the heavens in pieces, sliced in half by the merciless power of Farley's light beam. A flying ape-man spiraled downward directly above Katie, throwing off sparks as it fell, exploding twelve feet above her without a sound. A cloud of black dust rained down on Katie, making her cough.

Most of the imps, however, glided onward, undeterred by the gunfire. Mobs of them crowded into each of the Blackhawk helicopters, overpowering the pilots and gunners. The aircrafts tilted, spun, and dived, crashing in loud, fiery explosions in the distant pines, setting them aflame.

Scores of soldiers turned to run away through the dusty haze. The imps showed no concern either for their victims' or for their own lives. Throughout the field they dived from above, absorbing showers of bullets and plowing into the soldiers at lightning speed. Imp and soldier alike imploded in clouds of dust, leaving only shallow craters in their wake. Other imps snatched retreating soldiers by their arms or legs and hefted them over the treetops.

Twelve feet to Katie's right, a soldier dropped his gun and

screamed with such terror he made himself disappear. His attacker swooped past him empty-handed.

"They're just being awoken," Katie assured Clara. It gave her some comfort reminding herself that these poor people were just waking up. Only hers, Clara's, and Jack's lives were actually on the line.

Derek and Tamera remained visible above the far embankment. Katie figured they needed a clear view of the battleground in order to shape everything. Derek stretched his arms upward at a dark cloud that began forming above a crowd of imps to his left, near Damien. It solidified and took the long sleek form of an Apache attack helicopter, its cylindrical rocket launchers already firing at the throng of imps. A dozen creatures exploded in a thundering plume of flame. A score of airborne imps charged the helicopter and sent it flying into a tall tree where it tore itself into fiery pieces within the branches. The remaining imps on the ground turned toward Derek and charged.

Tamera stretched her arms out, then swung them back toward herself. The earthen embankment flattened and reshaped into a solid white concrete buttress. She and Derek disappeared below a concrete box lid, and thin vertical slits opened along the length of the bunker wall. Rifles protruded from the slits and gunfire flashed with the blasts of their gun barrels. Approaching imps twitched with every bullet, but they still reached the bunker and climbed all over it. They hefted rocks and hurled them at the walls or slammed them down on the massive lid. Nothing could penetrate it.

Katie stood for a look above the stone bulwark but fell back under the pressure of Jack's hands on her shoulders. An orange beam carved off the tops of the stones in front of her.

"That was close." Jack peeked over the now heated rocks, ducked, and turned back to Katie and Clara. "I don't see any soldiers left, but Farley's still holding his own out there. The imps can't get near him."

Katie ventured another peek over the rampart, and Clara joined her. Electronic blasts echoed from Farley's tail at random intervals, immersing the treetops in reflected orange brightness. Farley had secured gleaming blue scimitars from the fleshy pockets that ran along his segmented chest and he held the steel weapons in each of his six pincers. He danced in a circle, aiming his tail at anything that dared approach him. Imps hovered among the treetops all around him, snarling and growling, waiting for a chance to attack. Three imps charged him at once, but a single swipe from Farley's tail disintegrated them in flashes of sparks and smoke.

Katie ducked down again. "Nothing's getting past that tail of Farley's."

"We need to do something," Jack said.

Clara's eyes lit up. "Maybe we can distract him." She eyed the dislodged top hatch of one of the demolished tanks lying on the floor of the trench near her feet. She yanked the metal door hatch from its hinges with a loud steel crunch.

"What are you going to do with that?" Katie smiled at Clara's display of strength, so out of place from a teenage girl of such slight build.

Clara dropped the hatch door, letting it stab six inches into the dirt. "We're so much stronger here. I was thinking if all three of us sneak up behind one of those broken-down tanks, we can push it toward Mr. Farley and distract him."

"That might give the imps a window to attack him!" Jack grinned wide.

"It's risky, if he sees us," Katie said. "We don't know what that light beam will do if it hits one of us. It could burn us to ashes."

"We'll have to make sure he doesn't see us," Jack rushed along the trench floor, head lowered, until he arrived at a location where a crushed tank stood between him and Farley. Katie locked step behind Clara and they soon caught up to him.

Jack pulled himself over the rampart and helped the girls climb up. Katie moved with them across the field toward the tank, with her head down. She couldn't see Farley, but she saw two of the imps charging at him from opposite sides in the air, each taking a pulsing blast and vanishing in downpours of sparks. Another two beasts dove and took cover in depressions in the battlefield to his left when his back was turned, his light blast swiping the air above them.

Jack positioned himself with both hands pressing against the crushed tank, his feet planted firm on the ground, ready to push. Clara did the same, then Katie.

"On the count of three," Jack said. "One...two...three."

Katie pushed with all her strength, along with her companions. The tank rolled from the depression it sat in and tumbled toward Farley, rolling two times. Katie, Clara, and Jack fell to their knees as it left their hands. Farley's tail beam sliced downward, dividing the tank down the middle and forming a wide gap. The tank stopped short of hitting him.

The distraction, however, worked. The two imps hiding in the nearby crater rose into the air and pounced on Farley's barbed tail, throwing it to the ground and sitting on it. Their success triggered twenty more creatures to attack. The breeze from their flapping leathery wings brushed across Katie's face and hair. Ten of the imps pinned Farley's tail down and he dug his feet into the ground, groaning in his effort to free it.

Farley continued firing his grounded tail weapon, burning a deep hole in the side of the hill behind him. Ash trees toppled one after another in a row, their roots incinerated by the pulsating beams. The shaft of energy, however, slowly decreased in strength.

Other imps pressed upon Farley, but he held them at bay with his six swords, and the powerful snapping of his large pedipalp claws. He slashed through the air, crisscrossing his swords in the faces of any being within reach. The imps took turns lashing at him whenever his gaze turned. Three imps blitzed him, two taking wounds from the edges of his crisscrossing blades while the third perished in the powerful grip of his right pedipalp. Each imp wiggled and fell, sputtering to nothing but mist and sparks.

"Derek!" Farley slashed another imp to oblivion. "Help me out here! So help me, I'll have your mind wiped! Get me out of here!"

Derek had his hands full with the hoard of imps smothering his bunker. Gunfire continued exploding from the bunker across the battlefield and Katie laid low, hoping Derek and his companions couldn't see her behind all the tree branches and machine parts lying on the ground. Jack and Clara crawled over to her.

"I can't believe that worked," Jack said. "Good idea, Clara."

An imp dived behind Farley, carrying a large stone, and began crushing Farley's tail with it. Farley thrashed around, trying to slash at the imps behind him, but couldn't reach them. An imp caught one of Farley's right arms and yanked a sword away, along with the pincer-hand holding it.

A loud crack sounded from behind Farley and he screamed. The imps behind him backed away, and one of them launched into the air, swinging around a three-foot section of Farley's tail. The imp spun around and hurled his prize far over the hill behind him. The stump of Farley's tail darkened, now useless and unthreatening.

A trumpet echoed through the clearing and Ezekiel led his horse through the stone wall, past Clara, and stopped in front of Farley.

"My loyal servants!" Ezekiel's voice resonated louder than should have been possible. Every imp stopped and turned to face him. "Thine loyalty shalt be rewarded. It is time for thee to retreat and give this battle over to your master."

The imps didn't waste a second. They leaped into the air and darted for the shadows in the trees and undergrowth, some gliding over the hills.

Katie turned to Jack. "Are they calling it off?"

"I don't think so," Jack pointed over her shoulder.

She turned and discovered over thirty Ghost Knights had emerged from the trees in a long row, many with their lances raised. She turned the other way, looking over Jack's shoulder, and found another twenty Ghost Knights sitting similarly at alert on their black steeds.

Farley backed away three steps, his eyes wide.

"Spare our quarry," Ezekiel said. "Fire away!"

Missiles shot from the knights' lances in rapid succession, pummeling Derek's bunker in a symphony of explosions, buzzes, and loud cracks. Cannonballs shot from the lance of the knight ten feet behind Abby. Lightning buzzed from the lance of the knight next to him. Three knights took to the air on their steeds, blasting beams of blue and red energy at the bunker. Concrete chipped, cracked, and exploded, only to refill and heal itself seconds later.

"It's a mental battle," Clara said. "Each side is trying to un-shape what the other side shapes. We better stay out of their way."

"Back to the trench." Katie pushed herself to her hands and knees and crawled backward toward the stone wall, unwilling to look away from the battlefield for even a second. Clara and Jack did the same, though Jack moved at a slower pace, apparently too distracted by everything happening in front of him.

A thirty-foot-tall oak tree took form in the air above Derek's bunker and dropped, slamming down on it and making the earth rumble. The bunker split into two segments and part of the wall tipped over, exposing Barbara, Travis, and Carl. The tree transformed into gray dust and dispersed into a massive cloud that washed across the field in all directions.

A massive grizzly bear appeared in a flash of green light and charged through the opening in the bunker. Its six-inch claws swiped first at Barbara, then Travis, and then Carl, each of them vanishing in turn before Tamera shrunk the animal to the size of a squirrel and Derek re-formed the concrete barrier walls.

Katie couldn't tell who was shaping what. She helped Clara over the rampart wall into the trench and watched both Jeb and the tusked knight stare intensely at the bunker, weaving their hands through the air like they were practicing tai chi. A dozen other knights did the same. No doubt, Derek and Tamera were gazing out the slits in their bunker, shaping weapons and defenses as fast as they could think.

Two Apache helicopters started to form in the air, but then melted and turned to mush and dropped to the ground with a splash.

Three camouflaged K2 Black Panther tanks melded up from the ground in the clearing and fired on the Ghost Knights. A ten-foot-wide fissure wove along the battlefield, and the tanks tipped into its endless depths. The crack worked its way to the bunker and split its walls with a loud crack. The bunker healed itself. The fissure filled with dark soil.

A rounded shadow surrounded Katie and Clara and Katie looked up and screamed. A ten-foot boulder was dropping from the sky over

Jack, who still lay ten feet from the safety of the trench. Jack's Ghost Knight admirer stretched her arms out and a nearby tree uprooted, spun through the air, and cracked against the boulder, flinging it away like a golf ball. The knight sent the tree across the field where it crashed into Derek's bunker and blasted another wide gap in the concrete.

Ezekiel saw his chance and leveled his lance at the gap. A thin funnel cloud emerged from the lance's tip and stretched across the field, widening as it went, until it broke from the lance and became a full tornado. Ming flew from the gap, hanging onto a bar of twisted steel reinforcing, his legs wiggling in the air. Tamera then flew out of the gap and slammed into Ming, sending them both into the clearing. Tamera rolled several feet before Abby blasted her with a bolt of white light from her lance. Tamera disappeared.

Ming lay alone in the clearing, dazed and shaking, his eyes wide with fear.

"Ming's terrified," Clara said.

"We can't help him," Katie said. "He's on their side now."

Jack was about to climb into the trench but stopped and shook his head. "I don't know what they did to him, but he's my friend."

"He's a friend who won't hesitate to kill you." Katie reached for Jack's leg, but he'd already moved out of her reach.

Balls of steel flew all around Ming, slamming into the earth or crashing into the concrete bunker behind him. He threw his hands over his head and laid flat on the ground.

"Their guns can't hurt me," Jack said. "I'm going to help him."

"You have cracked ribs and bruises that tell a different story," Katie said. "Besides, he'll just wake up if they hit him."

"He'll wake up thinking I hate him. I'll be okay."

A lightning bolt carved a line through the battlefield near Ming and exploded at the bunker. Jack pursed his lips and charged toward his friend, zigzagging around craters in the ground and dodging flying steel balls and blasting bolts of lightning all around him. He winced when a bullet tagged him in the back of the neck, and again when one pegged his left thigh.

Jack arrived at Ming's side and took his hand, trying to pull him up. "Come with me!" He had to yell over the din of the battle.

"Just let me die!" Ming yanked his hand away.

"Come on, Ming. You're my friend. You'll be safe with us."

Ming looked up at him and stared for several seconds. He stretched out a hand and let Jack pull him up, but they ran only three steps before Ming vanished. Jack stood wide-eyed and confused, but Katie had seen the rifle barrels firing from the edge of the opening in the bunker.

Jack's face contorted with fury. His shoulder jerked and he winced when a bullet pelted him in the back. He turned toward his attackers and raised a clenched fist. "What's wrong with you people! How do you live with yourselves?"

Jack turned away from the bunker and marched toward Katie, his face showing only contempt.

The shooting from the bunker stopped.

"My gun stopped working!" Katie recognized Tony's voice yelling within the bunker. "Hurry! Derek, make me another one!"

Jack arrived at the rampart and jumped over it to the trench floor next to Katie.

Katie embraced him, astounded that he'd risked his life for someone who'd betrayed him.

"For what it's worth, he woke up knowing you forgave him."

"That's what matters." Jack smiled at her.

Katie released him and turned back to observe the battlefield. The gap in the bunker clouded up and solidified into concrete again, but Derek was working alone now. The Ghost Knights moved in closer, Jeb and the tusked knight taking the lead of six other knights, all shapers judging by the way they held their hands forward. The tusked knight let out a roar and jabbed his arms forward. The lid of the bunker cracked, flew upward, and crashed through the pines, disappearing in the meadow grass. Derek lifted his arms to restore it, but the front wall began resonating and it crumbled into a pile of stones, metal bars, and chunks of concrete. Derek, Damien, and Tony stood exposed.

Derek's eyes bulged, and his arms shook in his effort to reshape the bunker, but the dark dust dissipated only seconds after he shaped it. A boulder appeared in the air above him. Damien lurched, grabbed Derek's arm, and the two of them stood frozen a full second before vanishing. The remains of the bunker melted to liquid and flopped down, flowing into the grass.

Tony stood alone in the wreckage. He checked the ammo in his gun, grinned, and tried to fire it, but nothing happened. Jack had somehow rendered his gun useless. Tony snarled and charged in Jack's direction, laughing and raising his weapon high above his head like a club. He arrived within ten feet of Jack when a tall, branchless pine dropped from the air and stomped Tony into Materia. Jack's admirer ghost knight nodded her head at Jack.

He grinned and nodded back.

The Ghost Knights closed in on the trembling and wounded scorpion form of Francis Farley. Jack peered over the cold capstones of the wall. A hand pushed down on his shoulder for leverage and Katie swung herself over the barrier and ran toward Jeb.

"What are you doing?" Jack pulled himself up and rolled over the capstones.

"Wait! Give me a hand!" Clara reached up a hand, Jack pulled her out of the trench, and they rushed to catch up with Katie.

Jeb sat on his horse behind the circle of knights, the frog nestled on his back with only its green head visible below Jeb's grizzled hair. "'Tis best ye stay back." Jeb stretched a hand in front of Katie.

She shoved it aside. "Abby's my sister!" She darted past him, only stopping after squeezing past the steeds of the crowding knights.

Clara rushed past Jack, and he ran to keep up with her. He could only see Abby and Farley sporadically through drifting gray mists and the waving of horse tails. Clara pushed between two horses and the riders moved to let her stand next to Katie, allowing Jack a clearer view of the fight.

Farley extended his massive pedipalps, snapped them at the knights, and danced in a circle, waving his three remaining scimitars at them. "You think I don't know you ghosts are a bunch of cowards?" Farley snapped his right pedipalp at the tusked knight, who pulled his horse back three steps. Farley's furrowed brow and wide eyes exposed his inner terror. The red stump of his tail wobbled over his back when he moved, a constant reminder of his powerlessness.

"They'll be back for me," Farley said. "Damien went for reinforcements. You'll see. Touch me and you'll have to deal with the entire Intershroud. Your actions have already shredded the treaty of Phantasmagoria. Lynch won't tolerate that. You'll see."

The laughter of a woman erupted from a mounted Ghost Knight facing Farley, mocking and merciless. She removed her helmet, let it slip from her hand onto the ground, and swung her leg over her horse and hopped down.

Farley spun to face her. "Abby Frost? I figured you might be here somewhere, but I didn't think you'd *joined* these wingnuts. Not really your style, or so I thought."

Abby laughed again. "Enjoy your thoughts while they last." Her smile turned to a sneer. She tightened her grip on her lance and jerked it toward him. A blast of yellow light shot from its tip with a loud crack. The beam connected with Farley's chest and threw him backward, slamming him against the horse of the tusked knight. The knight jabbed him with his lance, forcing him to crawl, groaning and wincing, to the center of the circle.

He looked up at Abby. "Are you really this ignorant? You can't kill me. I'm in a coma."

Abby's face contorted with hate, her eyes swelling, teeth gnashing, and hands trembling. "Death is too good for you! I'm not just going to kill you. I'm going to disintegrate your mind, reduce you to a mindless, living corpse. You'll be nothing! Then, after you've rotted in a hospital bed, Katie will finish the job and pull your plug."

Farley cried out and lunged at Abby, his swords slicing the air. She zapped him in the chest, and he rolled backward, head over heels, three times before collapsing in a cloud of dust.

Katie placed her hands over her mouth and cried. Jack didn't know what to say to her.

Farley took several deep breaths and righted his scorpion body.

Abby walked around him. "So pathetic! Before I erase you, I want you to spend your final thoughts pondering on your stupidity. We knew you were hiding in these hills, but we also knew nothing would lure a coward like you out of your rathole. So, we tempted you with something we knew you'd think you could easily destroy—a small band of Ghosts Knights and a few naïve children."

"You used your own sister as bait?" Farley sneered. "You're no better than I am."

"Katie wants me avenged as much I do! Start the Rite of Vengeance!"

Ezekiel raised a hand and looked around. The sounds of trumpets, drums, and an ethereal chorus echoed from the trees, same as when Jack's Aspect had fought Avard's ghost. Farley trembled and glanced at Jack, his eyes begging for help.

Jack looked away and found Clara hugging her cousin.

"She's lying," Clara patted her back. "She's just trying to humiliate him. She wouldn't have used us like that."

Jack shook his head. "No, she wasn't. I saw the red-eyed knight blast a spy hawk earlier. Another one took off to the northwest hills and he let it go. He wanted it to go to Farley."

"You're not helping," Clara said.

"It's alright, Clara." Katie's frowning lip quivered. "I don't blame Abby for this, after what Farley did."

"But she'll disappear," Clara said. "We'll lose her forever."

"You heard Jeb. We already lost her. That's not my sister. It's just her tortured mind, obsessing with her pain and suffering, giving Farley what he deserves."

Farley lunged forward again, but a blast of yellow light struck the shoulder of one of his left pincers with another loud crack. Farley spun to his left and his pincer tore from its socket, his scimitar flying through the air and twanging against a tree trunk far behind him.

"That was for Elian." Abby leveled her lance at Farley's left side. "This is for his brother, Julian!" She fired, and the beam tore off the only remaining appendage on Farley's right side, spinning him around. His sword skidded through the dirt behind him.

Farley raised his only remaining sword and inched forward, but Abby's lance blasted off one of his two left legs. He tripped and stumbled forward onto his face, moaning.

"That was for James Durden," Abby said.

Farley started to stand up and she blasted one of his right legs, sending him rolling on his left side. "That was for Emily."

"I get it," Farley clawed at the ground. "You're going to name off everyone who died in the explosion. Just get this over with!"

Another crack echoed through the hills and yellow energy crashed through the hinged joint of the large pedipalp on Farley's right. The two halves of the claw tumbled in the dirt below two horses and the faint image of a normal human arm appeared at Farley's right side.

"That was for my friend, Jasmine, who never would have hurt a fly!"

"Don't kid yourself. You're just like me." Farley swayed from side to side, unable to stand up. "You're enjoying this."

Abby laughed.

Jack detected movement to his right, turned and gasped. Damien appeared out of nowhere, thirty yards away, his arms around two men in dark suits on his left and two women in grey pantsuits, to his right. They each held glowing violet staffs and stood frozen for two seconds, until Damien disappeared. The people he left behind positioned themselves a dozen feet apart in a curved line. Damien appeared again in another location, arms around another two women and men, each dressed in suits.

The tusked knight spotted the arrivals and stared at them for a few seconds before turning back to Abby. At least three other knights had also seen them, but did nothing.

"This one's for Sam," Abby blasted Farley's other pedipalp which spun from his arm socket and slammed into a tree, sparking and fading into black dissipating dust. "He thought you were his friend! He looked up to you!"

Four more people appeared with Damien thirty yards beyond the knights on the other side of Farley.

Clara slid next to Jeb. "Damien's bringing in people from Intershroud. They're forming a circle around us."

Jeb looked around and his bushy eyebrows rose up. "They won't interfere with the Rite of Vengeance. That'd mean war with the ghosts. 'Tis certain 'tain't good fer ye, though. Ye young'uns best be on yer way. Follow me. I'll get ye to me haunt."

"This is for Drake!" A thunderous crack sounded amidst a burst of light, and another leg flew off Farley's segmented underbelly. He laid motionless in the dirt, one leg stretched to his left side below a single pincer, still clinging to a scimitar.

"You call me a coward? How about giving me one fair swing at you?"

Jack ran to Katie and grabbed her arm. "Lynch is coming. We need to go."

Katie yanked her arm away. "I'm not leaving Abby."

"They're surrounding us," Clara said.

Another loud crack bathed the treetops in shadows and yellow light. Farley's last leg flung through the dirt. Two faint human legs appeared, stretching in front of him.

"That was for the last of us. Angela," Abby said. "I never liked her. She defended you when you were harassing me. Yet even that didn't stop you from murdered her in cold blood!"

Farley laughed. "Do you really think I'm going to start feeling guilty now? Your last attack is for you, right? Let's get it done."

"Oh no. Not yet. This next one's for all of our families whose lives you destroyed!"

Farley flung his last scimitar at Abby, but it disintegrated in the same burst of yellow energy that ripped the last appendage from his body. His stump of a tail faded, and his segmented chest shrunk down and flattened until it reformed into the tall wiry limn of Francis Farley, sitting in the dirt and leaning on his left arm. His bruised, hairy chest showed through his tattered black shirt.

Jeb steered his horse in front of Katie, blocking her view. She glared at him and pushed at his horse.

"I's truly sorry, miss. I know ye wants to see this, but yer lives be in peril. Intershroud ain't here for the ghosts. They be comin' fer ye. We have to leave, now!"

Katie turned to Clara, then Jack, then she looked around. Intershroud agents stood in a wide circle, each toting a vertical violet staff in their right hand. Damien appeared, his arms around Curtis Lynch, Fenton Murdock, and Derek. Katie's shoulders slumped. She nodded and said, "Let's get out of this nightmare."

LXI

Katie ran, Jack and Clara darting after her. Jeb rode on their right to block the view of Lynch and his companions. His tactic, however, didn't work. Every Intershroud agent nodded at Lynch in unison, raised their violet staff a foot high, and jabbed it into the ground. A violet web of laser-thin beams of light crisscrossed the terrain below everyone within the circle, each staff connecting a light beam to each other staff, forming a massive web of purple light.

Jack's leg muscles throbbed and weakened. The feeling reminded him of a time long ago when he'd accidentally touched an electric fence.

Katie and Clara stopped and turned to Jack.

"What is this?" Clara rubbed her thighs.

Jeb raised his hands toward two of the agents, then looked at his hands. He tried to turn around, but his horse only whinnied and wouldn't move a hoof.

The music of the Rite ceased.

"Who dares interrupt the Rite of Vengeance?" It was Ezekiel's voice, but it had lost its strength, now the normal baritone voice of a man.

Jack turned around and found that the whole scene had changed.

The sinewy forms of the Ghost Knights had reverted to the appearance of typical knights riding normal horses. Even the tusks had disappeared from the tusked knight's helmet. The ghosts jabbed their lances in the air toward Intershroud agents, but nothing happened.

"Their powers are gone," Katie said.

"This is an outrage!" Ezekiel unsheathed his sword and raised it toward Lynch. The other knights followed suit, raising their swords high. The knights, including Jeb, faded a little, allowing Jack to see Lynch and his Intershroud agents in any direction.

"I'll skewer you like a pig!" Abby jabbed her lance toward Farley, but no energy came forth. She tried to run at him but couldn't lift her feet. She screamed.

Farley pulled himself up, staggering and laughing. "I warned you. Intershroud looks out for its own."

"Silence, you imbecile!" All eyes turned to Mr. Lynch. "Intershroud values its relationship with the ghost population!" He faced Ezekiel. "I beg your forgiveness for this interruption to your sacred rite, but it was unavoidable. The inhibitor net was necessary to apprehend these three fugitives. Please, carry on with your business."

Farley's eyed bulged and he glared at Lynch. "What? These ghosts destroyed our camp! I've been faithful to you! I've brought you dozens of recruits and protected our secrets!"

"How long did you think we'd tolerate your incompetence?" Lynch nodded to Mr. Murdock, and the man pulled a pulsating violet orb from a pocket in his black suit jacket.

"The ghosts are entitled to their revenge," Lynch said. "It's your sloppiness that lost us our recruitment facility. We cannot allow you to now threaten our alliance with the ghosts."

Fenton held his hands forward and released the orb, his fingers stretched toward it. The orb hovered and floated to a point twelve feet above Abby and Farley. A transparent dome flowed out of the orb, encasing the entire Ghost Knight cavalry. Only Jeb and the three Dream Runners remained outside of the dome, along with all Intershroud agents. The glowing violet lines of the inhibitor net stopped at the dome edge and crisscrossed over the top of it.

The sinuous forms of the Ghost Knights instantly returned, and their horses whinnied and bucked amidst their dark mists, elated to be able to move again. Abby's lance again glowed with bright yellow energy and she grinned, her eyes bulging in her ecstasy. Then she bent her lance toward Farley's face.

He cowered, shaking his head.

"Any last words?" She laughed. Farley's mouth opened to speak, but Abby had no intention of letting words come out. She gritted her teeth and squinted at the bright yellow light washing away the features of Farley's face. She pushed all the power of her being into the energy of that lance. It crackled and brightened until Jack could barely open his eyes to watch. Farley's body shook and morphed to the color of the beam, then flickered out with a thunderous whump.

Farley was gone.

LXII

The sheer joy in Abby's face made Katie's stomach churn, yet she couldn't look away. She braced herself, expecting her sister to fade away at any moment.

"It's done!" Abby tossed her lance in the dirt. "I did it. He's gone. He's finally gone." She staggered in a circle, like a drunk woman, and laughed.

Jack looked at Jeb. "How much time does Abby have?"

Jeb raised an eyebrow. "Ye never know with these long-term ghosts. The memory pouch is already gone from her belt. I suspect she ain't got long."

The earth rumbled, and Katie leaned on Jeb's horse to regain her balance. The frog, still nestled in Jeb's hair, turned his head to see what was happening. He shook his head and pressed his face back into Jeb's hair.

The grass, rocks, and soil at the feet of the agents of Intershroud churned and heaved upward, broke apart, and made way for something huge emerging at a slow pace from the ground. Tree roots snapped, and stones tumbled away. Intershroud agents rose steadily on top of a gray wall of rough-textured concrete, over ten feet thick. Derek squinted and held one hand to his head and the other forward, palm down. A ten-foot-wide, studded-steel gate punctuated the ascending circular wall below Lynch and Murdock. In less than twenty seconds, a twenty-foot-high enclosure had surrounded the Emend Delegation, Jeb, and the Dream Runners.

"Release my people!" Ezekiel's voice thundered. He charged to the edge of the transparent dome and faced Lynch and Murdock. "This outrage shall not go unanswered!"

Dozens of angry threats resonated from the knights throughout the prison yard. "Infidels!"

"We'll wipe Intershroud from the earth!"

"This is war!"

"I'll destroy the lot of ye with me bare hands!"

The red-eyed knight raised his lance and sent a white blast directly at Lynch, but it fizzled out at the surface of the dome, absorbed by the inhibitor net.

Jack turned to Jeb. "Where are their imps?"

Jeb pointed upward. "Ye didn't notice the fog overhead?"

The three teenagers looked up. Sure enough, the yellow-gray sky had turned a light gray, with billowing clouds churning slowly, deep within the mists.

"'Tis the same fog dome they placed over Farley's camp. 'Tis certain ye noticed it if ye ever dreamed while ye was there. Anyone what enters the fog dome be findin' themselves exiting a thousand miles away. 'Tis certain no imp'll be penetrating that fog."

"Please, please, my friends." Lynch held his open palms out to his sides. "I assure you; we mean you no offense. The ghost population has been our faithful ally for decades. Surely, you know I could've wiped out your entire delegation if that were my intention. We ask only that you depart in peace and leave these three children in our care."

"We ain't gonna let ye bring harm to these young'uns," Jeb said.

Damien ran to the edge of the wall and looked down at Katie. "We're not going to hurt you, Katie. I promise. We'll take good care of you, and Clara."

"Lies!" Katie stepped forward and shook her fist at him, ignoring the numbing effect of the inhibitor net below her feet. "I could've died in that sleep lab! You knew it and you did nothing! I'll never trust you again!"

Damien opened his mouth to speak, but nothing came out. He lowered his head and took three steps backward, stopping near his father, who patted him on the shoulder.

"There shall be no negotiations," Ezekiel said. "Release my delegation immediately or deem our treaty with thee nullified."

"I understand," Lynch said. "I wished only to apprehend these children without inciting a battle with your renowned warriors. In good faith, I release you from the inhibitor dome and ask you kindly to depart."

Lynch nodded to Derek who then raised his arms and twisted at his waist. Derek's eyes followed the circle of Intershroud operatives standing at attention along the wall top. Horizontal grey clouds formed out of the atmosphere over their right shoulders, shrunk, and condensed into metal tubes with thick black bands at each end, and a short viewer scope secured to its top. The agents each raised their right hands in time to catch their missile launchers and train them on the Ghost Knights. They raised their violet rods from the concrete ledge in unison, and the glowing violet lines of the inhibitor net flickered out.

The heavy steel gates creaked and swung open with a loud metallic clunk. Horses bucked and galloped in a circle within the dome. Mr. Murdock reached his right hand toward the violet orb at the apex of the dome and it flew with lightning speed to his open palm.

The dome evaporated, and the dark, ghostly cavalry charged out the gates.

"Hold up," Jeb said, his voice drowned by the whinnying of the angry, spectral stallions. "These young'uns leave with us!" He signaled Katie, Clara, and Jack to follow him.

Ezekiel nodded his approval to Jeb, then galloped through the metal doors.

A hand landed on Katie's shoulder and she turned to find Abby, breathing hard and looking around in jerky motions. She'd abandoned her horse, plainly visible through Abby's semi-transparent body, trotting alongside Ezekiel.

"I can guide you to the haunt." Abby's voice spoke soft and shakily.

"We need to hurry before they close the gate." Katie pushed onward with all her strength but couldn't walk ten feet without having to weave around a pothole, loose rock, or stray branch. She glanced up and saw four knights waiting beyond the gates, including Ezekiel, the tusked knight, the red-eyed ghost, and the short knight that had taken a liking to Jack.

Jack arrived to within twenty feet of the opening when a billowing gray curtain began to drop in front of Ezekiel and his companions. The knights charged the gate, but the cloud touched the ground and hid them from view. The gate swung inward and slammed shut with a deafening clunk.

Katie and Abby caught up with Clara, Jack, and Jeb, all standing before the closed gate, and watched it fade to solid gray concrete. The ground rumbled and the walls moved and scraped, closing in around Jack and his companions until the yard shrunk to a thirty-foot circle. Intershroud operatives teetered and struggled to maintain their balance, many of them falling and waking up, until only eight agents remained, missile launchers still strapped to their shoulders.

Only Abby and Jeb remained of the Ghost Knights. Jeb shot his arms forward, clenching his broken yellowed teeth. A twenty-foot section of the concrete enclosure softened and waved in and out, and a circular hole broke open in the wall. The opening grew wider, then shrunk again and sealed up. Derek stood with hands stretched out and his face contorted with strain, matching Jeb's effort to un-shape the stronghold. Five seconds hadn't passed before Katie could see the wall beyond Jeb and his steed, through his fading body.

The frog clung to Jeb's hair, sitting in full view and looking around in alarm. "Cease this silliness!" He slapped Jeb's ear. "You're exposing me to danger! Stop this at once!"

"You're fading," Clara ran to Jeb and grabbed his arm. "It's not worth it."

"I've a new purpose now that I met ye. I won't let ye down."

Katie started when Damien appeared next to her. He winked at her, and laid one hand on Abby's shoulder and the other on Jeb's leg. Damien, Abby, the frog, and Jeb's horse stood frozen in place for two seconds. Katie jumped toward Abby, but she vanished with the others before Katie could touch her. Only Clara and Jack remained with her in the yard. Movement on the wall caught her attention. Damien had reappeared, standing by his father.

"Where did you take her?!" Katie clenched her fists.

Damien shook his head. "She's fine. For crying out loud, Katie. You know I'd never hurt Abby. She was one of my best friends."

"Finally, we can get down to business," Fenton Murdock said.

"Patience, my friend," Lynch grinned. "We mustn't forget the little gift I procured for our friend, Mr. Park."

Mr. Murdock walked to the far side of the wall, out of view. He returned several seconds later and shoved an old Asian man toward the wall edge, the man's hands bound tight behind his back and a blue glow emanating from his body. Katie couldn't imagine why Intershroud would capture such a harmless, humble-looking old man. He wore the simple, loose clothes of a monk, light mesh fabric over a gray band, and a baggy white shirt. Despite his situation, he faced forward bravely, his chin up.

Jack gasped.

LXIII

Jack recognized the old Asian monk instantly. He'd dreamed about him many times before, most recently when the man had attempted to help him fight off the imps. The man stood with his hands bound behind his back, his body rigid and glowing with a pulsating aura of blue light.

Despair darkened Jack's thoughts, a mental force connecting the monk's situation with Jack's mental state. Marina had said this man was his Shadow, his hero Archetype, the personification of his subconscious mind. He watched his subconscious hero standing there immobilized and defeated, and he knew Marina had been right. It explained the weight crushing down on his mind. Jack's arms and legs lost their strength, he staggered sideways, and clutched Katie's shoulder with his hands.

Katie clamped her arms around him tight, but he slid through them and fell to his knees. He stared down, his neck unwilling to bend. He knew no hope. He couldn't be saved. He wept comfortless tears.

Lynch laughed, a crackly, merciless laugh. "I see you recognized your Shadow. We caught him sweeping away your tracks with tree limbs, attempting to throw us off your trail. He's quite the hero. Must've taken out ten of my operatives before they immobilized him."

Jack jerked his head up and glared at Lynch. "What's the point of this? Don't you people have anything better to dream about?" He grabbed a nearby rock and raised it over his shoulder, but let it drop through his fingers. He didn't have the strength to throw it.

"Oh, I most certainly do." Lynch's expression grew serious. "That is exactly the point. Intershroud has great need of my services, yet I find myself wasting valuable time dealing with ignorant, short-sighted anarchists like yourself. I don't care about you. From what I can tell, you're just an Aspect waiting for his body to die. All I've wanted is the assurance that our secrets are safe. The security of the entire world depends on it."

"Secrets!" Jack's anger lent him enough strength to pull himself up on wobbly legs. He raised his fist. "That's all you care about! It never occurs to you that no one cares about your stupid secrets! I just want to be left alone!"

Fenton stepped to the ledge, his face rigid and frowning. "If you weren't so certain you were such a genius, Mr. Park, we could've explained reality to you. What do you think would happen if everyone on earth knew they were sharing dreams with everyone else? I'll give you a hint. There'd be no privacy. No personal secrets. No escape from unwanted harassments, stalking, spying, exhibitionism. Every witless kook would learn all your passwords, your bank account numbers, locker combinations, your social security number. You wouldn't be able to hide anything, anywhere, ever. It would be chaos! Intershroud is the only thing protecting this world from falling into complete and utter anarchy."

Katie stepped forward. "And who is protecting the world from you?"

"It's the lesser of two evils, so what of it?" Lynch said. "You can have a relatively peaceful dream world controlled by those of us who understand it, or you can have a disastrous, chaotic dystopia where the strong devour the weak. There is no real choice."

"The people with the power always say things like that," Clara said.

"My mom used to tell me that. The people with power always say it's either their way or the end of the world."

Lynch rolled his eyes and shook his head. "I see I'm wasting time."

"Then stop wasting it," Jack said. "Why are you harassing us in the first place? You admitted you think we're about to die."

"Who told you I wanted to capture you? I'm only here to make sure you've had no contact with the outside world. I wasn't interested in capturing you." He glanced at Fenton Murdock.

Katie's eyebrows furrowed. "Mr. Murdock? Why? You're my dad's best friend. He trusted you!"

"Exactly," Murdock shook his index finger at Jack. "That little vermin, that gutter rat, murdered you, the child of my best friend. He just about killed Damien! I can't allow him to escape payment for that."

"I didn't kill anyone," Jack said.

"Don't lie to me! Damien told me everything. You knew about the explosives in that mine and you lit a flame anyway. It was fire from your lighter that blew up that mine! Damien's in the hospital. They're saying he may lose an eye. It'll be months, maybe years, before we'll be able to dig out your bodies, and the bodies of the two staffers you killed. I had to inform Katie's father of her death myself. He's devastated."

Murdock turned to Lynch. "Now, can I get on with it?"

Lynch grinned and nodded, whispering something to Derek. A dark cloud appeared and revolved around Lynch's legs, condensing and shaping into a cozy brown leather lounge chair. The old man leaned back in his chair, propped his feet up, and sipped from a cocktail glass that had appeared in his hand.

Fenton turned toward the concrete wall to his right. The deep rumble of crumbling concrete echoed throughout the yard and a nebulous car-sized chunk of concrete scraped and separated from the wall. It hovered in the air, twisted brown rebar protruding from its ragged edges at odd angles. Mr. Murdock waved his fingers and the massive broken slab glided through the air, rocks and bits of concrete sloughing from its surfaces and pelting the earth below. The slab stopped, centered above the old monk's head. Fenton lowered his fingers. Clara screamed. The hunk of concrete crashed on top of the monk with a sickening crunch. The monk rolled over the ledge and plopped in the dirt with a thud. Jack's hero Archetype was gone.

Jack flopped to his knees and rolled onto his side. He forgot who he was, where he was. His mind filled with darkness, despair, unbridled fear.

"You're monsters!" Clara ran and kneeled next to Jack, her chin quivering.

Katie dashed to his other side, stooped down, and caressed his hand. "That monk was only an image you created. Remember what Marina said; you don't need to be saved. You're your own hero. Embrace who you are. Your hero isn't dead. He's always inside you. He *is* you."

"How can you side with that jerk?" Damien stood at the wall edge, snarling. "He killed you! He doesn't deserve your sympathy."

Katie stood and put all her weight into pulling Jack onto his knees. Jack looked up at her through vacant, moistened eyes. Her words had resonated within him. She was right, he had created his Shadow. He could create him again. But maybe he didn't need to be saved anymore. Maybe it was time for him to step up to that role. If there was any time to face his fear, it was now.

Jack tightened his grip on Katie's hand and pulled himself to his feet.

Fenton sneered and pointed at the same chunk of concrete he'd used to destroy Jack's Shadow. He gnashed his teeth and flicked his wrist, sending the mass of concrete and steel flying at Jack. Katie and Clara jumped out of the way, each screaming Jack's name, but it was too late for him.

Jack threw his hands up to protect his face as the concrete mass pounded into his chest, lifting him off his feet and carrying him through the air. He slammed into a solid wall, concrete cracking and crumbling into dozens of small chunks, raining down around his arms and legs. He opened his eyes and found himself buried two feet into the wall surface. Two screaming Intershroud operatives fell past him, hit the ground, and vanished on each side of his legs.

Jack surveyed the crumbled rubble, wondering how he'd survived. The dreamed-up concrete looked solid, but it felt as though a mere gale-force wind had picked him up and pressed him against an equally strong windstorm blowing in the opposite direction. Regardless, his ears rang, and his back, chest, legs, and arms ached with every movement.

He couldn't, however, just leave Katie and Clara to the mercy of Lynch and Murdock. He took a deep breath and, with a little moaning, stood and brushed cement dust from his pant legs and torn shirt. He glanced around and found all eyes wide and fixed on him.

Jack took three steps before another mass of concrete came flying his way. Murdock stood far enough away that Jack easily leaped aside, letting the six-foot slab crash with a deafening crack through the wall behind him. He dodged another one, the slab passing him on his right.

Clara and Katie ran toward him and he attempted to run to meet them, but the pain in his legs made him wobbly and off balance.

Fenton stood ready to yank another swath of concrete from the walls when Lynch grabbed his arm and lowered it. "Perhaps we're being too hasty. This boy shows exceptional invulnerability. He could be useful."

"He's worthless." Fenton gritted his teeth and stretched out his hands to his left, tearing away a bus-sized section of wall, giving no heed to the two female agents standing on it. They fell screaming and cursing into a twelve-foot gap, then journeyed back to the awakened world.

"I checked his background." Fenton let the chunk of concrete hang in the air. "Some superstitious crackpot thinks Park is destined to save the world. She's part of some odd dream cult in Korea. She found Farley and the fool promised he'd enlighten the kid. Park shouldn't have been invited to the camp at all."

Fenton faced Jack, his jaw rigid, and sent the concrete hovering over Jack's head with a brisk flip of his wrist. Twisted steel bars clung from it like vines. Jack slipped aside to dodge the rocks and small chunks of concrete raining all around him.

"I'm curious," Lynch said. "I've never seen a coma victim endure an attack like this."

"They can't be ghosts," Fenton said. "There's no wild threats. No demands for revenge."

"Dad," Damien said, "Katie's running to help him. You better take him out before gets there."

"We have to face the truth, Damien. Their bodies will expire any minute now, and Jack has poisoned those girls against you. This is their final dream. There's no point in prolonging it."

"Dad! No!"

Fenton raised his hands a few inches and rocketed the concrete slab upward another twenty feet. Clara and Katie reached Jack and wrapped their arms around him.

"Get back!" Jack pushed their arms away. "He's going to drop that wall on us."

"Katie, get away from him!" Damien teetered at the edge of the wall.

Fenton showed no mercy. The shadow of the concrete widened around Jack and the girls, and the enormous mass dropped and pounded them into the earth.

LXIV

Jack cracked open his eyes and stared into an inky blackness. He would've believed he'd really died this time, if not for the throbbing aches emanating from every surface of his body. He wanted to lay there for the rest of time, but he could hear Clara wheezing and Katie coughing.

"You two okay?" Jack shoved up a slab of rubble with his hands, ignoring the pain, and heaved it upward. Ragged strips of light peeked through fissures in the crumbled slab above him. He gave the wreckage another quick push and a large chunk of concrete rolled aside, allowing the cloudy sky to bathe him in light. He choked on cement dust for a few seconds, then grabbed onto two strands of bent rebar above his head. He yanked them down and pulled himself up and out of the debris. He searched for the girls in the crumbled waste around him, through dim and dusty air.

"I think I'm okay," Clara's muffled voice said. "I got the wind knocked out of me."

"I twisted my arm," Katie said.

Jack guessed where the voices were coming from and reached around the edge of a rough six-foot-wide slab, hefted it, and gave it a shove, letting it slide ten feet away down a shallow slope of rubble.

Katie and Clara sat up, reached a hand to Jack, and let him pull them both to their feet.

The dust settled and the men on the wall came back into view.

"Unbelievable." Damien smiled and looked at his father.

Lynch handed his glass to Damien, kicked down his footrest, and arose from his lounge chair.

Jack found that the chunk of concrete had landed with such force, the concrete wall to his left had split from top to bottom in two locations. Only three Intershroud operatives remained stationed along the wall, each staring at Jack and the girls with their mouths agape.

Katie and Clara shoved aside crumbled concrete, kicked away a few twisted strands of rebar, and climbed out of the three-foot-deep crater.

Lynch laughed. "Such resilience! I've never seen anything like it."

"You think you're so brave way up there on that wall?" Jack choked again on the dust, then rubbed his bruised ribs. "Why don't you come down here for a fair fight?"

"Are you kidding?" Damien grinned and folded his arms. "We just saw what you can do. Besides, who said this had to be a fair fight? There's nothing fair about a dream."

Jack fumed. All he could think about was how unfair it was for them to stand up there in the safety of that wall, throwing things at him and the girls. It wasn't right. He clenched his teeth and glared at the four men on the wall—then something happened that surprised even him.

Damien, Fenton, Derek, and Lynch vanished from the wall top and reappeared on the uneven ground six feet in front to Jack. Each man looked around with a blank expression. Damien's eyes widened, and he dived toward Lynch and Fenton, placing one hand on Lynch's shoulder and the other on Fenton's back. He squinted and tensed his arms, waiting three, four, five seconds before he relaxed and lowered them.

"What did you do to my powers?" Damien glared at Jack.

Before he could answer, Katie stepped up and punched Damien in the face. He vanished.

Lynch grinned and froze for a half second, then disappeared.

Derek took ten steps backward, tripping twice over small stones on the ground, and darted behind Fenton.

Fenton stepped backward at a steady pace and looked up at the three agents still standing on narrow sections of cracked and broken concrete wall. "You haven't won yet, boy. Fire all missiles!"

The loud whoosh of igniting rocket fuel descended from above. Jack caught sight of a spiraling missile flying at him and he ducked, wincing at the hot flame whizzing past his neck. He cringed again as the rocket exploded at the base of the wall twenty feet to his left. A force connected with his right side and spun him around, inflicting a sharp pain on his right hip. Another sensation of pressure from a nearby explosion sent his hands to his ears and he found himself flying ten feet forward and hitting the ground rolling. The world spun around him until his back flattened against concrete.

Katie and Clara yelled, but their voices couldn't compete with the ringing in his ears. Another explosion sounded to his left and a force of hot air, mixed with rocks and clods of dirt, sent his world spinning again. He stopped rolling, squinting through moistened eyes. The metallic odor of blood filled his nostrils. Fenton stood ten feet away, watching him and sneering.

Jack couldn't move. Katie and Clara attempted to run to him, but the earth below their feet heaved and flowed like a sheet in the wind. The girls teetered back and forth and up and down, until they fell onto their knees. They crawled forward, making slow progress.

"Enough of this!" Lynch's voice spoke. "The boy clearly cannot be killed with brute force."

Jack took a painful look around but couldn't see Lynch anywhere, then remembered that the man had the ability to shade, to turn invisible.

"Then I'll smother him!" Fenton Murdock reached his hands out in front of himself, palms up. He gritted his teeth and raised his quivering hands upward, and a ten-foot-wide circle of earth rumbled and arose from the ground. Severed tree roots dangled from the six-foot deep mass of moist, black, rocky soil. It rose up twenty feet and hovered sideways until it hung over Jack's body, showering him with loose dirt and small stones.

The terrain around Katie and Clara stopped moving, allowing the girls to stand and run toward him. Hundreds of chrome spikes shot out of the earth at random angles in a line in front of them, stopping them cold. Eight-foot-long sharp-tipped rods, thick as flagpoles at their bases, blocked their path. They grabbed them and shook them in aggravation. Clara grinned when one of the cylindrical rods snapped in two in her hands, ringing with a loud clang. Following Clara's lead, Katie snapped one in half, too.

A clod of dirt slammed into Jack's head and the thought of being buried alive provided him all the adrenaline he needed to roll onto his hands and knees and crawl with every ounce of energy remaining in his body. He scuttled toward the girls over fist-size rocks and shallow mounds of soft, moist soil, facing downward so he could breathe amidst the dust.

He glanced up again and watched Katie and Clara kick down four of the chrome spikes and step over them. Katie glared at Mr. Murdock and swung a broken spike toward him with all her strength, yelling out and letting the glimmering rod fly.

Fenton's eyebrows rose, and he started to duck, but the spike found him, penetrating his chest. He disappeared, and the chrome rod in his chest dropped and clanked against the rocky terrain.

The soil hovering over Jack now loosened and fell, turning his world dark in mere seconds. The weight of the soil pressed him flat on his stomach and he couldn't move. The musty odor of moist earth assaulted his nose and air stopped flowing from his lungs. His mind screamed for a quick merciful death.

The weight, however, lifted from his back and light again appeared. He sucked in air, choking on the dirt that came with it. The mountain of soil rolled to his left and dropped into the hole from which it had come. Jack laid there and moaned, vowing never to take a breath of air for granted again. He heard the crunching of feet on rocky ground and rolled himself onto his back.

Katie and Clara stood near him, each wielding a chrome rod. Katie swung her post and let it fly toward Derek. He jumped aside, and it crashed with a loud clang against a far concrete wall, cracking and collapsing a three-foot-wide section of it in a cloud of dust. An Intershroud operative teetered and fell, awakening within the crevasse.

Derek waved his arms around, forming rectangular clouds that densified into blocks of granite as large as cars. He situated them along the ground between himself and the girls.

"I just saved Jack from a horrible experience!" Derek said. "Don't blame me for this. I'm not your enemy. You know I can't go against Lynch and Murdock. I've been playing defense this whole time."

Clara snarled and threw her chrome rod at Derek and it tumbled through the air, missing him by a good ten feet, yet it still penetrated six inches into the concrete wall behind him.

"Three comatose Aspects with unprecedented super strength." Lynch's voice seemed to be everywhere. "It's unheard of. Unless…"

"Unless what?" Derek stretched out his arms and twenty grey clouds appeared in three rows along the ground in front of him, each densifying into blockades of granite blocks, stacked to the height of Derek's chest.

"Unless, they're Dream Running."

## LXV

"What?" Derek looked around. "They can't be. Everyone knows that's folklore."

"Not true. It's happened before, and nothing else explains their unusual strength."

Jack gritted his teeth and started to pull himself to his feet. Clara ran to lend him her shoulder for support. Derek form more stone block walls on each side of himself.

"They're scared of us," Jack said.

Katie looked at Jack and gave a wry smile. She stepped up to a stone block, placed a hand on each side of it, and lifted it up. She raised it over her head and let it fly toward the concrete border wall, below the last two remaining Intershroud operatives. The block crashed into the concrete with a deafening crack and a twelve-foot-wide section of wall collapsed. Vast chunks of slab twisted and tipped over, slamming into the pine trees on the other side of the wall. The two female agents, in their flashy red business dresses, vanished in clouds of cement dust.

The area had grown darker, and Jack looked up. "The fog dome is gone."

"I wouldn't be so sure of yourselves," Lynch's voice said. "You may be strong, but you are Material beings in an unpredictable, chaotic dream world. At my command, Derek could shower your vulnerable bodies with needle-sharp daggers and pierce your feeble hearts."

Derek looked at Katie, made a face, and shook his head. "I didn't sign up to murder people." He turned to Clara in time to see her launch a stone block over her head at him. He raised his arms, but the stone connected with his left shoulder and he disappeared.

Lynch laughed. "Are you not even wise enough to recognize your allies? We don't want to harm you. One of you has an ability that allowed you to Dream Run. If we can save you, you'll be invaluable to us."

Katie kicked aside a stone block. Clara picked one up and swung it aside, letting it crash through one of Derek's block walls.

"We'll never work for Intershroud," Jack said.

"More powerful men than you have made such claims. I already know Katie's power, and Clara's. So, it must be you, Jack. I watched you defy Damien's verger power and transport me and my companions to the ground. No doubt, you did something similar when you caused yourself and these girls to Dream Run. You're unique in the world and it would be a crime not to make use of your skills."

"Show your face, coward!" Jack clenched his fists. "I'll show you my skills."

Lynch laughed again. "Surely, you know you won't survive here without my help. No one has ever survived a Dream Run. Even if you continue to survive, you'll need a haunt soon, and there are no more haunts around here. Ironic that you blew up your only hope of escape."

"We'll find a way out," Jack said.

Katie grabbed Clara's wrist, pulled her to Jack, and she leaned into his ear. "We need to get to that haunt, fast."

"But we don't know where Mr. Lynch is," Clara said. "We can't let him find out where we're going."

"So, you do have a haunt," Lynch said. "How could you? The old miner! Of course. That old ghost has been hiding his haunt from us for so long, I forgot about it. I wondered why he was defending you."

"You better not hurt him!" Clara clenched her fists, searching for any sign of the man's location.

"I keep telling you, I have no desire to harm anyone. I want to help you, and if you were smart, you'd realize that you need my help. If you continue to fight me, your Material bodies will waste away in this place. No one will ever know what became of you."

"We don't need help from a coward that won't even show his face," Jack said.

"You know nothing about this world! There's no real Material air here. How are you even breathing? You only imagine it. You're dying of oxygen deprivation as we speak!"

Katie's eyes widened. She gulped several deep breaths and held her throat.

Clara ran to her. "Don't listen to him. We've been breathing fine all day."

Katie nodded and breathed softer.

Lynch chuckled softly. "Let's not play games, Mr. Park. We both know what is going to happen here. Even if you do escape Essentia, we'll never stop pursuing you. We'll track you down. You may sleep, but you'll never rest. Join me now or you'll be forever consigning yourself to a life of fear."

"Leave us alone!" Jack picked up a block of granite and tossed it in front of himself, hoping it would find Lynch. It crashed through the concrete wall and knocked down a ten-foot wide section. The steeple of a church in Silverton became visible through the cement dust.

"Your just wasting time," Lynch said. "Go ahead. Go to Silverton and find the old man's haunt. Just be aware that we'll be watching your homes and your friends' homes. Everybody dreams, Mr. Park. You cannot hide. Work for me, on the other hand, and you'll live like royalty."

"Shut up!" Jack grabbed another block of concrete and threw it.

"Don't say I didn't warn you," Lynch said.

A block of stone sat precariously on the edge of a block wall next to Clara and she looked up in time to see it teeter and fall. She jumped aside and it crashed into rubble at her feet.

Jack knew Lynch had shoved it. He clenched his teeth. "Show yourself!"

"Be reasonable," Lynch said. "Katie, you've lived the high life since your parents joined the company. Tell your friend to see reason."

"I said, show yourself!"

"You know, Jack, the Murdocks will be asleep again at any moment. All you've done is delay the inevitable. Fenton will be back with reinforcements. Besides, you'll have to sleep some time. Who'll protect you then, I wonder."

"You don't play fair! I said show yourself!"

A warm wave of energy rolled through Jack's body. The tattered walls of the enclosure looked wavy in the rising heat. Lynch appeared, leaning against a stack of granite blocks ten feet away.

The grin on Lynch's face vanished and he looked down at his hands and patted his chest. He gritted his teeth, tensed his arms, and tried to disappear again. He looked up at Jack and sneered.

Jack could hardly move his aching muscles, but nothing would stop him from staggering toward the old man. He lunged at Lynch with his fist pulled back and swung at the man's wide-eyed face.

# LXVI

Katie and Clara loped down a long, steep hill, each with an arm wrapped around Jack's back and holding his arms around their necks. Their speed increased with every step.

"We need to slow down. I'm about to fall on my face," Jack said.

"I know. I can't slow down," Katie said.

They reached the foot of the hill at a fast pace and Katie went another twenty feet before she could force her legs to stop. She gulped some air and looked at Clara. They both laughed. Katie walked again, aiming for the back wall of an old abandoned clapboard home. Light pierced the exposed rafters of its steep, half-missing roof. She reached the wall, eased Jack's arm from her shoulder, and leaned against the home's rough, sun-bleached clapboards, the peeling white paint tickling her fingers.

"There's a dirt road." Clara pointed to a narrow strip of pitted dirt that ran along the other side of the house, along a field of waist-high, yellow grass.

"Silverton's not far now." Jack winced and gingerly touched his throat.

"Oh no! What's that?" Clara ducked behind the corner of the house. A twenty-foot-wide strip of grass melted down flat and turned a deep black. The adjoining dirt road widened ten feet and adopted the same appearance. The new asphalt road turned off the formerly dirt road and curved away from the house to the base of the hill they'd just descended.

"Someone's coming! Don't let them see you!" Katie wrapped Jack's arm around her neck again and helped him limp to the far side of the house.

The neigh of horses joined the bumping of hard wheels on the new asphalt.

"I must say, ol' friend," a familiar bass voice said, "these paved roads are far more conducive to the practice of verbal intercourse. The smoothness of its surface greatly enhances one's ability to carry on a conversation. Ease of conversing is quite necessary for one such as me, you know."

"It's the frog!" Clara darted around the house.

"Clara, wait!" Katie let go of Jack, ran after her, and smiled, throwing her hands up to her face. Jeb sat on the boxed seat of a long wooden wagon, pulled by two sets of gray horses. The animals were a third larger than any horse Katie had ever seen.

The frog sat on Jeb's lap and rolled its eyes. "It would appear, Mr. Colton, that the deceased bodies you were so passionately determined to grant, as you said, 'a decent burial,' have not yet heretofore complied with the aforementioned criteria. I therefore recommend that we be on our way before they entwine us, once again, in a most perilous predicament."

Jeb ignored the frog and dropped his reins, climbed down from the cart, and ran to Clara, grinning wide. He embraced her, though Clara only dared pat him lightly on the back.

"I cain't believe me eyes. I spent a good ten minutes shapin' this 'ere wagon in hopes to make it dense enough to take ye lifeless bodies to me haunt. I couldn't bear the thought o' ye wastin' away here in Essentia. Never crossed me mind you'd be standin' here, free o' them Intershroud rogues."

"We still could definitely use the wagon," Clara said. "Jack can hardly walk."

Jack hobbled around the corner of the house and leaned on the front porch railing.

"We could use a doctor, too," Katie said. "I'm exhausted. It's hard to breath with bruises everywhere."

"Let's get y'all into me wagon. No time to waste." Jeb ran to unchain the wagon's backboard and let it drop open.

Clara and Katie rushed to Jack and lifted his arms around their necks. They guided him to the back of the cart and eased him onto it. The wooden slats creaked and bent under his weight but held firm. Katie climbed in and kneeled next to him, her back against the sideboard.

"Ye can sidle up here with me," Jeb said to Clara. He brushed the frog aside and it hopped from the seat and landed next to Jack, its face contorted with indignation. Jeb gave Clara a hand and helped her climb up to the wooden boxed seat next to him. She smiled and bounced up and down a few times after discovering the two bent metal springs supporting the seat. Jeb climbed up, sat by her, and the frog hopped onto his lap and folded its arms.

"It may have escaped your observation," the frog said, "but we were most contentedly immersed in a delightful conversation before you three came along and most egregiously disrupted it. It's most categorically impertinent, you know. Why, I'd have stayed back at the house if I'd known you'd be all alive and interrupting us like this."

Jeb grabbed the straw hat off his head and plopped it over the frog, then clamped his right hand on top.

"This is outrageous!" The sides of the hat bulged out in five different places where the frog kicked at it, but the hat didn't budge.

"You keep yer durn fly catcher shut or so help me, frog, 'tis certain I'll be roastin' ye legs fer me vittles this very night. These young'uns be me friends and they've endured an ordeal I wouldn't wish on me worst enemy, 'cept, o' course, that ol' vermin, but that goes without sayin'." Jeb grabbed the black pouch dangling from the left side of his belt and gave it a hardy squeeze. A tiny voice screamed, and Jeb gave half a smile.

"Yah!" Jeb yanked the reins and the cart jerked forward. The horses turned the wagon around and clip-clopped along the paved road at a rapid pace. They rolled past one dilapidated wooden home after another, each designed so simply, they reminded Katie of drawings she'd made with crayons when she was a child: rectangular box structures, steep pointed roofs, one front door, and a window to its side. Flowerbeds splashed bright yellow, orange, and pink along the bases of each porch. They were simple homes for uncomplicated people. Were it not for the constant dread of Lynch and his people returning, Katie would've enjoyed the wagon ride.

Not far ahead, rows of clapboard homes and small businesses lined both sides of Main Street, each painted in pastel blues, reds, and greens. They passed the old white church with the tall octagonal steeple. It wasn't much different than the homes, just larger and with more windows. They rolled by its adjoining cemetery, dotted with tilted crosses. They reminded Katie of a question that filled her with dread.

She looked at Jeb and steeled herself, gripping the sideboard. "Is my sister gone?"

"She was fading fast when I left her, but she may still be there yet. She was durn determined to see ye one last time, be ye live or dead."

Katie's eyes moistened. "When I saw she wasn't with you, I was sure she'd already moved on."

"Forgive me, miss. I shoulda let ye know how things stood. I left her at my ol' house.

That rascal in the black suit stole us to a road a ways down the mountain. I fixed to shape me one o' them flying machines, so I could come back in haste and help ye, but Miss Abagail convinced me it'd be no use. They had ye trapped below a fog dome. Best I could do was take yer bodies to yer material world fer a burying. 'Tis a blessing to be takin' ye there alive, that be certain."

"I suppose Abby didn't want to come with you," Katie said.

"She asked to wait for ye. The jostling o' me wagon was makin' her fade faster."

"I don't see the Ghost Knights around," Clara said.

"No. 'Tis certain they took a likin' to ye, but they fulfilled their mission. They're surely on their way back to their homeland."

The horses clacked down the main street of Silverton. The Aspect of a dreaming little boy, in blue shorts and a red tee-shirt, kicked a tin coffee can and it clunked along the road parallel to Jeb's wagon. A boy in blue jeans and a drab green tee-shirt stopped it with his foot and kicked it back to him.

A thin old man in his nineties rocked in a wooden chair on the wide porch of an old gray house, his long white beard swaying with the chair. Next door, a hefty middle-aged woman with a flowered white apron and a navy-blue scarf around her gray hair came out of the screened storm door of her pastel pink house and began sweeping dust into the street from her wooden porch. No one looked at Katie and her companions, or even acknowledged them.

"Not the friendliest people I've ever seen," Jack said.

"They won't even look at us," Katie said.

"They're Sleepers," Jeb said. "They aren't enlightened like you are. When dreamers don't know they're dreamin', they're only interested in the small world their own minds created fer them. That woman is thinkin' on sweepin' that porch, so there ain't nothin' in her dream world but that broom and that porch."

A distant rumble thundered from the forest, rattling nearby windows.

"Sounds like a storm's coming," Clara searched the sky.

"That weren't no thunder. We best be g'tting' to me haunt." Jeb whipped the reins up and back down and the wagon lurched forward at a more rapid pace. Jack sat up.

An old gray-blue clapboard house came into view. He remembered seeing it when he drove past it on the way to camp. It looked just like the other homes, with its raised porch below a wooden canopy, except it had two stories. Its porch columns leaned at an angle and the canopy sloped down to the right, giving the whole house an ominous tilt.

Katie, however, zeroed in on a woman in a white frilly dress, sitting on a porch swing hanging from a canopy beam, the white slats and thick metal chains of the swing visible through her semi-transparent body.

"Abby!" Katie threw herself over the wagon's sideboard and ran to the porch and up its creaky wooden steps.

"You made it." Abby's voice was soft and lifeless. She stood and forced a smile, then frowned again. "I'm so glad. I didn't think you'd make it."

Katie trembled and couldn't hold back a wide-stretched smile. She felt like Abby was seeing her for the first time. "Why are you so unhappy? You did it. You got your revenge."

Abby stared at her with watery eyes. She struggled to speak. "It wasn't how I thought it would be. It was exhilarating at first. I watched that monster descend into nothingness. But the feeling flitted away like a gust of wind. I feel empty, Katie. I can't bear it. I just want to be with you and Mom, and even Dad. I want to go home. I had forgotten it all. I turned it all away, and for what?" She dropped her face into her hands and sobbed. Her body faded more with every word.

"Stop it, Abby! You're dissipating. You don't have to go away. You can find another purpose. You could join the Ghost Knights! Fight battles for other ghosts. Please, Abby. Please don't go."

Thunder roared again, louder this time. The boards of the wooden deck rattled along with the window glass.

"You need to go back to Materia," Abby said.

"Not until you tell me you'll try to stay alive, that you'll try to find a new purpose."

"Don't you see? This isn't my doing. I could never join the Ghost Knights again. I don't share their obsession anymore. My eyes are open now. Those knights seek illusions. They fight for emptiness. I've wasted all these years."

"No, Abby, you brought that horrible man to justice."

Abby was barely visible now. She shook her head. "Actually, I've finally come to my senses. Justice, too, is an illusion. The mere molecule of pain I caused Farley couldn't possibly account for a trillionth of the anguish he caused me. It was pointless. I'm empty, Katie.

I beg you; don't do what I've done. I'm so sorry you saw me at the depth of my disgrace and shame."

"Don't go, Abby, please. I'm not ashamed of you. I'm proud of you. I've always been proud of you."

"I'd give anything just to hug you one more time." Abby's voice sounded distant. "Find Mother. She'll protect you. Tell her I loved her."

"Abby!" Katie darted forward and embraced her sister, then sensed the warmth of her soul melt away. She was gone.

# LXVII

Jack leaned against a white porch column and watched Jeb stare at the empty swing where Abby had been sitting, his eyes hinting of a fire awakening in his soul. Tears drenched Clara's cheeks and Jack looked away, afraid his own emotions might erupt. A thunderous crash shook him out of his somberness, and he turned around and looked down the street.

A cloud of gray-yellow dust wafted down the road and consumed every vehicle, person, and structure on either side of the street. The bald heads and bare, hairy chests of two massive giants came into view amidst the settling dust, each bearded and snarling, towering above the trees, higher than a four-story building. They stretched shaggy tree-trunk arms a dozen feet forward and sliced straight down through the trees, their enormous hands pounding the forest floor. They swept their arms sideways in opposite directions.

The earth shook, and Jack covered his ears against the deafening roar of hundreds of trees being wrenched from their roots. Countless tons of rock, soil, and trees flew right and left, landing hundreds of yards beyond the town and leaving massive dust clouds behind them.

The smell of moist soil again blanketed the town and the sky darkened.

"They're destroying the whole town!" Clara ran to Katie.

Three drab-green armored personnel carriers floated out of haze at the end of the town, hovering in the center of the newly made clearing. Twenty light armored vehicles rolled past them on both sides, each packed with camouflaged Sleeper soldiers with assault rifles hanging over their shoulders.

Two men in dark suits stood in the lead vehicle, their faces sour and resolute.

"It's the Murdocks," Jack said.

"We've waited too long," Jeb ran to the door and opened it, the frog nestled on his shoulder. "Get upstairs! Now!"

Jack set out to tackle the first step of Jeb's porch, but almost collapsed from the searing pain that shot through his right leg. He couldn't move to the next step until both feet rested on the first one. "I may be awhile. You guys run ahead. I'll catch up as fast as I can."

"We're not leaving without you, dummy." Katie ran to his side and Clara darted to the other. They pulled his arms around their shoulders and heaved to lift him to the next step.

Another thunderous rumble shook the house and Jack looked down the street. A fountain of water shot up from an enormous hole in the ground where the pink clapboard house had been. He saw no sign of the woman with the broom, nor of any other dreamers in the streets.

One of the giants held the little home against his bare belly, and a section of wooden flooring cracked and dropped from below the house, along with a wooden table, three wooden chairs, and an old flowery blue sofa. The furniture tumbled down the giant's tan loin cloth and bounced off a bare right foot twice the size of the Murdocks' flat-topped armored vehicle.

The giant raised the house over his head and launched it into the woods where it crashed and crumbled to pieces among the distant pine trees. The Sleeper soldiers swerved their vehicles to a stop in front of six other homes and businesses, jumped from their vehicles with rifles in their hands, and swarmed all over the street, making their way into each structure.

Clara and Katie eased Jack to the level of the porch, then helped him to the screen door Jeb held open. Clara started to cross the threshold but stopped and stepped back when a cheerful young girl in a yellow dress skipped out the door.

The frog hopped down from Jeb's shoulder and stood in front of the girl, staring at her and grinning larger than should've been possible.

The girl pointed at him, smiled, and laughed. "Mr. Toad! Are you back from another adventure?"

The frog opened his mouth to speak but didn't get a word out before Jeb rushed to the girl's side and shoved her into the door frame. She disappeared.

"Jeb!" Clara glared at him, her eyes showing shock.

Jeb shook his head "Had to wake her, miss. We can't waste a second."

Rumbles, cracks, and explosions of another home being destroyed reached their ears and Clara nodded. She and Katie helped Jack through the doorway and walked him across the ornate Oriental rug in the foyer. They arrived at a set of white-painted stairs.

Jack pushed the girls' arms away and took hold of the decorative newel at the base of the baluster. "Go ahead of me. I can make it up the stairs pretty quick holding onto these rails." He looked at Katie and Clara in turn.

"Okay, but you better be right behind us." Katie placed a hand on Clara's back to urge her up the stairs, then followed her up. Jeb darted up the stairs behind them.

Jack encountered the frog standing outside the doorway, folding his arms, frowning and staring at him.

"You can't come with us, Mr. Toad, "Jack said. "You better go hide somewhere."

The frog firmed his resolve. "That little girl Mr. Colton so rudely woke up was my originator! She dreamed me into this world. This insult will never be forgiven. Tell your crazy old miner friend that our friendship is heretofore terminated!"

The square wood-shingled roof of a flower shop bounded and

rolled along the street behind the frog and crashed into another building down the street out of Jack's view. Unintelligible voices of distant soldiers yelled things at each other. Gunshots sounded. Doors slammed and Jack winced at the sound of another home being torn from its foundation and tossed into an adjacent neighborhood.

"I'll be going now." The frog hopped along the porch and away from the mayhem.

Jack turned to the rickety stairs and grabbed hold of the wooden rails on both sides of the stairway. He put all his weight into his arms and swung his feet from step to step, passing photos on the wall of the little girl and her mother. Halfway up the stairs, he gained a clear view out a window across the room and watched a burly Sleeper soldier kick down the door of a house two doors down. Eight other soldiers invaded the home, hands on their rifles. Seconds later, they charged out the door and headed for the house next door.

The massive palm of one of the giants slapped against the side wall of the home two-doors down and it started to rise. A window crashed into shards and boards splintered from the walls. Water flew up and dripped from the house's foundation. Jack looked away and swung his legs to the next step and the next. Katie stood at the attic door with her arms out. She grabbed his hands and helped him through the attic door the moment he reached the landing.

Katie wrapped Jack's arm around her shoulder and helped him limp across the dusty wood-slat attic floor. Jeb shut the door and locked it.

Stacks of boxes of various sizes and shapes lined two of the walls, and a rack of dresses hung on a rod along the far wall. A black chest with chrome studs sat at the foot of a small brass, four-poster bed to Jack's right. Light entered the room through a single octagonal window, adding to the light from a single incandescent light bulb hanging from the steep rafters on a frayed black wire in the center of the room.

An earsplitting crack, followed by a rumbling noise, shook the house, and it creaked and swayed back and forth with such force that Jack braced for the structure to collapse.

"That was the house next door," Jack said.

"Where's the haunt? I don't see anything," Clara said.

"'Tisn't visible, only but a shadow." Jeb pointed to the floorboards. "Me haunt is the area in front of this old chest. Tis a space that exists in both worlds at once. To pass through it, ye must forget this world and think on Materia. If luck be with us, ye'll be walkin' into Materia."

The stomping of many boots echoed from the porch outside, followed by a loud crack at the front door. Clara darted to the area where Jeb had pointed, and Katie helped Jack limp to the spot.

Jeb pulled two silver-barreled flintlocks from the holsters at his waste. "I may have to create a diversion."

Jack smiled, but his smile quickly faded—he could see the row of dresses on the other side of the room through Jeb's body. The black bag no longer hung from Jeb's belt.

"You're fading!" Clara ran to Jeb, but he held his hands up to stop her.

Boots clomped on the wooden stairs and Jeb turned and waved his fingers at the paneled door. A dark mist formed in front of it and densified into a twenty-four-inch-thick block of black iron matching the size of the door and settling snug against it. Jack could barely hear the rattling of the doorknob, or the subsequent pounding of rifle butts against the door.

"That should hold 'em fer a minute'r two. Stay in the haunt and close ye eyes. Think o' the things that ye find only in Materia. Maybe a hot sun under a bright blue sky."

"It probably isn't daytime," Jack said. "There were people dreaming in the town."

"People may be dreamin' here from all over the world, and at any time o' day, but ye may be right. The lass we met at the door is a local gal. So, close ye eyes and think on starry nights and cold air. When ye feel the cool night on yer skin, you'll know ye be there."

Thumping continued against the wood door, but the iron block didn't budge. Jeb kept a gun ready in each hand and watched the walls near the stairs.

Katie placed a hand on Clara's shoulder, but she wiggled free and ran to Jeb.

"You have to come with us." Clara grabbed his arm.

"'Taint nothin' that'll stop them fer long, Miss Clara. They'll find a way into this room. Do as I says."

The butt of a rifle broke through a wall next to the door.

"Ye helped me find peace, Clara. I want nothing now except to save ye. Close ye eyes, me friend, and know that me soul will forever be grateful to ye. That be certain'."

The walls beyond Jeb grew clearer, his body more difficult to see. Clara's eyes welled up and she nodded but didn't move. Jeb smiled at her and wiggled his right hand. The floorboards in front of Clara heaved upward and she fell backward against Katie.

"Close your eyes," Katie said.

Clara frowned and closed her teary eyes. Jack waited for Katie to close hers before closing his own. He thought about the cool night air against his face and visualized a clear, starry night, for the first time realizing how much he longed to experience them again.

Pounding through the wallboard continued with blasts of gunfire.

"Stay out o' me house, ye vermin!" Jeb's voice faded into silence.

Jack's arms shivered against a sudden chill in the air and he opened his eyes.

# LXVIII

Jack drank in cool air and wondered how he'd survived without it. He opened his eyes to a room he hardly recognized. A half dozen brown boxes lay stacked against two of the walls, but the black chest was gone. There was no dangling light bulb, and a tall table now stood snug against the wall where the bed had been seconds ago. Drawings, a short stack of paper, and a square lamp on a flexible metal shaft sat on the sloped table surface, along with two small canisters of paint brushes and a flat box of colored pencils. On the opposite side of the room, stacks of books and magazines covered an old brown sofa where the row of dresses had been. A large, round, beige rug hid most of the glossy, refinished, wood-slat floor.

Jack looked at Katie and Clara and found them gazing back at him in the glow of the moonlight shining through the window. He stared at them, trying to come to terms with what had just happened. He wanted to believe what his mind kept telling him, that he'd just awoken from a bad dream, but such thoughts couldn't account for the bruises, the dull pain in his legs and back, and the fact that he now stood in the attic of a perfect stranger.

"What do we do now?" Katie broke the silence.

Jack looked down and shook his head. "You heard what Lynch

said. They'll be watching our families and hunting for us everywhere, even in our dreams. How do we run from that?"

Katie's shoulders dropped, and she leaned against the drawing table. "There's no one I can trust. My whole life has been one big delusion."

Clara sauntered over to the octagonal window and glanced down at the quiet street. Her eyes widened, and she gripped the dusty window frame. "That looks like Taylor!" She stepped aside and waved for Katie and Jack to take a look.

Jack limped to the window and became excited. The tall lanky blonde stood in front of a chain-link fence, staring up at the window with wide eyes and a big smile. Taylor glanced at the front of the house and his smile vanished. He tilted his head and pointed both his index fingers toward the back of the house, then ran that direction.

"Someone's here. He wants us to escape out the back door. Let's go." Jack started to move, but Katie grabbed his shoulder and looked him in the eyes.

"I hate to say it, but what if it's a trap? What if they got to Taylor?"

Jack felt sickened by the thought, but after pondering it a few seconds he shook his head. "He's my best friend. If they have him, they might as well take me, too." Jack limped to the door and swung it open. Katie and Clara followed behind him.

"Need any help?" Katie took his hand.

"I can make it down the stairs." Jack held the rails tight and swung his feet down two steps at a time. He cringed every time the old boards creaked but held onto the hope that he'd be out of the house before anyone came to investigate the noise. He landed on the bottom step and froze when someone pounded hard on the nearby front door.

Light flickered on to his left, emerging from below a paneled door. Jack looked back at Katie for a second, saw the fear in her eyes, and turned back around and swung his feet to the floor. He turned back down the hallway when his legs gave out and he fell forward a step. Katie darted to his side, caught him, and wrapped an arm around him. Clara ran to his other side and did the same.

"Who do they think they are, waking people in the middle of the night?" a woman said from the room to the left. The door handle shook.

Jack hugged the girls' necks and limped with them four steps down the carpeted hallway. The light from the adjacent room flooded the foyer. He leaned to his left and pulled the girls with him into a wide, open closet below the stairs. They pressed their backs against a line of fluffy coats and thick sweaters. Jack caught a glimpse of a robust woman with messy, light-brown hair and a cozy white bathrobe entering the foyer from the side room. She held a rifle under her right arm.

A row of framed photographs of the woman and a young girl hung on the hallway wall, one of which reflected a partial view of the front door to Jack's eyes. It didn't escape him that the people at the front door might be afforded a similar view of him hiding in the closet. He pulled a bright blue coat in front of himself.

Someone pounded on the door again.

"Give me a second!" The woman snarled, looked down, then smiled at someone outside of Jack's view. "Get back to bed, Sweetie. Nothing to be afraid of."

"I dreamed about Mr. Toad again, but I woke up," a little girl said.

"That's nice. Now back to bed. Hurry up now." The woman waited for the girl to close a door to her right, then unlocked the front door and opened it six inches. She leveled the gun barrel out the door. "What's the meaning of this? It's the middle of the night! You're scaring my daughter to death."

"We hate to bother you, ma'am," a gruff voice said. "We received a report that someone spotted some kids from the camp in your attic. We just need to check it out."

Jack recognized the gruff voice of one of the soldiers who'd taken Taylor away. He still couldn't tell if it was a man or a woman.

"Not those rumors again." The woman opened the door and stepped aside, her rifle still raised. "People in this town are always going on about my house being haunted. I don't see how anyone could've broken in. I keep my doors locked twenty-four seven. But you got me nervous now. Go ahead and check out my attic, but if you're still here in five minutes, I start shooting."

"No need to worry about us," the agent said. The soldier rushed up the stairs with a companion, and the woman followed them up at a leisurely pace.

Jack leaned out the closet door, pulled Katie and Clara with him, and limped down the hallway with the girls on either side of him. Furniture scraped along the attic floor above. He found a paneled back door on the far side of a small room on his left at the end of the hallway, opposite the kitchen area. Jack stepped past a pile of clothing on top of a washing machine. Katie turned the brass deadlock on the door and twisted the knob, opening the door.

"Sandy, are you out of bed again?" The woman called from the attic.

Jack rushed out the door, still sandwiched between Clara and Kate.

Taylor ran up the back steps and stood in front of him, looking him and the girls up and down. "Man, what did they do to you guys? You look like you stepped out of a zombie movie."

"Not far from the truth," Katie said.

"I'm so glad to see you," Clara gave Taylor a hug.

"You're telling me! Come on, the car's hidden down this back road a ways." Taylor pointed off to their right beyond a row of rose bushes and several tall sycamores. "Sorry I couldn't park any closer. Lynch's people have been wandering around."

Taylor motioned for Clara and Katie to move away from Jack, then he pulled Jack's arm over his shoulder and wrapped a strong right arm around his waist. Jack hopped down the steps, leaning heavily on Taylor, and limped with Taylor's help across the back lawn toward an open gate in the chain link fence.

"You have no idea how glad I am to see you," Jack said.

"Dude, my head's been on a roller coaster wondering what was going on with you. I totally meant to pick you up south of camp the other night, but those stupid guards wouldn't leave me alone. They followed me all the way to Kalispell and wouldn't leave even when I spent like fifteen minutes at the gas station down the street. I heard that huge explosion at the camp. It lit up the whole sky. I thought you died, man. I tried to head back to camp, but those guards wouldn't let me pass. I could've killed them."

They funneled through the back gate, turned to their right, and started walking as fast as Jack could limp down a dark narrow road canopied by tall, lush trees.

Taylor smiled at Clara. "I tried to ditch those stupid guards at the motel in Kalispell, but the jerks stole my keys. They didn't give them back until the next morning. I outsmarted them, though. I messed with their Humvee during the night, so when they gave me back the keys, I took off. The expression on their stupid faces was priceless."

Taylor laughed and directed Jack and the girls up a narrow unpaved side road. The moonlight reflecting off Jack's silver Ford Fiesta a few hundred yards up the path.

"Wish I'd been there, dude," Jack said.

"My life was all mental torture after I escaped from them," Taylor said. "Man, I didn't know if you were ever going to show up. I recognized a few guards from camp casing out the area yesterday, but that was good because it told me they were still looking for you guys."

"I was wondering why you stayed here for so long," Katie said.

"I wanted to give up," Taylor said. "I worried that I'd misunderstood you about meeting at the old house. I spent most of my time hiding between some bales of hay below an old metal canopy up the road from the old house. It gave me a good view of the area. It rained last night though, and I about froze to death trying to sleep in your car. Then there was another explosion up in the mountains somewhere. I seriously thought Farley had blasted you with something. But the next morning, there were still guards hanging around, looking for you."

"Why were you watching the attic? It seemed like you were expecting us to be there," Clara said.

"I was." Taylor arrived at Jack's car. The headlights turned on and the engine revved. Jack shielded his eyes. Taylor opened the back door for Clara and Katie, ran around to the front passenger door, and opened it for Jack. "A few hours ago, I was watching the house and saw someone walking along the fence, staring up at the attic window."

"Hurry and get in the car, guys," a woman's voice said from the driver's seat. "Lynch's thugs'll be swarming around this town any moment now. We need to hightail it out of here."

Jack lowered his head and grinned at Marina's bright blue hair. He sat down and closed the door. Katie and Clara climbed in a back door behind her and Taylor squeezed himself into the car behind Jack, his long legs pressing into the back of Jack's seat.

"Marina!" Clara leaned forward from her center seat and gave her a hug around the neck. "I was so worried about you."

"We aren't out of this yet." Marina yanked the gear selector into drive and the car lurched forward, swerving in an abrupt U-turn.

"Marina told me everything that happened to you guys," Taylor said. "I got to admit, I thought she'd lost her mind in that dream lab or something. She told me she'd found out that an old ghost was leading you to a haunt in that house and I needed to watch for you in the attic. Dude, I totally thought I was just playing along with her nutjob psychosis, but next thing I know, I look up, and Clara's staring out the window at me. Then those two guards showed up at the front door and you know the rest."

"Thanks for playing along with my nutjob psychosis." Marina gave a wry smile. "You were just in time, too. I saw those agents in a Humvee take off down that road." She pointed to her right. "If anyone from Intershroud recognizes me, I'm done for."

Marina turned the car down a poorly lit back road to the farthest edge of town, then swerved and drove three blocks to the only road leading down the mountain. She looked for anyone watching the road. The car lurched forward, swerving as she slammed the gas pedal down.

"Where are you taking us?" Clara leaned over the seat.

"I need to talk to you about that. Jack, do you know an elderly woman named Sion?"

"Doesn't sound familiar."

"Well, she knows you. She told one of my associates that an old friend of hers showed up at her door a few days ago, begging her to help her free you from the camp. Before you ask, I don't know who her friend was or how she knew you were at the camp."

"We better not trust her," Katie said. "Before we went to that camp, Jack and I shared dreams with a group of crazy cultists. I don't want to step out of one fire and into another."

"Sion is no cultist. You can trust her. She used to belong to my resistance organization. She sent her husband up here from Arizona to take you to his safe house. I met him once. They call him Skeets—nicest old Navaho man you'll ever meet."

The car screeched around a narrow curve and Jack gripped his seat and clenched his teeth. He glanced back at Katie and found her laughing.

"Hey, take it easy," Jack said. "This car wasn't cheap."

"You'll never see it again if Intershroud catches up to us," Marina said.

"I'm just glad we caught up with you again," Katie said. "I was sure Lynch found out you set off that landslide. He seems to know everything."

Marina shook her head. "I fooled them pretty good, if I say so myself. I told Carl and some others that one of you set off the rock-slide, then I followed you and saw you joining up with Abby. I told them Abby showed you an image of the house of someone who could transport you away. Then I just convinced them I needed to go find the house because I could only recognize it by sight. My ally among the camp guards offered to drive me there."

"Sounds like it worked to perfection," Jack said.

Marina nodded. "Except I slept in their vehicle and found that you were no longer at the railway station where I left you. I feared the worst."

"How'd you know we'd be in that attic? I didn't even know we were going there," Clara said.

"There are spies for the resistance even among the people who were attacking you. The Ghost Knights have no love for Intershroud either. I was able to piece together enough info to figure out that you were heading for Jeb Colton's haunt. I'm sad we lost it. That haunt was one of the few secrets we were keeping from Intershroud."

Light suddenly bounced around the car's interior, coming from behind them. Jack turned around and squinted at the bright headlights of a vehicle swerving in and out of view at every curve of the road.

"Crap," Taylor said. "I recognize those headlights."

LXIX

Marina slammed the gas and Jack stared wide-eyed at her surprisingly calm face.

"Our turnoff's coming up soon," Marina said. "I need to make some serious distance so that car won't know we turned."

Jack looked back. "I think we lost them."

"There's the turnoff!" Marina yanked the wheel to the right and the wheels screeched. Everyone lurched to their left. The car swerved, skidded, and drove at a slower pace down a tree-lined dirt sideroad.

"Why are you slowing down?" Taylor stuck his head forward between his knees.

"If we throw any dust around, they'll know we turned." The car circled a hairpin curve and Marina hit the gas again, speeding past hundreds of pines. A chubby, white-striped skunk stopped at the edge of the road in front of them, then waddled toward the trees. Marina narrowly avoided it, pine boughs scraping the windows on her side of the car.

She slowed down after a few minutes, then stopped the car near the edge of a high cliff, the engine still running.

"Why are we stopping?" Jack looked at Marina.

"This is where we get out. Your ride is tucked behind those trees."

Marina pointed to a set of tire tracks running along a shallow slope into a clearing beyond a thick cluster of spruces. She climbed out of the car.

Taylor opened his door and eased his long legs away from the back of Jack's seat and out the door. He stood and opened Jack's door, holding out a hand to him. Jack's legs were stiff, and he cringed at the pain of lifting them out the car door. Taylor secured a firm grip on Jack's hand and leaned back, pulling him out of his seat and onto his feet. Clara and Katie exited the opposite door and ran around the car to join Jack and Taylor.

Jack stood back from his car, looking at Marina. "So, what're we going to do with my car? Should I follow this Skeets guy?"

"Is there anything you need from the trunk? The glove box?" Marina stood next to the car with the door open.

"I don't think so," Jack said.

"I put everything from your car in my backpack." Taylor pointed a thumb at the backpack hanging from his shoulder.

"Good." Marina nodded, gave a subtle grin, and reached into the car. The vehicle started to slide backward. She kicked at the gas pedal with her foot. The car lurched forward, and Marina jumped back.

"What are you doing?" Jack reached for the moving vehicle and fell on his knees.

The view from the cliff was magnificent under the full moonlight. Grizzled outcroppings of stone peeked out from the undulating mountainside, caked with pines. Thousands upon thousands of trees hugged the steep cliff for hundreds of yards below them.

All Jack saw, however, was his precious silver Ford Fiesta rolling over the cliff, its back bumper rising upward, then disappearing from his sight with the rest of the car. Taylor, Katie, and Clara ran to the cliff edge. Jack closed his eyes and cringed at the sickening crunch of his car colliding with stone. He gritted his teeth at the swishing and clunking of his vehicle tearing through hundreds of pine branches, scrub oaks, and swathes of loose gravel and rock. He winced at the final distant thump that preceded an explosion. A cascade of orange, fiery light showered the distant trees.

Jack stared for at least ten seconds before turning to Marina. An approaching engine echoed from the roadway, and a camouflage-colored Humvee pulled up behind her. An Intershroud guard stepped from the passenger side and stood behind Marina—one of the agents who'd escorted Taylor away.

Jack's heart sank and his eyes teared up. "They got to you."

"You traitor!" Katie charged at Marina, but the muscular guard darted in front of her and, with a quick kick at Katie's legs and a twist of her arm, placed her in an arm hold.

"How could you?" Clara's voice trembled.

Taylor leaned down behind Jack, pushed his forearms below Jack's armpits, and lifted him to his feet. Jack looked at Taylor and realized that his friend hadn't reacted to the arrival of the two guards. He felt another wrenching pressure in his chest.

"No. Taylor. They got you, too?"

Taylor's eyebrows creased, and he shook his head. "Dude, what are you thinking? I'm not with Intershroud! Neither is Marina."

"Sorry, Jack," Marina said. "I forced Taylor to keep you in the dark. I knew you wouldn't let me send your car over that cliff, and it was too critical to our plan."

"You destroyed my car!" Jack shook his fist.

Taylor put a hand on his shoulder and Jack jerked it away. "Dude, I feel bad, but Marina's right. There's only one road out of these mountains. Lynch and Murdock know you made it to that haunt, and they'll be setting up blockades and sending out helicopters. They'd have caught us."

Marina looked Jack in the eyes. "Your only hope of escaping them is for me to convince Lynch's operatives that the roadblocks aren't necessary. We're going to tell them we were chasing you and didn't see you turn on this side road, where you swerved off the cliff. It'll take them some time to get down there to investigate the crash. By then, you'll be far away from these mountains."

"But, you're with those guards," Clara pointed at the driver of the Humvee. "They're so mean."

The two guards looked at each other and smiled.

Marina laughed. "These are the friends I told you about, with the resistance. They're perfect allies. No one ever suspects mean people of being good guys."

"Marina only told me about them a half hour ago," Taylor said. "Lynch ordered his people to see to it that I had a fatal accident on my way home. Marina sent these two, uh, people, to make sure I made it home safely. They actually let me give them the slip, but I didn't head home like they thought I would."

Jack heard branches moving and underbrush crunching behind him. He spun around. A forest-green van with no rear windows rolled down a shallow hill from beyond a cluster of blue spruces. Its wheels crackled against the gravelly road until the vehicle stopped next to Jack. An old Navaho man in a faded denim shirt and light-tan cowboy hat leaned his round face out the window. He had a pleasant smile and deep, brown, friendly eyes.

"I assume this is the boy I'm looking for. They call me Skeets." He reached a callused hand out his window and Jack shook it.

"This is your ride," Marina said. "My friends and I need to head out. Hopefully, no one will suspect Skeets if you four keep your heads down. Good luck."

Marina and the guard rushed to the Humvee and climbed in.

"Will we be seeing you again?" Clara followed Marina to the Humvee.

"I hope so. Skeet's wife, Sion, will teach you some Free Dreaming tricks to help you hide from Intershroud. With any luck, I'll see you in your dreams." The Humvee turned around and sped away.

"Good to finally meet you, Jack," Skeets said. "Your grandma's been raving about you."

"Grandma?" Jack's eyebrows rose, and he turned to Taylor and shrugged. "I've never met either of my grandmothers."

"That's not what she told me." Skeets pointed his thumb at the back of the van. "You best hop in quick now, before them agents show up. We'll have plenty of time to talk on the way. Your grandma's back there. I'm sure you're anxious to see her."

Jack looked at Taylor again, not sure what to think. Clara and Katie ran to the back doors, swung them open, and climbed in.

Taylor slid Jack's arm over his shoulder, helped him limp to the back of the van, and lifted him onto the gray-carpeted floor, easing him into a leather seat, facing sideways. Taylor climbed in and buckled himself into the seat across from Jack. He pulled the doors closed with a clank and the cabin went dark.

Jack looked for his grandmother, but only saw a van full of silhouettes in front of a deep-blue twilight sky. One of them was a short, curly-haired woman, sitting on a chair facing backward from behind the driver's seat. The van started to roll forward and Jack bumped against the van door. He felt around for his seatbelt. HE found it over his shoulder, pulled it down over his chest, and buckled it.

"It's dark in here," Clara said.

Taylor zipped open his backpack and pulled out a flashlight. "This was in your glove compartment. See, I'm looking out for you, dude." He flicked the switch and handed it to Jack. Light filled the van and Jack stared at the grinning face of an old Korean woman.

He dropped the flashlight.

LXX

The old woman's crooked smile reflected the light of Jack's flashlight. She wore a black outfit with a loose cotton cloth tied around her portly waist, one of the outfits Jack had seen her wearing in dozens of nightmares. Her humped back forced her to lean forward on her thick wooden walking stick.

The flashlight rolled near Clara's foot and she picked it up and aimed it in the woman's face. The woman squinted and put a wrinkled hand in front of her eyes to block the light.

"Let's keep the light off back there till we're off the mountain," Skeets said.

Clara turned it off.

"Grandmother?" Jack clenched his teeth. "You're not my grandmother." Even as he said it, he realized how much she resembled his father.

"No grandmother would do what you did to Jack," Katie said. "You have a lot of nerve."

"You're the whole reason I went to that camp!" Jack gripped the side of his seat. "You tortured me every night for months! You had me thinking I was crazy! I had no idea you were real. You had no right to invade my dreams! My whole life has been ruined because of you!"

"You're nothing but a monster," Katie said.

The woman nodded after every sentence.

"You brought Katie into it, too," Jack said. "You had people tie her down while monsters were roaming around. It must've been terrifying! What did she ever do to you? You violated our personal thoughts! And now you dare come here, after being completely absent all my life, and claim to be my grandmother? Let's get something straight. I don't have a grandmother!"

Ten seconds of silence passed before the woman finally spoke.

"Pak Jaegi, I can only beg your forgiveness. I deserve your anger. The scorpion man deceived me. He deceived us all. He promised me he would enlighten you, give you the power to understand your dreams. But then he kept you from me. We couldn't reach you in the Dream World. I deeply regret that we did you such great harm trusting that man."

"Don't try to blame him! You were behind all those nightmares. You made me fight snakes and monsters every single night. I thought it was all in my mind. I was terrified to fall asleep. I can't imagine what Katie went through. You had no right to mess with our dreams! You had no right!" Jack's eyes welled up and he clenched his fists.

The old woman nodded. "They were only dreams, young one. You and your friend were never in any danger. Katie's powers were necessary to help you prepare for what is to come."

"You're not a fortuneteller!" Jack kicked his heels on the floor of the van.

"I am not. But Zaqar is. The white cloud of prophecy came to me in a dream. He is an ancient Deisom, one of the greatest nightmares of the Dream World. He speaks pure truth."

The vehicle swerved around a narrow turn and Jack thumped against the van's door.

"This is just too much," Katie said. "You probably dreamed that cloud up yourself. His prophecies were the inventions of your own warped mind."

"My grandson knows that is not true. He witnessed the wrath of the Dark Mind. He wouldn't question my words even now if his guardians hadn't locked his memory of it within the flame. Zaqar is real and he informed me that a hero would arise in my family who would lead the effort to defeat the Dark Mind."

"Convenient that Jack can't remember it," Taylor said.

"She might be right," Jack said. All eyes turned to him and no one spoke for several seconds. Jack thought about his obsession with fire and couldn't deny the truth in her words. "I'm not saying she's right about me being a hero. But it's true that I have no memory of the years I lived in Korea. My whole life before coming to America is a blank. My parents told me I hit my head." He rubbed a small scar on his forehead.

"They lied to you," Jack's grandmother said.

"Like we can trust you," Katie said.

"I sold everything I owned to come to America and rescue my grandson from those men. That is how sure I am of his destiny."

"Then how about jogging his memory about what happened in Korea," Taylor said.

"I cannot tell him. His passion to find out the truth is the only thing powerful enough to help him regain his memory. He must fight for the memories himself."

A helicopter buzzed overhead, and everyone went quiet. Jack tightened his grip on his seatbelt. Skeets slowed the van down until the helicopter went away.

"That had me worried," Skeets said. "I don't think I'll breathe easy until we get off this mountain."

"This is pointless," Jack said. "You're telling me heroic tales about my future, yet the entire Intershroud is looking for me. I'm putting everyone in danger. I should just turn myself in and let the rest of you go home."

"I don't have a home anymore," Katie said.

"I go where Katie goes," Clara said.

"Dude," Taylor said. "We're with you until we figure out what to do about Intershroud."

"But that's just it," Jack said. "There isn't anything we can do."

"I know one thing," Katie said. "We can find my mom. I realize now that she's been hiding from Intershroud all this time. If anyone can help us, it'll be her."

"I need to talk to my mom, too," Clara said. "She's probably worried sick about me."

"We can't contact her," Jack said. "We can't go home or use phones or credit cards. They'll be listening for us and watching our homes. We're not safe anywhere, not even in our dreams."

"Maybe we can find a way for all of you to dream where I dream," Clara said. "Everyone is nice there."

"No way," Taylor said. "It's not natural to dream that way, Clara. It seems like someone is controlling you. If anything, we need to help you escape those dreams."

"It doesn't matter," Jack said. "We aren't skilled enough to hide from Lynch and Murdock in our dreams. I'm dead tired right now, but I'm terrified to even doze off."

Jack searched his pocket for his lighter, then shook his head when he remembered it wasn't there. Instead, he found the folded newspaper he'd retrieved from Farley's wastebasket in the research facility. He pulled it from his pocket and brought it close to his eyes.

"The Essential Expositor," Jack said. "This is it!" He waved the scrap of paper in front of Taylor. "Todd Price. This guy's standing up to them. He attacks Intershroud in public with this newsletter. He must be distributing it from somewhere."

"Maybe he can help us find my mom," Katie said. "You see Jack, your dream power doesn't just work in Essentia. Your mind's always working to put things right."

Jack leaned his head against the van doors. He found his grandmother smiling wide and staring in turn at him, Taylor, Clara, and Katie.

"What are you smiling about?" Jack leaned back and closed his eyes.

"I have never been so happy," she said. "I searched whole life for a hero in my family to fulfill the prophecy. The white cloud said he would lead three companions to defeat the Dark Mind. The pieces finally have fallen into place." She started to laugh.

Taylor rolled his eyes and shook his head. Katie grinned, and Clara laughed.

"When I was a child, I worried I'd forget the prophecy, so I made it into a song. You, too, must learn it, Pak Jaegi. I'll sing it for you."

Jack shook his head and folded his arms. His grandmother broke into a song that awakened a memory deep inside him:

> *A Demon to lead him,*
> *A Trickster to guide,*
> *A Senex to strengthen,*
> *A Hero provide.*
> *They fire upon her,*
> *With fire they bind,*
> *From fire they blind her,*
> *Defeat the Dark Mind.*

# ACKNOWLEDGMENTS

I'm pleased to acknowledge everyone who supported and encouraged me in the long road to bringing about this book. I especially have to thank my good friends James Wymore and John Peterson whose inspirational ideas helped build the foundation upon which this work was created, and whose encouragement kept me moving forward through thick and thin. I also express my deepest gratitude to my wife and children who endured many a night sleeping soundly while I stayed up way past my bedtime writing, rewriting, rewriting rewrites, rewriting rewritten rewrites, and basically doing a lot of tapping on that "accept changes" button.

I am highly indebted to Jason King, Holli Anderson, and other friends and staff at Immortal Works, to Ashley Literski for the excellent artwork, and to the army of editors assigned to this book, for all their time, patience, efforts, insights, and guidance that enabled me to bring this book to its highest potential.

# ABOUT THE AUTHOR

R.A. Baxter has always appreciated the arts, nature, religion, philosophy, and all the mysteries this world has to offer. He grew up loving animals, gradually grew interested in all aspects of religion, history, and science, and finally sought to ease his curiosity of the writings of the many authors of the past. His interests led him to pursue a Bachelor of Fine Arts degree in painting and drawing, a Science of Architecture degree, and a Master of Architecture degree. As an Architectural Specifier, R.A. Baxter spends much of his time manipulating words and instructing builders as to the best way to construct a coherent building. He would rather, however, spend his time with his wonderful wife and children, or lose himself in the imaginary worlds available to those who enjoy reading and creative writing. He and his longsuffering family live in the shadow of the Rocky Mountains in Bountiful Utah. If you have any comments, questions, or highly-overstated praise for R.A. Baxter, contact him at https://rabaxterauthor.wordpress.com/.

This has been an
Immortal Production

www.ingramcontent.com/pod-product-compliance
Lightning Source LLC
Chambersburg PA
CBHW020232110726
47898CB00004B/1235